GARY HAYNES

began writing seriously four years ago as a hobby, but it quickly became a passion. When he's not writing, he likes to keep fit by working out at his local boxing gym and going for long walks by the sea. He has three children and lives in Devon with his very patient partner.

Gary writes cinematic, fast-paced, action-packed thrillers, although not without a healthy smattering of humour. He plans on writing a series of novels based on his main character, Tom Dupree, a special agent in the US Bureau of Diplomatic Security.

You can contact Gary at garyhayneswrites@gmail.com and follow him on Twitter, @GaryHaynesNovel.

STATE OF
HONOUR

GARY HAYNES

W❂RLDWIDE®

TORONTO • NEW YORK • LONDON
AMSTERDAM • PARIS • SYDNEY • HAMBURG
STOCKHOLM • ATHENS • TOKYO • MILAN
MADRID • WARSAW • BUDAPEST • AUCKLAND

For my partner, Catherine, who makes it all so much easier, and my mum and dad, for their love and belief.

Recycling programs
for this product may
not exist in your area.

ISBN-13: 978-1-335-01506-8

State of Honour

Copyright © 2013 by Gary Haynes

A Worldwide Library Suspense/June 2018

First published by HQ Digital, an imprint of HarperCollins Publishers

www.Harlequin.com

Printed in U.S.A.

STATE OF
HONOUR

Writing is a lonely pastime, but to get a book into shape for publication, it becomes a collaborative process. I would like to thank Helen Williams at Harlequin for spotting my potential and for her encouragement and enthusiasm, and my excellent editors, Dean Martin, Victoria Oundjian and Lucy Gilmour, for their attention to detail and helpful suggestions.

PROLOGUE

Hindu Kush. North-west Pakistan

THE SHOOT-TO-KILL ORDER came through at zero one fifteen, relayed over a satellite radio. It'd been just three hours since the two-man reconnaissance team had reported the sighting.

They lay in a shallow dugout on a windblown ridge, the leeward slope falling away steeply to an impassable boulder field. A desert-issue tarp all but covered the hole, protected from view on the flanks by thorny scrub. Shivering, they blew into their bunched trigger-finger mitts. The daytime temperature had dropped twenty degrees or more, and fine sleet was melting on their blackened faces.

Darren Proctor extended the folded stock of his L115A3 sniper rifle. He split the legs of the swivel bi-pod and aligned the swivel cheek piece with the all-weather scope. Flipping open the lens cap, he glassed the terrain cast a muted green by the night vision. The tree line was sparse, a smattering of pines and cedars shuddering in the biting wind. Glimpsing movement on a scree slope fifty metres or so beyond, he focused in. The eyes of a striped hyena shone like glow sticks. He watched as the scavenger ripped at the carcass of an ibex or wild sheep. A second later it sniffed the air, ears pricked, and scampered off.

Too late, you're dead, he thought.

Lowering the stock onto a wrapped poncho liner, he glanced to his left. "You see anything, Mike?"

"Nothing apart from that weird-looking dog," Mike Rowe replied, his eyes fixed to a LION, a lightweight infrared observation night-sight. "This place goes into lockdown after dark."

He'd served alongside Proctor in Iraq and Helmand Province; elsewhere, too. But their presence here, a few miles east of the Af-Pak border, was illegal. The drone strikes had ceased three months ago in response to the spike in civilian casualties, and the withdrawal of all but advisory ISAF personnel in neighbouring Afghanistan had been implemented as planned. With the West resorting increasingly to using private military contractors for black ops in the region, they now earned ten times what they had as regular British soldiers. If they died in the process, the politicians wouldn't get flak from the media, or have to answer difficult letters from grieving parents. They were deemed to be expendable shadows, and they knew it.

Proctor shook his head. "It's a hyena, genius."

"Whatever. Fucking thing looks like it crawled up from hell. Even uglier than you, and that's not easy," Mike replied, snickering.

"Thanks, mate."

They'd grown wiry beards and wore local tribal dress beneath their ghillie suits: baggy pants, long cotton shirts and sheepskin vests. Otherwise, the two men were physical opposites. While Proctor was six-two with a clean-shaven head and bull-like shoulders, Mike was five-six and bony, his matted brown hair reaching past the nape.

Mike placed the LION onto a kitbag, to
camouflage helmet and picked up a Gerber too
the small blade, he began to strip the bark from
clearly bored.

They'd been on an unrelated mission, shadowing a
small group of Haqqani network fighters suspected of
the murder of a US diplomat in Islamabad. Once that
operation had been aborted, they'd maintained their
position high up in the foothills. The target was a pri-
ority. But they'd agreed that it could take days before
he showed again.

Proctor grasped the bolt-action rifle once more, his
eye glued to the scope, scanning.

The target—a phlegmatic Muslim cleric called Mullah Kakar—was hiding out in a cave complex a mile
away. The area was riddled with them, used for decades as bombproof bolt holes. Earlier, they'd seen frail
plumes of light-grey smoke curling over the craggy
overhang above the mouth. Now there was nothing. If
he'd been alone, they'd said they'd have risked an assault. But he was protected by four Afghan bodyguards
and hadn't come out since they'd spotted him. When
he did, they'd decided to take out everyone, using frag-
mentation grenades, if necessary. They had to authenti-
cate the kill. That meant close-up digital photographs,
and mouth swabs and blood samples for DNA. With a
seven-figure reward on the mullah's otherwise elusive
head, Mike had commented that this was going to be
the last time he slept in the open.

"You want a brew?" he said.

Proctor put an open hand to his ear. Freeze and listen. He chambered one of the five rounds and flicked
off the safety.

"Ninety metres at three o'clock. Rocky outcrop," he whispered, aiming the seven kilograms, long-range weapon.

Mike snatched up the LION. "Terry?" he asked quietly, army slang for Taliban.

Proctor raised his open-palmed left hand across his chest and pointed to the right. Move there.

Mike slipped the LION into a cargo pocket, picked up a suppressed Heckler & Koch HK416 assault rifle fitted with a thermal imaging sight, and eased himself out of the hole. Proctor followed him with his night-scope. The body moved in a low crawl, inching diagonally towards a cluster of stunted bushes; a vantage point from which he could spy behind the mass of jagged rock. Proctor lay perfectly still, controlling his breathing. He should have had his scope trained on the outcrop, making sure Mike wasn't in danger. But he'd lied to him. When he was some ten metres away, Proctor fixed the illuminated mil-dot reticle onto the back of Mike's bare head. At this range, the 8.59mm round would pulverize the skull.

"Sorry, Mike," he whispered.

He placed the ball of his forefinger on the trigger as he prepared to squeeze. A second later there was a muffled discharge, the noise and flash minimized by the fixed suppressor. Mike's body bucked as if he'd been Tasered, a thick spray of blood erupting from his head. He didn't move again.

Proctor removed his camo suit and put on a pakol, a woollen round-topped hat. Crouching, he sent an encrypted distress message to a Special Forces signaller in Kabul. Decoded it read: *Target down. Spotter down. Situation critical.*

Once sent, he wrapped up the tarp and shut down the portable SATCOM, GPS and VHF radio. Using a short-handled shovel, he hacked at the plastic and metal until he was sure the systems were inoperable, and shoved them into two canvas kitbags. He scooped them up and began filling in the hole with the relatively loose earth they'd dug out earlier. When he'd finished, he shouldered his rifle and walked slowly to the corpse. Kneeling down, he removed Mike's two-way radio, sidearm, and wristwatch. He thought about his friend's four kids, and his wife, Debra. Then, pushing aside the HK, he zoned out.

He spent the next half an hour digging a grave. After heaving the body in, he covered it with stiff clods of soil. That done, the equipment and gear had to vanish, too. He trudged along the ridge to a remote crevice, just wide enough to swallow the bags, and flung in all trace of their existence. Exhausted, he crouched down and lit a cigarette with a silver Zippo, telling himself that he'd earned it. He glanced up. The sleet had turned to snow. Trembling, he inhaled the smoke deeply, felt the frigid wind slice to his bones. The overcast skies rendered high-altitude recon drones useless, and it could be hours before a rescue team could be put together. He had time to spare.

A few minutes later, he zigzagged down the wind-ward slope, using the metre-long rifle to steady him. Below, the land was farmed in terraced plots. He'd seen the hamlet on the drone feeds, the timber houses stacked one above the other. But Mike had been right. The place went into lockdown at night.

Reaching flat ground, he walked to the bank of the turbulent river, the rapids exploding like geysers against domes of smooth rock. It was warmer in the valley floor and the wind had dropped to a cool breeze. He bent down, cleansed his hands of bloodstains and cupped the icy water onto his face. Lighting another cigarette, he heard the vehicle before he saw it. Braced himself. As it pulled into the hamlet along a mud track peppered with potholes, the lights were killed. He made out a red Toyota pickup truck with five men hugging AK-47s sitting in the rear. It stopped a couple of metres from him. He let the cigarette fall from his fingers, stubbed it out with his boot.

A man opened the passenger door and strolled over. He wore shabby sneakers and a dark-green flak jacket. His face was pitted, the grey beard extravagant. Proctor thought he looked older than the photograph of him he had hidden in his pocket. Being a fugitive doesn't suit him, he concluded.

They shook hands.

"Asalaam Alaykum," Proctor said. Peace be upon you.

"Wa 'Alaykum Asalaam," Mullah Kakar replied. And peace be upon you also. He looked up at the surrounding foothills, as if he were recalling time spent here. "Are we officially dead?"

Proctor nodded.

"Then get in. We ghosts have much work to do."

ONE

Islamabad was a city that reeked of fear. Martial law had been imposed by the Pakistani generals, and terrorist attacks were escalating. As a result, the US Embassy compound in the Diplomatic Enclave resembled a modern supermax, ringed as it was by security bollards, floodlights, high-definition surveillance cameras, blast walls and heavy fencing. To add to the deterrent, three Marine rifle companies guarded it in rotation day and night.

Halfway down one of its tiled corridors, two men stood either side of a soundproof, brass-inlaid door, their tailored suits masking holstered SIG Sauer P229 handguns. On the other side of the door, the US Secretary of State, the forty-three-year-old Linda Carlyle, worked alone in a windowless office.

"I heard the generals ordered all women to wear the hijab," Steve Coombs said, running his hand through his receding sandy hair, his broad back nestling against the wall. "It'll be the burqa next. My eldest, Cathy, is studying law at Yale. Beats the hell outta me."

"Me too," the younger man replied.

His name was Tom Dupree. He'd spent twelve years overseas guarding embassy staff. After another three in the office of investigations and counterintelligence, he'd reached a career summit for a special agent in the Bureau of Diplomatic Security: head of the secretary's protective detail. It had been his time. The scars on his body—a two-inch knife slash on his bicep and a chest seared by mortar shrapnel—were testament to his dedication. But now his time leading the protective detail was almost over.

"So you'll be stuck in DC, huh, Tom?" Steve said, picking sleep from his eye.

"Yeah. Chief nursemaid to the good, the bad and the ugly."

"Foreign dignitary detail ain't so bad. At least you'll get to snuggle down in your own bed some. When you gonna get yourself a little lady to share it with?"

"Who says I don't?" Tom said, adjusting his stance.

Truth was, Tom hadn't had a girlfriend in over a year. Not since Carrie, an analyst in the DS's passport and visa fraud division, had told him she couldn't deal with dating a man she saw less than her dentist.

"'Bout time you became a one-woman man, you ask me," Steve said, his tone preachy.

Knowing his friend was a Catholic, who'd been married since his nineteenth birthday, Tom chose to ignore the comment. He checked the time on his wristwatch: 08:36. They would be on the move soon, but he was dreading it.

"It'll get hotter than a habanero chilli out there," Steve said, yawning. "I sure hope that kids' hospital got AC."

"The kids' hospital is a bad idea," Tom replied, his brow furrowing.

"So why don't Lyric drop the line-up?" he said, using the DS's pro-word for the secretary.

"A photo op. Who knows? But it's making me twitchy as hell, I know that much."

The advance detail had carried out a security profile on the location of the kids' hospital, which was basically a threat and risk assessment: what could happen and the likelihood that it would. It was a dynamic process, and the additions Tom had made since arriving a few days before had been some of the most comprehensive he'd produced in his career. But after distributing the operational orders to his team, he'd realized that half of the countermeasures that would be required if security was compromised would be down to the host Pakistanis.

"Paranoia keeps you sharp. Don't forget that, Tom."

"Yeah. Paranoia till stateside."

It was the most important mindset DS special agents were taught. If any place made it a healthy disposition, it was Islamabad, Tom thought. The city attracted violence as Palm Springs attracted pensioners. He was constantly briefed on hot spots, and this one had been at the top of the list for months. But apart from his six-strong protective detail, there were eight back-up agents in the tactical support team. Part of the Mobile Security Deployment, or MSD, they travelled in armour-plated SUVs, and carried Colt 9mm sub-machine guns and Remington 870 pump-action shotguns. The drivers were experts in defensive and evasive techniques. They'd studied satellite imagery of the surrounding road network, so, if they had to evacuate the secretary at speed, they knew alternative routes back to the safety of the embassy, or the nearest hospital or police station. Still, Tom knew a hundred things could go wrong. Compromises had been made. A fleet of up-armoured Humvees shadowed by a squadron of AH-64 Apache attack helicopters would have been the ideal way to travel, but he knew that was as likely as Steve turning into the laconic type.

"A perfect record and only a week to go. It had to be here, huh."

"That's real helpful, Steve," Tom said, unbuttoning his charcoal-grey suit jacket.

But he's right, he thought. Back home, the advance detail would have been thorough. Local extremists and publicity-seeking whackos monitored. Pipe-inspection cameras poked into every cranny. Storm drains checked for explosives. The dumpsters removed. Manhole covers bolted, the public trash cans sealed. Then, on the day of her visit, scores of local P.D. would've been on the periphery and tried and tested counter snipers on the roofs. All vantage points covered. Discarded bottles and lumps of loose concrete removed within an appropriate radius. The Belgian Malinois bomb sniffers would've swept every inch.

"Corridor duty is as boring as those TV reality shows, ain't it, Tom?" Steve said.

"Can't argue with that."

Tom watched Steve weaving his head in what appeared to be a figure of eight. "The hell you doing?"

"My doc said it'll help with my headaches. Relieves neck tension."

"Didn't know you suffered from headaches," Tom said, a little concerned that his friend hadn't mentioned it to him before.

"They started a couple months back. Sometimes when I wake up at night, it feels like I'm wearing a vice."

"Get it checked out again. You got a physical coming up."

"Sure I will, Tom."

A couple of seconds later, Tom coughed into his fist and gestured with his eyes. But Steve's head was still animate. A stocky man with a weather-beaten face and short silver hair had entered the corridor from an elevator twenty metres behind Steve's back. He carried a bundle of papers in a manila folder under his arm, and walked like an ex-military type. When the man's footsteps became audible on the tiles, Steve stood ramrod straight. As he got closer Tom recognized him, and moved over to knock on the door before opening it.

"Thank you, son," he said. He turned to Steve, gestured towards the clear wire spiralling down from his earpiece. "That wire attached to an iPod, Agent?"

"No, sir."

"That's good," he said as he disappeared inside.

Tom closed the door, worried. He wondered if he'd missed something important in terms of the assessment. But the training his team underwent continually was based on repetition, the type that created confidence and long-term muscle memory. If an attack of whatever nature happened, be it a flung bag of flour or a multiple-armed assault, they would act instinctively, almost without conscious effort.

Steve sniffed. "The paper shuffler thinks he's a comedian."

"He's a deputy director of the CIA," Tom said, "and he ain't here to tell Lyric a joke."

TWO

Linda Carlyle looked up as the heavy door opened, hoping her rising sense of unease didn't show on her face. The dimly lit room was fifteen metres square, the few pieces of furniture functional rather than decorative. Sitting at an oak desk, she lifted a pair of black-rimmed eyeglasses off her aquiline nose. For the past forty-five minutes, she'd been speed-reading a departmental report she'd commissioned on the near-past disputes between Iran and Pakistan; all of which had stemmed from Islam's major schism. While Iran was ruled by Shias, Pakistan was Sunni dominated. In the nineties, they'd backed opposing sides in the Afghan Civil War, and had sponsored sectarian terrorism in each other's major cities. Now they were on the brink of a conflict that could ignite the whole region.

"Good morning, Madam Secretary," the deputy director said, walking towards her, his hand massaging the folded skin at his neck.

"You're not harassing my boys, are you, Bill?"

"Sometimes I forget I swopped fatigues for a suit."

Forcing a smile, she said, "Take a seat. I'll be right with you."

Deputy Director Bill Houseman, who had travelled to Islamabad with the secretary, together with the Chairman of the Joint Chiefs of Staff and the Under-Secretary of Defense, sat in a padded chair two metres from the desk and crossed his muscular legs.

Linda closed the marble-coloured lever arch file and tapped a remote. The room lit up. "So, let's have it," she said, switching off the antenna-like arc lamp she'd been reading under.

"The switchboard operator just got a call. I think we should ask the head of your security detail to join us."

"I'd like to hear what you have to say first. Please continue."

"A threat has been made." He clenched his teeth.

"I see."

"The caller said the Leopards of Islam would ensure that the US Secretary of State never leaves Pakistan soil. We're putting it down to a random individual. Low-level risk assessment."

"And why's that?"

Houseman cleared his throat, putting his hand to his mouth. "Because as a rule, the Leopards don't make threats before an attack, ma'am."

"That makes me feel a whole lot better," she said, shaking her head. "And the current situation here?"

"The Leopards are launching fresh attacks in Karachi, Bahawalpur, Lahore. The list goes on. There've been three bomb attacks in Islamabad in the past twelve days."

"Is civil war on the cards?" she asked, fearing the worst.

"We have reports that Shia elements of the army are joining the insurgency, so it's a possibility."

"And the Leopards are definitely backed by Iran?"

Houseman nodded. "No question. But the Sunnis brought it on themselves. The atrocities against the Shia minority were bound to result in an armed response."

"How serious is the Iranian threat?"

Houseman drew in an audible breath through his nose and shuffled his buttocks a fraction. "Satellite images and drone feeds show that Iranian Special Forces have already made incursions across the border. And there are three divisions of the Revolutionary Guard massed just four miles from the largest of Pakistan's five provinces—"

"Balochistan."

"That's right. Our analysts believe that Iran is planning to occupy the port of Gwadar and help themselves to the huge resources of natural gas in the province if Pakistan becomes a failed state."

"They're hoping to take advantage of the chaos," Linda said, leaning back in her chair and arching her fingers.

"They are, ma'am. But if the Iranians come over the southern border in force, the Pakistanis, despite their internal problems, are likely to go to war. They regard the Iranians as apostates."

"It's a mess." She massaged her temples with her thumbs and forefingers.

"My view is we back Pakistan with muscle and—"

"That's a decision for Congress."

"Yes, ma'am," Houseman said, nodding.

"Thank you, Bill. Send the agent in, will you? The tall one with the buzz cut."

Houseman got up, said, "May I speak freely?"

"You may."

"Don't go to the children's hospital this morning. Frankly, I don't think it's worth the risk; however small."

He has a point, she thought.

Pakistan had been a Frenemy for years. But the new Prime Minister had requested her visit to discuss the possibility of the US taking temporary possession of Pakistan's nuclear arsenal if matters got worse. Although they'd been distributed over the country for security reasons, they'd been brought back to Islamabad in recent weeks. They were safe for now. But if the Pakistanis refused to allow them into US custody, her brief also extended to ensuring that the likelihood of them being used if the Iranians came over the border in force was zero.

This, she had to admit, was the real reason for her visit. *Houseman knows that, too,* she thought, *which is why he's advising against the trip to the hospital.*

But, she said, "The president wants to show solidarity with the new regime on the issue of opposition to extremist acts of terrorism, if nothing else. Those children are their victims. I will ensure that the head of my security detail speaks with your people before we leave. Is there anything else, Bill?"

"No, ma'am," he said, barely able to conceal his concern.

TOM SAW THE door open. The deputy director came out, scowling.

"Is everything all right, sir?" Tom asked.

"Just peachy." He gestured behind him. "The secretary would like to see you."

He put the folder under his arm and straightened his tie before strolling off towards the elevator, taking a call on his cellphone after a few steps.

Tom moved through the door left ajar and saw the secretary standing in front of the desk, a neat, navy-blue box in her hand. Her shoulder-length chestnut hair was tied back with a flesh-coloured scarf. The scarf was a concession. Flowing hair was easily grabbed. Curtailing the possibility of that kind of embarrassing incident just meant one less thing to worry about. She also wore a ballistic pantsuit, as he'd asked her to, together with her specially made jewellery, a gold pendant shaped like a pear and a heavy emerald ring. The pantsuit was a pale hue of cameral. Soft body armour that could withstand a round from a handgun. The impact of the bullet was eradicated by a net of multilayered woven fabrics, which dispersed the energy over an extended area. Pure physics. He'd seen videos of Americans down in Columbia being shot at in their ballistic suits from close quarters. Something he wasn't about to divulge. It was useless against a round fired by a high-velocity rifle.

She smiled and stepped forward holding out the blue box. "I'd like you to have this." She handed it to him.

Tom opened the box. Inside was an expensive silver watch, an Omega with a large face studded with diamonds.

"I've had it engraved," she said.

Tom took it out, turned it over. He read the inscription: *To Tom with heartfelt gratitude. Linda G. Carlyle. US Secretary of State.*

"Thank you," he said, feeling a little embarrassed by her gift.

"I just want to tell you how much I appreciate all you've done."

"It's been an honour, ma'am. But I still have a week before I leave the detail."

"I know. I just wanted to give it you today... Oh, and

I should tell you that a threat has been made," she said, clearly doing her best to sound mundane.

"A threat. Why wasn't I briefed?" he asked, his jaw muscles flexing.

"It's not serious. An anonymous phone call to the embassy just a minute ago. The CIA will brief you before we leave this morning."

"I'd like you to reconsider your visit to the hospital, ma'am."

The faint lines on her forehead deepened. "The president gets ten threats a day. He got fifty on the morning of his inauguration. Where would we be if we succumbed to them all? Ensconced in a bunker at Fort Bragg, I imagine."

"But, ma'am—"

"No, Tom. My mind is made up."

He looked down at the watch. "This is very generous."

"Don't ask what the G stands for. I never use it, and no one knows apart from my parents. Don't ask about my birth certificate, either." She feigned a laugh.

His head snapped back up. "I'll get you safely home, ma'am," he said. "I promise."

"Yes, you will."

THREE

Tom sat in the front passenger seat of the third MSD
SUV, feeling agitated. The convoy was doing a steady
sixty-five along the eight-lane highway leading from
the embassy, police outriders front and rear. They were
ten minutes behind schedule. The secretary had had to
take an urgent call from the president on a secure landline. Sitting directly behind Tom, the safest place from
a protective viewpoint, she discussed the speech she'd
give to the army generals at Parliament House right
after her visit to the hospital. The speech writer had a
retro moustache and a servile tone, a skinny guy whom
Tom considered a hindrance.

After they'd agreed on the final changes, the secretary said, "The president wants the visit to the hospital
cut to twenty minutes tops."

"Yes, ma'am," Tom replied.

"That means no press questions."

"Understood."

"He mentioned the threat."

Tom turned around in his seat. "If the agreed procedure is followed, your exposure will be minimal,
ma'am."

She nodded, slowly.

Tom double-checked that her seat belt was fastened
securely, that the doors were locked and the windows
closed. He ran through the various evacuation scenar-

ios, depending on the nature of the attack and which vehicles might be taken out. She'd be plunged into the footwell. The driver would employ a full bootlegger's turn or resort to ramming. They played out like video games in his head, priming him for a potential en-route ambush.

Next, he tested his push-to-talk, or PTT, radio. The PTT button was inline and ran between the radio connection and the earpiece. It could be used either via the button or as a voice-activated unit, providing a hands-free facility. The destinations they'd be travelling to today had codenames. The hospital's codename was Cradle. He used them to communicate with his team, checking their radios were functioning in the process. Satisfied, he focused on the pre-planned arrival procedure. He'd alight first, opening the passenger door. The agents in the vehicle behind would form an open-box formation around her as she entered the building.

Check.

The Faisal Children's Hospital was a few miles from the Saudi-Pak Tower, a contemporary landmark known for its Islamic tile work. Nineteen floors high, the tower was visible from the tinted windows of the SUV. Tom worried that the hospital was outside the so-called Blue Area, the commercial centre of Islamabad. Together with a couple of his team, he'd walked the route the day before, liaising with a group of ISI operatives, the Directorate for Inter-Services Intelligence, the main Pakistan security service.

The lead operative had been called Awan. He was a beefy six-footer with leathery skin, who wore a sombre suit and black necktie.

"The road has been checked for IEDs. The hospital

is clean, at least in terms of bombs," he said, his wide face breaking into a crooked grin.

"What about all these people?" Tom asked.

"This isn't the West. If they do not work, they do not eat."

The street and those surrounding it lacked the Blue Area's greenery and modern architecture. The hospital abutted run-down buildings on either side. Brick-built retail stores with whitewashed residential accommodation above. Opposite, bland concrete apartment and office blocks rose three storeys to flat roofs. They cast an unbroken shadow over a line of flimsy stalls, selling reams of brightly coloured cloth, second-hand cellphones, fruit and vegetables and halal meat on hooks.

"I don't like it," Tom said.

"Then tell her not to come," Awan replied, shrugging.

Ignoring him, Tom said, "Your men ready for tomorrow?"

"As I told you on the phone, apart from yourselves, ten armed operatives will mix with the crowd. There will be fifty-two policemen. On the roofs, a team of snipers." He pointed up to the sky. "And a police helicopter with elite commandos onboard."

"Have the hospital staff been screened?"

"They were screened when they were employed. They're all well-educated Punjabis. Our problems come from frontier hills people. Shia illiterates."

Tom pinched his nose. "The main exposure is when the secretary leaves. A two-minute delay while she does her goodbyes to the official line-up," he said, knowing that a couple of Grey Eagle drones would be monitoring the scene from above.

"Everything will be okay, Mr Dupree."

Tom had wished he could've believed him.

He stood half a metre behind the secretary now, just to the right of her shoulder, his sense of unease unabated. The walls of the hospital ward were painted an insipid yellow. It was cramped with twenty small beds a fraction more than a body-width apart. If it had AC, it had been turned off. The competing smells of disinfectant and stale sweat were equally pungent. He figured the authorities were intent on making the experience both unpleasant and memorable.

A bearded doctor, with black bags hanging in folds like a bloodhound's, explained to the secretary in detail the nature of each of the children's injuries and what could and could not be done. Tom thought he looked like a coke addict, or a guy who drank a bottle of Jack a day, but put his jaded appearance down to a dedicated man who didn't sleep much. He watched the secretary listen attentively, and speak with each child in turn via a government interpreter before moving sullenly to the last bed.

The undefined nature of the threat had left Tom feeling even more paranoid than he would've been normally in such circumstances. Beside the bed, a young female nurse with exquisite feline-like eyes, and a mouth so naturally generous that no amount of collagen could replicate it, checked a saline drip. Tom slid over to her and eased a ballpoint pen from her hip pocket stealthily, placing it onto a window sill just out of her reach. Two separate attempts on the life of President Ford had been by women who'd looked like grade-school teachers, and a pen was as deadly as a stiletto. His antennae were up.

"The Leopards have no regard for human life," the doctor said. "Young or old. No matter."

The bed was occupied by a small boy who was almost completely cocooned in bandages. With his wide-eyed stare and lack of visible skin, he resembled a fragile hybrid. The secretary bent over the bed and said a few words. As she went to touch him the doctor spoke.

"Please no. Ninety per cent burns." He shook his head to emphasize that death was certain.

The secretary lowered her hand, looked close to tears but managed a closed-mouth smile. Tom fought the urge to wince.

"Excuse me, ma'am, but we're due at Parliament House in thirty minutes," a female aide said, bending towards the secretary.

Her thick red hair accentuated the paleness of her skin. She looked like a size zero, and what little make-up she wore had been applied with calligraphic precision.

"I visited a hospital just like this one in Iraq eight years ago," the secretary said to her quietly, without turning around. "The only difference being the bombs were ours. But the children looked just the same. This can be an ugly world, Miss Hanson; please don't add to the negativity with insensitive remarks."

Tom glanced at the aide. She was flushed with embarrassment, her beauty suddenly diminished.

"I'm sorry," she said.

"Don't worry, the TV cameras won't pick that up," the secretary replied, turning towards three news teams.

One was local, SAMAA TV, the other two from the States. There were half a dozen more in the corridor. Apart from the local crew, the teams had drawn lots. There just wasn't enough room on the ward.

The secretary shook the doctor's hand, thanking him and praising his work. She waved to the nurses and children, some of whom smiled and waved back, while others just carried on looking vaguely bemused. Tom retained his position, readying himself for the obstacle course that would no doubt occur in the corridors leading to the hospital lobby.

Once that had been overcome, she would shake hands with the security-vetted group and give a short statement to the news hounds. He would call up the tactical support team and usher her inside an SUV fitted with run-flat tyres. The windshields were made of glass-clad polycarbonate, which were both bullet-resistant and prevented glass fragments from showering inward. But the windows were constructed from layers of a laminated material known as one-way bulletproof glass. This prevented rounds from entering the vehicle, while at the same time allowing agents to fire out of it, as the unique combination of absorptive and flexible qualities of the layers responded accordingly. It was as safe a civilian vehicle as science could create.

But it was best practice to have the SUVs close to the exit point, parallel, in fact. In this instance they would block the view for the TV crews and the crowds, and Tom now knew that the secretary's visit was essentially a PR exercise, despite her sincerity. He told himself it would be fine.

That done, he would breathe easily for a second or two before the whole routine would begin again.

This, at least, was his plan.

FOUR

THE LOBBY LED to an incongruous-looking, clear-glass frontage set back about three metres from the narrow sidewalk. The excitable crowds were being held at bay by skinny, moustachioed policemen, wielding long wooden batons. Tom would've given a year's pay just to have had them all swept by portable body scanners before they'd gotten within a hundred metres of the secretary. Regular procedure stateside.

But he consoled himself by thinking that the plan was simple, and in his experience simple was best. The police would create a secure funnel, which the secretary would move down to be met by the lead MSD SUV parked twenty metres to the right, flanked by police outriders. The protective detail would walk around her. If there was a hint of trouble, they'd form the closed-box formation, so that she'd be covered by their bodies for a full three hundred and sixty degrees, each agent within half an arm's reach of her.

He stuck a couple of fingers inside his stiff collar, wishing he could loosen his dark-blue necktie. He put on mirrored shades. It was stifling, just as Steve had said it would be, even though it was only 10:13. He was to Tom's right, his face glistening with a fine sheen of sweat. They exchanged tight nods.

Still positioned behind her right shoulder, he kept his head up. The secretary stepped back after brief contact, as he'd taught her to do, and moved steadily from hospital staff to well-wishing local dignitary. A second agent walked further down the line-up, while a third was shadowing her movement from behind it, watching for a drawn-back fist or leg, or worse. The split-second advantage could be crucial.

Seeing a rotund man in a blue pinstripe with his hand in his jacket pocket, Tom leaned towards him. "Excuse me, sir. Please remove your hand from your pocket." He could speak good Urdu, but knew the majority of educated Pakistanis spoke fluent English.

The man looked bewildered, but removed it just the same.

"Thank you, sir," Tom said.

He scanned those nearby looking for pre-attack indicators. Most were subtle movements, but they could be exaggerated. He knew that it didn't matter if someone was smiling like a Baptist preacher, the average assailant exhibited at least one before an assault. A shifting body, rapid shallow breathing, trembling hands or dilating pupils. Traits brought about when the adrenal glands produced an adrenalin dump.

He stayed close to the line. The key distance was seven metres. Anything inside that and a trained operative had a chance to stop a person drawing a concealed handgun and discharging it; anything outside and the chances were they would get off a round. It didn't matter how good a person was told or thought they were; it was a fact.

He was aware of everything around him. The details that most people missed or weren't interested in even if they didn't. If there was a security lapse, he'd have to manage the natural adrenalin surge that would happen in his own body. Primed meant being one step from a

reaction rather than three. It meant avoiding being para-
lyzed by a sensory overload, or panicking, as the body
was swamped by hormones. It meant learning to run
at a person who had pulled out a twelve-gauge shotgun
rather than heading in the other direction.

Mentally, he saw someone lurch at the secretary, a
knife in hand. Stepping forward, he used his body as
cover for hers. He stretched out his left hand to grab her
arm, and manoeuvred her behind him, holding her back
to his. Simultaneously, he quick-drew his SIG, pointing.
Aggressive words and actions were generally enough to
subdue an assailant. But if he saw a handgun, he'd pro-
pel into the gap, and swing her to the ground behind his
legs, as he fired into the centre of the assailant's chest.
His team would bolt over, shielding her entirely in the
tepee-shaped formation.

Check.

Ten seconds later, he was drawn to a woman in the
front row. She was large-boned, a sweep of shiny black
hair protruding from her dupatta headscarf. She wore
a canary-yellow Shalwar Kameez, and was holding a
bunch of pink roses. But he was drawn to her because
the flowers were vibrating, just enough to mark her out.
She didn't strike him as a shy individual, so he eased
the secretary on before the woman could present them.

Something's not right, he thought. He couldn't work
it out at first. Then it hit him. A distraction, perhaps.
With that, a commotion started in his peripheral vision;
to his left. He turned. Four young men had broken free
from the crowd and had overpowered Sam Eddy. He
was a thick-necked ex-DEA agent. The type that didn't
go down easily. But he was on his back now, his jaw
slack, taking a vicious kicking.

Tom felt the urge to go to his aid. But the secretary was in front of him, and his first duty was to her. Besides, it was a rule that one attack tended to be followed by another, and there was no counterambush team on hand. He spoke briefly into his mic, part of the restricted radio network linked to the temporary command centre. Two agents dashed to Sam's aid, quickly followed by a dozen or more policemen who'd taken the initiative.

As he drew the secretary behind his back the woman with the flowers rushed forward and flung them into his face from the side. He parried most of them away with his free hand, but a thorn scratched his forehead, drawing blood. Half squinting, he glimpsed a muscular guy push through the crowd. The man threw a straight right, baring his teeth like a primate. Tom just managed to block the full force with his forearm, the fist grazing over his temple.

Before he had a chance to follow it up, Tom leaned forward and ploughed his elbow into the man's cheek. It wasn't hard enough to fracture the bone, but he needed to disable him fast. As the man's head jerked sideways Tom applied an arm lock, slid his right leg behind the front ankle, and struck him just under the throat with his palm, his fingers and thumb split in a V-shape. The man had no option but to fall over Tom's extended thigh.

As fellow agents took hold of the secretary and bundled her away, Tom decided to keep the lock on. He grasped the man's shirt, and lowered the body to the asphalt. Experiencing a hit of hormones, he heard gasps and half-muffled cursing, sensed the crowd moving back. The attackers had targeted him, not the secretary, and that had almost caught him off guard.

"Stay down!" he snarled.

Although the man was barely conscious, Tom didn't have the time or inclination to deal with him again, and he wasn't carrying cuffs. But the agent shadowing the secretary burst through the line-up, and grabbed the guy in a headlock.

Straightening up, Tom caught sight of the female slinking away, although people were pointing at her and calling out. Before he could get the police to arrest her, the agitated words of agents flooded his earpiece. The secretary, he thought, grimacing. He pivoted around. Two of his team, Dave Robbins and Becky Sykes, were jogging with her, Becky holding her elbow, Dave shielding her lithe but awkward frame. She was wobbling on her high heels, and Tom barked into his radio, told them to remove the damn things or lift her.

Seeing that the MSD team had alighted from the SUVs parked on the dusty roadway, he glanced back to see how Sam was faring. The male agents had restrained a couple of the young men, pinning them to the ground with their suited bulks, although their weapons were still holstered. Sam lay face up and looked to be in bad shape. A pool of dull-red blood had formed around his head, the consistency of mucus. The policemen were beating the other two men with their batons. If they kept it up, they'd either kill them or cause brain damage, Tom thought.

He turned, saw that the secretary had almost reached the nearest SUV. It couldn't drive up to her due to the fracas on the road. But the MSD agents had surrounded her with their body-armoured chests and backs, their weapons sweeping the crowd and the roofs of the surrounding buildings for any sign of a shooter. Evacuation was the best defence. He knew they'd manoeuvre her swiftly into the rear vehicle and exit at speed.

He had a gut feeling and decided to stay put. A sixth sense that had developed over the years. He checked the windows opposite, the tattered drapes half drawn. After a three-second scan, he saw what looked like the muzzle of an assault rifle disappear from view, although he couldn't be sure. He shouted into the radio and drew his SIG, releasing the safety. Two MSD agents raced towards the building's entrance, shoving people out of the way as they went.

He aimed his SIG at the window, deciding that if the image re-emerged he'd empty a full clip into the dirt-stained glass, irrespective of the outcome.

Then his worst nightmare began.

FIVE

SMOKE AND STUN grenades hit the ground first, quickly followed by tear gas and bursts of automatic fire. Flashes of white light erupted, the high-pitched blasts blowing people off their feet. Others flailed about, blood leaching from their bodies. The two agents who were sprinting towards the building were dropped at the double doors. Panic-stricken, the crowd began to stampede, desperate to escape the kill zone. The air was swamped by hysterical screams, the police rendered useless, hunkering down as bullets cut chunks from wooden beams and ricocheted off metal posts and concrete overhangs.

Tom swayed, disorientated, his ears throbbing. Shaking his head in an attempt to revive himself, he glimpsed at least ten armed men rappelling from open windows, their faces obscured by gas masks. They had what looked like HK sub-machine guns strapped to their backs, with scopes, which he guessed were of the thermal imaging variety and would allow them to see in the smoke. He half raised his SIG, thought he was going to black out. Before he had a chance to get off a round, they vanished into the grey haze rising menacingly from ground level. Due to the state he was in, he guessed he would've capped an innocent by mistake, even if he'd been able to squeeze the trigger.

He did his best to turn his head. He couldn't make out the SUVs or the secretary, either, now, and sensed the first tendrils of panic, his heart rate escalating. He just hoped the MSD agents had evacuated her already. As dopamine kicked in, the pain eased, and his muscles began to take in oxygen at an increased rate, counteracting his ebbing strength. He searched the roofs above as best he could. The snipers, he thought. Where the hell are they?

A massive explosion erupted, sending him to the ground. He landed on his left shoulder, the pain making him grit his teeth and moan. Blinking rapidly, he just about made out an SUV somersaulting above the smoke. He knew the car had an anti-explosion fuel tank laced with fire-resistant cladding, and was leak proof. This protected it from a high-velocity round or an anti-personnel landmine. But as flames engulfed it he figured it must have been parked over an IED. That and the force of the blast. He damned the Pakistani ISI. It was either incompetence or complicity. Either way, he blamed them.

Pushing himself up with his grazed hands, he stumbled forward, bursts from sub-machine guns tearing into flesh and bone about him. But he barely heard them, his hearing impaired by the blast. His eyes felt as if soap had been rubbed into them, the tear gas almost blinding him and making him feel nauseous. He began retching, and his shades slipped off. Looking up, he squinted as the bright light hit him.

Move, he thought. Keep moving.

As he got closer to where the SUVs were parked he felt the intense heat from the burning wreckage of the lead vehicle. The armour plating could withstand a grenade blast, but the IED had all but shredded the doors. The car had landed on top of a police motorcycle, the rider spreadeagled under the front right-hand wheel. As the smoke lifted a little he counted five bodies around it, bloody and contorted. But none was that of the secretary.

Another explosion erupted, taking out the façade of an office block, the shockwave flinging people to the ground. Many were hit or buried by falling masonry. As he buckled at the knees his eyes levelled on the bodies of his two agents, Dave and Becky, stacked against the second SUV like effigies. He half crawled, half scrambled over to them. Their heads had flopped forward. They both had centimetre-wide entry wounds in the backs of their necks. Executed, he thought, resisting the urge to gag. He'd known Dave for three years, and Becky had been married just two months.

As grey ash settled on the talc-like dust that already smeared his suit he inched over the rubble. His eyes felt as if they were melting, the stinging sensation so great that he groaned. But he knew he had to focus.

The rear vehicle was covered by chunks of concrete and twisted iron girders. Wincing, he caught sight of four MSD agents strewn around it. They looked as if they'd been hit by a hundred rounds, their bare heads lacerated and unrecognizable. He moved back and rolled under the middle SUV, his jacket tearing on a protruding piece of metal. As he emerged on the other side the smoke had almost cleared.

Then he saw her. An MSD agent ran by her side, pursued by five armed men. They wore ballistic vests, heavy Kevlar helmets, blast-resistant goggles and respirators. He couldn't risk firing his SIG because, although the crowd had thinned out here, there were still enough people to hinder a clear shot. If it hadn't been for the pursuers, he knew the agent would've flung her to the ground and covered her body to protect it from careering debris. Now the guy was doing the right thing by getting her out of the danger zone in the only manner available to him.

Feeling a surge of adrenalin jump-start his muscles, Tom pushed himself up and broke into a sprint.

As the secretary reached the remnants of a fruit store he saw one of her pursuers kneel. He raised what looked like an M4 carbine, his eye pressed to a scope, a red-dot laser beam showing up on the back of the agent's unprotected neck. A shot rang out, and the agent fell. The secretary stopped, her hands going to her head, clearly traumatized. When the men reached her, she was lifted off her feet.

"Jesus."

Rushing up the road, Tom vaulted over clumps of shattered bricks and mounds of concrete and steel. The men carrying the secretary turned down a side alley, flanked by jerry-built buildings. Three re-emerged and crouched down at the entrance, emptying their magazines into a small group of policemen who'd appeared on the other side of the road. They were all killed or maimed instantly. Tom kept close to the building line, his SIG hovering above a low wall. It was a risky position. If there was another catastrophic explosion, he could be buried. If it happened next door, the shock wave could travel down the wall and kill him.

Seeing the men disappear, he bent down and moved forward, just as a Pakistani squad car came screeching around the far bend. It raced up the opposite end of the road, its siren blaring. But the men returned, together with another, carrying a compact RPG. Tom fired a couple of rounds, although he had to dive for cover behind a concrete pillar immediately afterwards to avoid a volley.

After a few seconds, he risked glancing around it. The telltale trail of white-grey smoke was spewing out of the rear of the rocket launcher.

"Jesus Christ," he whispered, realizing that his hearing had returned to normal.

The police car was shunted sideways, a dust-filled cloud enveloping it. Shards of glass and red-hot chassis shrapnel ripped through the air. He hoped the occupants had died on impact, because the decimated vehicle was engulfed by flames soon afterwards, the tails of burning gasoline curling over the imploded windows and fractured bodywork.

Seeing the men retreat, Tom jogged forward, speaking into his radio to the temporary command centre, his laboured breath resembling an asthmatic's as he reported what had happened and where the secretary was likely to be. He was told that a helicopter was on its way. On its way, he thought. It was meant to be overhead.

He stopped a few metres from the alley entrance. He heard car engines revving furiously, then the distinctive sound of the helicopter above. He looked up and, squinting against the white sun, saw that it was the Pakistani police. He waved his arms, and pointed in desperation in the direction of the cars.

Reaching the alley, he ducked down as a swath of bullets was fired from a HK, brick fragments raining down on him. But he'd managed to glimpse at least five cars, parked hood to trunk, although it'd been impossible to tell which one the secretary was in. The helicopter hovered low, the wash from the rotor blades creating a whirlwind of dust and litter. Kneeling in the open side door, a police commando scanned the ground through the day-scope on his G3 assault rifle. The helicopter is her only hope, Tom thought.

But then he noticed movement below it. A man had appeared on the edge of the flat roof opposite, the unmistakable shape of a Stinger perched on his right shoulder. Tom shouted out to the commando, his words lost in the cacophony of voices coming from behind him, and the wave of sirens from fast-approaching fire crews and ambulances. He aimed his SIG at the man, but there were a good three hundred metres between them. He let off four rounds, but realized there was nothing he could do. The effective range of the handgun was a third of that on a good day.

Stunned, he watched the flash at the tail end of the Stinger's launch tube, the small engine falling away after about three metres, propelling the missile at a rate of over a thousand miles per hour. Using infrared to lock onto the heat in the helicopter's exhaust, the missile impacted the target with devastating precision. The explosion created a fireball and caused the rotor blades to buckle and the windshields to shatter. As the helicopter lost altitude, zigzagging like a massive kite, a second explosion occurred as the fuel ignited. It fell the remainder of the distance to the ground horizontally, black smoke spewing from the tangled metal. When it hit the asphalt, the rotor blades snapped off and splintered, sending a flurry of lethal fragments through the air.

Tom gritted his teeth and ran forward, ducking down as he reached the alley entrance. But the men had disappeared and the cars, half on the narrow sidewalk under awnings and store overhangs, sped away, each one taking a different exit along the rutted track.

He realized he had one option left open to him.

SIX

Tom turned towards the entrance of the run-down apartment block where the man had fired the Stinger. If he could capture him alive, it might be a start. He pressed the PTT button, waited for the static to clear, and reported his position, asking for back-up. He raced across the road, jumping over chunks of jagged metal and smouldering craters, oblivious now to the pepper-like stinking still in his dark, streaming eyes.

As he got to the door of the building he saw that the security system was one step up from a Yale lock. Phlegm rose in his throat, impeding his breathing. He bent over and spat it out, the taste in his mouth like pure acid. He ejected the clip from his SIG, took a fresh one from the pouch on his belt. Slipping it in, he chambered a round in what appeared to be one smooth action. Deftly.

He shielded his eyes with one hand and shot open the entrance door, the rapid impact of the rounds acting like a ripsaw, the spent cases spinning to his right and clanking on the glass-ridden floor. He ducked in, his pulse racing, his shirt sticking to his aching body. There was an elevator directly in front, a concrete staircase to the right. He decided to take the stairs.

He reached the top in twenty seconds. A slick of sweat covered his ribboned forehead, and he was breathing heavily, the debilitating combination of tear gas, inhaled smoke and the build-up of lactic acid taking its toll. He hadn't met anyone on the way up, but had heard muted shouts and cries from the apartments he'd passed. There was a solid wooden door leading to the flat roof, but it was padlocked. You don't shoot padlocks with a round—the ricochet could kill you, he'd told a rookie agent once. It was a good rule. One he wasn't about to discount now.

He spun around, saw a red firefighter's axe in a metal case on the breeze-block wall. Below it, a regular fire extinguisher and a couple of gas canisters. He used the butt of the SIG as a hammer on the Plexiglas cover. After the first hit, the plastic broke, and he jerked out the axe from its perch. He holstered his weapon, and held the axe firmly in both hands. He stood to the side of the door, and began hacking at the wood, knocking out the lock with the splintering chunks.

Dropping the axe, he drew his SIG. He kicked open the door, but ducked down behind the wall immediately afterwards. It was a sound move. A burst of automatic rounds tore into the doorframe and lintel, and peppered the wall to the rear. He felt blood run down his face, but felt no pain save for something akin to a paper cut. He brushed his forehead, pulled out a large splinter.

He glanced around the door, seeing a portion of the ill-kempt rooftop: an array of rusted TV aerials, mouldy tarps, and a weather-beaten awning hung over plastic chairs. There was no visible sign of the shooter. He moved back, picked up one of the canisters, and held it before him. Turning, he launched it into the centre of the rooftop.

As he sank down against the wall a second burst was unleashed. But he'd figured out the trajectory of the bullets. Smarting, he aimed his SIG around the doorway at the canister. Fired. The round pierced the metal and a huge mushroom of white smoke spewed out, the safety valve preventing it from exploding into a thousand lethal shards as he'd hoped it would. He stepped back, grabbed the axe and flung it, so that it somersaulted handle over blade to the left.

As it clattered to the concrete floor he darted out from the wall, using the smoke as cover. He dived into a forward roll to the right. Springing up into a crouch position, he glimpsed a man in black fatigues and a gas mask, holding a MAC-10 machine pistol: a stubby weapon fitted with a suppressor and a holographic sight. Just as the smoke was thinning Tom shot him twice in the legs, guessing he was wearing ballistic plates. The pistol fell from his victim's hands. He ran over.

The man was still, save for his twitching left leg. Tom didn't have the time to frisk him, the Stinger being nowhere in sight. He spoke into his mic, reporting his position and saying that one terrorist was down. Badly wounded.

He checked behind a pile of bricks, and noticed the curved iron handrails of a fire escape on the rear wall about four metres away. He sprinted over, saw a man descending three-quarters of the way down, the Stinger strapped to his back. The ground-to-air weapon weighed a mere sixteen kilograms, but it could hit anything flying below four-thousand metres. The helicopter had been hovering at less than thirty and hadn't stood a chance.

The fire escape was rusted and unstable, the steps grating against the concrete under the weight of the black-clad terrorist. But at least it reached all the way to the side road beneath, which was the reason the access door was locked, Tom guessed.

If the man had a handgun, Tom knew he would be ridiculously vulnerable. But if he used his SIG to shoot him from above, he wouldn't be any further forward. Unless he just winged him, and the man didn't die from the fall. Concluding that that was far too risky, Tom spoke into his mic and asked for back-up again, said that the area should be cordoned off. The short reply crackled over the radio: "With what?" He figured all the nearby local resources were still dealing with the devastation outside the hospital.

He eased over the ledge, his right foot hitting the third step. He saw the man look up, a tinted gas mask and woollen skullcap covering his face and head. The man half slid down the remainder of the steps, hitting the ground with a crunch of his boots. Tom hurtled after him, almost losing his balance twice, the fire escape threatening to bust loose from the wall and either swing under his weight or collapse backwards. Conscious that the man could escape, he placed his feet outside the steps. He plummeted the last five metres, crouching into a parachute roll at the bottom.

He heard a motorcycle engine and saw the man hobbling along, his left leg dragging behind him. He was heading towards a teenage boy sitting astride the bike. The boy, twisted around on the two-man saddle and wearing only thin white cotton and sandals, was calling out and beckoning with his hand. The man released the clip on the canvas bag, and the Stinger fell to the floor. In his condition, the dead weight was slowing him to a crawl.

The side street was narrow, bordered by open-fronted

stores, a smattering of people running about or point-ing at the flames and smoke rising above the buildings opposite. A motorcycle was undoubtedly the best op-tion. Tom broke into a run behind the shooter, saw him cock his leg over the back of the motorcycle and grab the saddle bars. He realized he had to act decisively. He stopped, bent down onto one knee, his lungs heav-ing. He raised his SIG, steadying his aim with his left hand, the tear gas still forming a milky sheen on his eyes. The motorcycle sped away, the engine screech-ing like a kicked cat as the back tyre skidded and threw up dust and grit.

You got one shot, Tom thought. Make it your best.

SEVEN

THE SIG BUCKED and the spent case skipped out. Tom didn't move. The motorcycle was doing maybe thirty when it lurched to the left at a ninety-degree angle, smashing into a stack of wooden cages full of chickens. The few people in the street ran for cover, the women pulling at their hijabs. Tom stood up just as the owner of the store stormed out, a rotund middle-aged man wearing a long white shirt. He dragged the boy up by his arm, and cuffed him over the head. But when he saw Tom running towards him, gun in hand, he rushed back into the store.

Tom pointed the SIG at the boy, gestured to him to stand still. The shooter was strewn on the ground, the motorcycle's battered fuel tank lying on his right thigh. He lifted his gas mask, clearly struggling to breathe. Gasping, he held it out for a second before letting it drop back. Tom didn't see his face, just the sunlight glinting off a gold necklace, half lost among the curling black hairs, damp with sweat. He was a tall man, Tom estimated, perhaps six-four, his limbs beneath his dark fatigues appearing well-muscled. But he wasn't strapped.

Holstering his SIG, Tom bent over, about to jerk the man up, put an arm lock on him and half drag him back to…what? he thought. The Pakistani police would get him talking soon enough, but that kind of harsh treatment made a man say anything to save his ass. He thought briefly if he should get the CIA to pick him up and take him to a remote, classified detention centre. Maybe he should ask him some questions of his own.

Halfway down, Tom saw the boy, who looked about seventeen years old, pull out a handgun from his waistband. He pointed it at Tom, who recognized it as a Kel-Tec P11 semi-auto; a little over thirteen centimetres long, with rounded edges designed for concealment. But it was chambered in 9mm Lugar and could stop a gorilla in its tracks. They were rare in this part of the world, so Tom figured it was a gift from the kidnappers; an inducement, perhaps.

The boy shouted at him to step back. Tom straightened up, told the boy in Urdu to relax. The boy's eyes were glazed, he noticed, his face unusually gaunt, the skin sallow and spot-ridden. There was something in those oyster-flesh eyes that told Tom the boy was both unstable and fearless.

The man managed to ease out from under the motorcycle and, grunting, struggled up. Tom stretched towards him, but the boy shot at the dirt between them and he stepped back. The man remained silent, turned and limped off. The boy smiled at Tom, his teeth stained a dull yellow. An opiate addict, Tom thought. He knew that, despite being a Muslim country, Pakistan was awash with drugs. The kid was high or coming down. Either way, he was capable of putting a bullet in his chest.

Tom offered him his watch and wallet. The boy just grinned. Seven metres, he thought, the takedown zone. The kid was less than two metres away, but the gun was pointing at Tom's head now, and making a grab at it would be suicidal.

He watched the man slink into an alley and cursed

himself. But even if he hadn't holstered his SIG, he knew he wouldn't have shot the boy. He'd joined the DS to protect people, and that meant he might have to kill. But not like this. Not a kid on drugs with no immediate and direct danger to his charge.

Tom said he should put the gun down, that he'd done his job and that he would vouch for him. Truth was, he needed him alive. With the man gone, he was a potential link to those who had abducted the secretary. Although he knew that meant probable brutality at the hands of the Pakistanis, there was nothing he could do to prevent it.

He could see that the boy was wavering, that, despite the drugs, he didn't have it in him to kill a man without cause. He would wait. The boy would succumb to his prompting, and if he didn't drop the weapon he would risk disarming him as he lowered it, just in case he changed his mind. He kept talking, his tone sober and sympathetic. The boy's head began to bow, his eyes blinking frantically, his mouth forming words he couldn't speak.

He's going to drop it, Tom thought.

A shot rang out. The boy buckled. Instinctively, Tom reached out to him, but he knew he was dead as soon as he slumped to the ground. A fountain of blood had spurted out from his left temple as the round impacted. A split second later, another round pinged through the air just centimetres from Tom's head. He drew his SIG, and, spinning around and ducking down, he heard rapid fire.

He saw Steve Coombs about six metres away, his gun raised towards the flat roof of an adjacent store. His face was creased, his body relaxed. He had both hands on his SIG and was leaning forward a little from the waist, as if he were on a range doing target practice. But the roof was empty.

Tom turned back around, holstering his SIG. He took off his jacket and, bending down, placed it over the kid's upper body and head. He heard Steve come up behind him, sniffing and clearing his throat. Tom figured the unknown assassin had killed the boy to prevent him from talking. He glanced over his shoulder just as his friend jerked out the silver crucifix he always wore around his neck. Placing it to his lips, Steve kissed the crucified Christ.

EIGHT

LINDA LAY FACEDOWN in the rear footwell of a car that was now travelling at a sensible speed. She had a boot on her neck and another on her ankles. Her hands and feet had been secured with flex-cuffs. She was gagged with grey masking tape and a hessian sack had been placed over her head. The car radio blared out what sounded like a string of Pakistani pop songs. She hadn't seen her captors' faces. They hadn't spoken. She'd travelled in the footwell before, after a nut had fired what turned out to be a starting pistol at her. An agent had covered her whole body with his and hadn't let her up for what seemed like miles. This time it was different.

She felt sweat bead on her forehead, and dug a fingernail into her thumb to stop herself from weeping. She thought about her husband, John, and her two girls. She cursed herself for agreeing to visit the hospital and for not heeding the advice of the deputy director and Tom Dupree. But she still had the presence of mind to know that that wouldn't help her now, so she did her best to concentrate on counting her breaths.

Two minutes later, she decided to survive by whatever means and fought to focus on something more positive to assuage her escalating fear. She told herself that her people would be looking for her, that roadblocks had been set up. They could follow her, after all, at US

Air Force bases, via drones, or whatever else they had that even she didn't know about.

Then she did her best to remember what Tom had told her about how to respond if she were ever kidnapped. Do not resist them, she thought. Act upon all reasonable instructions without complaint. Refrain from making retaliatory threats or unrealistic promises. Attempt to build up a rapport, but slowly to avoid it being considered contrived.

But then she began to waver again. For now she was in the hands of men with no humanity, who had snuffed out life as most people sprayed mosquitoes or swatted bugs.

She knew her see-saw emotions were reasonable in the circumstances. But she had to survive. For John. For her girls.

Oh, God, hear my prayer. Help me.

NINE

An hour and a half later, after undergoing an initial debriefing at the temporary command centre, Tom showed his blue and gold DS badge to a cordon of harried-looking policemen dressed in light-khaki pants and maroon shirts, guarding the now-shattered glass doors that led to the hospital lobby. The flanks were occupied by a platoon of US Marines, some of whom were handing out water bottles and the contents of med kits to survivors.

A CIA paramilitary operative stood immediately inside. He held an M6A2 carbine, said he'd just arrived from the embassy with ten colleagues. Edging past him, Tom was hit by the shocking sight of the aftermath of the attack.

The injured lay on gurneys or on blankets on the floor. Every centimetre of the ground-floor corridors seemed to be a mass of writhing bodies, their moans and shrieks reverberating in his ears. At least twenty doctors, nurses and paramedics were doing what they could, although it was obvious that they were overwhelmed by both the number of casualties and the severity of their wounds.

Tom knew for sure that three of his protective detail had been killed in the attack; another two badly injured, he'd been told. Mark Jennings, the youngest agent, a veterinarian's son from Arkansas, had been shot in the head. He'd been examined by a specialist who'd been flown in by an MH-53 search and rescue helicopter from Islamabad's Maroof International Hospital.

Tom eased by a woman doctor, her latex gloves soaked in blood. Two orderlies were holding down a young boy as the doctor attempted to give him a shot of morphine. A woman with angular features, whom Tom took for his mother, was hysterical, shaking her hands at the ceiling and wailing. He pushed open a fire door, and took the stairs two at a time to the third floor.

A muscular man in his mid-twenties stood guard outside one of the private rooms. He wore a flak jacket over a short-sleeved shirt, and held a HK sub-machine gun before his chest. He turned as Tom entered the corridor, nodded briefly. Tom figured he was CIA, too.

The door's glass pane was criss-crossed with wire, although Tom glimpsed a bed beside the far wall, a hastily boarded-up window above it. He strolled in, a closed-mouthed smile slicing across his face. It was all he could muster. The room was a dull white and smelt faintly of mould. But at least the AC was functioning, although it sounded like an antique generator.

As he walked over to the bed Tom saw half a dozen tubes coming out of Jennings, including an IV drip. He guessed the poor guy was lucky to be alive. When he reached him, he was lying flat with an expressionless face, a bloated dull-red-and-yellowish bruise on his left cheek like a piece of ripped plum. The top of his head had been bandaged, his hair shaved.

"Lyric?" he asked, as soon as he registered Tom's face.

"She's still missing."

"Goddamnit!"

"Don't worry. We'll find her before the day is out,"

Tom said, lying. There was no point in making Jennings feel worse than he already did.

"You think?"

"Sure."

"Thank God."

"You'll be here for a few days," Tom said. "Then we'll get you home."

"You gotta gum? I gave up the smokes five years since. I still get the urge, especially after getting shot in the head. And this pillow's as lumpy as hell and smells like it's had guinea pigs nesting in it."

"I'll be sure to get you a new one. What's the diagnosis?" Tom asked, handing Jennings a stick of gum.

"The doc told me that the chances of surviving a head shot are about five per cent. And of those who live, only one in ten escapes suffering permanent disability. A bullet likes to rattle around in the skull, turning the brain into scrambled eggs, according to him. It's a miracle, Tom, beating those odds. But they can't operate. It's too dangerous. Guess I'll have to carry it around as a souvenir."

"That's good to hear. I think," Tom said, glad that Jennings was taking it so well.

"It hurt like hell, Tom. Like a goddamned mustang mistook my head for a rattlesnake." Jennings winced, as if reacting to the initial impact. "How does it look?"

"Like that mustang had a grudge," Tom said, trying to keep the mood light.

"I collapsed. The sky turned red. Thought I was dying. I thought I was dying, Tom. And I don't mind telling you, I was terrified."

Yeah, too good to be true, Tom thought. He could see that Jennings was getting upset. It was a natural reaction. He knew that people who'd sustained head injuries, or sometimes just had their noses broken, often suffered severe depression soon afterwards. But at least the headshot had turned out to be better than a round in the leg or shoulder, where massive blood vessels were situated. In Nigeria, he'd watched a man bleed out in less than five minutes after being shot in the upper thigh. A medic had told him the femoral artery, which lay close to the surface of the skin, had been severed, and had retracted back up into the pelvis. And the shoulder housed a ball-and-socket joint that was all but inoperable if it got pulverised by a bullet.

Tom put his hand on Jennings's forearm. "It'll be all right. Trust me."

"Who were they?"

"We don't know for certain. But you did your job."

"The hell I did. I got shot and Lyric has been kidnapped by a bunch of psycho Islamic terrorists, the way I see it. We lost some good people, too. Becky was a fine woman. It's a goddamned disaster," he said, using his palm to wipe his eyes dry.

Tom sucked his bottom lip, nodding. "There's a CIA guy outside if you need anything."

"He should be looking for her. It's a waste of resources. Nobody gives a damn about me. You think someone's gonna creep up the fire escape and smother me with a pillow, or inject poison into one of these tubes?"

"No, I don't. Now get some rest."

He grabbed Tom's wrist. "Find her, Tom. Just find her."

"I made a promise to her. I *will* keep it."

"And kill them. Kill them for murdering our own and doing this."

Tom smiled, weakly. "Rest. Then home."

He patted Jennings on the arm and left.

"He'll be fine, thanks for asking," Tom said to the CIA guy, just wanting to take it all out on someone, but regretting it instantly afterwards.

The CIA man remained silent. Just stared hard. Tom guessed he didn't even have the kudos to rouse a response any more. Besides, often people who said nothing said a helluva lot; all of it derogatory.

He'd been told to return to the embassy where, no doubt, he would be subjected to the second of many frame-by-frame debriefings on what had gone so badly wrong. As he reached the fire door at the end of the corridor he shoved it open. He stopped at the top of the stairs and sank down, engulfed by a sense of guilt and failure that had no hope of personal resolution, and not for the first time.

Involuntarily, he saw his mother's face. He'd broken a promise to her, too.

TEN

THE CAR HAD taken a series of tight curves before slowing down to maybe fifteen miles an hour. Linda guessed she'd been in the car for an hour or more. She'd heard sirens and people shouting and screaming at first, but now there was just the sound of the radio. Her captors still hadn't spoken a word. No contact, either, save for the boots on her neck and ankles, as if they were restraining a bad-tempered dog.

The car stopped and the music died, but the engine remained ticking over. She heard what sounded like a chain being drawn across metal, the creaking of a door opening. The car moved forward slowly before coming to a halt once more, but this time the engine was switched off. The boots were removed from her neck and ankles. She felt the plasticuffs restraint on her lower shins being cut, and was manhandled out of the rear footwell. The cramp in her legs made her wobble at first, but strong hands grasped her upper arms, helping her to stand upright.

Apart from her pantyhose, her feet were bare, and as she inched over the gravel the edges dug into her heels. No one spoke. The hood still covered her head. Will they kill me now? she thought, the gag preventing her from pleading for her life even if she'd succumbed to the urge. She decided not to struggle, to maintain her dignity and continue to comply, just as Tom had told her to. Then she thought that that was a pathetic thought. What choice do I have?

She sensed she was going to retch, but gulped a couple of times and the bile eased back down her slender throat. If I get out of this, things will change, she thought. I will spend more time with John and the girls. Maybe retire from public life and take up a teaching post at a university. She realized then that she had to tell herself these things, because the alternative was to start to go ever so slightly mad.

She was led a few steps forward before her hands were cut free, and she rotated her wrists to help the blood flow freely there. A hand clasped her left wrist, and moved it to something cold and smooth, which she realized was a handrail. An arm linked hers, and she was led down a flight of steps. Underground, she thought. Dear God, why are they taking me underground?

At the bottom of the steps, she heard the same sounds of a chain being removed and a door opening, the crunch of more footsteps on gravel. A tug of her arm prompted her to move again, and she realized that she was going inside, because the sun had stopped beating on her head. It was cool now, a smell redolent of blocked drains.

She went through three more doors, hearing the hinges creak and the doors shut behind her. She suddenly sensed that her feet were moving across something that felt like tiles. Yes, tiles, she thought, feeling the line of grout with her toes as she shuffled along.

Finally, she was held still.

When the hood was removed and she registered the contents of the room, tears welled in her eyes.

ELEVEN

IN THE SITUATION ROOM at the White House, the President of the United States, the fifty-year-old Robert Simmons, a Nebraskan with the lean body of a marathon runner and swept-back greying hair, had already convened a meeting. He sat on a swivel chair at the head of a mahogany table surrounded by two tiers of curved computer terminals. The pensive faces of the commander of the Joint Special Operations Command—JSOC—and Deputy Director Houseman peered out from separate flat-panel videoconference screens.

Those members of the National Security Council who'd been in DC, including the Secretary of Defense, the National Security Advisor and the vice president, had joined the commander-in-chief here. It was 03:05 in the capital and everyone present had been woken from their sleep as soon as the crisis had begun.

The basement room was an intelligence management centre used to conduct secure communications. The president watched a CNN news report on a TV monitor, showing the aftermath of the secretary's abduction in Islamabad, the dishevelled female reporter's voice cracking with emotion as she spoke. She stood in front of a chaotic scene: black smoke belched from the remnants of a building, the blaze being tackled by three fire crews. The LED lights of ambulances and police cars flickered. Sirens wailed. The dead and injured were still being carried away on stretchers. People were crying and shouting, while others simply sat on the kerb, dazed and bloodied.

"The Pakistan military, which formed a provisional government after a bloodless coup eleven months ago, are blaming the Leopards of Islam, the Pakistani Shia terrorist organization, for the attack and the kidnapping of the US Secretary of State, Linda Carlyle," the reporter said. *"The Leopards, who carried out an assassination attempt on the Pakistani President in Washington DC on March 10th this year, killing thirty people in the capital, have remained silent. But a source at the US Embassy here in Islamabad has revealed that a threat against the secretary's life was made to the embassy by a man claiming to represent the Leopards less than two hours before this latest outrage. There is mounting speculation that the secretary may have been kidnapped in order to facilitate the release of twelve Pakistani men alleged to have taken part in the March 10th atrocity, who are currently in US protective custody at an unspecified location prior to their trial for multiple counts of murder and the attempt on the Pakistani President's life."*

"Turn it off, Angie," the president said.

The flat-screen cut to black.

"God only knows what she's suffering," he said.

"I hate to say this, Mr President, but she could be dead already," the Secretary of Defense said, preferring to be formal in such circumstances, the fingers of his right hand propping up his ample head as he rested his elbow on the table.

"Don't you think I know that, Jack; and how the hell did that reporter know the secretary received a death threat this morning?"

"The caller spoke to the switchboard operator, Mr President," Deputy Director Houseman said, his hard features filling the screen, highlighting the mottling on his cheeks and hawk's nose.

"I'm aware of that also. Find out for sure. What are the chances the Leopards are to blame?"

"Without any intelligence reports to go on, I'd say about sixty per cent, sir," Houseman replied.

"They'd do it just to humiliate us. I don't want the Bureau of Diplomatic Security dealing with this. The CIA will assume operational control. I will personally oversee matters from here."

"Mr President, the White House is on high alert, but I'd prefer it if you boarded Air Force One, at least for the next few hours," the secretary said, shuffling uneasily in his chair now, his forty-eight-inch waist spilling over his pants.

"That isn't going to happen, Jack," the president replied.

The secretary rubbed his flabby neck before shaking his head.

"I want the Joint Chief and the Under-Secretary back home today. I want the embassy closed in forty-eight hours. Is that clear, Bill?"

"Understood, Mr President," Houseman said from the screen.

"Closing the embassy might not be the best move," the secretary said.

"I don't want another US citizen killed over there. The DS has taken a beating. The country will be seeing quite enough coffins draped in the flag. Quite enough."

The president took soundings from each of the assembled group. At this stage, no one was able to come up with a coherent plan. Any plan, in fact.

"We have replays, Mr President," a defence advisor said, sitting in the second row of chairs behind the table. "On terminal two."

The president and the others watched in silence as the images of the kidnapping unfolded. The smoke obscured the view as it was intended to. The drone operators, fully trained pilots at Creech Air Force Base, had focused on the secretary being bundled down the alley. But the Pakistani police helicopter exploding into a white flash hadn't helped, and in any event it was impossible to make out which of the five cars that had sped off from underneath the overhangs and awnings had been used to carry her.

"They parked there purposely. They knew we'd have Linda covered," the Secretary of Defense said.

The president knew that drones could track insurgents with lasers to pinpoint them for pursuing Special Forces on the ground. But one of the few times he'd felt the multibillion-dollar technology would earn its keep, it had been rendered useless by a simple yet very effective diversionary tactic.

"Goddamn it, Jack. This is awful. I want everyone we have on this. Everyone, do you understand?"

"All leave has been cancelled for the FBI at the Hoover Building until further notice. The CIA at Langley and the NSA at Fort Meade, too," he replied.

"Mr President," Houseman said.

"Yes, Bill."

"I should point out that we have no evidence to date that the secretary was taken in a car. She could've disappeared into one of the buildings. The cars coulda been decoys."

"Either way, find her. Just find her," the president

said. "I want thirty-minute progress reports for the next twelve hours. And I mean *progress*."

"Yes, Mr President," Houseman said, his voice sombre.

The room fell silent again. The president stood up, followed by the assembled men and women. "I think we should pray now," he said, bowing his head, knowing the Secretary of State was a deeply religious woman.

Truth be told, he didn't know what else to say at this juncture. But he felt that a moment of reflection would, at least, assist a sharpening of minds. A resolve to follow every possible lead, legal or otherwise.

TWELVE

Tom was slumped forward in a grey, blow-moulded plastic chair. His head was in his hands, his elbows resting on a Formica table centimetres from an untouched cup of coffee. The interview room at the embassy was no more than twice the size of a suit closet; stuffy and windowless.

He'd been questioned by a fresh-faced counterterrorism agent who'd looked as if he'd belonged to a college fraternity for tiddlywinks. Tom recounted the attack outside the hospital, sucking in air to calm himself. The kid repeated the questions too often for his liking, as if he were trying to trip him up. Tom didn't have anything to hide. What he'd done was standard procedure, although he felt sick to his stomach. If the lead agent had to neutralize a threat, the support agents took his or her place. He'd acted professionally at all times, even though he'd failed. But when the kid had said that he'd recommend a psychological report be obtained, Tom had felt like punching the wall.

After the debriefing, he'd cleaned up in a restroom as best he'd been able. He'd put ointment on his forehead to heal the splinter wound, and checked his multiple bruises, which were deep-red blemishes covering a quarter of his body. He'd noticed that his angular features had hardened, the long shifts and many time-zone changes ageing him. But there was something else in the olive-skinned reflection that stared back from the restroom mirror: guilt at escaping almost without injury. He'd learned that all of the MSD agents were dead or seriously wounded. A total of twenty-three locals had died, another sixty-eight needing surgery of some sort. A third of the Pakistani police deployed there had died also.

Apart from the carnage, the secretary's GPS tracking devices weren't working. She could be anywhere, and as yet no one had a clue. He didn't even know if she was still alive. No ransom demand had been made. Jennings had been right. It was a disaster.

After changing into a sports jacket and fawn-coloured slacks, he'd returned to the interview room as ordered.

Still slouched in the chair, he awaited another round of questions. He fingered a small wooden Buddha he kept in his breast pocket. It wasn't a good-luck charm, but rather the symbol of a personal philosophy he'd cultivated over time.

Get it together, he thought. Just get it together and take it from there. He resolved to stop being so maudlin and see if at least he could do something positive to help find her. No, scratch that, he thought. I have to find her. He'd made a promise and he wasn't going to renege on it. But how? In truth, he had no idea where to start. Then it struck him. The guy he'd shot on the roof had to have been found and recovered. If he was still alive, that might be something. And the two people who assaulted him might have been found by now. He'd been told that the man had escaped in the confusion. He already knew the woman had. But they were known. They were on a list.

He heard the door open. A man with massive hands sat in the chair opposite him, struggled to get comfortable in the confined space.

"They build this place for midgets?" he said.

Tom looked up. It was Dan Crane, a near-legendary CIA operative. Crane smiled, the skin on his wide face crinkling around his robin's-egg-blue eyes.

"You look like shit," he said.

"You don't want to know what I feel like."

"I can guess."

Tom had come across Crane when he had spent two years in New Delhi, protecting the US embassy eight years ago. He'd seen him a couple of times since; once in DC and another at Langley when he'd been guarding the secretary. Crane had a reputation for sardonic humour of the un-PC variety, but he knew the Middle East and South Asia better than anyone else in the agency. He spoke five languages and had an encyclopaedic mind. He'd been held hostage by Hezbollah for three months back in the late eighties. He still had the remnants of scars on his neck and hands, off-white blemishes that looked like skin grafts. Tom didn't want to think about where else he might have scars. His fame had been assured after he'd overseen the analysts who'd pinpointed bin Laden in Abbottabad. That also meant that he could get away with a lot of things that for others would've led to a reprimand, or worse. Crane was an offbeat kind of guy to say the least.

"So, they all got away. Even the sonofabitch you say you shot on the roof and the one who fired the Stinger," Crane said, waving his hand through the air.

"Wait, the man on the roof was incapable of walking.

How the hell did he disappear?" Tom asked, straight-ening up.

Crane held up his hands. "You tell me?"

"You don't believe me?" Tom wondered if Crane had been sent to do what the kid hadn't had the experience or guile to accomplish: make him say something to in-criminate himself.

"I didn't say that. I just said he wasn't there when the command centre asked the police to pick him up."

"What about the man and the woman in the official line-up? They were all supposed to be vetted."

"They were," Crane said. "The Pakistani police raided their houses. Guess what? They weren't there. Now, let's go through it again."

Jesus Christ, Tom thought. Back to square one.

Tom was questioned for a further fifteen minutes. Crane nodded his approval for most of the time, and never once lost his temper or even appeared irritated. When he finished, he looked genuinely sympathetic.

"That's it. Same as I told the kid," Tom said.

"Don't beat yourself up too bad. The guys on the Kennedy detail let it affect their whole lives, even though everyone knows they did all they could. Now it's home for you. There's a flight taking the Under-Secretary of Defense and some brass back at fifteen hundred. You'll be on it."

"I wanna stay. Help out."

Crane sighed. "It's outta the DS's hands. POTUS's orders," he said, using the acronym for the president. "It's down to the spooks now."

"She's still my responsibility. I got a week left as head of the detail. A guy like you can understand that."

"It's not up to me. Besides, you're probably still in

shock. And don't assume you know what makes me tick. You don't," Crane said, pushing the chair back against the wall, attempting to ride it.

"Whatever. But I'm not leaving."

"You disobeying a direct order from POTUS?"

"He's at the top of the food chain. He don't concern himself with cleaner fish."

Crane raised his thick eyebrows. "Wow, you got some self-esteem issues there, Tom. You gonna sprout gills?"

Tom smiled, weakly.

"Seriously, you'll get through this. You're a nice guy, Tom. Go home."

They batted the issue around for a further five minutes. Finally, Crane agreed to pass it by Deputy Director Houseman, who was staying behind to coordinate matters on the ground.

"Appreciate it," Tom said.

Crane struggled to get his bulk out of the chair. "Interview rooms for midgets. Jesus. They'll be ordering us to carry stepladders next so they can climb up and feel less intimated."

"Technically they're called dwarves. Back home they like to be called little people. And they are the same as you and me," Tom said.

"I'm joking with ya. You know that, right?"

"Sure I do," Tom said.

"I know they're the same. They just come up to your goddamned waist."

Tom rubbed his temple and sighed. Crane was smart, but he was a jerk, too. He glanced up. "So come on. How do you figure that guy on the roof disappeared?"

Crane was looking serious, his eyes narrowing. "He was evidence. I guess the Leopards had some plain-clothes guys on the ground, who cleaned up before the Pakistani cops got there."

"Yeah. Sure they did."

"A conspiracy theorist, huh. Well, it won't come as any surprise to you when I say that if the deputy director lets you stay, don't trust anybody. You hear me, Tom?"

Tom thought for a moment. "That include you?"

THIRTEEN

AN HOUR LATER, Crane told Tom that he'd swung it, and that the old man had asked him to join them for an initial in thirty minutes' time.

The secure conference room was thirty metres square, the massive windows obscured by gleaming Venetian blinds. Tom sat at a large pine table on one of the matching rattan-wicker chairs, his brown loafers resting on coral-blue tiles. Crane said that it had been swept for bugs ten minutes before. Behind the locked door, two Marines ensured that they wouldn't be disturbed.

"The ISI are playing hard ball," Houseman said, cradling a fist. "But we have no jurisdiction here. They won't allow the FBI to investigate. Anyone else in the US intelligence community, either."

"They're in a difficult position," Crane said. "If they're seen to be too pro-West, they'll play into the hands of the Pakistan Taliban. And they got enough on their plate with the Shia Leopards just now. On the other hand, if they alienate us, they won't get what they want." He pinched an ear lobe, looking a little smug.

"Which is exactly?" Tom asked.

"About ten US divisions heading into Tehran," Houseman said.

"We should leave them to fight their own battles. The Pakistanis double-crossed us," Crane said, his tone surly. "Goddamned lying sons of bitches who caused the deaths of thousands of US and coalition forces."

Tom knew Crane was referring to bin Laden. If it weren't for the Pakistanis, he would've been captured in Tora Bora back in 2001. A bunch of al-Qaeda and Taliban lieutenants, too. After that, the ISI babysat thousands of insurgents in the Pakistan Tribal Areas. Then they just picked up where they'd left off. When bin Laden's six-year holiday in Abbottabad was factored in, Tom was inclined to agree with Crane.

"That maybe, but I want to know what we're going to do to find Lyric?" he asked, a little more bluntly than he'd intended.

"My money's still on the Leopards," said Crane. "Backed by the Iranians."

"The ISI had to be involved," Tom said. "The assault couldn't have happened if they'd done what they said they would. The helicopter didn't arrive on time. The snipers just disappeared. And it was too well organized."

Houseman cleared his throat. "Listen, son. The Leopards have ex-military in their ranks. They were capable of it. The Iranians equip them with top weaponry. We ain't dealing with farmers with AK-47s here. The building was razed to the ground by thermobaric charges." He snatched up a bottle of water, took a frustrated pull.

Tom saw Crane staring at him.

"When a country is going down the tubes, people start to do all sorts of weird things. It could be as simple as rogue elements," Crane said. "Or just plain corrupt ones. God knows it's a national disease. Besides, the ISI are saying it was Shia traitors in their ranks. Shia cops, too.

You remember when Indira Gandhi, the Prime Minister of India, got assassinated?"

Tom nodded.

"Then you'll recall it was two of her own body-guards. Peppered her with thirty rounds. Sikhs, who did it for revenge after the army stormed their temple and killed hundreds. Religion in these parts overrides any other affiliation."

Tom studied Crane's face. He guessed he'd been a handsome man once. But now his features looked tired, his eyes hooded, his mouth drooping at the sides.

Houseman banged the bottle on the table, as if he wanted Tom to stop staring. Clenching his jaw muscles, the old man said, "Up until the generals took over here, the Pakistanis were talking about declaring war on us if we attacked the Iranians. That gives you a hint at how complicated this area of the world is. They were buddies; now the Pakistanis regard Iran as an existential threat."

"I don't get it," Tom said.

"You obviously ain't heard of the Iran-Pak gas pipeline," Crane said. "The Pakistanis have an ongoing energy crisis. They figured sidling up to the Iranians would go a long way to fixing that. The thing is now, the new Sunni regime here wouldn't let an Iranian pipeline cross their land if their lives depended on it."

"I thought the Iranians wanted to invade Balochistan to get their hands on natural gas," Tom said.

"You're right. They've got the resources to find and extract it. The Pakistanis don't. All their efforts are focused on national security."

"And so what now?" Tom asked, pursing his lips, feeling a little out of his depth.

"There are no contingency plans for such a kidnapping," Crane said. "Not on foreign soil that ain't fully cooperative. That's the risk, and Lyric knew it." He sat back in his chair, began riding it, as appeared to be his habit.

Tom bristled. "What are you saying?"

Crane ignored him. "The flight to Kabul leaves in twenty minutes. Get what you need."

"Wait a second. Lyric is very likely to be right here in Islamabad. And we're leaving?"

"POTUS has ordered the closure of the embassy in forty-eight hours," Houseman said. "You come to Kabul with us or you go home."

"I'm sorry, sir," Tom said. "But why Kabul?"

"The flight time is thirty-five minutes," Houseman said. "We still got a fully operational set-up there. Otherwise we'd be flying back to the States and doing this from a computer screen at Langley. Now get outta here before I change my mind."

Reluctantly, Tom stood up and strode over to the door. They hadn't said anything explicitly, but he guessed the real meeting would begin as soon as he reached the corridor outside.

FOURTEEN

"YOU OKAY?" HOUSEMAN said to Crane after Tom had left.

"I guess."

"Anyone knows what she's going through, it's you, Dan."

"Yeah," Crane said, his mind going back.

He was walking down a narrow street in Beirut, Lebanon, the air thick with the smell of Arabic coffee and grilled chicken. It was midday, and he was sweating badly beneath his flannel shirt. The so-called South Lebanon conflict, the Israeli occupation, which had begun in 1982 and would last until 2000, was in its fifth year.

The small white Fiat came screeching around the corner with four masked men inside. His cover was that of an aid worker from Chicago and he wasn't strapped. But now he wished he had a weapon, if only to have the option of ending it before they took him. He knew what that would mean. The torture first, followed by the years of solitary. Then his corpse would be lifted from the trunk of a car and thrown into a drainage ditch. By the time it was found, the insects would've had a feast and his mother would have nightmares, because the authorities would not allow her to see his face when they flew his body home.

He didn't run, because the only place *to* run was back the way he'd come, and a second vehicle had already stopped halfway through a three-point turn, all but blocking off the street.

They exited the Fiat fast. He was fit and trained, but he knew they'd only make it worse for him in the close confines of the car if he fought them. There was a time for that and a time for raising your hands, he'd learned. He took an instep hard in the groin, and a cosh over the back of his head as he doubled over. He blacked out then.

The makeshift cell Hezbollah had kept him in in Lebanon was a bare concrete room, three metres square, without windows or artificial light. The door was wooden, reinforced with iron strips. When they first dragged him there, he lay in the filth that other men had made. They left him naked, his wrists and ankles chained. He was gagged with rag and tape. They had broken his nose and split his lips.

Each day they fed him on half-rancid scraps like he'd seen people toss to skinny dogs. He drank only tepid water. Occasionally, he heard the muted sound of children laughing, and smelt a faint waft of jasmine. And then he could not say for certain how long he had been there; a month, maybe two. But his muscles had wasted and he ached in every joint. After they had said their morning prayers, they liked to hang him upside down and beat the soles of his feet with sand-filled lengths of rubber hose. His chest was burned with foul-smelling cigarettes. When he was stubborn, they lay him bound in a narrow structure shaped like a grow tunnel in a dusty courtyard. The fierce sun blazed upon the corrugated iron for hours, and he would pass out with the heat. When he woke up, he had blisters on his skin, and was riddled with sand fly and red ant bites.

The duo were good at what they did. He guessed the one with the grey beard had honed his skills on Jewish conscripts over many years, the younger one on his own hapless people, perhaps. They looked to him like father and son. They took him to the edge of consciousness before easing off and bringing him back with buckets of fetid water. Then they rubbed jagged salt into the fresh wounds to make him moan with pain. They asked the same question over and over until it sounded like a perverse mantra.

"Who is The Mandarin? His name? Who is The Mandarin?"

He took to trying to remember what he looked like, the architecture of his own face beneath the scruffy beard that now covered it, and found himself flinching at the slightest sound. They had peeled back his defences with a shrewdness and deliberation that had both surprised and terrified him.

By the time they freed him, he was a different man.

FIFTEEN

THE ARIANA HOTEL was in the Diplomatic Quarter,
Kabul, near the US Embassy and the Presidential Palace. But it hadn't been open to the public for well over a
decade. The former hotel still housed the headquarters
of the CIA in Afghanistan. The compound and the roads
around it were some of the most heavily protected in
the capital, following a day-long siege by insurgents in
September 2011. Crane had grinned and had told Tom
that to the average Afghan, the quarter was as inacces-
sible as a Playboy Bunny.

"It's still off-limits to the local cops," he said as they
rode past a checkpoint with huge cement bollards in
an adapted Land Cruiser. "For how long, who the hell
knows these days?"

The boxlike, cream-coloured structure looked run-
down. Tom saw more than three dozen armed guards
on the perimeter, together with mobile rocket launch-
ers. Two IAV Strykers, eight-wheeled, armoured fighting vehicles fitted with M2 .50-cal machine guns, were
parked either side of the main gate.

"You're not taking any chances, that's for sure," he
said.

"Yeah, but looks are deceiving."

"The Taliban breach this?" Tom asked.

"Green on blue nightmares. You can't trust anyone
in an Afghan uniform. And on the streets it's worse

than ever. We've lost a total of fifty-two core collectors since the military pulled out; fifteen in the last month alone. We stopped making that official a year back. You know, Tom, more people are killed coming down off a mountain than ascending it. Leaving an occupied country ain't no different. They held off for a while there. To encourage us, I figure. But now they want as many dead as possible. I give it maybe three years before even what's left of us are gone for good."

"I'm sorry to hear that. I think."

"You still got your gun on you?"

"Yeah. You want me to hand it in?" Tom asked.

"You're a special agent, ain't ya? You just keep it close. A SIG?"

"Standard-issue."

"I favour the Kimber Eclipse Custom II," Crane said, easing the handgun out of his shoulder holster and weighing it in his hand. "Now that barrel alone is five inches, but it's a .45 ACP and is fitted with these here low-profile night-sights," he went on, fingering the back of the gun where the sights were mounted in rounded dovetails. "And it's only a four-pound trigger pull. I got it in 10mm, too, and that'll take a man's head clean off."

"A good piece," Tom said. "But mine allows an easy draw."

"You wanna hold it?"

"I'm fine."

"Suit yourself," Crane said, holstering it. He took out a slim cigar from his jacket pocket, lit it with a gold lighter. "You smoke, Tom?"

Tom shook his head. He looked at Crane. He took a long pull on the cigar before puffing little smoke rings out of the open window. He was a strange kind of guy.

SIXTEEN

TWENTY MINUTES LATER, Tom was feeling frustrated that
nothing positive seemed to be happening. He found
himself at another intelligence briefing in another secure conference room, although the security had been
ratcheted up several notches. He'd had to show a laminated badge to a Marine outside the shockproof door,
who'd checked his name off on a clipboard list, and
had noticed that the plaster had been replaced by lead-
lined walls to eradicate the threat from electronic listening devices.

Crane and Deputy Director Houseman were present, together with half a dozen CIA analysts, a couple
of high-ranking US Army officers, and a lieutenant in
the 1st Special Forces Operational Detachment-Delta, or
Delta Force, called Mark Sawyer. He was a troop commander in B Squadron, a six-foot blond with a boyish
nose and neat little ears, eyes the colour of cornflower.

B Squadron contained seventy-five operators split
into three troops, which were in turn made up of teams
of five. It was stationed at Pope Air Force Base, North
Carolina. The Delta Force squadrons, together with
SEAL Team 6, made up the direct action and reconnaissance element of the tier-one Special Missions Unit
of the US Armed Forces. Sawyer's troop was on standby
on the off chance something happened in the next day
or two. They'd been training Afghan Special Forces as

part of the US commitment to assisting the country's security services following the official withdrawal, which Tom felt was the only piece of good luck that had happened so far.

Like the façade, the interior of the Ariana wasn't exactly five star, but it had modern facilities and was clean. Apart from the flat-screens and the ubiquitous blue tiles, the basement conference room had a large moulded-plastic table and chairs. It was lit by fluorescent strips, which had added a clinical aspect to what had started as a frosty meeting. Tom knew it was the way when different departments with ultimately competing budgets had to get something done together, the continuing US debt crisis just making that dynamic more acute. But gradually everyone put aside their differences and concentrated on the clear-cut task of getting the secretary home safely, although they had nothing material to go on as yet.

After they had decided that gathering intel from Pakistani assets and sources was their best bet, the door opened and a young Special Forces officer with red hair came into the room without knocking, his face flush with excitement.

"You better have a real interesting thing to say, captain," a broken-nosed colonel said.

"I'm sorry, sir. But we've located Lyric," he said, his arms barely able to refrain from punching the air.

"The GPS," the colonel said, excitedly.

Everyone in the room now knew what Tom had always known. Apart from the tracking devices hidden in her specially made jewellery—her necklace and ring—she'd agreed to have one implanted under the skin of her upper left arm. But due to its sensitive location, it wasn't large or sophisticated enough to prevent jamming.

"Yeah, our techs designed them," Crane said, preferring to lean against the beige wall rather than sit at the table. "But don't hold your breath."

"Where is she, son?" Houseman asked.

"Upper Kurram Valley, sir. We lost the signal for a while there, but, hell, we've found her now."

"Federally Administered Pakistan Tribal Area. A stronghold of the Leopards," Crane said, soberly. "It's picture postcard. Northern Af-Pak border country. Less than a hundred and fifty klicks away, which means it's easily accessible by stealth helos. The two major tribes are the Bangash and the Turi. In Upper Kurram, the Bangash are Shia. The Turi are all Shia. They've both sent alotta young men to join the Leopards."

The assembled men nodded, all tacitly accepting that Crane was the expert in such things.

Tom held back from saying that they had to act fast. It was as obvious to everyone concerned as saying a diet of fries and pizzas wasn't a great idea if you wanted to lose weight. So he kept quiet and did his best to fade into the background, hoping that his presence would be accepted, even though in truth he had no right being here, at least as far as the president was concerned.

He watched Houseman report to the POTUS on a secure video link. After the input of more than a dozen people, including the Director of the CIA—who everyone knew was actually coordinating matters at Langley—a process that took forty-five minutes, the president decided that the National Security Council would consider a rescue plan.

The chances of finding bin Laden in the compound

in Abbottabad had been estimated to be forty per cent when a similar sounding had been taken. The chances of getting the secretary out alive were deemed to be half that at best. But no lines of communication had been established, and every minute that passed meant the chances of getting her out alive were diminishing. There really wasn't any other option, despite the odds.

Houseman turned to Crane. "Go along with Lieutenant Sawyer. He'll liaise with JSOC. Give 'em the benefit of your local knowledge. I want a plan ready to go in two hours."

Crane looked aghast. "That's not enough time. Even if we've got UAVs sending back photos of the brand of toothpaste they prefer," he said, referring to the unmanned aerial vehicles used for reconnaissance.

"I think we can do it in the timeframe, sir," Sawyer said. He turned to Crane. "Two hours is standard prep for a mission."

Tom saw Crane's pale-blue eyes bore into the lieutenant.

"Yeah, for a kill or capture mission. Lyric's life is at stake here," he replied.

"We haven't got time for a red team analysis, or for this. Get to it," Houseman said.

Tom left with Crane and Sawyer, figuring everyone was still too preoccupied to care.

SEVENTEEN

IN A SIMILARLY SECURE, adjacent room, Tom, Crane and
Sawyer were hunched over a large stainless-steel table,
doing final checks on the rescue site via the twenty
printed satellite photos spread out before them. The site
was an ochre-red fort abandoned by the Frontier Corps
of the Pakistan Army three months previously, after
it had been almost overrun by the Leopards, and all
supply routes had been cut off. Black-and-white drone
feeds were playing on laptops either side of the photos.

"I count at least thirty pax," Sawyer said.

Tom frowned.

"That ain't disrespectful," Crane said to Tom. "It's
military speak for people."

Sawyer looked quizzical.

"Tom's sensitive about such things," Crane said,
turning to Sawyer. "He thought you were calling the
locals Paks."

Tom shook his head, thinking that Crane was bait-
ing him deliberately, but let it go. He looked back at the
photos. A few hundred metres beyond the fort there was
a makeshift town, which all but surrounded it. A ragbag
collection of awnings, thin sheets of battered-out metal
containers, and mud and stone and wooden structures.
Home to four thousand Shia refugees from ransacked
and burnt-out towns and villages further south and east.
Innocent civilians who'd escaped from the sectarian

tyranny that was blighting the country. As a result, the helicopters couldn't land far enough away to enable an approach on foot, which Sawyer favoured. There'd be no element of surprise, or the advantage of sneaking up on the fighters before they had a chance to arm themselves. So a creep in, creep out mission was out of the question. They'd have to go in shooting from the off.

Sawyer had spoken with the JSOC Commander already. If the plan was a goer, it had been agreed that two Black Hawks from the 160th Special Operations Aviation Regiment's Night Stalker Unit, stealth helicopters fixed with anti-radar cladding, which could fly as low as thirty metres and at a hundred and thirty miles per hour, would carry the Delta troop as the first wave of attack. An MH-47E/G, multi-mission Chinook with terrain avoidance radar would transport a platoon of Army Rangers from the 75th Ranger Regiment, a light-infantry-combat formation, which was part of the US Army Special Operations Command. The Rangers were carrying out weapons training for their Afghan counterparts alongside the Delta troop, most of whom were ex-Rangers themselves. They would secure the immediate perimeter. Despite the ban on armed drones, Reapers loaded with Hellfire missiles would protect the assaulters from above, backed up by a couple of adapted AH-64 Apache attack helicopters.

A second Chinook would carry the civilians and double up as a flying ambulance for any wounded. Crane said he'd travel in the rear Chinook, together with a back-up interpreter and five CIA counterterrorist operatives whom he'd handpicked already. The entire search and rescue operation would be relayed in real time to Houseman, the Director of the CIA and the White

House Situation Room via state-of-the-art surveillance equipment: a squadron of MQ-1C drones, infrared cameras secured outside and onboard the gunships, and robust video cameras fixed to the lead operators' Kevlar helmets.

Tom had kept quiet about going along at this juncture, but he was desperate to be in on the action.

Crane scratched the back of his head. "I'm still not sure about it."

"With respect, sir, this is special ops not covert ops," Sawyer replied.

"You don't say. There was me thinking we could dig tunnels under them and pop up wearing Halloween masks and then blame it on… Who? The freakin' Chinese? Of course I'm aware it's a special ops, I'm just saying I'm not sure about it."

"If you would like to put forward an alternative, sir, I'd be happy to consider it with JSOC."

"What, in about two minutes? It takes me longer than that to make sure I've shaken all the drops off when I take a leak these days," Crane replied, stretching his back.

"He's right," Tom said to Crane.

"Is he, now? So, you're a trigger-happy Leopard and you see Sawyer here and his buddies arriving like the Seventh Cavalry. What are you gonna do, huh, feed the secretary grapes?" Crane gripped his forehead, clearly frustrated.

"They could move her any time. They could kill her any time. You want that on your conscience? Besides, JSOC know what they're doing, so why don't you ease up on the lieutenant here?" Tom said, feeling that Crane was being overly obstructive.

Truth was, the CIA's ultra-secretive Special Activities Division, the most elite section of which was the Special Operations Group, had worked in tandem with Delta since their inception in the late 1970s, and regularly recruited operatives from the squadrons. But it was obvious that the CIA had the upper hand, and Tom had heard rumours that Crane headed the Special Operations Group, or had done.

Crane seemed to relax. "Sure. What the hell do I know anyways?" he said, although not without a hint of sarcasm.

"We've successfully carried out eight similar hostage recues over here," Sawyer said, still apparently unfazed. "That's why POTUS wants to go for it. But if the NSC judge it's totally off the wall, they'll say so. I know there's only a twenty per cent chance of success, but we're ready and able to give it our best shot. If we don't try it, we're likely to be too late. Now I'm no politician, that's for certain, but why wouldn't they have made a demand already, if they wanted something?"

"Why wouldn't they have killed her already, if they wanted her dead?" Crane replied.

Tom thought that that was sound reasoning, although it made him shudder to think it could end that way. But you could bat this one back and forth for days, and you'd still be left with the same dilemma. He guessed that was why those who had to make such decisions would go for it. The alternative was inertia. And if the secretary died while they were procrastinating, well, that could be political suicide. Besides, although it wasn't a perfect plan, no plan was, especially with what they had to work with. But it was unlikely to be any different in a week's time, and with the passage of time came an increased likelihood of a leak.

"Are we done?" Sawyer asked.

"Yeah. Run it past Houseman," Crane said.

Sawyer headed for the door, a laptop and a bundle of photos under his arm. Tom saw Crane glance at him, although he looked preoccupied.

"I'll see what I can do, Tom. Just stick around for now."

EIGHTEEN

TOM HADN'T WANTED to push his luck, thinking that if he kept in the background Crane might be able to get him to go along on the mission. He got a cup of coffee from a vending machine in the lobby, and sat on a pleather chair. He thought about those who'd died already, and those young men who might lose their lives in the next few hours. He just hoped that their sacrifices would lead to a worthy outcome.

He sensed someone behind him and twisted around. It was Steve Coombs, holding the extended handle of a small suitcase on wheels.

"The hell you doing here?" Tom asked.

"Benazir Bhutto got a bomb threat. It's closed till further notice," Steve said, referring to Islamabad's international airport, named after the assassinated female politician. "I'm flying home from Kabul. The CIA said they had a couple more questions; asked me to come in on my way to the airport."

Placing the cup on the floor, Tom stood up. "Good to see you, Steve, anyhow."

They shook hands.

"And you, Tom?"

"I'm staying put for now."

"How's that?"

Tom shook his head. "Don't worry about it. You get home safely, you hear. And give Page my love."

Tom hadn't seen Steve's wife in maybe two years, but he admired the woman, and he knew that his friend was devoted to her. Steve was a lucky man in many respects, he thought. His parents farmed three-hundred acres in Eastern Pennsylvania split into cattle and soybeans. He had six siblings, all of whom were married and doing well. Steve had told him that growing up on a farm was like he imagined heaven to be.

As they parted company Tom thought his own early life couldn't have been more dissimilar. Up until he was eight, he saw his father about once every three months, if he was lucky. He gave him a toy or twenty bucks. He looked handsome in his Army officer's uniform. He was six-two with a natural muscularity, his black-onyx-coloured eyes and hair marking him out like a movie actor. He'd never married his mother, and Tom didn't have his name, Dupree being her surname. His father was uneasy around him, avoiding physical contact, and there would be long silences between them. He was Louisiana Creole, his forefathers being colonial French who'd settled in the southern states. Tom excelled at French at school; did it, he supposed, to make his father proud in some remote way.

He clenched his jaw muscles now and tried to focus on something positive.

"Tom."

It was Crane's voice. Tom looked over towards the row of elevators and saw him walking across the tiled floor, his big legs striding out, his confidence restored. Tom stood up.

"It's a goer. You ready for this?" Crane said, excitedly.

"Hell, yeah," he replied, thinking Crane's mood had turned a full one-eighty.

"We don't land until the Rangers have secured the site. You realize that, right?"

"How did you pull it off?"

"Apart from Houseman being sympathetic, which, I have to say, ain't his natural disposition, I told him that you were the only man suitable to go along who she'd feel instantly comfortable with."

"Thanks, Crane."

"You know how to use an MP5?"

Tom nodded.

"I'll make sure you have one."

"You getting paid to keep me alive?" Tom asked.

Crane grinned. "If I was intent on keeping you alive, I woulda made sure you went home on that plane."

NINETEEN

THE CAPITAL LAY in a narrow valley of the Hindu Kush on the banks of Kabul River. The convoy of adapted Land Cruisers moved at speed, Tom sitting in the second vehicle beside Crane. Both men wore fatigues and body armour, their Heckler & Koch MP5 9mm sub-machine guns upright between their legs. They were fixed with suppressors. Crane had explained that all of the assaulters' weapons were suppressed, so if they heard a round go off from a firearm that wasn't, it meant it was from a hostile source.

The distance to Kabul International Airport was ten miles, the North Side Cantonment of which housed the command centre for the Afghan Air Force. They would utilize the seven helipads there for the mission, although the Afghans had been told an elaborate lie. Crane had told Tom that if they knew what they were up to, they would've all been arrested. Bagram Air Base, which had been used as a staging point for Special Forces' missions along the northern Af-Pak border, was so depleted that it could no longer be used safely.

Kabul International was connected to the capital by a four-lane highway, shared with domestic traffic. As Tom stared out he saw the heat haze rising above it, the tarmac melting from the hours of intense sunlight.

"You wouldn't believe this was Afghanistan, would ya?" Crane said, smiling.

"No. It's changed a lot since I was here last."

"Don't get me wrong—you get outside the ring of concrete and steel and it's still a Third World hellhole as bad as any I've seen."

"You think we were right coming here?" Tom asked.

"It was a hornets' nest. But staying as long as we did, hell, no. They sit down and talk, but you can't tame these people. They're tough, goddamn it. Toughest people I've ever met."

"Nothing tough about IEDs," Tom said.

"A necessity. They couldn't fight a hundred thousand well-armed troops face-to-face."

"So that's all gonna be forgotten about now, huh?"

"Look, I do my job. Damn good at it, too. You know why?" Crane said, rhetorically. "Cuz I don't hold grudges. That gives you ulcers. I got enough bad habits as it is."

"That's not what you said about the Pakistanis," Tom said, massaging an aching bruise on his thigh.

"Always gotta have exceptions, Tom."

Tom glanced at him. "How will they've treated her?"

"That depends," Crane said, his voice serious.

"On what?"

"If she's been compliant, they've likely just ignored her most of the time. But if she's acted like the US Secretary of State, they've probably treated her worse than a stubborn goat."

Tom watched Crane staring into space now, and wondered what was going through his mind. He hadn't held back. He wasn't the type. Fingering his Buddha in his pocket, Tom just hoped she'd acted as he'd instructed her to if the worst happened.

The military terminal was marked by a ring of black,

red and green Afghan flags and what looked like relatively newly built redbrick buildings. As the Land Cruisers passed through the heavily guarded checkpoint, Tom felt a knot in his gut. He was both a part of it and a bystander; a voyeur, even. But as Crane opened the door and the sticky heat hit him he consoled himself by knowing that if she was there, she would be glad to see a friendly face at least.

Let her be there, he thought. Let her be alive.

TWENTY

THE SOUND OF the twin engines and huge tandem rotor blades scything the cold air was near-deafening as the special ops Chinook flew at almost two-hundred miles per hour. The Black Hawks had silenced rotors and engines, but by the time the Chinooks got there it would be game on. Dusk had fallen now and the clouds were high and wispy, the skyline above the mountains the colour of hacked strawberries.

Tom had been told to wear a seat belt and helmet to stop himself from knocking himself out if the helicopter had to take a sharp turn or got caught in downdraft. Although the cabin had been fitted out with padding, it still looked as if it was weeks away from being finished. But anything that wasn't functional was left out, especially on a mission. The operators called the helicopter the flying school bus, which Tom thought inappropriate.

He sat on a red canvas, aluminium-framed seat, his feet placed firmly on the metal decking with exposed rivets. Crane, wearing a clear earpiece attached to a PTT radio, sat beside him, talking to one of the other CIA men who were in flight. An iron-pumper with a black beard and square face, a real Cro-Magnon hard case, who was nodding as Crane talked in short loud bursts like a drunk in a noisy bar.

From the oval porthole opposite him, Tom could see a four-blade Apache attack helicopter. It was a state-of-the-art killing machine, the nose-mounted sensor hub housing the night-vision systems for its 30mm Chain Gun carried between the landing gear, and the Hellfire missiles and Hydra rocket pods on the stub-wings sticking out of the fuselage behind the cockpit. But he knew such weapons had been of little use in a guerrilla war where the combatants had dressed like locals and had lived among them, too.

The Apaches would fly ahead soon and be the second wave of attack, once the Black Hawks had landed at the insertion point and there was no further need for an element of surprise, however brief. Then they would buzz the valleys of the White Mountains in the vicinity, deterring any element of reinforcements. The drone reconnaissance hadn't shown up any other settlements nearby, but a group of Leopards could always be squatting under scrub or in dugouts.

Tom chewed his lip and grabbed the seat bar as the Chinook hit turbulence. He knew he was heading for a death zone.

The last time he'd flown in a helicopter had been on a short flight from DC to Richmond, Virginia, where the secretary had opened a library at South University. That was a fortnight ago. He'd thought that his time with her would end in a clean slate until he'd gotten the call from his direct superior, informing him that she would be going to Islamabad. He never knew why, in detail. He didn't have to know. He was only ever told her destination days before if her schedule changed. But he'd felt uneasy from the beginning, a nagging doubt that had played out as fretful dreams.

Crane turned to Tom. "ETA five minutes," he mouthed, holding up five fingers. He opened up a laptop to get the live feeds. "That's the view from Sawyer's video camera in Salt One," he bellowed. "That's the interpreter next to him. Bet he didn't sign up for this. The operators call it flying it into the X. Heavy shit, huh."

The interpreter was a Pakistani, his face obscured by a black ski mask. Tom knew that his whole family would be killed if he was ever recognized.

The screen was split into quarters, with different images appearing from the various cameras, including those mounted on the Black Hawks' fuselages. Briefly, Tom wondered what his first words to her would be. Whether it would be appropriate to apologize or simply say he was glad to see her alive? But what if they found her dead already? What if the plan failed at the last moment and she was killed or terribly injured? What would he say or do then? he thought.

As the amber LED lights were cut, he spent the next few minutes zoning out.

"They're moving in," said Crane, breaking into Tom's thoughts.

Tom looked down towards Crane's lap at the live feeds. "The Black Hawks are shaking a lot," he said, watching one of the helicopters hover above the fort's flat roof as the other lowered down to about ten metres above the courtyard. Each had a sniper aiming a suppressed rifle out of the cabin's open side door, scanning the rescue site for any sign of a fighter.

"Uplift of trapped air," Crane said. "It'll be fine. The Delta work top down, bottom up, and converge in the middle. Smooth and fast, smooth and fast. A breacher blows down a door, then the fire teams enter. They take out the resistance. The main dangers are trip wires, IEDs and blind firing around walls. If the whole place isn't rigged with Semtex, it'll be fine. Don't worry. If she's there, we'll find her."

At least Crane is still upbeat, Tom thought. He just hoped he had a right to be, despite the man's previous misgivings.

On screen, he watched Sawyer lead the assault on the ground. He fast-roped adroitly in leather mitts some seven metres from the bar jutting out from Black Hawk's fuselage, landing into a swirl of dust and small stones. After being propelled forward by the rotor wash, he took point in the dark courtyard, adjusting his head-phones before speaking into his cheek mic. The main building was directly ahead of him, a few outbuildings and vehicle ports left and right. He scanned around with his M4A1 carbine, fixed with a thermal scope and red-dot laser, his four-tube night-vision goggles allowing peripheral vision, but making him look as if he'd landed from another solar system.

After the main interpreter sprained an ankle on the descent and a medic had his ill-secured backpack almost torn off by the wash, the assault teams panned out and ran forward, their torsos clad in sixty-pound ballistic plates. The live feed showed a serious of controlled ex-plosions, bursts of automatic fire and swift movement.

"Alpha three down. Medevac," Sawyer shouted, looking over at an operator seven metres from him, his body splayed on the ground.

With that, another Delta was blown into the air three metres in front of Sawyer. He landed heavily, his legs a twisted mess. The operators couldn't use their frag-mentation grenades, because they had no idea where the secretary was being held. But the local fighters were using them to devastating effect. That and a triangulation of small-arms fire.

"Jesus," Tom said.

The movement ratcheted up to something approaching frantic. Gunfire crackled and breaching charges erupted. A flurry of tracer rounds flew through the air from a corner turret and, a few seconds later, there was a massive explosion coupled with a white flash. Tom heard the muted voices of the men on the ground.

"Salt Two down," said Sawyer. "A bird's down. A bird's down."

"Damn it!" Tom said.

With that, an Apache hovered before blowing off the turret. A funnel of flame exploded upward from the black smoke ball, the smashed clay bricks showering down onto the courtyard. Tom thought it might as well have been made of balsa wood for all the protection it had afforded.

"Wow," Crane said. "See that? Got those RPGs for damn sure."

As the operators moved into the main building they began to clear the warren of corridors. Their eyes were covered by helmet-mounted NVGs as they aimed suppressed, desert-tan HK416 assault rifles and Colt carbines, assaulting the building from top and bottom, just as Crane had said they would. The insurgents fell away like ghosts, or buckled under double taps to the head and body from relatively close quarters, after they were fixed with IR lasers. Once a section was cleared, an assaulter shouted, "Move," and his teammate would shout, "Moving," before taking a step. It was precise. Calculated.

Outside, a second Apache fired a rocket at the far

left-hand side of the surrounding wall of the fort compound, smashing a gaping hole in the clay bricks.

"There ain't enough room to put the Chinooks down in the courtyard and the gate is likely to be rigged. Hence the hole. We're going in," Crane barked. "And put your goggles on or you'll be picking grit out of your eyes for a week."

Tom felt a rush of adrenalin. He'd been in combat zones many times, but this was something else.

TWENTY-ONE

THE CHINOOK HOVERED before descending ten metres from the fort's outer wall. After it touched down in the landing zone, the tail ramp lowered so that they could disembark quickly without squeezing through the cabin doors. A bearded master sergeant, holding an HK fixed with an AG416 40mm grenade launcher, led them through the smoke and swirling dust whipped up by the rotors, over the chunks of bricks and into the main courtyard. The downed Black Hawk was burning up in the far right-hand corner, the other circling in front of the bullet-ridden walls of the main building. The Delta told them to follow his steps, saying that they hadn't swept the area and IEDs could be anywhere.

Tom saw a dozen bodies lying dead or groaning on the ground, including three operators, who were being attended to by medics. A group of women, hugging children and wailing, sat in the courtyard to the left. In front of them, a couple of Delta stood either side of the second masked interpreter as he attempted to comfort the innocents and obtain intel in the process. Directly behind him, four operators were securing those insurgents who'd surrendered or had been captured alive with plasticuffs before hooding them. At the doorways to the outer buildings, infrared lights visible only via the operators' night-vision goggles signalled that they'd been cleared of any threat.

Tom, Crane and the others were met at the central door by another five Delta, all wearing mismatched uniforms and padded gloves. One was holding a Belgian Malinois dog on a lead, its eyes protected by a ballistic visor, its torso sheathed in body armour. The dog snarled when they came close, bearing huge fangs. Its Delta handler jerked the lead and took point. Sawyer remained behind, organizing the ongoing security of the periphery with the rest of the troop, together with the Rangers who had disembarked from a Chinook beyond the wall.

The interior was thick with dust and stank of stale smoke and kerosene. Guided by the operators' helmet-mounted flashlights, the dog led the way, its snubbed snout tracking the scent of the secretary via an article of clothing taken from her bedroom at the embassy. The GPS had pinpointed the building, but the signal had faded en route, so it was impossible to tell her exact position in the many dark corridors and small rooms that constituted the fort proper. The corridors were on three levels and narrow, no more than two-metres high, creating a claustrophobic effect. The walls were uneven, the floors pitted and strewn with small rocks.

After five minutes or so, the dog, salivating now and snorting, moved down a slope below ground level. It stopped at a reinforced metal door at the end of a pitch-black corridor peppered with rat droppings. The air here smelled of something akin to rotting vegetables. An operator carrying an M4 Super 90 shotgun moved up before banging on the door and calling out. There was no answer. Tom clenched his jaw muscles, feeling anxious. Crane stepped forward and ordered the door blown open.

"We can't risk it," Tom said, intervening.

He knew that if the door opened inward, the secretary could be killed as it careered into her.

"Blow it down, son," Crane insisted.

Ignoring Crane, the Delta spoke into his cheek mic. "A metal door, sir. Lyric could be beyond it. No question of knocking out the hinges with Hatton rounds. It'll need an explosive breach." After getting an order from Sawyer, he said, "Copy that."

The rear operator came forward and placed a strip of adhesive breaching explosives over the lock, which would rip it apart. He primed it with two blasting caps, so that if one malfunctioned there'd be less chance of failure, and reeled out the connecting wires. Tom and the others retreated a way back down the dim corridor. As blast shields were held up in front of them they lowered their heads. Tom just hoped the door would blow back outwards.

"Fire in the hole," the Delta shouted.

After a two-second delay, the explosion was ferocious, making the shields almost buckle, the shock wave exaggerated by the confined space. An operator ran forward, with bolt cutters strapped to his back. He leapt over the blown-down door, his red-dot laser scanning the room. He flipped up his night-vision goggles, activated his helmet flashlight and double checked for any sign of the secretary, a booby trap or Leopard.

"Clear," he shouted.

The dog handler moved forward, closely followed by Tom and Crane. Tom saw the dog scratching at the floor. The Delta crouched down and used a gloved hand to clean the dirt from a small piece of flooring.

"It's a hinge," he said.

"Jesus," Tom said, fearing they would find the secretary's body beneath.

The Delta used the butt of his carbine to dislodge the
small padlock securing the hinge.

"Watch out, Chris. It could be rigged," an operator
called out from behind.

A Delta brought up a blast shield and, crouching
behind it, the man called Chris lifted the trap door.
Nothing happened. He shone his flashlight down.

"One body, likely dead," he said, clinically.

"Male or female?" Tom asked.

"Looks like a woman's body."

Tom's face turned the colour of wet clay. He scrambled forward. Peering down, he shone his handheld
flashlight into the hole. It was about two metres deep
and three metres square. A small body, its face shrouded
by a black square of muslin, lay against the far mud wall.

"Tom?" Crane said.

"It's her clothes," he replied. "The body is dressed
in her clothes."

The dog barked and strained at the leash, desperate
to descend into the hole.

"Go down, Tom," Crane said. "It's only right it's you.
But don't touch the body."

Tom tucked his flashlight into his webbed belt, slung
his MP5 over his shoulder and lowered himself into
the hole. He coughed, gagging on the smell of decay-
ing flesh. After taking out the flashlight, he held it up
and saw the emerald ring on the blackened finger, the
pear-shaped necklace lying on the flat breasts. Was she
burned? he thought, unable to conceive of such a death.

He pulled off his goggles and knelt down. Clenching
his jaw, he lifted the veil. He saw a stained skull. The

tracking device that had been hidden under the secretary's skin was lodged between the two front teeth.
They were black-green in colour, as if they'd been
sculpted from serpentine stone. He arched back and
slumped down in the damp earth. Breathing heavily, he
took off his helmet and winced. He figured the reason
for the intermittent signal from the sensors was down
to their subterranean position.

Crane dropped down into the hole, his bulk almost
filling the space. "This one's been dead for as long as
you've been waking up with a boner," he said, putting his hand to his nose. He scanned around with his
Maglite. "They threw a few dead rats in to make it smell
convincing. You gotta hand it to them—this is cute."

Tom didn't have the strength to punch him; couldn't
even bring himself to swear.

TWENTY-TWO

MULLAH KAKAR LIVED in a dingy house in one of the oldest and cheapest sectors of Islamabad, with narrow streets and poor infrastructure. He'd rarely ventured out at first, and when he had he'd always been accompanied by his four bodyguards, all of whom were from Peshawar, and had fought against ISAF in Afghanistan. But after meeting up with the British ex-SAS soldier called Proctor in the foothills of the Hindu Kush five months ago, he'd taken to moving about the city more often, at least at night. As far as the Westerners were concerned, he was dead, after all. Besides, when the call had come from one of Brigadier Hasni's men, ordering him to meet a driver at a coffee house a ten-minute walk away, he'd told his bodyguards that they would be leaving shortly. This was something that required little or no thought. When Hasni beckoned, a man moved, unless that man didn't care for moving that much, and was content to push himself around in a wheelchair for the rest of his life.

He switched off his fat, black-and-white TV, the grainy screen shrinking like a deflating balloon, and slipped on a pair of rubber-soled sandals, his mind fixed on the meeting at hand. Hasni, whom he knew on what he referred to as a professional basis, was as remote and dangerous as a snow leopard. But he'd controlled the ISI and therefore Pakistan's foreign policy for over a decade. And although he professed to be a practising Muslim, Kakar knew that Hasni, like most high-ranking ISI officers, was motivated by two things only: political power and patriotism. Despite its historically pro-jihadist stance in Afghanistan, the ISI was essentially a nationalistic organization, rather than a religiously motivated one.

Kakar moved the blue-and-white sheet that separated his meagre living space from the equally cramped kitchen. He walked through the dim passageway to the wooden front door, the familiar smell of damp and sewerage filling his nostrils. As he got to the door he took out the photograph of his wife and three children. They'd been killed in a HIMAR attack five years ago. He knew that the mobile rocket launcher was accurate up to a distance of almost two hundred miles. He'd thought, at first, that his family had been in the wrong compound at the wrong time. But over the years, he'd come to the conclusion that the Westerners had killed them out of revenge for what he had done.

He placed the photograph into the pocket of a woollen vest, hanging on a hook screwed into the bare concrete wall. He knew that he would join them in Paradise one day. He just hoped it wouldn't be too soon. He had a lot of revenge killing of his own to do first, despite the fact that he'd already murdered thirty-eight ISAF personnel since their deaths.

Apart from his young family, he had seen many people die in his country. Innocent men shot for talking on cellphones, the snipers having been told they were Taliban spotters. Others had been hauled off by security forces, tortured and never seen again, simply because their neighbours had wanted to earn a few hundred dollars or acquire a small goat herd, the neighbours making up some story to rid themselves of someone they disliked, envied or who had slighted them over a family marriage proposal. The Westerners had been murderers, their materialism an infectious disease.

By 2005, he had acquired the mullah title. It happened in the way some people acquired accents. The more a person used it, the more people accepted it, until, in some peculiar way, the user believed it to be real as well. He was by this time devoted to the cause, both as an active fighter and strategist. Two years later, he'd planned and executed the act that had made him notorious. The murder of the British Defence Secretary in London.

As a result of the assassination and his subsequent bloody activities, the US had offered a million-dollar reward for information leading to his capture, or death. That hadn't been revoked, so, unlike some Taliban leaders, who had received a tacit amnesty, he was still a wanted man. But ISAF had left his beloved homeland. God's will, he believed. And now, he was a ghost.

And so it was without too much trepidation that he stood up from the seat at the small table and walked to the door as the black Mercedes pulled up outside, a man driving without others. His bodyguards rose with him, their handguns tucked into their belts, concealed by long shirts and vests. As Kakar approached the car the driver's window slid down.

"Just you," he said.

Kakar didn't like his tone. Nothing short of dismissive, he thought. He nodded to his bodyguards outside the coffee house, and sat in the back of the sleek car, which eased into the traffic like a shark moving among its prey.

The ISI driver hadn't said a word for a full twenty minutes, despite Kakar's attempts to strike up an innocent conversation with him on three occasions. The man wore shades even though it was dark, and chewed gum noisily. He had a thick, sweaty neck, and Kakar felt the urge to take off a sandal and beat him over the head with it. But he sat tight. There was nowhere to hide apart from Pakistan. The alternatives were either too risky or too dire to contemplate. Yemen. Somalia. Syria. West Africa…the list got progressively worse.

En route to the Blue Area, the wide corridor that abutted the length of Jinnah Avenue—the city's main highway leading to the principal government buildings—the view outside the car's windows became progressively affluent. The roads became wider, the darkness rendered less oppressive by the increasing amounts of streetlights.

A few hundred metres up from a smoked-glass skyscraper, the car pulled into a tarmac driveway edged with black metal security posts shaped like water hydrants. Initially, the house reminded Kakar of a Hollywood mansion, with its terracotta-tiled roof, smooth pillars out front, and pale-cream walls, the entrance barred by a huge electronically controlled, wrought-iron gate. But then he noticed the extra security: concertina razor-wire atop the walls, and at least twelve armed guards, two of whom walked the perimeter with Dobermans.

As the well-lit gate opened the driver nodded to a guard, his sub-machine gun on full view. He fears assassination, Kakar thought. He knew he feared spies even more. They were everywhere, like the rats that plagued his dilapidated sector.

He shuddered involuntarily. He had never been to Hasni's home before and he'd heard rumours that the man had built torture cells beneath it.

TWENTY-THREE

WALKING THROUGH THE DUSTY, narrow corridors, Tom felt desolate, his head hanging, his shoulders bunched. Crane was in front of him, shining the Maglite on the floor. He knew the secretary could be anywhere now. The thing about most kidnap victims was, if they weren't found in the first twelve hours, they probably wouldn't be found until they were released or... killed, he thought, shaking his head to help him remove the image. But he knew that the chances of finding her quickly without a Pakistani wanting to make easy money were remote.

Crane told him to watch out for a chunk of metal sticking out of the wall and shone a quick beam of light onto what looked like a rusted nail. He suggested that Tom tucked his pants inside his boots, adding that the scorpions were deadlier than the locals in these parts. Tom thought Crane sounded oddly parental, couldn't figure it out. Ruminating on that brought other images into his head.

The house he and his mother had lived in was one up from a trailer, a tiny bungalow resting on breeze-blocks, a yard no bigger than the living room. On his eighth birthday, she was sitting at the kitchen table in a floral nightgown, her mascara doing an Alice Copper; her hair uncombed. Tom had come home from school, excited to see his father. But when he asked if he would be coming soon, she told him that he was never coming again. That he didn't love them any more; that he had someone else in DC and would have other children; that he'd forget all about them.

She'd started crying herself to sleep that very night, kept it up for a full month. He cried along, too, at first, but grew tired of it and took to placing his head under his pillow instead. Tom hadn't seen his father again until he was sixteen, several weeks after his broken promise to his mother had led to a tragedy so great that he'd felt like drowning himself in a bayou.

A MINUTE LATER, Tom strolled out into the evening air, which stank of the aftermath of weapons' discharge and burning gasoline. Ahead of him, he watched Crane scratch his blond-grey hair and light a cigarette. The Black Hawk was smouldering in the courtyard. It would be subjected to delayed explosives a short while after they'd left the site, which would destroy the communications systems and sensitive onboard data. In front of it, operators were carrying the remaining wounded on stretchers to the Chinook outside the fort to be flown back to Kabul for treatment. A worried-looking medic knelt by a Delta who lay on a poncho liner, his ballistic vest a metre or so away. He was holding two pads, part of an automatic external defibrillator, as another medic pumped the man's chest with his palms. Those who'd fallen were already encased in black canvas body bags, positioned in a sombre row by the large hole in the clay-brick wall.

The seized weapons had been stacked in a pile. An operator was crouching down beside them, priming explosive charges with a delayed detonator. Two more

Delta were snapping away at the haul with digital cameras, an activity called sensitive site exploration, or SSE.
This was more a political necessity than a military one,
something to counter any subsequent accusations that
they'd just decimated a peaceful settlement occupied
by harmless refugees.

Tom rubbed his eyes, feeling even more inept than
he had onboard the Chinook. But there was another
emotion, too: a deep sense of grief for those who had
perished here. As he took off his helmet and wiped the
sweat from his forehead he saw Crane speaking to the
back-up interpreter before walking over to him.

"We leave in five minutes tops," Crane said.

Tom reckoned the Pakistani Air Force had scrambled jet fighters.

"The Shias thought we were Pakistani Special
Forces," Crane said. "Hence the rumble. But here's
the thing. The interpreter questioned a man about that
corpse in the hole. A married woman got caught with a
local male twenty years ago. They stoned her to death.
Some outsider paid the headman to have her dug up
and put down there, together with the clothes and GPS
jewellery. Guess they lodged the sensor that was under
Lyric's skin between the skeleton's teeth, too."

"That's real nice. But I still think the ISI have to be
involved," Tom said.

"That's like saying JFK had to have been killed by
two shooters."

"Excuse me?"

"Speculation based on zero proof and an obsession.
Classic traits of a conspiracy theorist. I knew you were
one," Crane said, taking a pull on his cigarette. "In any
event, the chances of us tackling the ISI are about the

same as a Bernstein becoming the next Pope. You can't see the risks, for Chrissakes? Pakistan is a nuclear state that refused to sign the no-first-strike treaty. And just now it ain't exactly a stable country."

They walked together to the hole in the wall, seeing the Chinook ahead of them. A line of Rangers with snipers on the flanks were ensuring that civilians or random insurgents didn't get within a hundred metres of the fort.

"You still think the Iranians are behind it?" Tom asked, questioning his own reasoning.

"If they are involved, there's alotta folks back home who'd like the opportunity to kick their ass. And the Israelis are straining at the leash, that's for goddamn sure. The Saudis, too."

"Do the Iranians have nukes?"

"Not yet. Still, this gets outta hand, New York will be as safe as the Swat Valley. But nowhere near as goddamned beautiful."

They reached the Chinook, and Crane stubbed out his cigarette after getting berated by the huge crew chief.

"At least the dog's still alive," he said as the Belgian Malinois started barking.

"Jesus, Crane, don't you ever let up?" Tom shook his head, exasperated.

"What you want me to say?"

"That my men died well," Sawyer said, coming up behind them.

Tom turned first. Sawyer's night-vision goggles were flipped up on his helmet. His face was streaked with blood, his carbine hanging limp from the belt clip.

"Yeah, they did, young man," Crane said, turning around. "But I just happen to be an animal lover. And it ain't nice to listen into other people's conversations, except if you're getting paid to do it like me."

"You might want to keep your wisecracks for when we get back to base, sir."

"You think I haven't seen men die in the field before? My own men. You deal with it your way, and I'll deal with it mine. What are you, twenty-seven? I've been in the field longer than you've been eating solids. And don't forget who's really in charge here," Crane said, with a dismissive flick of his hand.

"That's fine with me, sir. I'm just telling you that if you speak like that again, you and me will have a problem."

Sawyer was standing ramrod straight now, his eyes narrowing.

"You talk to me like that again, son, I'll stick your fucking carbine up your ass. Truth is, I think you'll enjoy it," Crane said, jabbing the air between them with a thick finger.

Tom saw a couple of operators getting interested in what was being said, their sleeves rolled up, as they took snapshots of the perimeter.

"Enough," he said, putting his hand out between them. "You two wanna dance, dance back in Kabul."

The co-pilot appeared on the Chinook's tail ramp, called out, "You guys need to get over here. A video has appeared on YouTube."

TWENTY-FOUR

BRIGADIER HASNI, HEAD of the ISI's Joint Intelligence X Department, which coordinated the other seven departments, was a tall, heavy-set man with a thick moustache and greased-back hair. His face was wide but hard, as if chiselled from a slab of caramel-coloured marble. Dressed in a white pathani suit, he sat at an ornate desk, his hands folded in his lap. The room was his study, the polished wooden floor half covered with expensive hand-knotted rugs.

Another man sat opposite him on a padded armchair. He was of paler skin and flabby, his bald head speckled with liver spots. His name was Asad, and he was Hasni's deputy. Gripping a Mont Blanc, he'd just handed Hasni a draft report on the events that had happened outside the children's hospital.

"General Malik is being suitably apologetic by all accounts," Asad said, referring to the new Foreign Secretary.

"The man has the manners of a monkey and the morals of a street boy."

Asad grinned.

"But it's not the generals we have to worry about," Hasni said.

Although the new breed of younger high-ranking military officers were too radical for his taste, Sunni hard men, no one but the illiterate poor harboured any doubts about who wielded the real power in Pakistan, at least as far as foreign affairs were concerned.

"Indeed, sir."

But we still need them, Hasni thought.

The generals' predecessors had ruled Pakistan on and off for a total of over three decades, the first military era occurring for a thirteen-year period from 1958—just eleven years after independence from the British. As far as Hasni was concerned, it was as natural as night passing into day. The generals held all of the ministerial offices. There was no way that the population, riotous as they were, would allow the ISI to openly control the country's international dealings. But it was a temporary measure, or had been sold as such. The previous civilian government just couldn't deal with the security crisis and the army had stepped in. For now, the people saw it as an expedient measure. A strong if interim government.

After scanning the typed pages of the report, Hasni said, "Make sure it emphasizes the fact that four police officers identified known Leopards as the perpetrators."

"Of course."

"Underline it."

Asad nodded.

"And you should add that they drove the cars. That the secretary was definitely abducted by them."

"As you say, Brigadier."

"That ought to keep the Americans off our backs for a while at least."

There was a knock at the door and a young woman dressed in a turquoise and gold Shalwar Kameez entered. Her hair was the colour of a raven's breast. It was tied back tightly from her make-up-free face in a ponytail, accentuating her high cheekbones and luminous eyes. Her name was Adeela; Hasni's daughter. He allowed her to remove her hijab inside the house. His own view on the headscarf was that it was oppressive and cumbersome, especially when coupled with the face-obscuring niqab. But outside, she had to keep up appearances, at least until another less dogmatic regime took over.

"A man is here to see you, Father."

"Did he give a name, my dear?" Hasni said, smiling.

"Only that he was The Mullah, Father."

Hasni leaned in close to Asad. "The fool thinks he's a holy man." He glanced over at his daughter. "Give me five minutes, Adeela."

"Yes, Father."

She left, closing the door quietly.

"Have you contacted the Saudis?" Hasni asked, smoothing down the ends of his moustache with a thumb and forefinger.

"Yes, Brigadier."

"And?"

"Our brothers there are most concerned that Iran will invade Balochistan," he said, referring to the Pakistani province that bordered south-east Iran.

"Our Saudi brothers have their own agenda."

Asad looked puzzled.

"Don't worry, everything will become clear with time. As for the Iranians, with the addition of a little more evidence about their involvement in the abduction of the secretary, they will be too focused on appeasing the Americans to seriously contemplate invading Balochistan."

"Let us hope so."
"Later, then," Hasni said.
Asad rose and left.

TWENTY-FIVE

A FEW MINUTES LATER, Kakar was ushered in by Adeela, a resigned look on his bearded face. Hasni remained seated, and gestured to the armchair left vacant by Asad.

"Some tea, Father?"

"Tea, yes. Thank you, my dear."

Kakar sat in the chair, his hands going first to the arms before he finally placed them in his lap, mimicking Hasni's.

"Thank you for coming to see me at short notice."

"When the Brigadier summons, his servants respond," Kakar said, bowing his head.

Kakar wasn't subservient by nature. He was too well educated for that. But despite his usefulness to Hasni, he knew the man demanded respect, and he had to make out as if he knew his place. Besides, he feared him. Or rather, the power he wielded.

Hasni tapped the report lying on the desk with his forefinger. "This is evidence that the Leopards took part in the abduction of the US Secretary of State. Police evidence. This is to be expected. This is what you will say to your Taliban friends."

"Of course, Brigadier."

"If all goes well, the ISI will continue to support your cause. But I expect the Taliban to do their duty in return."

"We know the whereabouts of several of their leaders in the Upper Kurram Valley. My men know who their guardians are."

Hasni grinned.

Kakar had been on the ISI's unofficial payroll since 2001. He resented this, but could do nothing about it. The alternative was to face almost certain death. Those Taliban leaders who'd escaped to Peshawar, but who'd refused to bend to the ISI's will, were found bound in gutters, their throats slit. The price to be paid for sanctuary on Pakistan soil was obedience. Besides, he viewed Iran as a common enemy. In 1998, after the Taliban Sunnis massacred the inhabitants of Mazar-i Sharif, a Shia town, Iran deployed three hundred thousand troops on the border and threatened war. A nuclear Pakistan, the Taliban's main ally, had been a major deterrent, Kakar believed.

Hasni leaned forward, arching his fingers. "I have heard that some of the Leopards responsible for this atrocity are still here in Islamabad. Your men will no doubt find them and hand them over to me tonight."

"But, Brigadier, how can—?"

Hasni slapped Kakar hard across the face.

As his head spun Kakar had to force himself not to urinate. With his breath reduced to shallow gasps, he felt his cheek throb. Apart from making him feel humiliated, Hasni had now given him an impossible order.

The door opened and Adeela brought in a tray with china cups and a silver teapot. Kakar was relieved. He knew that if Hasni hadn't been in his own home, well, anything could've happened. Then he remembered the torture-cell rumours. He resolved to provide Hasni with bodies, as long as they were Shia ones.

"Ah, tea. Excellent, my dear," Hasni said, wiping a slither of spittle from his bottom lip.

"Shall I pour, Father?"

"Please," Hasni said. "We don't want tea spilt on my rugs."

Kakar saw that Hasni had glanced over at his lap. His hands were shaking.

TWENTY-SIX

THE CO-PILOT WAS a lean-faced guy with a trace of teen-age pimples, who spoke with a Midwest accent. He sat on one of the flimsy seats in the Chinook's cabin, a laptop balancing on his closed thighs.

"It's been taken down, but I guess it's been downloaded and seen worldwide already," he said, clicking on the saved video.

Tom, who was seated one side of him, Crane the other, as Sawyer sulked to the side, winced. The secretary was slumped in a wooden chair, bound and gagged with a bare-stone wall behind her. She wore a T-shirt and cotton pants. Next to her on a stool was a radio playing a news report.

"It's the BBC World Service. The report was aired ten minutes ago," the co-pilot said.

"They want us to know she's alive," said Tom, just glad that she was, despite her predicament.

A masked man walked behind her carrying an old-fashioned tape recorder. He switched off the radio and turned on the recorder. The crackly recording began, the sound of a thunderstorm breaking the silence.

"They like the sound of thunderstorms," Crane said. "Taxi drivers play it all day long as an imam recites apocalyptic verses from the Qur'an. Still, I suppose it beats most of the shit we get stateside."

"This is where the guy speaks," the co-pilot said.

A male Pakistani's voice spoke in English as the eerie sound of the thunderstorm drained away.

"The Leopards of Islam, the true followers of the faith and the Prophet Muhammad, peace be upon him, will bring the Westerners to their knees and avenge the deaths of our brothers and sisters. The US Secretary of State has confessed to being a murderer of children and a desecrator of mosques. Despite her vile crimes, Allah is Most Merciful. The Westerners will release our brothers being held in the United States, the heroes of the Shia jihad. The Westerners will pay ten billion dollars for crimes against Shia Islam. If these demands are not met in full within seventy-two hours, the Secretary of State will be beheaded live on the Internet."

Tom ran his hand through his close-cropped hair and groaned, a deep sense of personal failure and shame engulfing him.

Crane stood up and put his hand on Tom's shoulder. "I'm sorry, Tom."

Tom knew that the chances of the president agreeing to the release of those who'd attempted the assassination of his Pakistani counterpart and the payment of the ransom were non-existent. The Leopards had killed thirty innocent men, woman and children in the attack, simply because the Pakistani leader had escaped unscathed. They'd gone on a killing spree. Besides, her kidnappers hadn't said that they would release her, just that they wouldn't kill her within the three-day timeframe.

But then his training kicked in and he glanced at his wristwatch. The clock had started ticking at 19:40 Pakistan time.

He got up and walked to the cockpit, asked for a satphone. He'd spoken with Vice Admiral Theodore Birch, the head of DS and an Assistant Secretary of State, a couple of times already. After a few minutes, Tom was speaking with him again. He asked him if there was anything their people in the office of counterterrorism division could do. Anything at all. But he knew what the answer would be before it came.

He rubbed his temples with his thumbs and forefingers, his mind racing in a hundred different directions, trying to find a way to get a lead, anything other than accepting the status quo. He'd seen the ligature marks on her wrists and ankles, and had watched her eyes as the recorded voice had fallen silent. It was clear to him that she hadn't been aware of her fate up until then. He wondered what kind of impact that had on a person's mind, even one as strong and resourceful as the secretary's.

Crane came up to him. "The Pakistani fighters are closing in. We're outta here now."

TWENTY-SEVEN

CRANE WAS SLUMPED in an armchair in his small suite back at the Ariana. He wore a dark-blue bathrobe and picked at his fingernails, as if he were still trying to remove the dirt from the fort. The living area was neat but tired-looking, with sickly pea-green walls and furniture that looked as if it had been brought in flat-packed. The light bulbs were of the energy-saving variety, and gave off a jaundiced glow.

"Helluva day, huh? But don't let the white towels and clean bed sheets fool you, Tom. This is still Kabul, so keep alert. I know at least five analysts who sleep with the light on and cuddle a Smith and Wesson Sigma like a comfort cloth. You gonna take a shower? You smell like a rodent."

Although he'd removed his dusty jacket and had slipped on a white shirt previously, Tom was still dressed in combat pants and scuffed boots. He hadn't washed yet. He was anxious for answers. He bent over an oval table and placed down two glasses, with heavy serrated bases. He poured a large whisky for Crane, a smaller one for himself. Crane said that despite sampling almost all of the world's alcoholic drinks in their natural environments, he loved Scotch above all else. It beat ouzo, schnapps, rum, sake... He rattled off another five national drinks, most of which Tom had never heard of. Ignoring him, Tom walked over to the armchair and handed him his drink.

"How did they disable the GPS sensor under her skin?" he asked.

"You can buy a tracker defence device on the net. A small unit with enough power to jam a signal within a five-metre radius," Crane replied, almost nonchalantly.

Still standing, Tom took a sip, felt the alcohol warm his throat. "Why would they lead us to the fort? They must have known we would kill the men there."

"They kill their own by the dozen a day. Internal feuds. One tribal warlord taking another's land. Think suicide bomber. Think a country where you sell your twelve-year-old daughter for two hundred bucks. Think—"

"I got it, okay."

"Besides, we just used up all our resources on the proverbial wild-goose chase. I'd say that was kinda smart."

Tom walked back to the table, put his glass down. Turning, he said, "Is Brigadier Hasni still around?"

"Hasni?"

"I heard about him when I did my spell in counter-intelligence."

"Yeah, he's still around. Like a bad smell," Crane said, smiling at his own jibe.

"I guess he knows the answer to my conspiracy theory, as you call it."

Crane laughed hard, his chest heaving. "And I know for a fact that man has tortured to death over twenty people. He's a butcher. But in his own way, he's as passionate about Pakistan as POTUS is about America.

Besides, he's an untouchable, so any little caper you've dreamed up won't be worth a dime."

"You think," Tom said, eyeing the older man and nodding.

He had a plan, one that he needed Crane's help to accomplish, although he'd already decided that it was more of a desire to act, rather than a coherent strategy.

"I don't feel inclined to score points here, so I'll just say that if you're planning on going back to Islamabad, I'll do my best to dissuade you," Crane said. "You go back there, you'll go it alone, and that, I can tell you, is just plain suicide." He took a gulp of whisky, licked his lips. "Besides, I got a duty to have you arrested by the Marines, you talk like that."

"I made a promise to Lyric, and I'm not about to renege on it. You're the only man I know who can help me out. If things go wrong, I won't mention your name."

Despite Crane's scepticism, Tom still believed the ISI were responsible. Even if they hadn't executed the abduction, there was no way the secretary could've been taken if they hadn't sanctioned it.

"If the ISI know you're a loner, you'll say my name. You'll fucking sing it," Crane said, scratching the back of his head. "They have these machines that turn your vitals into the size and consistency of plums. Get it?"

Tom walked over to a taupe-coloured sofa opposite Crane, dropped down onto it, said, "Then give me someone who knows the city."

"You'll put them in danger, too. I've had five assets arrested and imprisoned by the ISI this year already. I'm not inclined to lose any more."

"So what are we gonna do, huh? Sit on our asses

until Lyric's head is cut off on YouTube? Just gimme a break here."

Crane eased forward, spread his arms. "And if I don't?"

"I'll go back anyways."

"Don't you think we are talking to everyone who might know something? Jesus, Tom, we got close to five hundred people on this," he said, cradling his glass of Scotch as if it were a panacea.

"I just can't go home and do nothing."

"You won't make it. I'm telling you the truth. So just forget it. And if you persist, I *will* have you restrained."

"No, you won't," Tom said, getting up from the sofa.

He figured Crane was old school, too. He sure as hell wasn't a stuffed-shirt Ivy League type out to play the game in DC by the time they were thirty-five.

As he got halfway to the door Crane said, "Wait."

Tom turned. Crane seemed deep in thought. He rubbed the rim of his glass with his forefinger, and looked oddly sad, given that they weren't exactly tight.

Looking up, he said, "You didn't even ask the right question."

"What do you mean?" Tom said.

"Sit down."

Tom walked back to the sofa and sat back down.

Crane pursed his lips. "You shouldn't have asked how the GPS sensor under her skin was deactivated. You should have asked how they knew it was there. I told you not to trust anyone. Don't."

Tom shuffled uncomfortably on the sofa. He hadn't asked the right question. But his mind was made up. His eyes locked with Crane's and, for a second or two, he had a notion that he was going to tell him something extraordinary. But when the man spoke, it was practical.

"Whatcha got in mind anyhow?"

"I could pass for a Pakistani, least at night," Tom said. "I'm good at finding weak spots in security. Buildings, in particular. I make them strong. But this time I'll exploit it. You know Hasni has to be implicated in some way. Just let me check his place out. Then maybe I could plant some of those bugs your techs make, the ones that look like stones or moss. People feel safe in their gardens. They say all kinds of things."

Tom knew that satellites and drones could pinpoint a man or woman from thousands of miles away, but it still took a bug from relatively close quarters to hear a conversation that wasn't taking place on a cellphone.

Crane groaned. "How do you know he has a garden?"

"I was busy when you were taking a shower. Took a peek at some satellite imagery."

"Houseman would crucify me for even having this conversation with you. You realize that, right?"

Tom nodded.

"Okay," Crane said, sighing. "I'll put you in touch with someone. His name is Sandri Khan. But don't ever repeat that. Now listen."

TWENTY-EIGHT

LINDA BLINKED OPEN her eyes. She lay on a ragged floor mattress in a small cell, feeling heady and limp. She'd been drugged. To ease the trauma of the video her captors had taken of her and keep her docile, she imagined. The cell was stone-built. A single battery-operated LED light hung from a hook below the dome-shaped ceiling about four metres above her. She rubbed her sore wrists, chafed by the restraint, and realized she could move her feet as well. She raised her head slightly, but felt as if her skull were cracking open, and slowly resumed the foetal position.

She'd been moved from the cell where the video had been made. But only down a corridor and a short flight of flagstone steps, the ceiling so low that she'd had to duck down underneath the lintel, her guards almost doubling over. She'd seen from the interior walls and the height of the passageway that it had been built maybe a couple of hundred years ago.

The air was damp, but there was a hint of salt hanging there. She focused and heard the faint sound of waves breaking on a shore. If she hadn't been drugged for days, she guessed she might be on the south coast of Pakistan. Karachi, Pakistan's largest city and main seaport, perhaps. She felt a sudden throb in her upper left arm, looked down and saw that it had been bandaged.

The images of the underground room she'd been taken
to after the car journey flooded her mind.

Two women, dressed in white lab coats with light-
blue latex gloves and surgical masks, had stood by a
small operating table. A number of surgical instru-
ments, including a scalpel and clamps, lay on a cloth
on a stainless-steel tray beside it. An oxygen tank, fixed
by a tube to a respirator, stood in a rack at the head of
the metal table. She trembled with fear. Perhaps they
were going to remove a finger or an ear, she thought.
But then she realized what they were going to do. Her
GPS necklace and ring had been removed already, so
they were going to remove the sensor that had been implanted under her skin in her upper left arm.

She'd been led to the table and had heard the men
leaving behind her. The women stepped forward and
began to undress her. She resisted at first, wrapping her
arms around her body and pushing her chin down. But
they were strong and firm and she relented, deciding
that if she put up too much of a struggle the men would
return and do it anyway. Be compliant, Tom had told
her. Follow instructions. Don't antagonize a kidnapper.
Standing in her underwear, she was led onto the table.
She began to grind her teeth, her breathing becoming
rapid and audible. One of the women smoothed her forehead, her touch like a mother's calming a child. The
other woman put a long finger to her lips and shushed
her. She looked over and saw a burqa hanging on a hook.
The garment gave her a degree of hope. They will dress
me in it afterwards, she thought. The mask had been
put over her nose and mouth and, trying desperately to
refrain from crying out, she'd drifted off.

She clasped her left arm lightly now, and began to

rock back and forth. Despite the terrifying words that had come from the tape recorder as the video had been made, still no one had spoken to her directly. Not that she relished being called a bitch or worse, but the silence was burrowing away at her brain like a trapped insect. Men of violence come with barking threats, someone had once told her, but real killers say nothing.

If they were intent on carrying out their threat to kill her, she had three days left to live, or less. She worried that her girls would've seen the video, or been told about it. She prayed to God to give them strength. But God had not heard her prayers, or, if He had, He had chosen not to act on them.

She wondered briefly if there was some higher purpose to her incarceration, if her fate was that of martyr for a cause that she did not believe in, for she could see only revenge benefitting. Surely God was not involved in such things, she thought; and then she realized that her mind was still drug weary, her reasoning skewed.

She knew that men and women captured in the line of duty were at their most vulnerable to interrogation during the first seventy-two hours. And since no one had questioned her, she had a notion that they were bluffing. Maybe they weren't Shia jihadists after all. Maybe it was all about the multibillion-dollar reward.

She told herself to focus on being released.

Two minutes later, she was contradicting herself in her mind. Although she knew that ransoms had been paid for US public officials and members of the military in certain circumstances, paying those who had taken her, without proof of their innocence of the Washington atrocity, would be both politically and morally unacceptable. If they were members of the Leopards, releasing the murderers of the Washington atrocity was even less likely.

And they know this, she thought.

Focusing on the burqa folded on the floor a few metres away, she guessed she would be on the move soon, too.

She bit the inside of her lip, tasted blood, as she tried to revive herself fully. Her complicity was beginning to sicken her. In the short timeframe her kidnappers had imposed via the tape recorder, she knew her only hope was to escape.

TWENTY-NINE

CRANE'S KNOWLEDGE OF Pakistan had appeared limitless, and Tom had found himself warming to him.

After he'd finished tutoring, he told Tom what to say and do if he was picked up, a crash course in CIA counterinterrogation techniques. Things over and above Tom's basic SERE training, which, he said, was as useful as a eunuch to a sperm bank in the circumstances. Then he made a few calls and informed Tom that a CIA operative would drop by his room and give him some essentials, including the camouflage transmitters, although she'd be oblivious to what was going on. Jabbing a gnarled finger, he added that she'd had a rough time over here, so he'd be obliged if Tom was courteous.

Finally, he got all serious and offered Tom a capsule about the size of a pea that he'd taken from an antique snuff box.

"What's that?" Tom asked.

"You know what it is. If, and that's a massive if, you need to take it, crunch it on your back teeth, or it will pass through your system like a marble."

"No, thanks."

"Okay. But remember. This is just covert recon. Nothing more. You check out his house, drop off the bugs in the garden, and then come back over the border. If it don't have a weak spot, don't take any risks. I'll do my best to get the idea sanctioned by Houseman in the interim. But that could take twenty-four hours or more, once everyone with an opinion has their say, including the lawyers. Fucking bureaucracy is breaking my balls since waterboarding hit the headlines."

"You think we'll have time to get something incriminating?" Tom asked.

"The truth. No. But don't even think about trying to get into Hasni's house."

Tom shot him a look that said: you're telling me? He knew the doors and windows would likely be fitted with magnetized sensors and vibration detectors, the floors covered by portable pressure mats. Silent wireless alarm systems throughout. All kinds of stuff. He planned to position a spy camera first, which would be utilized to check out the garden via a secure satellite website on a cellphone. If it was clear of people, he'd plant at least three disguised voice-activated listening devices. It was a long shot, he had to admit.

But he was grateful to Crane for letting him go over the border and facilitating his as yet unofficial mission, although he wondered why he had agreed so easily.

He could have done many things to stop me, Tom thought; not least calling Birch. It was something of a mystery for now.

The phone rang.

"Get that, will ya?" Crane said, sinking back into his armchair.

Tom walked over to a pine dresser where the secure landline was and picked it up. It was Houseman.

"Where's Crane?"

"He's here, sir."

"Switch on CNN," he said. "Do it now. And tell him to ring me when the item finishes."

Tom put the handset back in the cradle and grabbed the satellite TV remote. Thumbing it, he told Crane what Houseman had just said. The screen showed three hooded and cuffed men, their heads being pressed down as they were made to duck into a Pakistani police vehicle. It looked to be in real time and staged, the scene illuminated by portable floodlights.

"The Pakistani authorities have three men in custody who have been charged with the abduction of the US Secretary of State, Linda Carlyle, state terrorism, and multiple counts of murder."

"They hood them so you can't see the beating they took," Crane said, nodding sagely.

"The three as yet unnamed men have confessed to being members of the Leopards of Islam. They will stand trial in Pakistan. Official sources have indicated that an internal report of the ISI, the Pakistan intelligence agency, highlights the fact that Pakistani police officers recognized some of the men directly involved at the scene of the kidnapping as being members of the Leopards. This is Debbie Cann for CNN news, Islamabad, Pakistan."

Tom switched the TV off. "The hell did CNN get this before us?"

"The Pakistanis ain't naive. They know the power of US public opinion."

"I didn't know that the police had seen known Leopards. The men I saw were all masked," Tom said, walking over to the sofa.

"We got a copy of the report over an hour ago," Crane said, a little sheepishly.

"And you didn't tell me."

"No point. Your mind was made up already. But now the world will believe they have those responsible."

"You think?" Tom asked, resting his hands on the back of the sofa.

"What I think don't matter diddly-squat as far as this is concerned. Perception, Tom." Crane waved a finger at him. "It's all about perception. And this little scene says the Leopards are guilty. The Iranians, too."

"Which makes what we've agreed all the more important," he said, straightening up.

"As I said, you've made up your mind already," Crane replied, draining his Scotch. "Just get me another one of these before you leave, eh, Tom." He held out his empty glass, as if Tom were a waiter.

"Don't forget Houseman wants you to call him."

"When I've finished my whisky."

"It sounded important," Tom said.

"No shit."

THIRTY

TOM WAS IN the snug bedroom allocated to him by a non-CIA manager, who was responsible for mundane matters at the Ariana. It was a high-security building, but no one expected operatives or analysts to clean restrooms, and he was surprised by the number of diverse civilians who worked here.

He was stripped down to his boxer shorts, in need of a shower. He didn't know how long it would be before he would get the chance again, and, as Crane had pointed out, he smelt like a rodent. He placed his small Buddha onto the nightstand and patted it. He would be on the move again in twenty minutes, going to what could be his death. He accepted it with a calmness that, paradoxically, worried him. He was not a risk taker; all of his training had been the opposite. A DS special agent on a protective detail was taught to eliminate risks. But he would not let the secretary go without doing what he could. Although he knew all too well that even if he successfully planted the bugs, there was no certainty that they would reveal anything useful, especially in the short timeframe.

There was a knock at the door. He slipped on a shirt and walked over to it. It was the CIA operations officer Crane had mentioned. She was a fellow Southerner with short blonde hair and a deep scar on her forehead. Her eyes were cerulean blue and as hypnotic as any he'd seen. After some brief small talk, she handed him a manila envelope containing car keys, a forged Pakistani passport and papers to enable him to cross the border, and the web address for the satellite imagery, which he hoped would result in a successful scan from the spy bug. She eased a canvas bag off her shoulder and gave it to him, too, saying it held a disposable cellphone, some clothes, a marked map, a Maglite and Pakistani rupees, together with the bugs. He noticed something about her. Something he couldn't pin down. She seemed a little agitated; nervous, even. Crane had said she'd had a hard time here, so he decided not to dwell on it.

After she'd left, he walked across the azure tiles to the cubicle shower, feeling both lethargic and energized. He stepped in and put the showerhead directly above him, turning the dial to blue. He picked up a bar of soap and shivered as the cold water drenched him. He soaped his bruised body down. Placing the soap back into the cradle, he began to massage his aching muscles.

He'd weighed a little shy of thirteen stone for the last ten years, retaining the physique of a light-heavyweight boxer. He watched what he ate and ran most days. He'd trained in Muay Thai when he'd done a three-year stint at the US Embassy in Bangkok. He'd kept up the training, honing his techniques and working out with dumbbells or doing calisthenics when they weren't to hand.

Bangkok had been his first long-term overseas posting. He'd been abroad on duty many times before, but he'd sampled as much of the culture as the average air steward did. It'd been a bar and a hotel room, then home. But after a week of late nights with a couple of other DS agents, he started to spend his days off exploring the city. The Buddhist temples were called *wats*, his cab driver said, and the best time to visit them was in the early morning when it was cooler and less busy. It was 13:02, sweltering and as packed as a subway at rush hour, the local workers being anxious to spend their lunchtimes offering the saffron-robed monks food parcels called *tam boon*. A way of attaining a better life the next time around, the cab driver had said with a sardonic grin as he'd driven Tom home.

The following day, the cab driver had arrived early and had taken Tom to the Grand Palace. Situated within the grounds, he explained, was the most important *wat* in Thailand: the Temple of the Emerald Buddha, *Wat Phra Kaew*. The Buddha was carved from a single block of jade, and sat adorned in garments of shimmering gold, an elaborate headdress twice its own size atop its cherub-like face.

A woman came up beside Tom. She wore canvas sandals and a purple cheesecloth dress that reached down to about twelve centimetres above her ankles. She had long, curly grey-brown hair, with lengths of beads dangling among the wildness. She looked to be in her mid-fifties with light-blue eyes glinting like sunlight on a glacier.

They had spoken to one another for a minute or two only.

But on his second visit, she'd managed to convince him to light joss sticks in memory of his mother.

THIRTY-ONE

THE MAIN A1 highway from Kabul passed through Jalalabad all the way to Torkham, the Af-Pak border town. Crane had told Tom not to stop, especially in Jalalabad, saying that the locals were as mad as hell. If the vehicle broke down, he should get a cab. There were more cabs in between Kabul and the border than there were wannabes in LA, he'd said. It would take about three and a half hours without a hitch, which would mean Tom would arrive in the early hours of the morning.

The vehicle Tom was driving was a rusted Ford pickup that'd been waiting for him in the Ariana parking lot, and which, he'd guessed, would tend not to arouse suspicion. But he quickly realized why the A1 was called one of the most dangerous stretches of road in the world, especially at night. The route snaked through mountain passes and was full of old ten-ton trucks that would give a traffic cop a heart attack, the car drivers risking their lives with a jaw-dropping regularity to overtake them. He'd had to drive off-road and await the passage of an Afghan military convey about midway between Kabul and the border. But at least the route lacked the numerous checkpoints manned by local police or security forces, whose presence clogged up the opposite side of the road.

At the border, the road was flanked by pedestrian walkways and metal fencing. Jagged rock faces towered above, rising to the foothills of the Khyber Pass. Tork-ham was a small town with dilapidated-looking hotels and poky, flat-roofed houses. He passed through without incident. But it was different for Afghans entering Pakistan. Those who didn't have bribe money were openly beaten by the administration officials and members of the Khasadar Force, the local militia. He sat tight and watched as skinny men covered their heads and buckled under the vicious strikes from wooden batons and rifle butts.

Entering Khyber Pakhtunkhwa, formally known as the North West Frontier Province, Tom felt equally vulnerable. It was a radical state, where even the liberally minded didn't care much for foreigners, Americans in particular. Apart from the threat posed by the Pakistan Taliban, kidnapping was rife, the average official even more corrupt than their Mexican counterparts. The locals seemed to have a penchant for Kalashnikovs, which they carried slung over their shoulders like fashion accessories. Tom was glad he was wearing the clothes of a blue-collar Pakistani: sandals, a white collarless shirt and cotton pants, and had added his wallet, SIG and a suppressor to the contents of the bag that the CIA operative had handed him. His swarthy skin and dark hair were a plus, too, although the lack of streetlights meant the chances of getting hard stares were limited in any event.

After leaving the border region, he kept on the N-5 National Highway, concentrating on driving on the left: a throwback to British rule. Along the roadside, people ate at dimly lit little stores. Roasted corn kernels wrapped in newspaper, green bananas and chicken wings. The road led all the way to Peshawar, the state capital, where he'd be picked up by one of Sandri Khan's men and driven to Islamabad. He estimated that the thirty-five-mile journey would take less than an hour.

Apart from the traffic, the only other signs of life were a single-pump gas station and the four Pakistani police checkpoints he was stopped at. He knew that the average local felt about as safe around them as a Chihuahua in a basement full of pit bulls. But Crane had told him to put a couple of hundred Pakistani rupees— a little under two dollars—inside his passport to ensure he wasn't held up. It had worked.

The land flattened out as he got closer to Peshawar, the fields filled with cash-crops: rice, sugarcane and tobacco. Stray buffalos and kids on mopeds still made driving hazardous, but as he saw the lights of the city, the mud-brick houses giving way to concrete blocks and pylons with sagging power lines, he started to adapt a little to the alien conditions. Crane had said that the streets of Peshawar were a dusty maze, and so he'd arranged for Tom to be picked up a mile from the outskirts, halfway down a private road flanked by broad-leafed shisham trees. The landowner would be paid to take care of the pickup, the man being an asset whom Crane had used often.

When he cut the lights, nothing stirred. Tom wound down the window. The night air was warm, the sky matte-black, the stars shining with the intensity of phosphorous bombs. He checked the map. It was roughly one hundred miles to Islamabad. He decided to get out, and walked over to some scrub. He squatted down beside it, put his bag by his feet and took out his suppressed SIG. Cocked and loaded, he placed it by his right foot. The main threat here was roaming bands of trigger-happy, anti-Leopard militia, paid to protect the city.

He saw the beams from a pair of full headlights approaching at speed, passing the remnants of a long-abandoned fort. The car stopped about seven metres from his vantage point, and the high beam was dipped. Tom reached into the bag and lifted out the Maglite. He signalled the three short, four long flashes that Crane had said to use, and waited for the four long, three short flashes from the headlights in return. Once registered, he bagged his SIG. Standing up, he walked out from the natural cover, and jogged towards a dark-green Mazda. As he got to it the front passenger door was opened and, bending down, he caught sight of his driver, a smiling middle-aged man with bad teeth and a lazy eye, who wore a ragged Shalwar Kameez and canvas flip-flops.

"Get in, please," he said.

"Thank you," Tom said, getting in beside him. He put the bag in the footwell and looked nervously about.

"My name is Jameel. We will be in Islamabad in less than two hours," he said, putting the car into gear and driving off.

"Where are we meeting Mr Khan?"

"His house. You like music?"

"Sure," Tom said, looking in vain for a seat belt.

"I always drive better to music. One day I will learn to drive properly and get a licence, and then I won't need the music to calm my nerves," he said as he turned on a cassette player and the sound of a Pakistani pop song belted out.

Despite Jameel's disconcerting statement, they reached the western outskirts of Islamabad safely, and travelled through a slum settlement, the track barely wide enough for the Mazda to pass. As Jameel turned down the volume on the cassette recorder the car's head-lights picked up the acid-like eyes of wild dogs and the gappy smiles of barefoot street kids. The only other lights were the yellow glows coming from oil lamps in corrugated shacks. Jameel pointed out that the shacks masqueraded as all-night food stores or eateries, but were, in fact, brothels and drugs dens. Even inside the car, the stench was appalling, assaulting Tom's nostrils, and he forced himself not to retch.

Leaving the slum, Jameel drove along a crater-ridden road before pulling into a back alley, which had a rivulet running down the side of it. As Tom saw the façades of a few three-storey tenements and derelict warehouses, Jameel stopped and cut the engine.

"Make sure you step over that," he said, nodding to-wards the fetid flow. "Or your foot will be amputated."

Tom wondered what manner of man this Sandri Khan would be.

THIRTY-TWO

THE RUST-FLECKED METAL front door led to a narrow stairway lit by an oil-filled hurricane lamp, hanging from a length of wire. The bare floorboards creaked, and plaster had flaked off the walls. At the top of the staircase, a potbellied man in an old undershirt sat on a wooden stool, an AK-47 resting on his knees. He was squinting at a newspaper but looked up as they ascended.

"He will frisk you," Jameel said.

"No, he won't," Tom replied, jutting out his chin.

"Then turn around and go."

As Tom reached the top of the stairs he held up his hands and the man did a thorough patting down. He snatched Tom's bag from him and lifted out the SIG.

"He will give it back to you when you leave," Jameel said.

Tom thought it useless to argue.

Jameel knocked twice on a first-floor door and, after a short pause, it was opened by a small man, about five-six, with a sinewy body and stubble. He wore a white robe that was stained and frayed at the bottom. His eyes were dull and flecked with red motes; his hair, bedraggled, hung to his shoulders.

"Come in. Mind the cats. They have free rein, but they will scratch and bite you if you approach them. They feel uneasy around strangers," he said, grinning.

Tom saw that the room was as unkempt as the man

Crane had called Sandri Khan, with piles of dirty laundry stacked high against damp-blackened walls. There was no furniture to speak of, save for a small sofa draped with a pale-red bed sheet, sprinkled with cat hairs. There were four cats. Their tails were almost furless, their bodies near-emaciated.

"They are my children. I am unable to have children, you see. And what woman would marry a man who could not give her children? So I live with my cats."

"That's a tough break," Tom said.

"It is God's will. I am a Christian," Khan said.

Nodding, Tom thought that a little strange.

"You look surprised. We are the largest minority religion in Pakistan. There are almost three million of us, and yet we are persecuted lepers. Some tea, perhaps? I have no milk or sugar, but the tea is good."

"No, thank you," Tom said.

"Please sit."

Tom risked attracting fleas and sat on the sofa, putting the bag down beside it. Khan filled a battered kettle from a tap that groaned and squeaked as a weak flow of water stuttered out. He put the kettle onto a single-ring gas burner before turning around and squatting on the floor.

"So you are an American. The problem with Americans is that you arm someone one day and fight them the next. Then you leave after you have wrecked the place."

"I'm not sure I follow you," Tom said.

"You armed Saddam against Iran, and then invaded Iraq. You pulled out of Iraq and the place descended into hell in a week. You armed the Afghans to fight the Russians and then invaded Afghanistan. Now you've left, the same will happen there, despite the politicians' words. You don't understand the region. Period, as you Americans say."

"That's a good speech. But I like to think we have a coherent strategy."

"No offence. You have a coherent strategy in this part of God's world like I have three balls."

"I think maybe I have come to the wrong place," Tom said, wondering if he should cut the meeting short and leave, although, in truth, he knew that would be self-defeating.

"No, no. Not at all. I am merely pointing out that you Americans have a habit of changing your minds. Think hard before you ask me to do something for you."

"Did Crane ask you to say that?"

"I don't know anyone called Crane," Khan said, smoothing a cat as it passed by him.

"This is bullshit."

Khan's expression changed. "First you insult me by not accepting my hospitality. Then you insult me by questioning my discretion."

"All right, I'm sorry."

Khan nodded, his eyes narrowing. "Well?" he asked, raising his palms face up.

Tom looked at Jameel.

"Ask what you have to ask," Khan said. "Jameel is my brother."

"Okay. Do you know where Brigadier Hasni lives?"

"He is a ruthless killer and exploiter of men. What do you want with such a man?"

Tom blinked slowly, gathering his thoughts. He would need Khan. And if Crane trusted him, so should he. After all the dancing around, he figured his best option was to be honest. At least he might be taken seriously.

"His house. I'm looking for a soft spot," he said. "I'd like to add a few bugs to his garden."

Khan laughed, dismissively. The water from the kettle began to boil over, making a whistling noise through the old-fashioned spout cap, and Jameel began to laugh, too.

"Even the kettle thinks it is funny," Jameel said.

"Make the tea, Jameel," Khan said.

"The tea, of course, brother," he said, appearing suitably rebuked.

Tom saw Khan looking at him. He'd seen that look before. It was the look of a man who could mix it with the best of them, despite his diminutive and shabby appearance to the contrary.

"Many men have tried and many men have failed. Hasni is well protected. His house is a fortress. A pretty fortress. But a fortress nonetheless. He sees assassins everywhere."

"So, you know where he lives?"

"I do," Khan said, nodding. "I also know where the President of the United States lives. Would you try to find a way to bug his garden also?"

Jameel slurped from a dirty cup and smiled. "Would you?" he mimicked.

"Will you take me to where he lives?"

"If you wish," Khan said. "First, I will drink tea with my brother. It may be my last."

THIRTY-THREE

SANDRI KHAN DROVE Tom in the Mazda past Hasni's house. He parked up beside a row of kachnar trees, their dense foliage minimizing the glare from the highway's LED streetlights. Hasni's house was on the other side, forty metres back, the front entrance illuminated by powerful floodlights. It was relatively isolated; the length of a football pitch from the nearest building. A twenty-storey, apex-roofed skyscraper jutting up from a pink-slab plaza. Tom told Khan to wait in the car, leaving the bugs in the bag. He'd do an initial recon first, without any incriminatory evidence if the worst happened. Khan just shook his head. But Tom had guarded buildings for years. If this one had a soft spot, he'd find it. He wouldn't even have to scale the wall around the garden. The bugs' robust design meant they could withstand a drop of twenty metres onto a hard surface and were pliable enough to remain operational after being run over by a family car. But he still needed a soft spot from which to launch the bugs into position.

Getting no more than a few metres down the sidewalk, he saw a white Rolls-Royce pull into the driveway leading to Hasni's home, small Saudi flags hanging limp above the hood, diplomatic plates front and rear. The car stopped and an armed guard ducked down to the front window. A few seconds later, the gate opened and the car moved forward.

In his experience, the rears of buildings were always less well protected than the façades. He hoped this one wouldn't be any different. He'd look out for gaps in security cameras. A patch of dark, or an overhanging tree. An area not protected by static guards, or outside their line of vision. Potential cover created by bushes or long grass. A back door not fitted with a video entry system. A window covered by shutters or hinged grilles. Anything that would allow him to toss the spy camera over the wall and into the garden undetected.

As he jogged across the street, he darted left, following the dark flank of the walled house from a suitable distance. But as he closed the gap to about fifteen metres, the whole area was lit up by floodlights. Shielding his eyes from the white light, he made out a bunker half sunk into the ground in front of the wall, the muzzle of a heavy machine gun sticking out of it. Knowing he had set off an invisible microwave beam, or a passive infrared variety, the modern equivalents of a tripwire, he stepped back. A second later, he heard a dog barking and the sound of pounding boots behind him.

Turning, he saw two guards in dark-blue combat fatigues emerge from the shadows. They both wore ball caps, emblazoned with the *No Fear* logo, a favourite of Pakistani elite forces. One of them was looking at him through the iron sights of a sub-machine gun; the other holding onto a black-and-tan Doberman that was already on its hind legs, straining at the leash. As it snarled white froth oozed from the sides of its mouth. Tom was ordered to raise his hands and stand still. As the one without the dog got to him he drew back his sub-machine gun, threatening to thrust the butt into his face. Tom winced involuntarily. But he wasn't hit.

Instead, the guard shouldered his weapon and frisked him brusquely. Satisfied, he gestured with a flick of his head that Tom should move. Passing in front of him, his hands still raised, Tom was kicked hard in the left buttock with the guard's heavy boot. The crude message was clear enough: keep moving or else.

Feeling humiliated, Tom was led towards the front of the house, the guard with the dog bearing off halfway down. He figured he was checking to see if he'd been alone. About ten metres from the gate, he counted the steps behind him from a given point. The guard was less than half a metre away. Swiftly, he returned the kick, as he thrust back with his right leg, catching the guard in the lower stomach with his heel. The man groaned as Tom twisted around. As the guard raised his head, Tom struck him under his jaw with his open palm. He'd not hit him hard enough to break his neck, but the blow had rendered him unconscious.

He heard the dog barking again. He decided that if he grabbed the man's gun, he would evoke a shoot to kill response, so he opted for a less obvious choice of weapon. Tom unhooked a pair of metal cuffs from the man's belt, a makeshift knuckleduster, and straightened up. As the guards on the gate began shouting out, he darted for the shadow, quickening his pace as he saw the street. He began to sprint. The barking got louder. He figured the brute had been unleashed. Risking a glance over his shoulder, he saw it bounding up to him. If he kept running, it could catch him, pin him to the ground and take a chunk out of his neck.

Tom stopped and turned. As the dog got within range he saw it launch into the air. He flung himself to the right, the dog passing a few centimetres from his shoulder. Pivoting around, Tom saw that it had landed badly, its front legs twisting. He bunched his right-hand fingers around the bottom half of the cuffs and, as the dog struggled to reverse, he bent over and yanked up one of its hind legs, immobilizing it. He used the makeshift knuckleduster to hammer it into submission, pummelling its ribs as it twisted its head, desperate to get a hold on him. After the fifth punch, it made an agonizing sound, its hard body going limp. Tom dropped the leg and ran towards the street, a couple of rounds whizzing through the air about him. He guessed that the guards were firing randomly in his general direction, since the men he'd seen lacked the benefit of night vision, and he was still shrouded in darkness.

As he got to the street, he heard the Mazda's engine revving, and noticed that the front passenger door was open. Before ducking in, he saw powerful lights scanning the grass where he'd felled the dog. Other guards were shouting and running about, as a monotonous, high-pitched Klaxon alarm system started up. He knew Khan was right. It was impenetrable, at least without a company of Screaming Eagles parachuting down inside the walls to back him up. He banged the door shut.

"Are you satisfied now?" Khan asked.

Tom nodded, crestfallen. He turned around and saw that a couple of the guards had all but reached the sidewalk. "Let's get the hell outta here."

THIRTY-FOUR

KHAN STOPPED THE car after about ten minutes, opposite a partially lit government office block.

"We should split up," he said. "At the very least they'll be looking for two men in a dark Mazda."

"You're right," Tom said, his mind fighting to control a rising sense of panic.

Khan turned sideways in his seat. "Before you ask, the property has a concrete tunnel running underneath, secured with eye-recognition blast-proof doors. There are three safe rooms on different floors with metre-thick walls lined with steel plates and filled with sophisticated comms. And when he travels around the city, he is accompanied by military vehicles in a limo that can withstand an attack by an RPG. You should go back over the border and go home. Never return to Pakistan."

"So why did you bring me here?" Tom asked.

"I was ordered to do what you asked, within reason."

Tom figured Crane had wanted to make a point. He had. But it was helluva way to go about it, he thought. He had a vague notion that Crane's motives for letting him come here were more complicated. But for now, they would have to remain unknown.

"But I will tell you something," Khan said. "There is only one way to get to Hasni. His son, Mahmood."

"No," said Tom. "I don't hurt children."

"He is not a child. He is, I think, twenty-two. A student at your Harvard University," he replied.

Tom thought about it. Mahmood was barely a man and likely innocent of his father's crimes. But he knew he had no other option to get to Hasni in the short timeframe imposed by the video. It took ten years and billions of dollars to find bin Laden, and, despite the most sophisticated surveillance equipment in the world, if it hadn't been for waterboarding the CIA would still be looking for him. He didn't like it, but it was a fact.

"Very few people know of his true identity. He goes by an assumed name. You should know that Mahmood is protected by a bodyguard. Do not underestimate this man. Hasni would only entrust his son's safety to one who is formidable. His name is Zafar. A squat man with a bearded face; eyes like black diamonds. Mahmood is scrawny and clean-shaven. And before you ask, I do not know where he lives."

"Why are you telling me this?" Tom asked.

"Hasni is responsible for killing many of my friends. He would kill me, too, if he knew what I'd done."

Tom figured it would be a waste of words to ask him what he'd done. Truth was, he didn't care.

"Mahmood's assumed name is Hassan Rind. I prayed about this on our way here. God has spoken to me. He has told me I can trust you, American, despite your lack of manners."

Tom heard the sound of a car pulling up close behind them, the headlights flooding the side-view mirror. The lights were extinguished and the engine turned off. He watched Khan check the rear-view, a worried expression crossing the Pakistani's hollow-cheeked face.

"Who is it?" Tom asked.

"ISI."

THIRTY-FIVE

TOM GRABBED THE rear-view and twisted it, scanning the car behind. Two thick-set men sat in the front seats of a black Mercedes, the half hidden bulks of more behind. He saw the front passenger door open and a man got out, his broad-shouldered frame swaggering towards them as if he'd watched too many dubbed Mafia movies.

Tom heard a shout just as Khan twisted the ignition key. As the car drove off a handgun was discharged. The round hit the rear windshield, the impact sending tiny shards of glass onto the back seat. It passed between them with a loud *hiss* and penetrated the plastic dashboard. Khan hit the gas and zigzagged into the outside lane, careering past a taxi. He honked the horn at a man on a moped, who wobbled but remained upright. Tom turned around and saw the Mercedes speeding up behind them. With that, the car engine started to splutter, and small geysers of hot steam rose from the air vents. Khan swerved behind a gold-coloured Lexus and slowed down.

"Damn them to hell," he said.

The steam was obscuring the windshield and Khan tried frantically to clear it with his sleeve, but to no avail. Tom wound down the window and put his hand over a vent, but the steam burned him and he winced. Khan swung the car to the left, cutting back into the inside lane, and accelerated off the asphalt highway. The car dipped into a storm drain runoff, and rose up the kerb of the sidewalk before crunching forward onto a piece of waste ground between two apartment blocks. If the car had shocks, Tom figured they weren't functional ones. As the car barrelled ahead he held the passenger door handle tightly, rocking with the impact, too preoccupied now with the recklessness of the manoeuvre to worry about the ISI. Khan was driving blindly.

"Stop the damn car!" Tom said.

Khan slammed on the brakes and the car shuddered to a halt. Tom nearly hit his nose on the dash, but put up his free forearm just in time, banging his forehead on it. Ignoring the throbbing pain, he ducked down and pulled his SIG from the bag in the footwell, chambering a round. As he straightened up Khan put his hand gently on his right forearm. Tom felt bad, but he knew he couldn't save the secretary from a Pakistani prison cell. He nodded and picked up his bag before opening the car door, hearing the Mercedes coming up close behind.

"I won't—"

"Go," Khan said.

As Tom propelled himself out of the car, he swivelled his head and saw the Mercedes bouncing forward, its headlights blinding his eyes. He turned and raced over the waste ground. Hearing rounds being fired behind him, he stopped instinctively. Twisting around, he watched Khan knock out one of the lights and aim at a front tyre, a round ripping open the rubber, flattening it.

The muzzle of a sub-machine gun poked out of the rear window of the Mercedes. Tom dived for cover onto the hard ground, grazing his knees. He saw the flash as a burst was fired, but the car had dipped into a small crater as the weapon had been discharged. The spray of bullets cut a shredded line less than a metre from his prostrate body, the stony soil peppering his face. If it hadn't been for the uneven ground, the burst would have likely cut him in two.

He pushed himself up, turned and ran, leaping over mounds of hardened cement and rusted girders, the land being an abandoned construction site. He skirted around behind a blackened, portable cement mixer, and saw that Khan was keeping the ISI men at bay, his rounds bouncing off the Mercedes' hood and slamming into the open doors. He's a brave man, Tom thought. He spun around and sprinted towards the end of the site, careful not to sprain an ankle on the lumpy earth. Fifty metres on there was an industrial chain-link fence, about three metres high.

Reaching the fence, he heaved his bag to the other side. He stepped back before running at it. He managed to scramble over, ripping his linen shirt on a protruding piece of wire. He crouched down, the lack of streetlights adding to his sense of isolation but keeping him hidden.

THIRTY-SIX

A FEW HUNDRED metres from the fence, the streets of the Blue Area were almost deserted. A cool breeze played across Tom's face, although he still felt clammy. He shuffled along the sidewalk, his ankle beginning to ache from the drop. As he passed a large, detached house surrounded by a brick-built privacy wall he saw a man watching him from an upstairs window and did his best to speed up. He wasn't sure where he was going. He just wanted to get the hell out.

He thought about ringing Crane. But what could he do? he asked himself. Maybe he could get an asset to pick me up? As he took out the cellphone from his bag, he watched a police squad car slow down as it levelled with him. A white Honda Civic with a dark-blue stripe down the middle, the words "CAPITAL POLICE" on the side. An officer peered over and shone a flashlight into Tom's face.

"You. Stand still," he shouted in Urdu.

The car eased into a rest stop about three metres ahead, and Tom sensed his heart rate race. As the cop opened the passenger door Tom risked walking towards him, doing his best to calm himself down. The cop was maybe twenty, clad in dark pants and a light-blue shirt, a black beret riding high on his thin, pockmarked face. He figured the cop had taken him for a vagrant or worse. He was filthy and dishevelled, his clothes ripped. Not your average Blue Area occupant. Then: maybe the ISI has put out an APB already, he thought. But the cop's hand didn't go for his handgun in a leather holster on his hip.

"What are you doing here?" the cop asked.

"I'm lost," Tom said as he reached him.

The cop raised a hand to his lapel radio, said, "You're coming with me. You—"

He didn't get the rest of the sentence out. Tom had taken advantage of the raised hand, whipping out a stinging right hook to the liver just below the floating ribs. The cop groaned and sank to his knees. Tom thought about bringing his elbow down onto the back of the cop's neck, just hard enough to keep him quiet, but the punch had left his victim gasping for air and it wasn't necessary. Instead, he reached into the bag and pulled out his suppressed SIG. Rushing forward, he ducked down into the space where the car door had been left open. The other cop was older, probably in his mid-forties, with a bushy moustache and double chin. His left hand was pulling at a Steyr AUG rifle lodged upside down in metal brackets between the two front seats.

"Don't do it," Tom said, the SIG raised.

The cop's hand hovered over the rifle before slowly moving back to his waist.

"Take off your radio," Tom said.

The cop obeyed. Tom reached over and took it from him, threw it to the ground and stamped on it. Pointing his suppressed SIG, he shot the car radio with a round, the circuit spitting out sparks. The cop almost leapt off his seat with shock.

"Ease your sidearm out. Toss it over here," Tom said, motioning to the seat next to him.

The cop did so. Tom unclipped the rifle's magazine and slipped it into his bag, together with the cop's Beretta before ducking out.

"I'll just disarm your friend. Then you can drive him away. No one is going to get hurt here."

"He looks hurt to me," the cop said.

"Maybe his pride, is all."

"You will never get out of Pakistan," he said.

The cop grinned. For a fleeting moment, Tom thought the cop knew something. He had no idea how, unless the ISI had in fact distributed his description. Either way, he needed to move. His grinning face had rattled him. He walked over to the winded man, smashed his radio and disarmed him. He started to run, sprinting for a hundred metres or so, ignoring the pain in his ankle.

He saw an alley bordered by a small, wooded park area to the left, and the side security wall of a hotel to the right. He checked the wall for CCTV cameras and shielded his eyes as he spotted one. He guessed he had less than half an hour before the cops reported the incident back at the station. He took off down the side alley, deciding to get out of Islamabad on his own, remembering what Crane had said about using a cab if his car gave up on him. With luck, it would be the quicker option.

THIRTY-SEVEN

LINDA COULD STILL smell the sea. She had been given a meagre meal of fish and rice, together with a bottle of water and a fresh set of clothes to wear: sweatpants, a black T-shirt and sweater, although the burqa had been left in the cell. The effects of the drug had abated fully, and she was lucid. She had no idea how she would escape at this point, but just the thought of it made her feel strangely elated. Sitting against the wall, she nodded, her mind made up.

A couple of minutes later, the cell door was unlocked and a man came in, his face obscured by a ski mask, his hands gloved. She noticed at once that he carried a long pair of hairdresser's scissors, a mirror and a plastic bottle. He placed the items on the stone floor and stepped back.

"Cut and dye hair. Like this," he said, taking a piece of paper from his pocket and holding it before her face.

She glanced at it. It was a childlike sketch of a head, the hair coloured in with a marker pen.

He tossed it to the floor. "I come back later," he said, and left.

She pushed herself off the floor and walked over to where the items had been left. Be compliant, Tom Dupree had said. She was resenting it now, but, if she wanted to escape, antagonizing her captors wasn't a good option. She picked up the mirror and stared at her face. Her make-up had been removed and her eyes were puffy and red, the crow's feet more pronounced, her forehead creased with sleep lines. She thought she'd aged ten years. She'd never been motivated by an ability to grab the attention of people by her natural beauty. But she was careful to look her best, and if that meant that she appeared attractive in front of the cameras or at some function, so be it—things that now seemed part of another world and time.

Bending down, she picked up the scissors and sketch, and walked to the small wooden table pushed against the wall. Propping up the mirror, she noticed that the table was unstable. She crouched down and checked the legs. The one on the left, wedged into the corner, was wonky, a single rusted screw keeping it in place. Ignoring it, she looked at the sketch, knelt, and began to snip. An act that soon became frenzied as she hacked away in order to finish the job quickly.

She wondered if it was an attempt to humiliate her further, but then dismissed the notion. They could do a thousand things to humiliate me if they were so inclined, she thought. It must be simply to disguise me. But from whom? There was the burqa for that. Even if they decided to move her again, she guessed that she would be hidden from view in any event. Still, she had no choice in the matter.

After she had done her best to recreate the image on the paper, the frenzy being replaced by a modicum of care before applying the dye, she slumped against the wall. Hearing the door opening again, she looked up. A similarly masked man was standing there, with a trash bag in his hands. But he said nothing. He walked over and picked up the items before placing them into the bag. He started to gather her cut hair, being fastidious to remove even a single strand. She wondered if they would use it to prove they had her, since it contained her DNA. But they had the video, she thought. It was simply to cover their tracks, then. He walked out without saying a word, the door left ajar.

The same man who had ordered her to cut and dye her hair appeared. She could tell from his size, his clothes, and the way that he moved: languidly, as if he were bored or some reptile hybrid. He stood before her, appeared to be examining her attempt. He nodded, grunting approval.

"Change into burqa," he said, pointing to the full-face garment folded on the floor.

He turned to leave.

"Do you believe in God?" she asked.

He stopped. "God is Great," he said.

"Did he tell you to kidnap women? To threaten them with murder?"

"You are Kafir. An unbeliever. Allah is not your God."

"You don't believe that."

He shrugged and left.

She got up and paced about, her mind active.

Her father had told her that the higher she climbed, the lower her sense of injustice would plummet, not because she would become self-serving, but simply because she would become aware of the competing influences, the otherwise secret agendas and the interplay and complexity of geopolitics. He'd been right, to a degree. But she fought hard and long to ensure that America left Afghanistan. The US would not become fully embroiled in another war while she had a say, although she'd agreed with the rationale for the initial invasion: the defeating of the Taliban regime. But she knew that her death could negate all that. There would be another war. The thought of more young men and women coming home in boxes, or spending the rest of their lives in wheelchairs or on antipsychotic drugs, gave her the impetus she needed to act quickly.

Two minutes later, the outline of an escape plan began to form in her mind.

THIRTY-EIGHT

TOM CROUCHED DOWN behind a brown-brick wall that abutted the sidewalk. His face was dripping sweat. He hadn't seen Khan get out, but he hadn't seen him killed, either. In truth, he felt confused by the whole episode. But had to admit that Khan, or whatever his name was, had saved his life and had given him his only lead.

After a few minutes, he saw a beat-up Suzuki sedan with the words "For Hire" emblazoned in red on the side, along with some Urdu painted green. He stepped out from the wall, still clutching his bag, and walked to the edge of the kerb before attempting to hail it down. The cab passed him but stopped and reversed. He opened the front passenger door and leaned in, seeing a slim-faced man with a high forehead and an unkempt moustache, the hairs peppered with white spots, as if he'd just eaten a sugar doughnut.

"Do you speak English?" Tom asked.

"Oh, yes," the driver said. "Very good English. Where are we going to?"

"Peshawar," Tom replied, deciding to pick up the Ford there and drive back to Kabul.

"Oh, no, sir. I work only in Islamabad. And I am having sleep in one hour. Besides do not go to Peshawar. Very dangerous."

"Listen. I need a car and fresh clothes."

"I only drive taxi, sir."

"I have three thousand American dollars," Tom said, all that he had in his wallet.

He liked to carry cash, especially abroad. In his line of business, he'd thought he might need it one day. Now that day had arrived.

"I know a very good car dealer. My cousin. You can have clothes, too. He is broad man like you. Get in, get in," he said, his hand beckoning Tom frantically.

Tom got into the back seat, something that felt like a busted spring jutting into his thigh. The driver pulled away, hammering at his horn as a car swerved to avoid his clumsy manoeuvre.

"How long till we get there?" Tom asked.

"A few minutes, sir. You want cigarettes? Marlboro Lights," he said, grinning in the rear-view.

"I don't smoke."

"Are you an American?"

"Australian," Tom said, lying.

"Ah, surfing and very pretty girls. You like very pretty girls?"

Tom checked below the car's dash. "Can you turn on the radio?"

"Sure. No problem," the cab driver said. "You like boys?"

"Just drive, will ya?" Tom said, figuring the guy got a cut from local pimps for providing foreign customers.

As the cab driver turned on the radio Tom took out the disposable cell and rang Crane, hoping that he would wake from his drunken slumber. He had to ring three times before he was greeted by a grunt on the other end, rather than voicemail.

"It's me, Tom."

"Jesus, what's that noise?" Crane asked.

"I'm in a cab. I'm still in Islamabad."

"Can you talk freely?"

Tom told him what had happened, including his encounter with the Pakistani cops, and that he'd arranged transport. He left out what Khan had told him about Hasni's son, Mahmood. He didn't want Crane interfering. He might get him picked up and moved to a safe house in order to avoid an embarrassing diplomatic incident. He just couldn't risk it.

"If they have Khan, he'll talk. Not right away, because he's tough. But he *will* talk," Crane said, his tone morose. "And you can't risk going over the border by yourself. I'll have someone meet you on the Pak side. They'll bring you back to Kabul. Ring me when you get close to Torkham. But avoid the major roads. Use the map."

"Can you get me on a plane from Kabul to Boston?" Tom asked, checking on the driver, who was still shaking his head to the music.

"Why Boston?"

"I got a buddy there. I thought I'd meet up with him," Tom said.

It was half a truth at least.

THIRTY-NINE

THE ARAB'S NAME was Rahul Al-Dhakheel, a leading confidante of the House of Saud, the enormous Saudi ruling family. A slight man, Hasni always thought, almost frail, with plump lips and a well-trimmed goatee, who wore metal-rimmed eyeglasses, a pristine white dishdasha and keffiyeh headdress. He occupied the armchair that Kakar had sat in earlier. But Hasni's manner had been entirely different. The man was the Saudi ambassador.

After knocking, Hasni's acne-scarred butler, Jarrar, entered, carrying a folded note on a silver tray, which also held a silver coffee pot and handle-free cups. Jarrar had been with him for two decades, and for fifteen years with his father before that. Hasni employed his whole extended family and trusted him more than any man he knew. Jarrar presented the tray to Hasni, who took the note, thanking him. The butler shuffled over to a table and poured the coffee. The note informed Hasni of the incident outside his home. But it didn't perturb him. Such things were to be expected, especially given the current situation in the country. Besides, he had more important things on his mind.

The Saudis had had a special relationship with Pakistan for decades. They'd funded the Islamisation programme in Pakistan when General Zia had imposed martial law in the 1970s. A man, Hasni knew, the new

generals were anxious to emulate. That influence had
continued and the Saudis still paid for Madrassas here.
Places the US called a breeding ground of militant
Sunni extremism. Hasni found it difficult to argue with
that. But he went along with it, because the Saudis had
also secretly funded Pakistan's nuclear-weapons programme. If and when Iran developed strategic nuclear
weapons, Pakistan had agreed to hand over a number
of their warheads to the Saudis. The Arabs never did
anything without a payback.

But he didn't blame them for this. The Gulf states,
and the Saudis in particular, had been terrified about
Iran becoming a major regional power after the Shia
revolution in 1979. He also knew that they'd feared a
rising up of Shia terrorist groups in Sunni-dominated
countries. Their fears had been borne out soon enough
with the founding of Hezbollah in Lebanon. In response, the Saudis had funded fundamentalist Sunni
movements all over the region, including those who had
massacred Pakistani Shias in the nineties, something
Hasni had been against, as it had fostered instability.
History was repeating itself, but even Hasni was pow-
erless to control such internal aggression.

And then as now, he had to do the Saudis' bidding.
Without them, the lights would go out and industry
would grind to a halt. The generals' encouragement of
the Shia killings had not only sabotaged the chances
of an Iran-Pak gas pipeline, but had also alienated the
Russians, the Iranian's allies. That and the fact that the
previous civilian government had failed to address the
predicament of millions of Pakistanis who lived without power. So there was nowhere else for Pakistan to
turn to for essential natural resources. The Saudis were

well aware of this, which was why they had been able to manipulate him.

Without a hint of emotion showing on his face, Hasni updated the ambassador in detail on the abduction of the secretary.

"The attack in Kurram will act as a counterbalance," the ambassador said, referring to the illegal incursion of Pakistan's territory by Delta Force, which had been reported on the local TV networks just a few minutes ago.

"Well, for some perhaps," Hasni replied, sipping at his coffee.

"They killed innocent Pakistani citizens. That's enough to warrant an apology from the US president," the ambassador said. "Is that not so?"

"Shia troublemakers. The country is better off without them," Hasni added, sounding sincere.

The ambassador smiled, nodding approvingly before pointing out that the Saudis had done all they could to stem the flow of Shia ambition. In Syria, they'd backed the Sunni revolt against the Iran-friendly Shia regime, supplying them with RPGs, machine guns and satphones. In neighbouring Bahrain, they'd sent their own Special Forces across the King Fahd Causeway to help quell the Shia uprising against their ally.

Hasni listened politely, but he had little time for sectarianism. The fissure in the Muslim faith dated back to the death of the Prophet Muhammad in the sixth century, when the essentially political dispute arose over the leadership of the burgeoning religion. With the passage of time, the division developed into a theological one, with both denominations referring to the other as rejecters of the true faith. But now, he had to admit, the

Shia uprisings were in danger of extending Iran's influence to the point where they could destabilize even Pakistan and Saudi Arabia. They had to be stopped. He agreed with the Arab on that, at least.

Twenty minutes later, the ambassador said, *"Ma'asalama."* Farewell with peace.

Hasni forced an open-mouthed smile and nodded.

He ambled back to his study and sank down on the chair behind his desk, wondering what the future would hold and how he might manoeuvre matters to Pakistan's advantage. He took out a Cuban cigar from a teak case and severed the closed end just above the faint line with his silver cutter, recounting the conversation he'd had with the Arab. He lit the cigar with a match, never a lighter, and began to puff, twisting the cigar around evenly to ensure it burned at a constant rate, just as his father had taught him.

Never inhale, my son. Draw in the smoke slowly. Savour it.

A knock at the door brought him out of his short reverie. Adeela entered. He'd told her to retire to her room before the ambassador had arrived, and to stay there. He didn't like the way the Saudi looked at her. He didn't mind her serving Asad and Kakar. If they had shown a hint of lust in their eyes, he would have blackened them. They knew it, too. Besides, since his wife had died from a massive heart attack three years ago, Adeela had become the woman of the household, and he had indulged her, allowing her to appear useful, partly to assuage her grief, he supposed.

"What are you still doing up at this hour?" he asked.

"I couldn't sleep, Father. Do you need anything?" she asked.

"Only a kiss, my dear."

She smiled and walked over to him. Bending down, she kissed his forehead gently. Straightening up, she said, "I'm scared, Father."

He held her hand. "Would I allow anything to happen to you?"

"No, Father," she said.

"Then go back to bed."

Watching her leave the room, he realized how much he missed his son, Mahmood. He loved his daughter, but Mahmood was his heir. One day he would help to shape Pakistan's future. America's power was waning, but it would be decades before they stopped asserting their influence in the region. He had come to understand that in order to deal with the US effectively, it would be necessary to think like them, and the best way to do that was to be educated by them. And so he had sent his son to Harvard.

FORTY

HOURS LATER, TOM was nearing the border, driving on a zigzagging back road he'd checked on the map. Crane had said that he couldn't rely on an Internet connection due to the mountains. The car was an old rust-ridden Toyota Corolla for which the cab driver's cousin had charged him three-thousand dollars. He guessed it was his own fault for letting on how much he had. The cousin had thrown in some clothes for free and had acted as if he were a major philanthropist. Tom had been ripped off, but was just glad that they hadn't tried to turn him over to the authorities and were only interested in making a living, even though it was a dishonest one.

It was morning now. The light-blue sky was blemished only by a few high, translucent clouds, although he couldn't see the horizon, the narrow road being flanked by steep, rock-strewn hills. He'd had to swerve twice already. Once to avoid a glittering, multicoloured bus with young men sitting precariously on the flat roof; the other, to avoid a small herd of wild mountain goats that'd wandered into the road. The car didn't have AC, and sweat constantly beaded on his forehead before running in tiny rivulets down his face and into his eyes. He was a short distance from where the road forked, and then, after a mile or so, linked up with the N-5 National Highway.

A few minutes later, as he passed a sharp bend, he

saw a couple of men directly ahead, a small truck a little further up, the tailgate hanging down. The two on the road had AK-47s slung over their shoulders, and were motioning with their hands for him to stop. They stood in front of a makeshift barrier: a gnarled log suspended on two oil drums. Straining against the glare, he noticed that two more were sitting on the truck bed, smoking what he took for hashish.

He knew the border area was dangerous, and guessed that his luck had finally run out. It was an unofficial roadblock. They could be anyone from bandits to members of more than a dozen known insurgency groups, he thought. He felt a desire to speed up and smash his way through. But the car wasn't exactly an up-armoured Hummer, and he didn't want to add hit-and-run charges to the list of offences he'd committed in Pakistan already. Besides, after the near miss by the single round in Islamabad, he thought the chances of getting capped by four assault rifles was too high a risk to take.

Slowing down, he took out his SIG from the bag and held it by his thigh, clicking the safety off. As he came to a stop he eased the door open a fraction. A car was a convenient way to travel, but in a firefight it was a metal coffin.

A man who looked to be in his twenties, although the bottom half of his face was wrapped in a black-and-white-chequered bandana, bent down and peered in.

"Papers," he said in Urdu.

Wondering why he hadn't spoken in Pashto, the local language of the majority Pashtun in the region, Tom reached slowly under the dash with his free hand, sensed the man edge closer.

"My brother is working in Jalalabad. He had an accident on a construction site. He is very ill," he said, handing his papers to the man.

Crane had told him that a lot of Pakistanis worked in Afghanistan's major cities, especially in construction, so it was common for them to pass over the border. That would be his reason for doing so, too, if he had to explain himself, he'd said. Tom had decided to mix it up a little.

"Where do you live?" the man asked, his eyes scanning the passport.

"Islamabad. But I come from Sindh."

After Crane had told him that his Urdu had sounded like a hog farmer reading Shakespeare, he'd explained that apart from Pashto many Pakistani regions spoke different languages. It would be best if he made out he was from Sindh. They would know, he'd said, that Urdu was likely to be a second language to Sindhi.

"Where in Sindh?"

"Sukkur."

"What river passes by Sukkur?"

"The Indus. Sukkur is on the west bank," Tom said.

He knew that if the questioning went much further, the little that Crane had been able to tell him in the short time they'd had at the Ariana would be exhausted.

"Why are you on this road?"

Good question, Tom thought.

"There was a traffic jam. Miles long. And as I said, I'm in a hurry."

The man stepped back, and took a cellphone from his green combat jacket. As he started to thumb it, Tom checked the position of the other three. The two in the truck were still smoking their reefers, while the third man was starting to get interested in what was happening.

The man looked at the cell and then at Tom.

He recognizes me, he thought. How the hell does he recognize me? But then he realized that the Pakistani guards or the cops he'd disabled might have given his description to a sketch artist, which, given the time-frame, could've been emailed nationwide.

Tom shifted into overdrive. He heaved the door open, just as the man was bringing his AK up in an arc. The door caught him in the kneecaps with a sickening thud, and he doubled over. Tom flung himself out and sprang up from behind the partially rebounded door. He shot the upright man in the shoulder, the impact spinning him around, his AK kicking in his hand, as he involuntarily let off a short burst to the side. A second later and the man would have had him.

Moving out from the door, Tom pistol-whipped the man he'd hit with it and ran forward, pointing his SIG.

The men in the truck were fumbling for their AKs, their close proximity and the drugs temporarily disorientating them, Tom guessed. He squeezed off two rounds above their heads and shouted out in Urdu, ordering them to hold up their hands. He fired twice more, emphasizing that it would be a good move. They couldn't duck down behind the sides for cover, because the truck's rear was facing him where it had parked on the road. Wavering for a second or two, they did as they were told. He barked at them to get off the truck and lie face down on the ground. They did so, albeit with reluctance.

He turned. The man he'd hit with the butt of his SIG was struggling to get up. Tom jogged backward, keeping an eye on the two on the ground. As he got parallel with the man, he punched him hard on the jaw. He fell sideways, groaning, a trickle of blood oozing from his crooked mouth. Tom picked up the AK and walked over to the man he'd shot, dipping down to gather up his weapon, too. The man's face was contorted in agony, his good hand grasping the bloody entry wound in his shoulder.

Tom ran to the back of the truck and pulled off the other two AKs by their nylon straps. Grabbing them one at a time from the barrel, he swung them to gain momentum before tossing them up among the jagged rocks. He thought about disabling the truck by shooting the tyres, but walked back towards the car instead. The man he'd punched was reviving, his hand groping for something under his jacket. As Tom reached him he bent down, snatched the man's hand away and pulled out a hand grenade, pocketing it.

The cellphone, he thought. Seeing it lying about two metres away, he walked over and picked it up. He checked it. His face stared out at him and he went cold. The photo had been taken in Islamabad just hours before.

Tom went back over to the man he'd shot. He stuck the SIG into his waistband and crouched down beside his bare head, the man's greasy hair falling to his shoulders. He saw fear in the amber-coloured eyes. As he grabbed his cotton shirt, the man winced. But when he ripped off the sleeve and used it as a tourniquet to ease the blood flow, the man's expression turned to one of confusion.

Then he frisked him, taking out his cellphone. Checking it, he saw his photo. He walked over to the two men who'd been on the truck, their heads still face down in the dirt. He did the same routine, pocketing their cells before pulling one of them over onto his front. He looked petrified, but said nothing. Tom stuck the muzzle of his SIG into the man's hairless cheek.

"Where did you get a photo of my face?" he said in Urdu, harshly.

The man shook his head a fraction.

Unless he spent the next half an hour or so doing things to them that he didn't relish, he figured he wouldn't get anywhere. Besides, they were foot soldiers of the uneducated variety. The chances of them knowing anything of significance were slim.

Straightening up, Tom nodded towards the wounded man. "He needs urgent medical attention. If you follow me, I will kill all of you."

The man he'd questioned nodded.

If he'd had to kill them, he would have. The thought made him question if what he was doing was right. But too many questions were already spinning around in his head, not least how they had a photo of him on their cells. Too many questions, he told himself. As he walked back to the Toyota he felt a searing pain erupt from the side of his neck. A split second later, he heard the clattering of metal on the road.

He twisted around deftly, pointing his SIG. The man he'd spoken to was wearing shin-length boots, high enough to hide a knife. Tom raised his free hand, stroked his neck with his fingers, seeing the blood as he held them before his eyes. Although he was sure it was just a flesh wound, he cursed himself for being sloppy.

The man, still standing, held up his hands and made a pushing movement with them, his tongue licking his bottom lip as he breathed heavily. Tom groaned, the pain making his eyes water. He cocked the SIG. The man covered his face with his arms and seemed to shrink to half his former size. He said he had two children and started praying to Allah.

After a full fifteen seconds, Tom lowered the SIG.

Too many fresh corpses were buried in this earth, and beneath them the yellowing bones of thousands more. Like the splintered roots of a dead forest, he imagined. He wasn't going to add to that if he had a choice in the matter.

FORTY-ONE

LINDA HAD PUT on the burqa, as she'd been ordered to do. There was no need for a niqab, her face being covered almost completely by the garment's lace net. But at least the man hadn't trampled on her dignity by staying in the cell as she'd changed. She remembered that the men had left the room at the makeshift operation theatre where her tracking device had been removed from her arm. Another confirmation that they were Muslims. Something that she'd decided to take advantage of.

Propped up against the stone wall, she clasped her hands. She'd accepted there'd been a chance, albeit a remote chance, that she could be injured or assassinated while performing her public duties. But now the worst had happened, and if her plan didn't work she'd likely die here. She guessed that being executed in a burqa would be a political statement for the Leopards. But then she remembered that the wearing of the burqa was very rare in Shia countries. Most women opted for and were permitted to wear only the hijab, a simple headscarf. The realization puzzled her. If she was in Pakistan, maybe the Leopards, being Shias, were intent on blaming it on the Sunnis. But what about the words on the tape recorder? Besides, although the generals had passed a law that all women wear the hijab, Pakistani women only wore the burqa in the Tribal Areas and Balochistan. She wondered if she would be taken to one of those regions. Her thoughts made her head ache, that and the dehydration she was suffering from.

She pictured John and her girls. John hadn't said anything expressly, but she knew he had been unhappy about her visit. It was a dangerous place with no respect for Western women, after all. And she recalled an unfamiliar sense of foreboding as soon as she had arrived in Pakistan. Something that had prompted her to ring home far more than usual.

In her temporary office in Islamabad two hours before she'd been kidnapped, she'd decided to wake John and the girls. After the girls stopped yawning, she told them she loved and missed them, that she would be back on Tuesday and that they would all watch a movie together. She asked them to look after their father and to remember that he was a dear man. The girls had just grumbled at being woken up and had gone back to bed.

John had been confined to a wheelchair two years ago, his spine shattered in a hit and run while out for an early morning jog. He'd done his best to cope with the physical and mental trauma of his disability, but she knew he was struggling. When he'd asked her if she was all right, she'd brushed it off, saying that it was the jet lag and heat getting to her.

She got up and paced about now, finding the garment both restrictive and degrading. For those who chose to wear it, good luck to them, she thought. But she felt genuine sympathy for the millions of women who were forced to live in them daily before being effectively locked away at night behind closed doors. She smiled, despite everything. The burqa would play a part in helping her break free from the men who guarded her.

She said a prayer for her family and then one for herself, as she did every morning and evening, although she had no idea of the time. She'd asked God to give her the strength to carry out what she'd set her mind to.

FORTY-TWO

THE PERSON CRANE had arranged to meet Tom just before the Af-Pak border drove a faded blue saloon. She was a striking-looking woman, who said she was an American, the daughter of first-generation Pakistani immigrants. She was a little under six feet in flats, her shoulder-length hair dragged back from her flawless skin by a jet-black hijab. She was heavy-boned but lean, her eyes the colour of red cedar wood. Confident.

When he asked her name, she just smiled before pouring him a coffee from a Thermos, sweetened with sugar to the point that it resembled liquidized molasses. Then she patched up his neck with Vaseline and a bandage, and gave him some painkillers from the glovebox. It eased the throbbing sensation a little and he thanked her.

Despite her calm demeanour, the incident with the ISI and his face on the cells had still left him feeling shaken. That and what Crane had said when he'd rung him a few miles from Torkham, as he'd asked him to.

"How did they get a photo of my face?" Tom had asked. "It was only a few hours since I was in Islamabad."

"There were only two men who could've taken your photo—that's what you're thinking right now, ain't it?" Crane said.

"Yeah. Khan or the cab driver. But the cab driver was random, so it had to be Khan."

"The eyes play tricks, especially in stressful situations. You got one of the cells on you?"

Tom dropped the disposable cell onto the front passenger seat and pulled over onto a stony verge. A little way beyond, the edge of the verge fell away a hundred metres or more to the base of a red-earth ravine. He jerked out one of the cells he'd put in the bag. He thumbed the image open.

"Damn!" he said, smacking his forehead.

He was wearing a white shirt in Islamabad, and had been given a similar one by the cab driver's cousin. But the white shirt he had on in the photograph had a different collar. He picked up the disposable.

"What is it?" Crane asked.

"It's a different shirt."

"Think. When were you wearing it?"

"I... When we came back from Kurram, at the Ariana. With you, Crane," he said, knowing there were scores of people at the former hotel who could've taken his photograph.

"What did Khan tell you?"

Tom was a little taken aback by Crane's abrupt change of subject. "Only where Hasni lived," he said, lying, still conscious that Crane could spoil matters for him.

"You sure?"

Wait, Tom thought. Crane might have set the whole thing up. After he'd been insistent about going over the border, he figured Crane might have seen an opportunity and ordered Khan to tell him about Mahmood. By why all the subterfuge? Maybe Crane was covering his tracks if things went to rat shit. Is he using me? Tom thought.

Then he decided that he was starting to think like Crane, and did his best to zone out the internal dialogue. It would simply confuse him.

"Yeah, I'm sure."

"Are you done this time?" Crane asked.

"I'm done."

"Looks like you got Khan killed, too," Crane said, disconnecting.

Tom thought that that was a vicious jibe, given the secretary's sentence. But he guessed that Crane had a right to be angry. Still, if Crane hadn't engineered the whole thing, the only person who knew what he planned to do in Boston was Khan, he thought. Unless he'd crumbled under torture, if in fact he hadn't made it out. The realization that Hasni's men could be waiting for him stateside as he went after his son, Mahmood, didn't exactly fill him with confidence. But he'd told himself to shape up. He might be getting somewhere.

As the saloon got close to the border a stream of trucks packed with food and white goods from the port of Karachi were waiting to enter Afghanistan. The woman pulled over and told Tom to hide in the trunk, covering his body with a stack of Pakistani silks wrapped in clear polythene. His leather holdall was in there, too. He figured that Crane was serious about wanting him to quit. As he curled up into a ball, just as the dome light was fading, he inhaled a couple of gasps of fresh air.

After crawling along towards the border-crossing proper, the car slowed to a halt. He heard the door open and the voices of the Pakistani border guards and the woman, but they were faint. He sensed that his whole body was covered in a sheen of sweat. The trunk was flipped and he tensed, refusing even to breathe. He felt something prodding him that he took for a baton. The silks were pulled off. Tom turned around and stared at the dark faces of two border guards, standing motionless outside the car. The woman said nothing but offered them a brown-paper package.

The guards looked at one another.

"A million rupees," she said in Pashto. "And we leave now."

Tom's face was frozen in an open-mouthed stare. He could go for his SIG, but what was the point? he thought. If he wounded or killed them, the cop's words in Islamabad would come true: *You will never get out of Pakistan.*

The younger of the two raised his long baton, and Tom flinched involuntarily. But the older one, his yellowing eyes fixed on Tom, motioned with his hand for him to lower it. The younger one hesitated before complying. The older one nodded to the woman and snatched the package from her hand, closing the trunk slowly afterwards. Tom breathed out audibly and brought his hand down over his face, furrowing the skin.

"Jesus Christ," he whispered.

Crane had told him that the average Pakistani wage was PKR 250,000 per annum, about $2,500. His freedom had just been bought for ten thousand dollars. But before the car pulled away, he heard two muted cracks, as if they'd whacked the car's hood with their batons, although it'd sounded as if something had smashed. He wondered if the windshield had been hit.

Fifteen minutes later, the woman stopped opposite a clump of sprawling banyan trees. The trunk was opened and Tom felt the dry air swamp him. He clambered out and got back into the front passenger seat, realizing the windshield was still intact. They travelled in silence, the woman manoeuvring past the various hazards with apparent ease. They weren't held up at the dozen or so Afghan police and security services' checkpoints, either, due in no small part to the plastic wallet which she handed over.

But by the time they reached the steep summit of Kabul gorge, the wind was gale force and a dust cloud hit them. The cloud was so dense that the woman slowed down to a near stop. Lightning struck nearby and thunder boomed. Tom noticed that she was gripping the leather steering wheel tightly. The voltage from the storm clouds was almost palpable.

"Maybe we should stop for a while. Till it clears," he said.

"He said no stopping."

"You known him long?"

She just stared ahead, not even a flicker or a twitch in response. But then she pressed a switch underneath the dash and began to drive with confidence again, despite Tom realizing that the headlights had been knocked out. After he asked if she'd been a cat in a past life, she explained that she'd activated the night-vision section of the windshield, together with an infrared camera sited in the plastic casing of the rear-view mirror. The IR scanned the road ahead, projecting any life forms onto a small video screen beneath her side of the dash. The faded bodywork made the saloon look like a wreck, but it was carrying close to $250,000 worth of equipment.

The disposable cellphone rang. Tom took it out of his pocket.

"You safe?" Crane asked.

"Yeah. We're just coming into Kabul," Tom said, thinking Crane's mood changed quicker than a crack addict's.

"There was a bug in my room, hidden in a clock radio. The room is swept once a week. The last time was three days ago."

Tom didn't doubt that that was possible.

"And, Tom. Dump the cellphone the female operative gave you at the Ariana. Do it now."

Crane didn't have to say why. Tom knew that was how the men at the roadblock had known he'd be arriving there, despite their incompetence once he had. And if they knew that, they'd know where Khan lived. He just had to hope that Crane would be able to get a message to him before he returned there, if he'd gotten out. Then he realized that whoever had been tracking the cell would know he'd been to Hasni's home, too. It was all bad. But he had a gut feeling that things would only get worse.

FORTY-THREE

By 14:02, Tom was inside Kabul International Airport. He'd cleaned up in a restroom, changed into jeans, a khaki shirt and sneakers, and had dumped the SIG a mile away after wiping it down. He got a cup of coffee from a fast-food restaurant in the departure lounge and eased himself into a low-slung plastic seat. He looked around, feeling eyes on him. A different form of paranoia now, one that he didn't care for at all; one that was playing with his mind and making him feel jittery.

He took out his smartphone from his holdall and emailed Lester, the friend he'd told Crane he was seeing in Boston, but not why. He hoped he'd pick up the message quickly on his cell. The man's full name was Lester Wilson. He owned a private security business. When Tom had asked him how he'd swung that, Lester had told him that this was America, and even a man who'd gotten thrown out of the Marines could prosper. Lester had been a US Marine for eleven years, three of which he'd spent in military custody for various offences, the most serious of which was punching an officer. An act that had also led to his dishonourable discharge. But Tom and Lester had become friends.

He asked Lester to meet him at Boston Logan airport in 5.5 hours, if he could, stating that he was on a scheduled flight from Kabul. The email also stated that he needed a Taser, plasticuffs, steel bracelets, duct tape, an MP4 player and a remote lock-up near Harvard. A rental car, too. He requested that Lester emailed back either way, pointing out that it was real important.

Allowing for boarding and the thirteen-hour flight, it would be 20:00 local time when he reached stateside, Kabul being eight and a half hours ahead of Boston time. And when he did, he would have just over forty-one hours to find her. Less than two days.

Sipping the bland coffee, he felt that he was missing something. Something that had happened on the morning the secretary had been taken. He started to piece the events together, his mind focusing on the man who'd fired the Stinger. He picked up his smartphone again and went online, scanning web pages on Islamic customs.

He was interrupted twenty minutes later by the flashing inbox indicator. He checked his email. It was Lester.

I'm in New York. Sure I will man.

Tom grinned. He was one person he could rely on. Besides, Lester owed him. He'd dragged his battered body from a heap of rubble after the US Embassy in Nairobi, Kenya, had been bombed in 1998. Lester had been a young jarhead, Tom a rookie agent. Afterward, he'd said that Tom's constant encouragement had given him hope as he'd lain in the darkness. And that that was a gift.

Hope.

With his head resting against the back of the cabin seat en route to Boston, Tom wondered what kind of hope the secretary had right now. She was a remarkable woman, he thought. By his reckoning, she deserved to be the first woman president. A good, family woman, too. A devoted mother.

Maybe it was the tiredness or the after-effects of the adrenalin dumps, but his thoughts kept wandering. He saw his own mother in his mind's eye, a woman who had been beautiful but for whom a life of stress and poverty had taken its toll. By the time he was sixteen, she looked old, her teeth nicotine stained, her eyes heavy with bags. Her once thick, lustrous hair was dull and ridden with split-ends. What little money she had from working the reception at a local machine shop went on heating and food.

The last time he'd seen her, he'd convinced her to go to the grocery store to buy eggs and bacon, because they had nothing in the fridge or cupboards for lunch, save tins of weak soup, which, for a hungry teenager, hadn't been exactly appetizing. Tom's granddaddy had taught him to drive the previous summer, and had spent the equivalent of three months' pension on a twelve-year-old Buick, which the old man had made roadworthy over a period of six weeks. Tom promised his mother he'd pick her up in it after he'd changed the oil. But when he'd finished, a high school buddy had come by, and he'd gone fishing with him instead.

Forcing himself back to the present, he asked the flight attendant for an English copy of the Qur'an and, after it was handed to him, he began checking the references he had seen online.

Two hours later, the Holy Book fell from his hands as he drifted into a deep sleep. But he'd found what he'd wanted.

FORTY-FOUR

THE PRESIDENT HAD only left the Situation Room to snatch a few hours' sleep and had changed into slacks and a fresh shirt, the relatively mundane affairs of state being carried out by the vice president, aided by the White House chief of staff. He couldn't concentrate on anything else. But he would have to get back to work soon. Besides, the narrow oblong room was beginning to feel like a tomb and he was becoming increasingly convinced that the secretary, whom he had known personally for eight years, wasn't going to be found.

He sipped at a cup of coffee, his eighth of the day, and nodded to Jack, the Secretary of Defense, who'd sat by his side for the duration. The president was a pragmatic and determined politician, a man who'd put himself through law school after being a probation officer in a tough neighbourhood for over a decade, but he couldn't have felt any worse if his younger sister had been taken.

"I should have never let her go," he said, rubbing his tired eyes.

"You don't build relationships by talking down a chunk of plastic, Bob. You can't blame yourself. Linda knew the risks."

"Yeah. But we never think they will materialize, do we, Jack?"

"Guess not."

"If the worst happens, the Iranians will have to pay the price. You realize that, don't you?"

Jack nodded, resolutely.

A couple of minutes later, there was a single knock at the door. It was opened by a black-suited Secret Service agent, the spiralling wire from his clear earpiece disappearing behind his protruding neck muscle to his collar. The White House chief counterterrorism advisor, Martin Rosenberg, a sixty-three-year-old with a Romanesque nose and narrow shoulders, walked through, his soft brown eyes catching the president's gaze and holding it.

"We have a lead, Mr President."

"Thank God," the president said, stiffening up.

"Deputy Director Houseman is on a secure video link from Kabul. I've liaised with the Director briefly already. He said it's your call," Rosenberg said, referring to the head of the CIA.

Rosenberg walked over to the table, picked up a remote and aimed it at the third flat-screen to the left of the secretary. The screen blinked open. Houseman's face almost filled it, his eyes dark-rimmed, his skin sallow.

"Give me the good news, Bill," the president said.

"One of our assets in Islamabad, Mr President. I have reason to believe that Lyric is being held at an old, abandoned watchtower just south of Karachi. On the coast."

"What reason?" the secretary asked, his tone inquisitorial.

"One hundred thousand of them, Mr Secretary," Houseman said, referring to the amount of dollars that'd been paid for the intel.

"You pay that amount, a man will swear he saw Elvis

serving fries at his local Burger King," the secretary said, dismissively.

The president saw that the old warhorse on the screen could barely conceal his contempt for Jack. He knew Bill had never cared for the Defense Secretary. Jack had a tendency to make his point in such a manner that didn't court friendship.

"How sure of this are you, Bill?" he asked.

"He ain't let us down before, sir."

"So what do we do?"

"We have the Carrier Strike Group in the Strait of Hormuz," Houseman said, referring to the waterway between the Persian Gulf and the Gulf of Oman. "But there ain't any Special Forces on board."

The president knew the aircraft carriers were there due to the Iranian crisis. In particular, their threat to close the major oil route if the US went to war. He turned to Jack, said, "Where's the nearest Special Forces' detachment?"

"Yemen, sir."

"Yemen, huh."

"I got eight CIA paramilitaries in Karachi, Mr President," Houseman said.

"And why's that?"

On screen, Houseman looked a little taken aback. "Since Lyric was kidnapped, we got over a hundred in Pakistan, Mr President. And the ones in Karachi are good men. The best."

"Jack?" the president asked.

The secretary craned his neck forward. "I'm not sure." He sniffed. "Could be riskier than sending astronauts to Mars."

The president knew that she could be moved repeatedly. It could be his only chance to get her out. He knew, too, that although the plan to rescue her in the Upper Kurram Valley had been put together swiftly, the short timeframe imposed by the Leopards since then demanded an even faster response.

"What do you mean by *could be*, Jack? And I don't want a bullshit answer based on your dislike for CIA paramilitaries. You got me?" he said, the lack of sleep and constant tension making his patience wane.

Jack nodded. "Yes, Mr President." He cleared his throat. "If Deputy Director Houseman says they're good men, I'll go with that in the circumstances."

The president rubbed the back of his head. "Do it, Bill," he said.

FORTY-FIVE

AT BOSTON LOGAN International Airport's Terminal E, Tom headed for the lower-level arrivals hall, carrying his leather holdall. He felt better for the long sleep he'd had. He didn't usually sleep well on planes, but he'd been exhausted. He was looking forward to seeing Lester. The guy could put a smile on a rock face. He bought a spare disposable cell and went to a restroom to check underneath the bandage on his neck. The wound had stopped bleeding and it didn't look too bad, and the fleck from the splinter on his forehead had almost healed. But the bruises on his body still appeared savage.

After he'd walked back into the hall, he saw Lester standing by an advertising board wearing jeans, hiking boots and a dark-blue windbreaker. He looked fit and muscular, his hair shaved. As Tom walked over, he could see Lester register that it was him, and his friend's slim face broke into a wide grin. They shook hands.

"Man, it's good to see you, Tom," he said, taking the holdall.

"You, too, buddy. Appreciate you coming."

"That was some shit over there. Anything broken?"

"We can talk about it later. I need to get to Cambridge," Tom said, holding back that he was going to pay a visit to a student called Mahmood at Harvard University.

"Massachusetts or Maryland?"

"Massachusetts."

"Good, cuz that ain't far."

They walked past the hall's restaurants and gift stores, out into the vapour light of the airport's exterior. It was an overcast evening, already dark. The lot was directly across from the terminal, where Lester had said his black VW van was parked. After they'd clambered in, Lester drove out of the lot. As they entered the Sumner Tunnel, beneath Boston Harbour, he put on his sat-nav. It was 20:12 and a frail mist hung in the air like gossamer.

"You ready to tell me what happened?" Lester asked.

Tom filled him in on the details he felt it appropriate to disclose, basically recounting what had happened outside the hospital, including the body count, but leaving out everything after the cars had sped away along the alley. The events that had happened afterwards were, he considered, classified. But in truth, he simply hadn't figured them out in his own head yet. Besides, at this stage, Lester didn't need to know more. If and when he did, he would tell him.

"As far as you're concerned, I'm just hiring your services like anyone else."

"Yeah, but it's got to do with the secretary, ain't it?" Lester said, taking a left onto Cambridge Street.

"It has. I got a hunch, Lester, no more than that, and a lead of sorts. You okay to help me out for the next couple days?"

"Hell, yeah."

"And I need you to put a small team together. But you have to work fast for obvious reasons. Anyone you can spare right away?" Tom asked.

Lester glanced at him. "You got something in mind, brother?"

"Nope. But I want all options available if my lead comes good."

"All my people are freelance. I just hire them on a need-to basis. It's cheaper and I don't have to put up with nobody bitching about the lack of healthcare."

"How about Johnny Silver?" Tom said, referring to an ex-DS agent he had introduced to Lester a few years back.

"They're looking to give him a lethal injection up in Nebraska. He popped a cap in an off-duty cop he mistook for an armed robber he was chasing down for some bail bondsman."

"Goddamnit. Poor Johnny. Anyone else we both know who ain't in jail?"

Lester pursed his lips. "I see Skip Howard around, but he's into salad now."

Tom shot Lester a puzzled look. "Salad? That street talk for drugs?"

"Nah. Lettuce and shit. He loves the earth, or so he says. Calls it his mother, though his mother lives in a trailer park in Idaho. Anyways, he wouldn't raise his hand to anyone no more. Skip thinks he's a hippy. I don't have the heart to tell him he's fifty years too late."

Tom grinned, nodding. "Just do what you can, huh? But I only want people with a sound background. No third-rate mercs or amateur adrenalin junkies." Now he was stateside, he figured he could be picky.

"Talking of which, we got a tail," Lester said, peering into the rear-view.

"You sure?" Tom asked, checking the side-view.

"Damn right, I'm sure. A big white Lexus SUV. It had blackouts, it'd be a regular pimp wagon. Been following us all the way from Logan. Though he thinks he's a sneaky mother."

Tom thought about it. Maybe Crane had put a tail on him, just to be sure.

"Now if we was in DC," Lester said, "I could lose him no problem. But up here in Disney World for smart-asses, I doubt it. That's why I got Davina giving me directions on the sat-nav."

"Davina?"

"That ain't her real name. I made it up," Lester said.

"You don't say."

"And the shadow?"

"Let him stay where he is," Tom said.

Figuring it was best to find out who it was, why he was following them and what he knew, Tom took out his smartphone. He hadn't noticed anyone onboard the flight from Kabul who'd looked like a shadow. It was weird, he had to admit. Unnerving, too. He spent a minute looking at satellite imagery, checking for nearby non-residential areas.

"There's a reservoir and park called Fresh Pond a few miles away. We'll take him there." Tom leaned over and programmed Davina.

Fresh Pond was a hundred-and-sixty-acre kettle-hole lake, with a further one hundred and fifty acres of surrounding forest and wetland. It fitted the bill.

"He still following us?"

"He is. At a distance. You strapped?" Lester asked.

"I just got off a schedule flight from Kabul. What do you think?"

"I got our favourites under your seat."

Tom put his hand underneath the seat, felt a bundle and took out an oily rag. As he unwrapped it he saw a pair of SIG Sauer P229s. He took one out, weighing it in his palm.

"It's too heavy for a 9mm."

".357 SIG," Lester said.

"Nice. But that's a bigger kick and muzzle blast."

"Yeah, but no one's gonna stay upright, either. Besides, I got suppressors, too. And it's a DAK. That's a 6.5lbs trigger pull, not 10lbs. Standard-issue for the Department of Homeland Security."

"Thanks for telling me. But we ain't going on a killing spree," Tom said.

Cutting through Harvard University with the Yard on their left, they headed for Concorde Avenue, which led all the way to Fresh Pond.

"He's getting closer."

"Just the one guy?" Tom asked.

"Yep. Unless he's got a shy friend lying on the back seat. He's wearing shades with a ball cap pulled down low. Who the hell wears shades in the evening, 'cept ageing rock stars?"

FORTY-SIX

LINDA SAW THE door open and the same man in the ski mask entered, leaving the door ajar. She lay on the floor mattress dressed in the burqa, her breathing audible. He held out a plastic bottle of water.

"Take it," he said.

She struggled up and inched over the flagstones, her right hand seemingly lost among the folds of the burqa. As she reached him she took the bottle limply with her left hand. A second later, she stumbled, losing her grip on the bottle, which bounced on the hard floor before lying flat.

"I'm sorry," she said, weakly. "I feel so light-headed."

She wavered, her head swaying, but remained upright. He went to steady her, but she flinched and he stepped back.

"Would you?" she said, gesturing towards the bottle.

He grunted something in response, but bent down low to pick up the bottle. It was then she thrust her right hand out of the armhole in the burqa, and hit him over the head sharply with the loose table leg that she'd yanked off before wedging the table back into the corner of the wall. He groaned like a ghost, teetered for what seemed like seconds, but finally collapsed sideways, the back of his mask becoming wet with blood.

She put her hand to her veiled mouth, struggled to remain calm. She thought about hitting him again, but couldn't bring herself to do it. Stepping over him instead, she peered into the low-ceilinged corridor outside. As far as she could tell, no one was there. Dropping the table leg, she ran from the room as swiftly as the restrictive garment would allow. The walls of the dark corridor were mossy and cobweb-ridden, the air cool and damp. She stopped, moved her head around, her peripheral vision impaired. But the corridor was empty.

Halfway down, she saw a large wooden door to the left, a chink of light just visible underneath it. She tried the circular iron handle. It was unlocked. Opening it, she felt both exhilarated and scared as a rush of adrenalin kicked in. She would keep the burqa on until she reached safety. She would find a cab or public payphone, and then she would be rescued.

Outside, the early-morning sun blinded her, despite the veil. Shielding her eyes, she saw a walled courtyard. In the centre of the wall was an archway, the path beneath leading to what she hoped would be the surrounding landscape. She heard waves breaking loudly to her right, and smelled the salt from the sea spray as it drifted down. As if God deemed it appropriate at this moment to give her a sign of hope, she heard voices, and, although they were faint, she made out English but no Urdu.

She felt that she had been saved, either because a deal had been struck, which hadn't involved huge sums of money or the release of the Leopards in the States, or because a Special Forces team had found her. This is it, she told herself. Freedom. Home. Family. As she ran towards the archway, she saw a group of white men appear, wearing military fatigues, with sub-machine guns slung over their shoulders. She thought the lead man was an American soldier, judging by his appearance. He was broad-shouldered and clean-shaven, with short brown hair and hardened features. Registering her, he beckoned her over with his hand. She tore the veil from her face and rushed towards them. But as she got to the lead man he grabbed her by the arm roughly. She struggled to break free, her heart sinking.

"She's a feisty one, I'll give her that," he said with a distinct British accent.

"Let go of me," she said, her sense of confusion tangible.

He raised a huge fist and, almost casually, punched her on the jaw. The impact caused an explosion of white light behind her eyes. Her legs buckled; her head swam. Hanging from the grip still on her arm, she felt cold and nauseous. A second later, she sensed vaguely that he was dragging her back towards the open doorway she'd escaped from.

Inside the cell, she was forced onto her back. Still dulled by the blow, she saw a hypodermic syringe through a watery haze, a gnarled thumb on the plunger, the needle oozing a bubble of the drug from its bevel. Her left foot was held up, her shoe tugged off. She felt fingers dig into her trembling skin with a fierceness her lack of struggling didn't warrant. Blinking erratically, she glimpsed the man who'd punched her administer the drug. He did so via the soft area of skin just below and to the right of her ankle bone. She sensed the quick prick of the needle.

And then she felt no fear, no disenchantment, or dread, as her world was bathed in calm.

FORTY-SEVEN

REACHING FRESH POND, Lester eased off the gas and took a tight left off Concorde onto a track of stabilized aggregate leading into Lusitania Field. A half-acre area of meadow with tall grasses and wild flowers, which was obscured from any prying eyes staring out of the buildings that bordered nearby Wheeler Street by thick hardwood woodland. Tom lurched to the side, hitting Lester on the shoulder. He knew the plan they'd agreed wasn't great, but it was all they had, and he couldn't take the risk of having a tail on him when he went after Mahmood.

Lester swung the VW halfway off the track after hitting the loop around the meadow. Slowing down, Tom opened the door and jumped out, rolling onto the damp earth and drawing the SIG. A DAK meant a cartridge could be carried safely in the chamber, but he'd checked it beforehand just to be sure. He'd left the suppressor in the van. He'd told Lester that the muzzle blast would scare the driver and give him an initial advantage. He watched his friend pull away, the rubber kicking up mud and grit.

At the bailout point, Tom low-crawled behind some thistle, hearing the SUV as it approached the bend. He felt the stagnant water seep into his jeans and shirt, thinking that he'd become a target for a number of unknown pursuers on two continents already, and worrying that he'd gotten Lester into something that was beyond his ken.

Three seconds later, the Lexus came into view, its xenon headlights piercing through the darkness. It did a wheelspin around the bend, the rear tyres cutting semi-circular grooves into the narrow track before powering on. Tom raised his SIG, deciding to go for a tyre rather than the front windshield, worrying that it could be an FBI agent or a CIA operative. He just didn't know.

He shot out the driver-side front tyre, the SIG bucking in his hand and the spent case somersaulting to his right. He heard the tyre burst, glimpsed the flayed rubber dragging on the ground as the front end of the vehicle sagged down a couple of notches. The exposed wheel dug into the stony surface as a cloud of burnt rubber smoke spewed out from the damage.

The Lexus veered off to the left, out of control, and came to a jolting stop in the damp meadow. He waited. No movement. He figured the driver had injured himself; maybe even knocked himself out. He raised himself up and moved forward slowly, pointing the SIG before him.

As he reached the edge of the track he crouched down again, half hidden behind a swath of rye grass, uncertain of how to proceed. He couldn't see into the car, because it was as black as hell here, the moon covered by scudding clouds. Seeing the driver's door swing open suddenly, he dipped and rolled. He raised his head and saw the man lurch out, the back of his ball cap the only thing visible. Tom watched him squat down, using the door as cover.

Tom leapt up, and sprinted to the left as a shot rang out, the bright flash followed by the bullet that pinged past his right ear. He felt the cold air part between the round and his skin, the sensation causing him to smart. He flung himself to the dirt, letting off five rounds, conscious that he was in the open. The DAK's double-action design allowed rapid and devastating firepower, the bullets penetrating the metal door with ease. But no one fell; no cry emitted from the driver.

He's moved, Tom thought. And I'm exposed. He dug deep and pushed himself up, duck-walking forward as a half-muffled blast came from the far right. He heard a groan, the sound of a body falling. A second round was discharged, followed by a concerned shout. It was Lester's voice. He saw his head emerge from behind a clump of yellow-headed tansy plants, his SIG in his hand. His friend broke into a sprint toward the Lexus.

"No! Lester, no! Let it go!" Tom barked, racing over to meet him at the car.

Breathing heavily, Tom met Lester by the car's trunk.

"He was gonna cap ya."

Lester's face was fierce-looking, his eyes two slits, his jaw muscles flexed. Tom loomed over the man who was face down in the mud, a body length from the trunk. Blood was oozing from the exit wounds in his back. As Lester picked up the man's handgun lying a few centimetres from his twitching fingers, Tom bent down and turned the body over.

"Guess what, it's a SIG," Lester said.

Tom looked into the contorted face, blood and spittle running from the man's lips. "Jesus Christ."

"You know him, Tom?"

"It's Steve Coombs. A member of my detail."

"Say what?"

Tom straightened up and stepped back, a jolt of disbelief hitting him like a lump hammer. He grasped his forehead. It was the last person he'd expected to see. He shook his head, feeling dizzy.

"Tom!" Lester shouted.

Tom looked at his friend. Unlike him, he was focused.

"Do what you have to do," he said.

Tom forced himself to act. Despite the shock, he needed answers. He crouched back down, his mind beginning to join the dots. He grabbed the back of Coombs's head, eased it up.

"The tracking device—did you tell them? Did ya?"

"Yeah," Coombs said, faintly.

Coombs groped for the silver crucifix he always wore around his neck. Tom pulled it out from his shirt and laid it over Coombs's fingers. He figured once a Catholic always a Catholic, and it was confession time.

"Thanks, Tom," he wheezed.

"My photo; was it you? The cellphone? Did you know that CIA woman? The terrorist who disappeared on the roof in Islamabad; that you, too?"

"Me, yeah. Forgive me… Tom."

"And the bugging of the room at the Ariana?"

"I…" He groaned and spat blood.

"Where is she? Where?"

"Father, forgive me," Coombs said, fingering the crucifix.

"Where is she?"

"I can't breathe," Coombs said as a croaky sigh emitted from his purple lips.

"Where?" Tom asked.

"I don't know, Tom. I'm… Forgive me, Lord."

Coombs strained to lift the crucifix to his lips. Then

his head flopped to the side, his bloodshot eyes staring blankly into the night.

Tom shook him. "Where, you sonofabitch? Where?"

He felt Lester's hand on his shoulder. "He's gone, Tom. He's gone."

FORTY-EIGHT

AFTER TOM HAD flipped the Lexus' trunk, they hauled the body up, using a green tarp that Lester had fetched from his van. Tom didn't want to give an early-morning dog-walker a heart attack, so he locked it. He hid his growing concern as best he could, but he knew that Crane's words were ringing true: *don't trust anyone*. Apart from that major obstacle, he still didn't know where Mahmood lived, and he had less than two days to find the secretary if her captors were intent on carrying out their horrendous threat. In truth, he didn't have any reason to doubt it, especially after what had just happened. But part of him still couldn't believe it. Coombs had been a stand-up guy.

As they walked along the track to the parked van an owl broke from the branch of a beech tree, twisting in flight to avoid them. Lester ducked down and drew his SIG.

"Easy, man," Tom said.

"Never did like the country."

"We ain't in the country."

"I can't see a building, I'm in the country," Lester said, holstering his SIG.

He unzipped one of the outer pockets of his windbreaker and took out a cell that he'd taken from Coombs's corpse. He handed it to Tom, who began searching the call and email history. There wasn't anything of significance. He figured Coombs had been smart enough to delete anything incriminatory and had probably used at least a couple of disposables for his traitorous comms in any event. There was no way that Coombs could've been working alone. But for now, it suited him to let any accomplices think that he and Lester had been killed, since that could give them some time before another assassin came looking for them. He took out his own smartphone, transferred his contacts list to his spare cell, and smashed it under foot before gathering up the pieces. He would dump it later. He'd keep the untraceable disposable he'd bought at the airport for now.

"You okay, Tom?" Lester said, before quickening his pace towards his van, which was parked on the southernmost part of the circular track, opposite the windswept edge of the vast lake.

Tom waved him on, taking a moment to process what had just happened.

He'd worked with Coombs for six years and he found himself questioning his own judgment. He couldn't make out how he hadn't got an inkling of his true nature. The man's duplicity staggered him. It struck him that the world he had entered was many times more corrupt and complicated than he'd first imagined. It was capable of turning a federal special agent, a sworn law-enforcement officer, as all DS agents were, into a traitor. But at least he didn't have to worry about any repercussions over his death, and there was nothing more to be done about it, at least for the next couple of days.

By the time Tom reached the van, Lester already had the engine ticking over, the headlights on. As he climbed in he asked Lester to head back the way they'd come.

"I'm covered for this, right, Tom?" Lester asked.

"It was self-defence. Besides, I pulled the trigger and you were lying in the grass."

"Get outta here. A man starts making up stories 'bout a thing like this and he makes mistakes that gets him life in the sore-ass house," Lester said, driving along the loop to the straight portion of the track that led up to Concorde Avenue.

"The sore-ass house?"

"Well, that's what my momma called jail to keep us boys on the straight and narrow."

"Your momma called it that?"

"Yeah. What?"

"Nothing. But this one's real simple, Lester. As I said, I pulled the trigger."

As Lester headed back to the densely residential streets of Cambridge Tom still felt miserable. He just couldn't figure it out. But then he recalled the motorcyclist high on drugs in Islamabad. He hadn't seen anyone on the roof that Coombs had been firing at, nor did he have a ballistic report on the bullet that'd killed the boy. Coombs could've been the shooter; could've been the person who'd taken a pop at him, too, for all he knew. He wondered who else might be involved; how high the conspiracy might reach. But he had to put all that to the back of his mind and focus now. Coombs had admitted his sins.

When they got to Inman Square at the intersection of Cambridge and Hampshire Streets, Tom asked Lester to pull over. He took out his disposable cell. He rang Carrie, his ex-girlfriend, who still worked at the DS's investigative department, which concentrated its resources on uncovering incidences of passport and visa fraud.

They'd dated for over two years, but his constant travelling had been too much for her, which was why she'd said she couldn't continue dating someone she saw less than her dentist. Still, when they'd parted, there'd been no hard feelings between them.

When she answered, he asked her a favour, saying he was worried about a guy from Pakistan, and asked her to check that everything was kosher as soon as she got into work. He needed Mahmood's address, suspecting that he lived off campus. Maybe even close by. But he gave her Mahmood's alias, hoping that Khan hadn't put him on a false scent. She asked him if he was okay, and he said he hadn't been hurt in Islamabad, but that this was very important, so he'd appreciate it if she went to work early tomorrow morning. She said that not everyone was a workaholic, but that she'd do as he'd asked.

Tom slipped out of the van into the half-light of the nearby streetlights and changed out of his mud-ridden clothes. He put on a fresh pair of jeans and a sweatshirt, and zipped up a waterproof jacket that had been rolled up in his holdall. He climbed back into the passenger seat.

"Now what?" Lester asked.

"I have to do something alone."

"I ain't gonna get all preachy on ya, Tom, cuz, hell, I ain't no saint myself. But if you're planning what I think you is, there won't be any self-defence plea. You'll get life in federal supermax, and that's hard time."

Thirty minutes later, Lester reluctantly picked up the keys for the rental car at an all-night office. It was a metallic-silver Ford Focus that looked and smelled brand-new and wouldn't draw any adverse attention. He handed Tom a small backpack, which he said contained the other items he'd requested by email en route from Kabul, together with a piece of paper with the address of the lock-up.

Tom drove off and parked up in a rest stop in Cambridge. If things didn't go well, the last thing he wanted was to alert Hasni to the fact that he had Lester on board. Hasni had the kind of reach that could end up with his friend being found hung up on a meat hook in a slaughterhouse.

But thinking that Coombs might have been in cahoots with the ISI and had passed on that information already, he closed his eyes and did his best to zone out.

FORTY-NINE

JARROD RIPLEY, A CIA paramilitary operations officer in the Agency's National Clandestine Service, sat in the first of three civilian open-top SUVs. He was five-nine and appeared slim when dressed. But his muscles were like weaved steel and he could bench twice his body weight. Like his fellow operatives, he had a thick moustache, his being dyed rook-black, as was his hair.

Deputy Director Houseman had called him a little under four hours ago and had said that he should implement Urgent Restoration as fast as possible. After receiving all the necessary encrypted details, satellite imagery and drone feeds via a secure laptop, he now knew that Lyric was in an abandoned watchtower on the coast a mile west of Karachi.

But due to the lack of detailed intel and need for speed, the mission was as basic as it was dangerous. Use covert means to get in. Leave with the secretary alive. Transport her to the US Consulate there. Bottom line, if he screwed up, the US would be sending Reaper drones over the Iranian border, followed by the 82nd Airborne Division. Then God only knew what the outcome would be. Ripley figured that this was the most important mission of his life.

The sun was blazing, even though it was only mid-morning, a heat haze hanging a metre from the parched ground. The SUVs raced up a hard-packed dirt track towards the dilapidated stone structure. Ripley and his men wore the black polo shirts and matching ball caps of the Elite Punjab Police—a counterterrorist quick-response force—and were armed with the MP5A3 sub-machineguns and Glock handguns the police used.

The watchtower's original doors had been replaced by a rusted gate that resembled a portcullis. The first SUV skidded to a stop a few metres from it, sending up a fine dust cloud. They'd agreed to go in fast and confident and overpower the guards before they had a chance of spotting they were Americans. But there appeared to be no resistance. Something that Ripley put down to the garb they'd kitted themselves out in. The SUV's doors swung open and Ripley and four other CIA paramilitaries jumped out, aiming their weapons at the top of the wall and the tower's tall flat roof as they crouched down.

A small wooden door opened to the right of the gate. An old man edged out, his face streaked with deep lines. He held up his skinny arms, although he appeared to be unable to straighten them fully. Despite his emaciated state and unthreatening demeanour, one of the operatives ordered him to lie flat on the ground. He did so as quickly as his worn-out body allowed, his bones creaking.

Ripley didn't have a problem with that. The Pakistani was an old coot, but he could have a suicide vest under his shirt. A body-borne IED, typically six kilograms of C4 studded with two hundred or so ball-bearings that could reduce the pride of the Special Operations Group to something resembling lumps of Swiss cheese.

As it turned out, he didn't have anything more un-pleasant under his shirt than a visible ribcage, and Ripley ordered his men to search the abandoned watchtower thoroughly.

After the hour-long exercise, the result was a distinct lack of any signs of occupation, save for a small room with an oil lamp, a floor mattress and a half-eaten plate of near-rancid food. That done, Ripley squatted down beside the old man, who was in the habit of breaking into a toothless grin for no apparent reason. Ripley spoke Urdu fluently and, after making some small talk, questioned him in a friendly manner. He said the room was his. He was the caretaker. The watchtower was going to be demolished by a construction company and he had been employed to make sure no squatters occupied it in the interim. They were going to build a luxury hotel here. No one had been here for weeks.

Leaving the man in the room with two paramilitaries, Ripley walked out into a dark stairwell and rang Houseman on a secure satphone. After telling him what had happened, Houseman ordered him to question the caretaker "more robustly". Ripley sighed. He'd done things to men he wasn't proud of. But at least when he woke up in sweat at night, he could tell himself that the majority were murdering jihadists. This was something different. And when Houseman said "more robustly", it was a euphemism. It meant be a real sadistic sonofabitch. The White House had officially banned waterboarding, but at times like this the suits simply developed something akin to a collective amnesia.

He walked back into the room, ordered the two men to leave. The Pakistani grinned his toothless grin and Ripley found himself nodding back. He thought about breaking the old man's fingers, one at a time, with the butt of his Glock. But if he were innocent, he might as well cut his hands off for all the use they would be to him afterwards.

Ripley saw a wooden bucket half filled with water in the dimly lit corner of the room. He walked slowly over to it. Bending down, he noticed that the water was stale and speckled with dust. Hell, there was even a shredded cobweb hanging from the handle. He stood up and turned, studying the old man's now concerned-looking face; then his hands. He asked him to remove his sandals, which he did, although it appeared to be such an effort that Ripley thought he was watching the action in slow motion. He was clean. But the water hadn't been used for days; weeks, perhaps. Not until now, he thought.

After the third prolonged dunking, at which point the old man appeared so breathless that his whole body went flaccid, he admitted weakly that he'd lied, just as Ripley knew he had. He'd been there for a few hours only.

When Ripley rested the muzzle of his Glock against the old man's temple and told him to ask Allah's forgiveness for his sins, he wheezed a feeble response at first. But after Ripley cocked the weapon, the Pakistani became suitably compliant and, clearly fearing for his life, swore on his six children's lives that he hadn't lied further. He'd been given the equivalent of a year's pay to be here and say these things by a man he had never met before.

Lowering the Glock, Ripley believed him.

FIFTY

Tom HAD SPENT the night curled up on the back seat of
the Ford, putting a plan together and drifting in and out
of a fretful sleep.

Carrie rang him a little before 06:33. He squinted
as the glare from the early-morning sun played on the
windshield. She gave him Hassan's/Mahmood's address. He asked her not to mention it to anyone, not
least for the next couple of days. She asked him if she
could trust him, but quickly recanted, saying although
he'd been an absent boyfriend, at least he'd been a loyal
one. She told him to take care and disconnected the call.

He relaxed his muscles, readying himself for the violence that would inevitably follow. But he wasn't on
a protective detail. He had no security profile to utilize. He would have to rely mostly on his intuition and
wits. He glanced at his wristwatch. Thirty-one hours
left, he thought.

He entered West Cambridge, near the Charles River,
thirty minutes later. He pulled over at the edge of a redbrick wall twenty metres or so from the black security
gates he'd passed. Carrie had said that the address was a
twelve-storey, upscale apartment complex. Tom hadn't
been surprised. It was a relatively isolated area, and
he got out and walked back to the gates, the backpack
over his shoulder. Knowing it was commuter time, he
figured he wouldn't have to wait long before the gates

opened. He could try scaling them, he thought, but that could just bring the cops down on him.

Ten minutes later, the gates opened and a red Porsche Cayman S nosed out. Tom pressed himself against the right-hand face of the wall, shielding his body from view behind the plain pilaster, which jutted out about ten centimetres. He hoped the car would turn left, since that was the road leading to the centre of Cambridge. He was right. Once in, he jogged along the asphalt roadway lined with grassy banks and cherry trees. After rounding a bend, the limestone block came into view, a substantial building with neo–Art Deco styling utilized on the entryways and aspects of the façade. Each apartment was set back from the outer wall, creating a placid terrace area. He guessed it cost more than a year's salary to live in for a month.

He crouched down by the exterior wall of the communal ground-floor garage, waiting for a car to come up the exit slope, so he could duck in. If Mahmood was going to make it to Harvard this morning, he'd have to show sooner or later. If he didn't, Tom would risk taking him in the apartment, but that had so many drawbacks that he'd have to rely heavily on luck to pull it off.

Five minutes later, Tom was bent over, tying a lace by a blue cinderblock wall as he checked the interior for CCTV cameras, a search that came up blank. After a couple of banker types dressed in bespoke suits stepped out of the garage elevator, Tom saw a man who matched Khan's description of the bodyguard. *A squat man with a bearded face; eyes like black diamonds.* The man's name, Tom recalled Khan saying, was Zafar. He wore charcoal-coloured slacks and a dark-blue shirt, and was walking towards a Bentley Turbo. His biceps were so huge that Tom decided the only way he could scratch his back was on a tree like a bear. As the bodyguard scanned the area Tom grasped his chest and moaned, feigning a heart condition. He collapsed to the floor. Zafar looked over, apparently puzzled. Tom called out for help, lying on his back.

"My pills," he said. "Get my pills."

Zafar strolled over and looked down, standing by Tom's side, his brow furrowing.

"In my jacket pocket," Tom said, nodding down to his left.

As Zafar bent down to put his hand in the pocket Tom thrust a Taser, shaped like an old-fashioned cellphone, into the man's neck. Zafar jerked, gritting his teeth, and stumbled sideways. But as he fell he managed to strike out, catching Tom on the jaw with a lazy right. Despite the imposed, half-hearted nature of the punch, Tom's head spun under the impact, the Taser falling from his grip. Still dazed from the blow, he struggled to get up, a trickle of blood running from the corner of his mouth.

But Zafar was on all fours, a mixture of spittle and white froth spewing from his quivering lips. He managed to get off his knees and charged forward like an injured rhino, headbutting Tom in the chest with the flat of his skull. Tom felt as if he'd been hit by a sledgehammer and fell backwards, the wind knocked out of him. Zafar's momentum kept him going, and he landed heavily on top of Tom's outstretched body. With Zafar's great bulk pinning him to the ground, Tom groped around for the Taser on the tarmac floor. But Zafar jammed his thumb into Tom's jugular notch at the base of his throat where it met the sternum, blocking off the airway. Applied for too long and a man would pass out and die. Tom felt as if a stone were lodged in his windpipe. He gasped for air, and started to panic, knowing that his options were limited. The pressure increased, and he saw red dots floating in front of his blinking eyes. In a few seconds, he'd fall into unconsciousness.

With that, the tips of the fingers of his right hand touched the Taser's plastic case. Summoning all of his waning strength, he brought up his arms like curved horns, hitting Zafar ferociously in both ears with his clenched fists. The bodyguard groaned, his hands instinctively retracting to cover the sides of his head. Tom stretched out and grabbed the Taser, and thrust it into Zafar's kidney. The man growled, his back arching before he slumped sideways. Tom rolled over and Tasered him again in the side of the neck, only easing off when he saw Zafar's eyes roll back.

Feeling dizzy, Tom almost retched, the pain in his throat severe. He did his best to keep it together. The man was a colossus, he thought. But he'd be sure to check a Taser had enough juice in it if and when he had to use one again to take someone out. It had nearly cost him his life. He grabbed Zafar under the arms and dragged his disabled body to a small room at the far end of the garage—used to store the janitor's equipment— where he'd left the backpack. The Pakistani's body had felt as if it had lead weights strapped to it. Tom cuffed him hand and foot with flex-cuffs, and propped his limp body up against a breeze-block wall. He slumped down beside him, and focused on controlling his breathing, leaving the door open so he could keep an eye on the elevator.

FIFTY-ONE

LINDA WAS STILL only half awake, feeling something like a terrible hangover engulf her, which, she realized, was the after-effects of the drug. She panicked and did her best to keep her eyelids open, sensing as if she were still in the throes of the morbid nightmare that had recurred throughout her life: being buried alive. Something that had haunted her in the way some people feared death by fire or drowning.

Then she noticed that her nose and mouth were covered, and she moaned. Her hands had been tied, likewise her feet, such that when she pulled up with her arms the noose around her ankles tightened. She was trussed up like the proverbial chicken; the blackness swamped her, and, although she couldn't see anything, she knew she was in a confined space. She felt as if she were having a panic attack, her deep gasps for breath taking the respirator to its limits. She tried to roll, but she just hit something like a hard cushion that had no give. She thought about screaming. But the mask was her lifeline and she was afraid of dislodging it.

Unbeknown to her, the drug that'd been administered back in Karachi had been a gift, for once it had taken effect fully her limp body had been lifted and taken up three flights of steps, where it'd been lowered into a mahogany coffin inlaid with brass. Her face was covered with a hard-plastic mask attached to breathing apparatus, a monitor strapped to her arm. After the lid had closed, the coffin had been draped with black silk.

The coffin had been taken from the watchtower, its walls built above the Arabian Sea, and had been loaded into a private ambulance. It had been driven for five miles to Pakistani Air Force Base Masroor in the Maripur area of Karachi, the largest airbase in Asia. After an enforced stoppage, the coffin had been removed and placed onto a loader, and guided into the baggage bay of a small white plane surrounded by men holding MP5 sub-machine guns.

As the afternoon sun had broken from a bank of cumulous cloud, the only blemish in a sky that had been otherwise the hue of blue coral, the aircraft had risen from the runway. After the undercarriage had retracted, it had headed west, its destination near Abu Dhabi, the capital city of the United Arab Emirates. A Sunni Muslim country fearful of the Shia jihad and an aggressively ambitious Iran.

FIFTY-TWO

WHEN ZAFAR HAD revived enough to be coherent, coughing up phlegm and groaning from the after-effects of the volts that had passed through his body, Tom began to speak.

"I've only got one question," he said, bending over him. "You answer it correctly, you live."

"Do you know who you're dealing with?" Zafar said, his eyes blinking.

"Brigadier Hasni, and you're the bodyguard, Zafar. Thing is, you don't know who you're dealing with. So I'll make it real easy. When the kid gets in the car, do you open the door for him or not? That's it. But if you lie to me, I'll come right back and put a hole in your forehead. Do we understand each other?"

Zafar nodded, awkwardly.

"The kid's going with me."

"What will you do with him?"

Tom figured that the bodyguard would be told anyway, so he said, "I'll make a phone call to the Brigadier. The kid will sound distraught, but I promise you I won't kill him, or even come close."

"How do I know I can trust you?"

"You don't. But you don't have too many options, either. So tell me and you'll walk away from this. You can tell the Brigadier there were five of us. Deal?"

"No deal."

Tom drew his SIG, forced the muzzle underneath Zafar's lips, the metal grating across his teeth. "Don't push it. You'll regret it. Deal?"

Zafar nodded, faintly. Tom removed the SIG and holstered it.

"Here in the garage, I wait in the car with it revving. The brat is always late, so I don't get out. Outside, I get out."

"Good. Keys?"

Zafar gestured down to the right-hand pocket of his slacks. Tom took out a key ring and noted the winged Bentley logo. He gagged Zafar with silver duct tape, slung the backpack over his shoulder and closed the storeroom door. Then he walked over to the Bentley, using the remote fob to open it and turn on the ignition. The car had dark-tinted windows, the type that were opaque from the outside but allowed him a twilight view of the world, which suited him just fine.

About ten minutes later, a young man appeared from the elevator and walked towards the car. He was lanky, almost anorexic-looking, and wore a pair of dark-blue jeans and a red sweater. He ducked down and sat in. Tom locked the doors remotely. He turned around and pointed the SIG at Mahmood's surprisingly undaunted face.

"Do you know who I am?"

"Yeah, I do," Tom replied.

"My father will kill you."

"Yeah, he might at that. But the way I see it, you're the only one who can identify me. So if I was you, I'd be nice," Tom said, turning back.

"Where is Zafar?" he said, still a hint of cockiness in his voice.

"He had to lie down in a storeroom. I shot him in

both temples. Now some may say that that's a waste, it should only take one bullet to kill a man. But I got plenty left. Whether or not I have plenty left in about a half-hour from now will depend on your father and how loud it's necessary to make you scream."

Tom checked the rear-view mirror. Yeah, that did it, he thought. The kid was wide-eyed, his left hand pressed against his floppy black hair, his full mouth twitching. Terrified.

He had no intention of beating on Mahmood, let alone shooting him. But if Hasni didn't believe he would, he wouldn't get what he needed, and that meant making Mahmood believe he was dealing with a killer. He didn't like it, but he felt he had no choice.

"Take out your cellphone and drop it in the footwell. You go for it, you'll end up the same as Zafar."

FIFTY-THREE

Tom HAD DRIVEN Mahmood to the remote location that Lester had arranged for him. The kid hadn't spoken again, the interior of the car remaining as silent as a diving bell. Tom had glanced in the rear-view mirror on a couple of occasions. Mahmood had just kept staring blankly out of the tinted window, his body motionless.

Tom parked the car in an alley dark with shadow, surrounded by derelict warehouses and industrial units. He did a last check on Mahmood before stepping out. He opened the rear passenger door.

"You make a run for it, I'll put a bullet in the back of your knee."

He took out a woollen scarf and blindfolded Mahmood.

"Are you going to kill me?" Mahmood asked, his hands shaking.

"Shut up, kid."

Tom stooped and picked up the cell from the footwell, dropped it into his jacket pocket. He patted Mahmood down just to be sure, feeling the outline of a wallet and keys.

"Now bring your hands out in front of you. I gotta cuff ya."

Tom cuffed him with a pair of metal bracelets that allowed a semblance of movement. But metal was better than plastic from a psychological point of view. It conjured up images in the captive's mind of dark basements.

"Walk," Tom said, putting his hands on Mahmood's shoulder.

Five minutes later, Mahmood was chained to a steel pole in the brick-built lock-up. Still blindfolded, he was half naked on the bare, gasoline-stained floor. A single battery-operated lamp hung from the ceiling. The place reeked like a wet dog. Tom found the whole scene repugnant, and resolved to get it over with as soon as he could.

"There's an old chest freezer against wall. That's where I'll leave you if your father doesn't give me what I want," Tom said, standing about two metres from his victim.

"You're not crazy. I believe that. If you want something from my father, he will give it to you. Please don't hurt me. He'll give you whatever you want."

"Let's hope so," Tom said.

Tom checked the contacts on Mahmood's cell. He thumbed the entry for "father" and put the cell on speaker. After four rings, it was picked up.

"Mahmood, my boy, how are you?"

"To tell the truth, he ain't great," Tom said.

"Father, help me. Help me."

"Who the hell are you?"

"Your boy here is chained in a lock-up. Now you think long and hard about how you'll live with the manner of his death if this goes wrong. You're on speaker, so let's be nice and businesslike."

"How much are we talking about?" Hasni asked, pragmatically.

"I don't want money."

"Let's cut the bullshit, okay. You have my attention. What is it you want?"

He's angry all right, Tom thought. He figured a headman in the ISI wasn't used to a family member being a victim, let alone a son.

"It's not complicated, and it won't take more than a few seconds. Then we can all go home, including your boy. Where is the United States Secretary of State, Linda Carlyle?"

There was a pause. "How do you expect me to know that? It was the Leopards. The ransom demand and the police statements prove it."

"Look, we can do this any way you want," Tom said. "Mahmood, what way do you want it done?"

"Father, please, tell him if you know. I'm scared, Father. Please."

"Hassan, don't be frightened. I won't let anything happen to you. Be brave."

"That's nice. Just be glad your boy's not squealing like a pig in the background. But if that's what it takes, I can start right now."

"Father!"

"All right. But I am in an impossible position. I can't tell you what I do not know."

"*'The Messenger of Allah, Allah bless him and give him peace, said, gold and silk has been permitted for the women of my community, and forbidden for its men,'*" Tom said. "*'The Messenger of Allah, Allah bless him and give him peace, said, whoever believes in Allah and the Last Day should not wear silk or gold'*... I could go on."

"So you know certain verses from the Qur'an. So what?"

"The Leopards of Islam are fundamentalists. They don't get decked out like an Aztec prince. Am I right?" Tom said.

"You are talking in riddles."

Tom knelt down, placing the cell on the floor. He took out the roll of silver duct tape from the backpack and walked over to Mahmood. He grabbed his slender wrist with his free hand and twisted it around almost a hundred and eighty degrees. Mahmood wailed.

"You bastard. What are you doing? Answer me," Hasni said, his tone a mixture of frustration and deep concern.

Tom ripped off a length of tape with his teeth and planted it on Mahmood's quivering mouth. Then he took out the MP4 player and put the earplugs into the boy's ears, sliding the volume to max before moving back towards the cell.

"I saw a man in Islamabad shoot down one of your police helicopters with a Stinger. It just happened to be right where the secretary was taken. You'll no doubt have that in one of your reports. The thing is, I chased him. He got breathless and lifted his gas mask. He was wearing a gold necklace."

Hasni didn't say anything for at least five seconds. Then said, "I see."

"The Secretary of State, Hasni. Where is she?"

"Listen to me, American. Even if it wasn't a Leopard, I still don't know anything," Hasni replied, his confidence seemingly restored.

Tom picked up the cell off the floor. "You and me both know that it couldn't have happened without the ISI being involved, or agreeing to it. I'm going to kill your boy now, slowly, because you're taking me for a fool."

"You won't do that."

Tom thought for a moment. He stepped forward and ripped off the duct tape from Mahmood's mouth before putting his hand around the boy's neck and squeezing, just enough so that he coughed and spluttered without choking.

"Your son's dying, Hasni."

"All right, all right."

Tom released his grip and Mahmood began to sob.

"You need to speak to an ex-CIA operative called Billy Joe Hawks. The attack wasn't carried out by the ISI. But I don't know more than this," Hasni said, miserably.

"Why Hawks?"

"He was the ISI's contact."

"Who does he answer to?" Tom asked.

"I don't know. I swear. The ISI didn't plan it. You should talk to Hawks. That's all I know."

"Where is she?"

"I don't—"

"I *will* kill him."

Tom took out his SIG and shot at the floor a few centimetres from Mahmood, such that he was showered by tiny fragments of concrete. The blast was accentuated by the confined space and was near deafening. Mahmood's sobs were replaced by screams, the sound of the discharge clearly audible above the music.

"Stop! Please stop," Hasni shouted above the din. "I don't know where she is. I swear."

Tom holstered his SIG. "All right, then."

"My son?"

Ignoring him, Tom said, "One more thing. Was Steve Coombs on your payroll?"

"I've never heard of him."

Tom couldn't tell if he was lying or not. If it wasn't Hasni then maybe Hawks had put Coombs up to it. But he figured with Coombs dead, it didn't matter a whole lot anyhow.

"My son?" Hasni said again, his tone verging on desperation.

"He can go, as I said. His bodyguard is safe, too. There were five of us who took him down, so don't be too harsh on him."

"And the American authorities?"

"Here's the deal. You keep your mouth shut, I won't repeat what you've said. But if you've lied or talk to anyone about this, you'd better leave that fine house of yours and find yourself a cave to live in, because your life won't be worth spit."

"Okay."

Tom had lied about not telling anyone. But so, he knew, had Hasni. He'd have to work fast.

FIFTY-FOUR

ALMOST TWO HOURS LATER, the private plane carrying the secretary touched down at a French base known as Camp de la Paix, or Peace Camp. The base was constructed in 2009 at the request of the United Arab Emirates. It was home to all three services of the French military and, apart from the airfield, had a naval port and an army camp, the latter of which housed a detachment of The 13th Demi-Brigade of the Foreign Legion. The base overlooked the Strait of Hormuz, although the three services occupied separate geographical sites, albeit within relatively close proximity of one another.

French Air Base 104 Al Dhafra was situated about twenty miles from Abu Dhabi. As the plane taxied on the shortest of the two asphalt runways, a black Renault van emerged from the side of the communications centre and drove up beside it. The plane's passenger door opened and the man who'd dragged the secretary back to the makeshift cell in Karachi emerged. He blinked slowly like a lizard on a rock, put on a pair of wraparound shades to protect his eyes from the strong, late-afternoon sun. Hands akimbo, his mouth cracked a lazy grin. Not long now, he thought. Not long.

He felt safe. No one at the airbase was aware that the coffin held a live human being, let alone the US Secretary of State.

He marshalled a small group of men with bullpupdesigned FAMAS assault rifles slung over their shoulders—standard-issue for Legionnaires. They removed the coffin and placed it into the cargo bay of a French Air Force transport plane, together with numerous wooden crates and boxes of faulty ordnance. He spoke to a couple of French officers and handed over a manila envelope containing fifty-thousand Euros before ascending the flight of steps leading to the plane's clamshell door. He stopped briefly at the top, seemed to sniff the air like a predator.

Ten minutes later, the transport plane took off.

A CAPORAL-CHEF, A short, squat man with a bulbous nose, had been watching the curious events unfold, half hidden behind a hangar as he took an unofficial cigarette break. He hadn't decided yet whether he should report it. He would have to explain his presence, and that could get him in deep trouble with the commandant. As he watched the plane bank left before climbing at speed he decided that the best way forward was to spend some time mulling over whether it would be worth the hassle.

FIFTY-FIVE

IN THE OVAL OFFICE, the president, flanked by the American flag and the flag of office, sat behind the Resolute Desk in front of three panelled windows with the view of the South Lawn beyond. Bright, early sunlight shone in through the panes, making the room feel more voluminous, airier. The Defense Secretary sat on a padded chair a metre or so from an ornate fireplace, advising the commander-in-chief that now was not the time to reduce the defence budget by the agreed $250 billion a year over the next decade, despite the US debt crisis.

Hours before, there'd been a knock at the newly hung reinforced-security door. As it opened the president caught sight of a couple of Secret Service agents: a tall, slimly built black man and a thick-necked white guy with cropped blond hair. Rosenberg, the White House chief counterterrorism advisor, entered, and relayed the bad news with an apologetic tone, although no blame attached to him. He said that Deputy Director Houseman had informed him that the CIA paramilitaries had been too late. But Lyric had been in the watchtower in Karachi, of that there was little doubt. The president thanked him. As Rosenberg left his face was awash with a mixture of embarrassment and depression. The president knew he was thinking what everyone was thinking: that perhaps the last chance to rescue her had eluded them. She'd been removed to another unknown location and the clock was ticking.

Standing up now, the president loosened his neck muscles. He'd picked at a plate of food prepared by his favourite chef, otherwise he hadn't eaten. Jack, the Defense Secretary, had had no problem with devouring his cooked breakfast. No further intel had come in since the CIA's asset had told them about the abandoned watchtower in Karachi. Jack had demanded that Houseman tell him the name of the asset, so he could do his own checks on the man via the Defense Clandestine Service, the Pentagon's equivalent of the CIA's espionage unit. Houseman had resisted at first, but had finally said he was called Sandri Khan, a Pakistani Christian who lived in Islamabad.

"What are the chances this Khan will come up with more intel?" the president asked, knowing that almost all foreign intelligence came at least initially from local sources or assets controlled by the CIA.

"Slim," Jack said, still seated.

"The truth."

Jack sighed. "Non-existent."

"I want a war cabinet put in place in six hours," the president said, his taut face showing palpable signs of stress. "Apart from me, it'll comprise the same thirteen post-holders as used by George W after 9/11. And make that public. I want the Iranians to think long and hard about this."

"Yes, Mr President," Jack said, standing upright.

The president knew that the Iranians could save her, due to their influence over the Leopards. They could sign her death warrant, too. And if that happened, the American people would demand an aggressive response, and he had every intention of satisfying that desire. He did his best to convince himself that his campaign trail, which began in three months' time, had nothing to do with his decision. But in truth, if she died, he would have a moral duty to act, especially given Iran's imminent invasion of Balochistan and their defiance over their nuclear programme. The West had been putting off the latter for years. It had to be confronted. Now he would obtain the backing of Congress, for sure. Even the Chinese and the Russians would have to suck it up.

FIFTY-SIX

TOM DROVE THE Bentley in silence, the doors locked. He'd untied Mahmood and had removed the cuffs and earplugs, eager for the kid to know his ordeal was over. He would drop him off at his apartment block. It was, he felt, the least he could do.

"You okay back there?"

Mahmood didn't answer.

"Mahmood, you all right?"

He checked the rear-view mirror. The young man looked to be in shock. He was staring blankly into space and his head was shaking a little, as if he had Parkinson's. Tom stopped the car at the next rest stop, got out and walked to the back passenger door, opened it and leaned in. Mahmood spat into his face, his eyes filled with hate.

"If my father doesn't kill you for this, I will."

Wiping the spittle from his cheek, Tom thought the kid was a lot tougher than he'd made out.

"Were you acting back there, too?" he asked, easing out.

"Drive me home."

"My name's not Zafar."

"Zafar will be whipped with bamboo for this."

Mahmood made a dismissive *hiss* through his teeth before slamming the door shut.

As Tom reached the wide road that led to the affluent apartment block in West Cambridge the evergreens lining the sidewalks were dripping rain from a heavy shower, which had stopped a mile or so beforehand, the slate-grey cloud breaking and a hint of sunlight inching out. At the gates, Tom stopped the Bentley, removing the fob key. He got out and opened the rear passenger door.

"Zafar is in the janitor's storeroom at the end of the garage," he said, handing Hassan the fob key.

"I hope they cut the bitch's head off," Mahmood replied.

"Get going, kid," Tom said, harshly.

Hawks was next on his list.

He walked beside the redbrick wall back to the rental car. He drove off, stopping about three miles away at a busy grocery-store parking lot. A light drizzle was falling, the sky clouding over again. He took out the cellphone he'd bought at the airport and punched in the speed number for Crane, agitated.

"Crane, it's Tom. Do you know a guy called Billy Joe Hawks? He's ex-CIA."

Tom heard Crane sigh.

"The hell are you up to now? You promised me you were done. Twice already. You carry on like this, you'll end up dead for sure."

"I gotta lead of sorts. It's Hawks."

"And where did ya get that intel?"

"Hasni."

"Hasni? How?"

"I won't tell you that. But if you pull Hawks in he will deny everything. There's no proof; nothing at least that will stand up in a federal court."

"Why's that?"

"You don't wanna know. But if you help me out, I'll keep you informed all the way," Tom said.

"The last time I helped you out you nearly got one of my men killed."

"Khan—he's okay?"

"Yeah, he's okay," Crane said.

Tom grasped his forehead, feeling relieved. "Thank God. But, Crane, come on. It's our only chance, unless you got something better."

Crane didn't reply for a few seconds, although Tom heard his breathing down the phone.

"Okay. Hawks went overboard on the waterboarding, so to speak. He liked to add a little oil to the water, considering it ironic. Now, in the context of what was going on at that time, it wasn't the worst thing in the world. But a journalist got a hold of the story and… well, he had to go."

"I've never heard that story. What happened to the journalist?"

"She died in a car wreck in Greenwich Village," Crane said.

"Goddamn him."

"The last I heard, Hawks was working for ADC, a major US arms manufacturer in Arlington County. Head of security, I think."

"What does he look like?"

"Five-ten, broad-shouldered. He had thick black curly hair back in the day. His eyes are grey. Blank-looking. His mouth is full, almost feminine. Walked like he owned the earth."

Being observant went with the territory, Tom thought.

"I'll ask you one more time, Tom. If you have something, you need to give it to me."

"I told you, nothing that will stand up. He's a US citizen. You can't torture his ass in Morocco or somewhere."

"That's history. Official. But you obviously ain't up to speed on the National Defense Authorization Act."

"I've heard of it," Tom said, watching a young mother push a shopping cart across the lot, her smiling blonde daughter hanging onto it as she swung a wicker basket in her free hand.

"Google it when you get the chance, cuz it means the president can treat a US citizen like a mad mullah. You carry on the way you're going, you'll have a bag pulled over your head. You'll be bundled into a van and locked up underground for ever without trial. You'll disappear, got it? You ask for due process, you'll be pissing in the wind."

It was a sobering thought. But Tom had come this far and he wasn't about to back down now. "Forget about me. And even if you could do it to Hawks, by the time you find out anything, Lyric will be dead. Besides, I'm not sure he's in on it yet. As I said, there's no proof."

"You're way out of your depth, Tom. Give it up before it's too late."

"You mean you actually want me to stop looking for her?"

"All right. But I've warned you, don't say I haven't. What in the hell is driving you?"

"Loyalty, I guess," he said.

But that was only part of it. Although he had a strong sense of professional duty and a deep affection and respect for the secretary, he wasn't going to let his broken promise to her end in the same way as the broken promise he'd made to his mother. Unwittingly, perhaps, he was seeking atonement, too.

"Loyalty is a good thing, Tom. One thing I've never questioned is your loyalty to Lyric."

"So what have you questioned?"

"Whether or not you're concerned about reaching your next birthday. Hawks is a dangerous sonofabitch. A real piece of work."

Tom rested his free hand on the steering wheel. "Steve Coombs, my second-in-command, tried to kill me."

"Jesus!"

"He was the one who told her kidnappers where the GPS sensor was. He either organized the removal of the shooter on the roof back in Islamabad or did it himself."

"I'll run some checks on him. Get back to you. How can you be sure it was him?"

"He confessed before he died. He was Catholic. They're particular about deathbed confessions."

"You killed him?" Crane asked.

"Self-defence."

"He say anything else before he croaked?"

"Yeah. Those guys at the roadblock in Pakistan, he sent them my photo from Kabul."

"What about the bugging of my room at the Ariana?"

"No," Tom said.

"Does anyone else know what you're up to?" Crane asked.

Tom thought about Lester. "I'm working alone."

"Uh-huh."

"Damn, I forgot. That CIA operative you're so concerned about, the one who gave me the cell back at the Ariana, she was working with Coombs for sure."

"Don't worry about it. She was found hung in her

room," Crane said. "After what you've said, I guess she likely bugged mine, too."

Tom didn't know if that was suicide or something more sinister. But she was dead, and, as far as he knew and hoped, the secretary was still alive. And up until now, Hawks was the only person he knew who could answer his questions. The guy might be a real piece of work, as Crane had said, but his blood was up.

FIFTY-SEVEN

TOM HAD AGREED to meet Lester at an all-day eatery just off Cambridge Street. A modern redbrick building called The Lincoln, set back from the sidewalk at the far end of a sprawling parking lot.

He parked the rental car on the opposite side of the road thirty metres down, deciding to leave it there just in case Mahmood had spotted him driving off in it and had called the cops, although he figured Hasni would've ordered him not to. But he couldn't be sure.

As he walked back up the road he noticed dappled sunlight reflecting off the puddles on the gravel lot, and heard small birds chirping from the sweetspire bushes that formed a natural border with the crowded McDonald's next door. The weather seemed to change with the same regularity as his mood of late. Striding out, he wondered whom Lester had been able to sign up.

The interior of the place had dim lighting and a patterned carpet that had seen better days. Soft background music was playing. The smattering of people seated at the dark wooden tables looked more like professor-types than students. He saw a woman sitting next to Lester at a window booth, both cradling cups of coffee. She looked healthy. Her hair was short and black, cut unevenly but stylish. More like a fashion model's than a punk's. He figured she was maybe in her late thirties. She wore faded jeans and red sneakers. There was a passing remembrance to the secretary, too, roughly the same height and weight, and he wondered what kind of state she was in right now, telling himself that she had to be alive.

They both rose as he walked over.

"Karen Booker, Tom Dupree," Lester said.

She smiled and shook Tom's hand. "Pleased to meet you, Tom."

"Likewise," Tom said.

He noticed her eyes, the colour of liquid honey. She and Lester resumed their positions on the padded bench and Tom sat opposite them.

"Karen's ex-Army. Been a freelance communications expert for the last eight years. Worked for Blackwater for a time in Iraq. Speaks fluent Spanish," Lester said. He gestured to Tom. "Tom here speaks French. A few other languages, too. Despite the way he looks, he's smart."

Tom nodded. "Yeah, yeah."

She smiled.

"Karen's willing to help out," Lester said.

"I'm a trained medic, too," she said, patting a backpack by her side.

"That's good," Tom said.

She said she was very serious about her work, and Tom detected a faint lisp in her otherwise perfect diction.

"Ex-Army, huh?"

"Yes. The Signal Corps. Spent my first years at Fort Gordon, Georgia. Don't ask me how I got into it. I wanted to be a doctor, but my grades weren't up to it. But I'm glad I didn't. Watchful for the Country, the Corps motto. It still means a lot to me."

"Well said," Lester commented, nodding appreciatively.

She smiled again, and Tom saw that her slightly hard features softened into a pleasing face.

"Lester, can I have a quick word?"

"Sure."

"Would you excuse us for a minute, Karen?"

"Of course, Tom," she said, nodding.

Both men stood up and Tom walked Lester out of Karen's earshot over to an imitation-marble counter where the bored-looking wait staff were resting their elbows.

"That's it?" he asked.

"Hey, you ain't sexist, are ya?" Lester asked, glancing back at Karen.

"No, of course not. I mean, just the one."

"My people are freelance, as I said. And in the timeframe, I'd say I got us a good one."

"What's she doing up here?"

Lester frowned and his head jolted back a few centimetres. "Her brother is a lab tech at Harvard. She was visiting."

"She Mexican?"

"She's from Connecticut."

"Her roots?"

Lester's face showed his displeasure again. "Mine are from somewhere in Africa, but that was like two hundred years ago. How far do ya wanna go back?"

Tom leaned in a little closer. "You know what I mean, Lester."

"Not sure I do at that."

"I'm just trying to get some background info here."

Lester shrugged. "You wanna ask her if she prefers nachos to burgers, go right ahead."

"Okay, buddy, let's forget about it," Tom said, tapping the fingers of his right hand lightly on Lester's protruding bicep.

"No problem," Lester said.

They walked back to the booth and sat down.

"I have to level with you, Karen. This could be hairy," Tom said, his head nodding slightly.

"Just what's this all about?" she asked, her face taking on a concerned expression.

Tom thought if she was going to risk her life, she had the right to know. "The Secretary of State."

"Wow."

"I'm the head of her protective detail. I think with a lot of luck, I might be able to find her. But I'll be honest, if you get involved, you might not make it."

"I thought I might not make it a few times back in Iraq. A few other times, too."

"It's my duty and Lester and me go way back. Why are you willing to take such a risk?" Tom asked, his tone a little more inquisitorial than he'd intended.

"Well," she said, turning her palms face up, "some girls like Friday nights out and chocolate. Me, I like danger and intellectual challenges."

She smiled again. That smile could melt a block of ice, Tom thought. He sighed.

"Listen, if you don't want me on board, I can live with that. But the way I see it, the secretary has been kidnapped by men I've been fighting in one way or another for most of my adult life. I'd say it's up to me whether or not I do my patriotic duty here. Besides, I haven't got anything else to do right now. And I've got a 32 gigabyte laptop and some other equipment in my pack that might just come in useful."

"What about your brother?" Tom asked.

She shot a glance at Lester. "He's busy. He's always busy. He only agrees to see me so our mom won't call and shout him out."

Lester looked at Tom and grinned.

"Okay, then. But if this all goes to rat shit, I take the rap for y'all," Tom said, his voice serious and uncompromising.

She nodded.

"I'll pay you twice your daily rate. A bonus if we pull it off."

"I'll gotta hand it to ya, Tom, you're one helluva negotiator," Lester said.

Tom couldn't stop himself from snickering.

"See. I told you he was one of the nice guys," Lester said. "What now?"

"Arlington County," Tom said.

"I just came all the way from New York. Jesus, Tom, you're a real pain in the ass."

FIFTY-EIGHT

HAVING FOUND NOTHING in her mind to calm her, Linda prayed to God for her safety, and asked Him to forgive the sins she had committed in her life. But when she finished, she did not feel His grace; there was still nothing but the terrible reality of what she now knew was a coffin.

Wait, she thought. The respirator. If they want me dead why go to all this trouble? They could have just shot me. She couldn't conceive of anyone being as cruel as to plan a gradual death in a coffin, unless the Leopards were going to use it as terrorist propaganda. But they've already said they would behead me, she told herself. Something that now seemed perversely preferable.

She heard the lid being wedged open. The bright, artificial light hit her eyes and she squinted. The face of the man who'd punched her appeared.

"You're still alive. That's good. It won't be long now. I'll just check around here," he said in his British accent as he thrust his hand in and tugged on the ropes that bound her.

Then he fiddled around with the breathing apparatus. Presumably satisfied, he lifted another hypodermic syringe, the needle glinting before a tear of liquid ran over it. He brushed the burqa up her forearm, revealing bare skin. She felt her lower forearm being slapped harshly before he injected a vein with an unknown drug and lowered the lid. She strained to soak up the last of the light, her sense of confusion only matched by the terror of her further confinement in the coffin, the dread of claustrophobia and the sense of being buried alive.

Faintly, she heard what sounded like metal claps being snapped down. Then was nothing but her dreams and nightmares as she passed into an induced unconsciousness once more.

FIFTY-NINE

AFTER RETRIEVING THE backpack from the rental car, which he'd left in situ, Tom sat between Lester and Karen on the VW's front-bench seat. He'd asked her to check out ADC online via the powerful laptop balancing on her thighs, find out what she could and see whether or not there was any reference to a head of security called Billy Joe Hawks. He'd said the HQ was in Arlington County, or had been.

After she'd logged on, he'd watched her fingers move over the keypad using all ten digits, her flow interrupted only by a meticulous scanning of the many web pages she'd brought up. He could tell that she was speed-reading as she navigated the sites. She seemed keen and intelligent, and he found himself thinking that under different circumstances he might have asked her if she liked Thai food.

Five minutes later, she said, "The CEO is called Peter Swiss. DoB May 2nd, '62. He's a naturalized US citizen, a former French national. Ex-French Foreign Legion officer. The 2nd Rep."

"Paratroopers. Damn good, too. I was seconded to the Legion for six months back in the day," Lester said, his eyes darting around for road signs, despite the oral instructions coming from Davina.

"You didn't tell me," said Tom.

"I don't tell you everything, man."

"Thank God for that."

"ADC has major contracts with the US military," Karen said. "It builds assault helicopters and land-to-air rocket systems. A lot else besides. The corporate HQ is still in Arlington County, near the Pentagon. But there's no mention of Hawks. Here's Swiss."

Tom leaned over and she showed him a photo of the CEO. It looked like a studio shot. His face was taut and tanned. There was a distinct lack of lines around the clear blue eyes for a man of his age, and his hair was blond, without a hint of grey. He was sort of elegant-looking, Tom thought.

"I need to be sure Hawks still works for ADC," he said.

"You want me to call them?" Karen asked.

Tom nodded.

Karen took out her cell. She thumbed in the number as she read it online, put the phone on speaker. Five seconds later, a young woman with a New York accent answered. After Karen asked to speak with Hawks, saying she was a major at the Pentagon, the woman put her on hold. About ten seconds later, she said that he was unavailable presently, but that she could speak with his PA. Karen declined, saying she would call back later.

Disconnecting, Karen said, "So what now?"

Tom pursed his lips.

"Listen, Tom. I know you don't wanna tell us much so we can just act dumb if this all goes to hell, but we can't help unless we know what we're looking for," Lester said, accelerating past a pale-brown Winnebago.

Tom sighed. His friend was right. He told them what he knew about Hawks, which wasn't a great deal, and that he might be involved in the secretary's abduction.

He said that he didn't think all the men involved were Muslims.

"If I'm right, then I figure the way forward is to trick Hawks into contacting whoever has her. That's it. That's all I have."

"Surveillance and hacking equipment installed covertly might be the key to finding the whereabouts of the secretary," Karen said. "And it's a plus that Hawks is head of security."

"How come?" Tom asked.

"Because he'll think that the building, phones and computers are bug and virus-free," she said. "They'll be swept on a regular basis, which means he feels safe."

Tom nodded. "Lester?"

"Normally you'd bribe a low-paid worker like a cleaner to place a bugged calculator or electric plug inside a room. Or blackmail an insider, depending on their tastes or shortcomings. Or use one of your own to make out they're an electrician. And although I agree with Karen, it takes time and that's somethin' we ain't got, right?"

Resting his head against the metal bar behind him, Tom clasped his jaw. "Right. We don't have time. Besides, I don't even know who else is involved. It might be just Hawks and nothing to do with ADC. If so, he's unlikely to use any company equipment. Come to think of it, even if ADC *is* involved, they won't risk it, either."

Lester braked at a red stop. "He'll use a disposable cell, too," he said.

"What about if we spook him, get him into the open and trace the call he's dialling?" Tom asked.

"A hidden monitoring device can capture the telephone number dialled by a touch phone, but not a cellphone," Karen said. "It processes the dial tone. But I don't know of any equipment we can utilize quickly that could do the job on a cell, at least without getting our hands on it first. If we knew the make, there are ways to activate the mic, and we could listen in on his real-time conversations, assuming he had the cell on him. But we don't."

"Can you see if ADC own any other buildings in the area?" Tom asked.

"Sure, Tom," she said, her fingers flying over the keyboard again.

"Whatcha thinking, Tom?" Lester asked.

"That I'm sick of sitting on my ass."

"'Bout time," Lester said, nodding.

SIXTY

AFTER AN ALMOST seven-hour flight, the man who'd checked on the secretary stepped out of the military transport plane they'd travelled in from Abu Dhabi. It was a grey day, the rain coming down in sheets, a westerly wind cutting in from the coast. On the French Air Force base tarmac runway, he oversaw the coffin being taken from the cargo bay and lifted by four men into the back of a dark-blue Citroën van. The secretary would be driven to a remote location in Normandy, northern France. One of the last places on earth that the US intelligence community would be likely to look for her.

He walked over to two French Air Force officers, spoke with them and handed over a package, same as he'd done at Air Base 104 Al Dhafra. Half then, half on successful delivery. The officers weren't habitually corrupt, but they'd taken the bribe just the same. They'd been told that the corpse in the coffin was that of a French national, the son of a wealthy Paris businessman, who'd died in a prison cell in UAE after being found with drugs in his suitcase. The businessman hadn't wanted any bad publicity, and had asked that his son be brought home this way in order to avoid it. It wasn't a great story, and the officers were putting their careers on the line, but it had worked.

The payment made, he got into the front passenger seat of the van, glancing at the two SUVs parked waiting behind. The team were all ex-French Foreign Legion or former European Special Forces' soldiers: six French nationals, three French-speaking Belgians and a couple of Brits. The little cortège pulled away, heading west.

One of the Belgians asked him a question, using his name. He threatened to break his neck for being so unprofessional. The Belgian had called him Proctor. As far as the British and Americans were concerned, he'd died in the Hindu Kush, and he wanted it kept that way.

He'd been a model soldier. His old mates would've never believed he was capable of murdering his spotter, Mike Rowe, whom he had shot in the back of the head with a sniper rifle. Although they'd been promised half of the million-dollar reward put up by the US government if they killed Mullah Kakar, he'd already been offered ten times that in pounds sterling for his role in the treachery. After over a decade of war, he'd realized that adrenalin rushes wouldn't compensate for an early death or blown-off limbs. Proctor now planned to spend a long retirement on a beach so remote that it barely showed up on a map.

SIXTY-ONE

LESTER HAD DRIVEN at an illegal speed for most of the way from Massachusetts to DC, getting there in just over six hours, which made it late afternoon. Checking his watch, Tom had calculated that he had twenty-three hours left. He'd rented a car, a metallic-black Honda Accord. Lester had said he had to pick up surveillance equipment and specialized weapons from a subterranean armoury beneath his basement garage, taking Karen with him. They would meet at the agreed place and time.

Tom waited for an hour at a lot off Interstate 395, and then drove the short distance to Arlington County, Virginia, over the Potomac River via a four-lane road-bridge from the capital.

The ADC HQ was an office complex, a three-storey glass-and-chrome monstrosity. It sprawled over a ten-acre site, the interlinked corridors branching off from the main hub, as if the architect had been fascinated by the complexity of a spider's web. There were no signs that it was the HQ of a major arms manufacturer, except that the security on the gate was backed up by an array of CCTV cameras, perched on poles above parallel chain-linked fences, glittering like a mirage in the sunlight.

Now that he had a physical description of Hawks, at least one that was eight years old and from someone with as keen an eye as Crane, he waited in the Honda fifty metres from the entrance, a line of yellow buckeye trees opposite. So far there was no evidence that Hawks was working with anyone else in the US. But he had to be, Tom thought. He couldn't be doing this alone.

The one key factor that was missing as far as Tom was concerned at this juncture was motive. If the Leopards had taken her, which he now had reason to doubt, motive would not have been a problem. But why would a Westerner or Westerners be involved? It made no sense to him, unless they'd just been used as mercenaries. He thought about taking Hawks to a remote lock-up as he'd done with Mahmood. But the guy was ex-CIA and he guessed that, unless he produced a blowtorch, he wouldn't talk, and he wasn't prepared to do that. Even if he did, Hawks would likely make up a story that couldn't be verified one way or the other in the timeframe. It just wasn't a viable option.

He took his cell from inside his jacket pocket and rang ADC. He asked to speak with Hawks and said it was very important. When the receptionist asked who it was, he said Tom Dupree from the Bureau of Diplomatic Security. After a twenty-second delay, and Tom getting tired of the bland music being played in his ear, Hawks took the call.

"Mr Dupree, how can I help you?"

The voice was low and guttural. From the north-east. Boston, perhaps, Tom thought.

"I'm in a car outside your office. Maybe we could talk."

"What about?" Hawks asked.

"You know what about."

"I'm sorry, but you have me at a disadvantage."

"Your Pakistani friend and the secretary."

There was a five-second pause. "You still have me at a disadvantage, Mr Dupree."

"I don't think so. Listen, we should have this discussion face to face. But it has to be now."

"Good day, Mr Dupree."

"You hang up on me, you won't last the day."

"Is that a threat?"

"Yes, it is," Tom said, matter-of-factly.

He could almost hear Hawks's brain ticking over on the end of the line. He's thinking where, Tom thought. If he didn't say the warehouse, which Karen had located on her laptop in Lester's van, Tom would suggest the nearest motel. It was a mile from the warehouse and he would take it from there.

"Okay. But not here," Hawks said.

"There's a motel fifteen miles away called The Morning View. You know it?"

"I do," Hawks said.

"The parking lot."

"Give me a half-hour."

"Sure," Tom said.

"Alone."

"I'm happy with that. But I'll watch you come out and follow you there."

There was another pause. "Okay," Hawks replied.

Tom drove up almost parallel to the open entrance gate and pulled over.

SIXTY-TWO

Twenty minutes later, a man matching Crane's description of Hawks—thickset with curly black hair—walked across the front parking lot to a dark-blue BMW SUV. He wore a light-grey suit, which hugged his muscles as he strode out. Despite his size, Tom noticed a certain degree of agility and gracefulness in his movement, a gait that spoke of a trained body. Hawks got into his SUV and pulled out of the space, stopping level with the gate. The barrier lifted and he looked around. He's clocked me, Tom thought. Good.

As Hawks drove out onto the road Tom started the Honda. He followed him out of Arlington County into the pig farms and cattle pasture of rural Virginia, seeing Hawks peering into the rear-view mirror on a number of occasions, checking he was behind him.

After driving past miles of whitewashed split-rail fences, Tom swung the Honda around a tight bend with acres of swaying crops on either side. He saw a rusted pickup truck blocking the road some thirty metres ahead. It appeared to have smashed into Hawks's BMW. The hood was up, the windshield shattered, the scene looking kind of unnerving. There was no sign of Hawks, or anyone else for that matter.

It started to drizzle, the fine drops smearing the windshield, as the automatic wipers activated in slow mode. Tom saw a white guy stand up from behind the far-back door of the pickup. He started to walk toward the Honda as Tom slowed to a stop. He wore an expensively cut suit and didn't appear to be concerned, his face grinning as he ambled along. Traits and apparel that didn't sit well with the vehicle he'd been apparently driving, let alone the car wreck. He held up his hand, fingers splayed, and gestured to Tom to get out of the car, as if he were in need of jumpstart leads, or just a lift to the nearest auto garage. As he got closer Tom could just about make out that the guy's hand didn't have a spot of dirt or oil on it. No chance, he thought. He guessed that the scene was the best that could've been concocted in the short timeframe.

He stayed put, locking the doors remotely.

When the white guy was a metre or so away, he went for what Tom knew would be a piece under his armpit. He jerked the Honda into reverse and floored the gas pedal. Putting an arm over the top of the passenger seat, he twisted around. He concentrated on steering straight one-handed, ensuring he wouldn't career into an oncoming vehicle, although the back wipers made visibility difficult at first.

After five seconds, Tom knew he was travelling as fast as the car would go in reverse, the engine sounding as if it were on the point of disintegrating. He jerked the steering wheel to the left, simultaneously engaging the parking brake. The car spun around roughly 160 degrees in what appeared to be a controlled skid, the tyres squealing under the pressure that the moonshine manoeuvre exacted.

But then the car tilted for a second, threatening to roll. Once he was sure the tyres had reengaged with the asphalt, he released the emergency brake and shoved the stick into drive mode, accelerating as fast as the automatic gearbox would allow.

Just then, a ten-wheeled truck turned into the bend, and Tom had to brake hard to avoid hitting it. He checked the rear-view. The white guy was running towards him, a cell to his ear and a handgun held upright at chest height. He turned back around. The truck had blocked the road with its grey bulk. It had feigned jack-knifing, which wouldn't look untoward to a random car coming up behind, and meant that the driver of the truck was a consummate pro.

The cab door opened and a black guy jumped down. He wore blue overalls, a ball cap and shades. He was carrying a pump-action shotgun in both hands. Tom couldn't drive off-road, because irrigation ditches separated the asphalt from the fields. Accepting the situation, he rested his hands on the steering wheel just as the white guy got to him and levelled the handgun at his head.

SIXTY-THREE

PROCTOR REVIVED THE secretary with smelling salts, her head snapping back as he put them to her nostrils. She lay on a single bed with fresh linen sheets, the make-shift cell, a damp basement room, formally used by servants. There were no windows, but there was a small wooden table and two chairs, and a table lamp with a white metal shade. She could read the books that were strewn on the table if she desired: a Bible and several tattered novels.

The burqa had been removed and she wore the Western-style clothes she'd been given in the cell back in Karachi. The burqa was literally an extra layer of security. If for any reason the coffin had been checked en route, there had been a good chance that no one would investigate further, the drug he'd administered paralysing the body and feigning death. That and the fact that most Muslim men would rather let something like that go undisturbed, rather than interfere with another family's business. In France, there was no reason to be stopped, he'd figured.

He walked a few steps to the door, leaving her lying on the bed. "I'll get you something to eat and drink," he said. "It won't be much." He turned around and saw her nod weakly. "Do you need medical attention?"

"I've had enough drugs already," she said, her voice little more than a murmur. "Can I speak with my family?"

"What do you think?"

She suddenly looked fully revived, her pale-green eyes alert, searching his face.

"Wait," she said. "I don't know what you're being paid for this, but if you help me I'll give you my word the US government will pay you double. That and a presidential pardon."

She's serious, he thought. She's a resourceful woman. "Are you asking me to help you escape?"

"Yes. That's it. You're English. We'll give you a new identity, everything. Call it a gold-plated witness-protection programme."

"That's interesting."

"Where am I anyhow?" she asked, straightening up.

"Well, you're not in Pakistan."

"So you'll help me?"

"Me? You're not a person." He sucked his teeth. "You're a symbol. You became a symbol by virtue of your own ambition, and you'll die a symbol by virtue of your own ambition."

"They'll find me," she said, defiantly.

"Well, they'd better hurry up."

He saw the uncertainty return to her eyes, decided to play on it. "No one will find you. No one would dream of looking for you here. Read your Bible, but remember, there is no such thing as God. Man just made him up to make sense of the senseless. We all die, missus, and then there's nothing. You'll just beat a lot of people to it."

SIXTY-FOUR

"GET OUTTA THE CAR," the white guy said.

He was still pointing the handgun at Tom's head. An Israeli Jericho 941, his hands overlapping on the grip. Tom unlocked the door and got out. The guy stood sideways on to minimize his exposure and guard his vital points. He had a lean, high-cheek-boned face. His eyes were pale blue and red-rimmed, which Tom put down to hay fever, because his body was well-muscled. The type that was addicted to steamed fish and al-dente vegetables, rather than drugs or liquor.

"Hands behind your head. Kneel like you're saying your prayers."

Tom raised his hands, sensing that the black guy had come up behind him. He felt vulnerable. They could cap him here, take his body away in the truck and toss him in the Potomac, or bury it in a slurry pond. No one would even suspect anything, other than Lester and Karen. Crane, too, of course. But putting them in danger was exactly what he'd wanted to avoid. He calmed himself down, hoping that Hawks, an ex-CIA operative, wouldn't kill him until he was absolutely sure that he'd extracted everything he knew. And he wouldn't do that on a road, not even one in the Virginia countryside.

"Tom Dupree. You killed four Islamists with your bare hands in Afghanistan. A year later, you saved the

Secretary of State's ass again. Took a bullet for her. I'm right, ain't I?" the white guy said, smirking.

"That's cute," Tom replied.

The guy hadn't recognized him, Tom thought. He was reading from a script. One which was designed to humiliate him and make him feel as bad as possible in the circumstances. Then he felt the muzzle of the pump-shotgun jab between his shoulder blades.

"The man said kneel," the black guy behind him said. "I don't give a racoon's ass who you are."

Holstering his handgun and pulling out the cell he'd been speaking into a couple of minutes before, the white guy smiled and turned face on. A mistake. Tom kicked him hard in the groin. As he pivoted around, he caught a glimpse of him wincing and doubling over. Using his extended elbow, Tom struck the shotgun on the barrel. A shell discharged sideways into the air, the black man's face turning from cocky to screwed in an instant. Tom kicked him hard on the outside of the kneecap. As he buckled sideways Tom hammered the hard edge of his palm into the black man's temple. He crumpled to the asphalt.

Just as he turned to finish off the white guy, Tom was struck by what felt like the butt of a handgun, bludgeoning him on the back of his head. Falling, he got another whack before he hit the ground. But they were designed to immobilize him rather than smash his skull. He landed in a heap, moaning. A hand grabbed his shoulder and pulled him over. He stared up into Hawks's dull-grey eyes, and just saw the blur of the right hook before it connected with his jaw. The impact made him bite his cheek, drawing blood. Hawks pointed a Glock at him, and for a spilt second Tom thought he was dead.

"Get up," Hawks said.

Tom struggled to his feet just as the white guy was rising, the other's cracked mouth gulping air.

"Don't even flinch, or I'll shoot your balls off," Hawks said.

Tom believed him.

Hawks nodded to the white guy, who grinned in return. Tom took an instep full in the groin and nearly passed out with the pain. He had tears in his eyes and clenched his already aching jaw to stop himself from crying out. Feeling as if he were about to puke, he heard the black guy getting up behind him and could guess what was coming next.

"Turn around," Hawks said.

Tom turned, still half bending at the waist, and caught the stock of the pump-shotgun on his head, just behind his ear. It spun him around and he hit the ground again, wondering if this time his skull had in fact fractured. Jesus, he thought. Jesus Christ.

As the light rain fell they patted him down. Tom had left his SIG with Lester. If he was carrying, they would've expected him to use it, and if he had he would've had to kill at least one of them, which wasn't his purpose, at least at this juncture. But he was thinking differently now. He hoped to hell that he hadn't made a big mistake.

They secured his legs with gaffer tape from ankles to knees, and pulled his arms behind his back before taping them, too. Then his mouth got the treatment. He counted five layers. They weren't taking any chances, he thought. He saw the cars move aside, and a black minivan appeared. They picked him up underneath his armpits, and dragged him forward across the slick ground as the van's rear doors opened. The drizzle turned to a heavy shower and the sunlight disappeared.

SIXTY-FIVE

TOM LAY GAGGED and bound in the back of the van. The men said nothing to him, and hadn't attempted to torment or abuse him further. The tarp that'd been thrown over him as he'd landed on the metal floor of the van smelt of gasoline and mould and obscured his view. But the tyres hadn't hit any potholes or zigzagged, so Tom was fairly confident that they hadn't gone off-road or down a dirt track to somewhere quiet and remote like a quarry or woods. He decided to use the time to think things through, partly to dampen his growing fear.

Hawks appeared to be a resilient character, one who had partaken in shameful torture, according to Crane, but had had the ability to secure a top job with a major US corporation. That meant that either ADC had an inept HR department, which he doubted, or that ADC wasn't particular about the violent tendencies of those it employed, which he also doubted. Hawks then had been employed for the particular talent he had displayed on the road a few minutes ago, and so Tom figured that ADC didn't have the same core values as Starbucks. He concluded that those involved in the kidnapping with Hawks were ADC. And that meant the CEO and founder, Peter Swiss, was a prime mover; maybe *the* mover. But still he couldn't work out the motive.

He sensed the van ease to a stop, but the engine kept ticking over. He guessed a gate was being opened, and strained to hear the telltale signs. But he couldn't discern anything above the rattling, even though the engine was front-mounted. The van took off again, this time at a sedate pace, and swung around in a semicircle before the engine was finally killed. He braced himself for what was about to come, hoping that Hawks didn't have a supply of oil stashed at their destination, together with a penchant for reliving the good times back in the day.

The back doors swung open and the tarp was ripped off. He felt rough hands on his ankles. He was dragged down the metal floor, and pulled upright. After his feet were freed with a butterfly knife, he was bundled forward by a couple of men with cropped hair and lean faces, who looked ex-military and wore off-white overalls and paint-stained construction boots.

As his angst spiked Tom told himself to be strong.

SIXTY-SIX

THE WAREHOUSE HAD cinderblock walls and a red-tiled roof, a metal fire escape at the far end, the lot surrounded by an industrial chain-linked fence topped with razor-wire. Steel poles held searchlights and infrared cameras in place. The lot was empty save for a Land Cruiser and a few dumpsters, overflowing with splintered plywood and polythene sheets.

Still gagged and breathing heavily through his nose, Tom was thankful that at least Karen had been right about the ownership of the place. Despite the violence that he knew was soon to be meted out to him, or perhaps because of it, he allowed his mind to wander to the contours of her face, the slenderness of her neck, and the gentle slope of her shoulders. He found himself thinking that he hadn't been quite so attracted to a woman in some time.

As they got to the side door a punch in the kidney made him double over, and he groaned into the gag.

"Not yet," said Hawks.

Tom winced involuntarily as the sun broke from a patch of cloud and cast shadows before him, his captors looking like giants on the cinderblock wall. Hawks opened the wooden side door and flipped a switch, activating harsh fluorescent strip lighting, which gave his face a pallid, light-blue glow, as if he were freezing cold.

The interior of the warehouse resembled an aircraft

hangar and smelled musty. Tom guessed it hadn't been aired for weeks. The floor was covered with stacked pallets, cardboard boxes, black-plastic trash bags and man-size rolls of polythene. A couple of red forklift trucks were parked around a staircase that rose to a steel mezzanine floor, its surface matching the shambles around him. Tom was flung to the dust-ridden ground. He still had his hands tied behind his back, and he landed heavily, his already aching head jarring.

"Now pick him up," Hawks said, fetching over a metal-rimmed chair.

He nodded to it, and Tom was pressed down into the seat, the two men standing either side of him. Then his makeshift gag was cut free. He took a couple of gulps of air before steadying himself.

"So, here we are," said Hawks, standing about three metres from the chair.

"Beats life in a supermax for kidnapping," Tom replied.

"That you or somebody else?" Hawks said, grinning.

"You made a big mistake taking her."

"You think? For someone who won't last the day, looks like I'm doing okay up to now."

Tom spat blood. "You Swiss's attack dog?"

Hawks smirked. "You know how this works. So, what do you know?"

"About what?" Tom replied.

Hawks nodded to one of the two men. Tom was punched hard on the cheekbone, his head twisting under the impact.

"You want to look like a piece of raw beef, that's your concern. But you'll talk."

"About what?"

This time the punch came from the man on the other

side, chipping a back molar and making Tom's vision blurred.

"What do you know?" Hawks asked, his hands going to his lean hips.

"About what?" Tom said, his head feeling as if it'd been trampled by a carthorse.

Hawks walked over to the side of the warehouse, picked up a piece of hardwood about a metre long. He tapped his hand with it as he strolled back.

"We'll see what gives first, your nose or the wood. My money's on your nose."

Tom heard the two men snicker. A forearm scooped under his secured arms behind his back, pulling him upright, as his head was grasped in a vise-like grip about his ears. He struggled to keep his head down, but it was forced up so that he was staring at the mezzanine floor.

He saw the plank of wood being lowered slowly toward his face, as Hawks measured the strike. This is going to hurt, he thought. Bad. A second later, he felt an oddly numbing pain, followed by a sharp pang like an electric shock passing through his brain. The sound was like two bricks being slammed together. He groaned, knowing that his nose had broken, the blood covering his nylon jacket and jeans. He barely kept it together, his head swaying back and forth, the grip being released at the last moment.

"Home run, I'd say. So what do you know?"

"About what?" Tom murmured.

"Okay. Now let's see what gives first, your shin or the wood. My money's on your shin."

Tom felt his ankles being gripped, then his shoulders. If Hawks shattered his leg, he would be out of action for weeks. As he was about to yield the door to the warehouse swung open. Tom half squinted. A man who looked like the photo that Karen had showed him on her laptop of Peter Swiss walked through, flanked by what he took for bodyguards rather than accountants. A tall, dark-haired, Slavic-featured woman wearing a charcoal pantsuit, and a guy with a big head, his stocky frame wrapped in a short woollen overcoat.

Swiss walked over. Stopping a few metres from Tom, he took out a packet of cigarettes and lit one with a gold lighter. After inhaling, he pursed his lips and blew out a cloud of smoke.

"This is messy. I don't like messy, Mr Dupree. Names of those you're working with. Everything you've found out. Then it'll end. I promise you it'll be clean."

Tom had detected only a hint of a French accent. "And if I don't?"

"Think of the worst thing possible. Then double it."

"You—"

"You what? I would have mentioned that your parents would have gotten a visit from Mr Hawks here, too. But your mother's dead and your father, well, he could be anybody, couldn't he? Did she like to screw around with the trailer trash, Mr Dupree? Father unknown. That's a hell of a thing to have on your birth certificate."

Tom resisted the urge to shout back a string of obscenities. Instead, he watched Swiss twiddle a heavy signet ring on his middle finger. He caught a flash of the red-and-green enamel, together with the exploding-grenade emblem. French Foreign Legion. 2nd Rep.

"I was given Hawks's name," Tom said.

He glanced at Hawks. The man was looking nervous. "Who by?" Swiss asked.

"Brigadier Hasni gave him up as easy as a junkie who needed to score."

Tom watched Swiss's left eye twitch. He was barely able to contain a mixture of anger and disbelief.

"He's a fucking lying—"

Swiss cut off Hawks in mid-flow with a raised hand. "What else did he say?"

"That's it. Just Hawks."

"Are you sure?" Swiss asked.

"Do you think I'd be sitting here if he had?" Tom said.

"Not a good answer. Carry on, Mr Hawks."

As Hawks raised the hardwood and walked forward Tom watched Swiss put his right hand inside his suit jacket and take out a Manurhin MR 73 revolver. As he cocked the gun's hammer Hawks's eyes closed briefly in recognition of the sound. He mouthed one word: Damn.

Coolly, Swiss shot Hawks in the back of the head with the heavy .357 Magnum round the French hand-gun was chambered to use.

SIXTY-SEVEN

HAWKS COLLAPSED LIMPLY to the ground, as if his muscles had disintegrated. A pool of black-red blood formed around his lifeless face, flowing steadily from the nickel-sized hole in his cranium. Tom clenched his aching jaw, trying his best to remain calm. The bodyguards looked twitchy, their open hands hanging loose at their sides. Tom breathed shallow breaths through his swelling mouth. Things weren't going well. He decided to improvise and offer Swiss a deal of sorts; one that didn't depend on him trusting the Frenchman.

"I wanna speak to the secretary," he said.

"Why would you want to do that?" Swiss asked, holstering his revolver.

"To know she's safe, for now at least. To say I'm sorry. I never did get to tell her that. I'm sentimental that way. Then I'll tell you all I know," he said.

"Everything, Mr Dupree."

Tom nodded.

Swiss took out a cellphone, and walked over to a corner of the warehouse out of earshot. The bodyguards looked nervously about. It was an isolated spot, but Swiss's revolver wasn't suppressed, and there was no way that they could've foreseen what had just happened.

A minute later, Swiss came back and put the cell to Tom's ear.

"Ma'am."

"Tom. Is…is that you?"

Her voice was frail, but controlled.

"I'll keep my promise. I swear it."

Swiss jerked the phone away, disconnecting the call. "It's not nice to give people false hope, Mr Dupree. Now tell me."

Tom stayed silent.

Swiss's face didn't react this time. He just put his cell in his breast pocket. "Call me if he decides to speak," he said, addressing the two men who were still standing on either side of Tom.

"And if he don't?" the one to Tom's left said.

"The fuck you think Mr Swiss is paying you for?" the heavyset bodyguard said.

Swiss began to walk away, but stopped and turned around halfway to the door. "Your friend, Steve Coombs," he said, tapping his pocket. "He was right here. Took his blood money with a filthy grin on his face."

Money, Tom thought. The guy had sold out for money.

Swiss left with his two bodyguards, the door banging shut behind them.

After a few seconds, one of the men moved around in front of Tom and took out a chisel with a narrow blade, filed to a point at the end. As the sound of Swiss's car could be heard driving away he grinned.

"We get paid by the hour," the man said. "So me and my buddy here figure we'll make it last till morning."

Just then, Lester appeared on the mezzanine floor above, levelling his suppressed SIG.

"Make like starfish," he said as he began to descend the metal staircase.

They hesitated. Tom figured after the beating he'd received they'd better do as they were told quickly. Lester had a look on his face, one that he'd seen a couple of times before. He was mightily aggrieved. If they weren't compliant soon, he'd cap them, probably feign a less-than-lethal shot to start off with before killing them outright. Lucky for them, they assumed the position without a scene.

Lester walked over to Tom, bent over him and cut his hands free with a Stanley knife. Tom rubbed his wrists and stood up.

"Thanks, man," he said.

"No problem. That hurt?" Lester said, staring at Tom's bloody nose.

"Not any more."

Lester grinned, handed Tom a SIG and walked over to the two men on the ground. He knelt down and began putting flex-cuffs on them. Harshly.

Tom looked up to the mezzanine floor. Karen was standing there. "Did you get everything?"

"Oh, yes," she said, nodding.

Tom had banked on being taken to the warehouse. Hawks would be cautious. Apart from being involved in something that could get him a life sentence in solitary, he was ex-CIA. He wouldn't take a man anywhere to beat on him. He would have to be sure that he was in a controlled environment where there'd be no nasty surprises, like hidden CCTV cameras, a nosy cop or a vigilant security guard. The warehouse was the only building owned by ADC in the vicinity.

Tom had resolved to make his part in it as convincing as possible, and, since they would have been expecting to tackle a DS special agent, that meant he'd had to make it difficult to take him. But the road trap had been a genuine surprise.

When he'd gotten to the warehouse, he'd known he'd have to take a beating. If he'd cracked too early on, Hawks would've suspected something. The plan was going well for a while. Hawks had admitted his involvement. But the arrival of Swiss and two handy-looking bodyguards hadn't figured in Tom's plan, either. And now Hawks was dead and Swiss was gone. But at least he knew that Swiss was in on it up to his immaculate blond hair.

Karen, who had walked down from the first floor, carrying a canvas bag, strolled over to him. "Let me," she said. She touched Tom's nose gently with her thumb and forefinger. "You want me to fix it?"

"Sure."

"It'll hurt more than when he broke it."

"Go a—"

She twisted it hard. There was a sharp crack.

"Jesus," he said, tears forming in his eyes.

"There, there," she said. "It looks fine."

Lester walked over to them. "You think I shoulda tried to tackle Swiss and his bodyguards?"

"No. Too risky," Tom said.

"That's good, cuz Karen here had an idea," he replied.

"You did?" Tom asked.

Karen walked over to the two bound men, crouched down beside them. As she took a couple of glass phials from the bag, she turned and smiled. She said she'd fill him in on the way out to the VW. Then she drugged them. By the time they woke up, the secretary's fate would have been decided.

It had already been agreed that Karen would set up surveillance video cameras as evidence. When Swiss had arrived unexpectedly, she had decided to act.

Swiss's dull-gold Range Rover had been parked beside the other car in the lot. She'd opened the chained fire door that led to the fire escape with Lester's bolt-cutters, ducking down as she'd checked that nobody was standing guard. After descending the metal steps, she'd jogged over to the Range Rover. She'd taken out a couple of magnetized objects each the size of a matchbox, and placed them onto the car's chassis: a listening bug and a location transmitter. Any onboard detection system would be rendered inert by the third object, an anti-alarm tremor field that repelled the signature probes, which she'd placed under the front, driver-side wheel arch, tilted to an angle to avoid all but the most diligent sweep by a mirror. That done, she'd run back to the fire escape and let herself in. By the time she'd settled down beside Lester behind a stack of cardboard boxes on the mezzanine floor, Swiss had been on his way out.

SIXTY-EIGHT

KAREN KNELT IN the back of the van, her hands twiddling plastic dials on a black-box receiver, her ears covered by padded headphones. There were two large plastic suitcases, too, containing, Lester said, "kickass equipment". He was driving back towards the Potomac, with Tom sitting beside him.

"Those bugs gonna work, Karen?" Tom asked, turning around.

"I'm on it," she said.

"Why don't we just get the feds to lift him? We got the evidence," Lester said.

"We do that, the secretary could be dead in an hour. We know Swiss is in direct contact with her kidnappers. They might think he'll cut a deal. I can't risk that. And, more importantly, we don't know where she is. Swiss is the only man who can lead us to her. Thanks to Karen."

He had an idea now, too.

They stopped at a gas station to fill up. There was a convenience store to the right. The sun was still out, the highway on either side slithering into the distance like glistening eels. Karen said she fancied a candy bar. Tom put on shades, got out first and walked over to a payphone, leaving Lester to pump the gas. He didn't want the man he was about to ring to have the number of his disposable cell. As he reached the payphone he was feeling a little apprehensive. He was about to ring his father.

They hadn't spoken in a while and even when they had it'd tended to be a short conversation, almost businesslike. After Tom turned eighteen, his father paid for his college education and seemed genuinely pleased that he was going to be studying French literature at Florida State University. But he didn't attend Tom's graduation and disappeared for weeks at a time. When he tried to find out where, he always drew a blank. Even his phone number had been unobtainable.

Tom punched in the number of his father's office at the Pentagon, which was less than a twenty-minute drive away in Arlington County. The Pentagon housed the rapidly growing Defense Intelligence Agency, the military's primary intel-gathering and special-missions organization, which worked in tandem with the CIA. Its core collectors, or frontline operatives, were drawn from both the military and civilians. Tom had a feeling his father was something to do with the DIA, or at least was affiliated to it.

"Major General Dupont's office," a woman's voice said.

"I'd like to speak with the general, please."

"He's in a meeting. Whom may I say called?"

"Tom Dupree. It's a private matter."

"He's due out in forty minutes."

"He'll take my call. Please tell him it's urgent."

Tom watched Lester at the pump. His friend smiled and waved. Tom forced himself to wave back. Karen had ambled into the store. He could see her through the windows, scanning the shelves. Ten seconds later, he heard his father's voice.

"My God, Tom, where are you?"

"Here in Virginia."

"Are you okay? I've been trying to contact you. Nobody knew where you were."

"I'm fine," Tom said.

"I was worried after I saw what happened over there."

"Can I ask you something?"

"Uh-huh."

"Do you know a guy called Peter Swiss, the CEO of ADC?" Tom asked.

"I've heard of him, but we've never met. Why?"

Tom thought that was a little strange, his father being a big shot at the Pentagon. But he left it. "Can I see you?"

"I guess. I'll be free around six."

"I need to see you now."

After a long pause, his father said, "All right, Tom. I'll organize a pass."

"Not at the Building," Tom said, the name its occupants used for the Pentagon.

SIXTY-NINE

PENTAGON CITY WAS in the south-east urban district of Arlington County, near the National Cemetery. The bar they'd agreed to meet at was just off the Fashion Centre Mall complex, twenty metres up from a large apartment building called The Metropolitan at Park Row. Tom kept on his shades as he walked in. An old edition of *Friends* was on the flat-screen TV above the optics. He sat at a small, round table in the corner of the bar with a view of the door and the sidewalk. He hadn't seen his father in two years, and guessed another two years would've passed by if he hadn't called him.

A minute or two later, he saw him get out of a black limo, dressed in civilian clothes: a sharp black suit, red tie, and white shirt. He looked fit and healthy, his smooth skin belying his sixty-four years. As he pushed open the glass door Tom stood up, gave a half-hearted wave across the room. The place had emptied of the business and political types he guessed he used it to power-lunch and it was too early for dinner.

His father's handshake was firm, the eyes dark and sparkling.

"You look thin, Tom," he said, sitting down.

Removing his shades, Tom saw the shocked look on his father's face. Although Karen had fixed the shape of his nose, the impact of the wood had caused his eyes to swell and darken, and the outline of a bruise had already formed.

"It looked real rough over there."

"It was," Tom said, nodding.

"Is that where…that happened?" he asked, using two fingers to flick between his own eyes.

"Not exactly."

The general called a waitress over and ordered a couple of black coffees without asking Tom if he wanted one.

"What can I do?"

Tom took out his cellphone and pressed the video-camera button, pushing it over to his father's side of the table. His father watched silently, his forehead creasing in a frown. Karen had downloaded the video taken at the warehouse onto Tom's cell. It showed just about everything that had happened, although Tom leaned over and stopped it before Swiss shot Hawks and had deleted the sound already.

"That was taken in a warehouse near Arlington County about a half-hour ago."

"Jesus, Tom. From what I heard about Swiss, he didn't seem the type."

"But you've never met him," Tom said.

"As I said, no."

The waitress came over, a skinny thing with her hair in a ponytail. She placed the cups and saucers down, together with the check. "Enjoy," she said.

"What's this all about, Tom?" his father asked.

"The secretary."

His father sighed before standing up. "I'm taking this to the FBI," he said, snatching up the cellphone.

SEVENTY

SANDRI KHAN HAD contacted his CIA handler on a couple of occasions since he'd done his little recon of Brigadier Hasni's house with the American called Tom Dupree, and had left him to his own devices in the Blue Area of Islamabad. He'd reported that things had gone sour but that he'd escaped unscathed, utilizing flash grenades, which were designed to disorientate and disable temporarily, rather than maim or kill. Still, he'd said he had to cap two ISI men just the same. They were chasing after the American. If he hadn't, the man would've been dropped by a fence. That hadn't happened and he'd seen him scamper off to what he'd considered to be safety.

After that, Khan had made his way to one of the many safe houses that the Agency provided for its Pakistani assets and sources in Islamabad, and which were used in rotation. If any were raided by the ISI, or officers from the Intelligence Bureau or Military Intelligence, the whole set-up was changed. It had been quite a successful arrangement up until a year or so ago. But many had been arrested in the interim, most of whom were never seen again.

He sat in front of a flat-screen, checking on his emails. His Glock 17-9mm was on the table within a hand's reach. It had three independent safeties, which made it the safest handgun in the world. The frame was made from a synthetic stronger than steel, but it

was eighty-six per cent lighter. It was virtually inde-
structible. It was also the most accurate handgun in
the world. The deadliest. He liked his Glock. He never
went anywhere without it, although he was always accompanied by his three bodyguards. Their wages were
paid from the significant sums that were transferred
into a bank account on a regular basis by the CIA via a
front IT business registered in Germany. His cover was
that he worked freelance for the business, one of many
outsourced services from the West. He was essentially
a bridge agent, acting as a courier and a go-between.
Apart from the money he kept for himself, he used the
remainder to obtain intel, which he then passed on for
a profit. It was a lucrative business. But he preferred
to appear poor. Besides, due to the run-down locations
the safe houses were situated in, it also meant that he
didn't draw any attention to himself.

He'd bought a lamb-and-lentil curry with rice and
roti bread from a stand on the sidewalk that he knew
sold the freshest food in the district. As he clicked open
his mail he used his fingers to scoop up some meat from
the thick sauce. Chewing methodically for thirty-two
times, a habit he'd acquired in childhood when a bowl
of plain rice was all he'd had to eat for the day, he read
an email ostensibly sent from a relative in the US, but
which had in fact been sent from Langley, Virginia.

The email was encrypted and informed him to lie
low for a couple of days and refrain from using his cellphone to contact his handler. There was nothing remarkable about this. It often happened at sensitive times,
and, even though Pakistan had a plethora of sensitive
times, the abduction of the US Secretary of State had
put every other covert surveillance and intel-gathering

job on hold. It was, then, to be expected, he thought. He would get paid even if he did nothing for weeks, so it was with a certain degree of contentment that he shut down his computer and concentrated on his meal.

Five minutes later, he heard a muffled groan and what he took for a chair toppling over. His hand went for the Glock as the door was kicked open and five men bundled through, holding the bodyguards in front of them as human shields. Khan knew the bodyguards well. They were more like friends than employees. Looking at their terrified faces, he didn't have the heart to shoot them to get at the men he knew to be from the ISI. Even if he did take that drastic course of action, he guessed the chances of him surviving the subsequent and inevitable firefight would be minimal. But knowing what was to come, he thought he might be better off dead. The ISI could keep someone alive for weeks, using blood transfusions and drip-fed cocktails of mild amphetamines and nutrients. Even if victims were found alive lying bound and naked by the side of the road, they were no longer any use to anyone.

He laid the Glock on the table and raised his hands, seeing the relief in the eyes of his bodyguards, their mouths clamped firmly shut by the huge hands of those who had overcome them. He wondered how they had been taken so easily, but as he was punched in the solar plexus with an uppercut he got the answer. His men were released and told to leave. They had betrayed him, he thought.

Still smarting from the blow, he had his hands cuffed and he was punched in the ear, the impact so great that he felt as if his eardrum had ruptured. He collapsed to his knees. His computer was snatched up as he was dragged from the room, two men remaining to ran-sack it. His cellphone would be seized and analyzed, too, although any money they found, together with his collection of watches, gold jewellery and rare coins—his pension—would be kept by those who found it. But there was his stash. In foreign banks. Nobody would find that, he told himself.

Not that he felt he had much use for it now. They would break him in time. Everyone broke in time no matter how tough they thought they were. It was, he knew, not a matter of courage or the strength of one's mind; it was simply inevitable. Even if he could hold out for a couple of days, he would not be able to hold out longer. Theirs was a tried-and-trusted methodology of torture, and those who meted it out were proficient in it and were both highly prized and well paid.

He was pulled like a lazy dog down the narrow stairs, kicked and spat upon, a barrage of insults about his sexuality and parentage shouted out, although he only heard them in one ear now. As he reached the open front door he saw the Mercedes car in the darkness, its rear door already open, a grinning thug in the driver's seat. He was heaved in, two muscular men squeezing onto the seat either side of him shortly afterwards.

As the car sped off they began to taunt him about what he faced, how his body would quake, his screams go unheeded. How he would beg for it to end, but it would not, and which parts of his anatomy the torturer he faced favoured and why. He gritted his teeth and even managed a closed-mouthed smile on a couple of occasions, but his eyes betrayed his true feelings. The eyes always did.

When they reached the end of Faisal Avenue, he saw

the four one-hundred-metre-high minarets of the Faisal Mosque rising from an elevated piece of land, illuminated by golden lights. The mosque was shaped like a nomad's tent and had been funded by Saudi Arabia. This, he knew, was the northernmost point of the great city, lying at the foot of the Margalla Hills, the western foothills of the Himalayas. The taunting stopped. Not even ISI operatives deemed it appropriate to say such things within sight of the National Mosque of Pakistan, the largest in South Asia.

The hills beyond were covered in pine, oak and fig trees and rose to over a mile high, the slopes dotted with little villages. For men such as Sandri Khan, they were also known for being the graveyard of hundreds of enemies of the state. Just as this thought registered a blindfold was tied tightly around his head.

His darkest fears had materialized.

SEVENTY-ONE

IT WAS 18:02 and the general stood on a muddy bank overlooking the Potomac. The Pentagon, where he'd worked in the Department of the Army for the past eight years, was a few miles upstream, obscured by the tree line. But the Washington Monument was clearly visible across the waters; a granite, marble and bluestone obelisk rising over one hundred and seventy metres above the National Mall. He put his hand into a plastic bag of dried white bread and fed the ducks, his broad back accentuated by his heavy black overcoat. The sun had disappeared once more, and the clouds were low and gunmetal-grey. A strong breeze was whipping up the surface of the river, the ducks bobbing up and down and struggling to remain close enough to the bank to take advantage of an easy dinner.

Tom sat in the back of Lester's VW van in between Lester and Karen, his eyes flicking between three flat-screened monitors. They were all wearing headphones. The van was parked on a lot next to a cluster of picnic shelters. There were five other vehicles parked there. They could have parked the van two hundred metres away amid a poplar copse, using camouflage netting to cover its bulk. But Tom knew that Swiss's bodyguards would be vigilant, and sometimes being visible was the best way not to stand out.

Besides Lester's van afforded perfect cover for surveillance. It was equipped with covert cameras in the grille and roof vent, together with a couple of parabolic microphones, which were linked to satellite-like dishes disguised around the headlights. The type that could pick up a whisper a third of a mile away. Their movement was concealed by steady pegs, which locked the van's suspension in place, and the interior was soundproof. The windows on the sides could be used for taking photos, but if someone outside peered in it looked as if the van were empty, a projected image showing on the glass.

The general had agreed to speak with Swiss, although it had taken Tom ten minutes to convince him that he wouldn't do anything afterwards that would ruin his career in the DS or leave himself open to a federal rap, or worse. He'd also agreed to wear a microphone hidden in a fountain pen. Tom had figured this would be their only chance to get Swiss talking, and, if anything went wrong with Lester's clandestine equipment, he wanted a back-up.

Five minutes later, Swiss's gold-coloured Range Rover with tinted windows appeared on the asphalt roadway and moved towards the general at a sedate pace. He didn't look up, just continued to feed the ducks. Tom had never known any details of what his father did, except that when he'd seen him as a late teenager he was always in uniform. He'd supposed he was regular military. But after he'd qualified as a special agent, he'd gotten the impression that his father's past was more complicated, although he never talked about his work, or anything else in his life for that matter. He was the most secretive man Tom had ever known. Like Crane, he was an enigma. Tom had gotten the idea that his father worked in intelligence after he'd found three passports in his suitcase when he'd visited him in DC one summer.

"We're on," Karen said.

The car stopped about three metres from the river-bank and Swiss and two bodyguards got out, the same pair who had been at the warehouse. The Eastern European woman and the meathead. The general didn't turn around. Swiss, flanked by his bodyguards, walked over to him and stood behind his right shoulder.

"Appreciate you coming," the general said. He gestured to the ducks. "The thing about ducks is, they're all controlled up top, but underneath they're paddling like crazy. Least when they see something that'll fill their bellies. And it don't matter who's feeding them, they see food, they just go for it."

"You said it was an urgent matter of national security."

"The weeding out of people who threaten the stability of government is always an urgent matter of national security, Mr Swiss. Or should be, even for people who weren't born here."

"Is that a slight?" Swiss asked.

"A slight?"

"Because I was born French and became a US citizen."

"The truth is, we're all immigrants of different degrees here. But the one thing that binds all Americans, or most of us, I like to think, is an allegiance to the Constitution. A belief, too, that despite our frailties, of which there are many, we stand for something good and positive in the world. It maybe old-fashioned, and God knows we've sinned, but there's still something about the freshness of the air that makes people from all over want to breathe it."

"What did you want to see me about?" Swiss asked, his tone agitated.

"You can tell your people to step back some. Then we can talk."

Swiss waved away the bodyguards like some ancient warlord.

"The CIA has been up to no good. Now I know a man with your credentials is aware that they've been up to no good for some considerable time, despite saving our asses from God knows how many 9/11s. But they've overstepped the mark."

Back in the van, Karen adjusted the monitoring devices for greater clarity as Tom studied every move both men made.

"And how have they done that?" Swiss asked.

"They're planning to utilize the situation in Pakistan to their own advantage. Their budget, like the military budget, is to be cut massively. Like a smack in the face with a catfish, as my daddy used to say. But we have information that implicates them in the abduction of the Secretary of State."

The general put his hand into the bag and scattered the bread, as if he were sowing seeds. The ducks squabbled with one another as ducks did, without any real aggression or damage being done. Swiss looked around. He motioned with his hand again, and the bodyguards started to move towards the lot.

In the van, Karen said, "Look, Swiss's finger is tapping his thigh. He didn't expect that. He's worried."

"I thought you were a communications expert," Tom said. He knew it was a subtle movement that only a trained operative could have picked up, something he'd been taught during his surveillance training.

"All forms of communications," Lester said. "That's what your résumé said, right?"

"Of course. I can lip-read and sign, too," she said.

"Okay, okay," Tom said, still transfixed by the monitor.

After the pause, Swiss said, "That's absurd."

"That's a fair comment, but it is a fact," the general said.

"You said 'we'."

"Patriots, Mr Swiss. Those who believe folks still got a right to breathe fresh air, despite everything that's gone on in the last decade or more."

"And why would the CIA do such a thing?"

"Like all people who fear their power is waning, they have to make themselves seem indispensable. They need a new enemy. They want the secretary to be the proverbial sacrificial lamb. They want to stir it up and make the Leopards and their Iran backers the new supreme bad guys, so that another war don't seem far-fetched no more. The ongoing uprisings in the Middle East, the build-up of the Chinese military, the North Koreans, and the al-Qaeda-backed insurgents in West Africa are all genuine security problems, but they won't spark another war. They always have to have a supreme bad guy, else they can't justify the billions they spend. Close to ten billion at the last count," the general said, still facing straight ahead. "The ugly death of the US Secretary of State will give them what they want."

"Even if I bought all this, which I don't, what do you think I can do about it?"

"I'm sorry you think that way, Mr Swiss."

"Okay, let's assume for the purposes of this conversation I do believe it."

"You father's lying, right?" Lester said.

"He is," Tom said, frowning. "Check on the body-guards."

"You have a vested interest in a war with Iran, Mr Swiss. You, no doubt, would supply the weapons. It's no secret that corporations like yours saw their stock rise fourfold during the wars in Iraq and Afghanistan. Like brokers, you make money irrespective of whether your customers win or lose."

"And, General?"

"When the secretary dies, as we all know she will, we want you to do your patriotic duty."

"Which is?" Swiss asked.

"We'll tell you how when the time comes. For now, just keep paddling beneath the surface and remain calm up top."

"So, you suspect me of something?"

"Did I say that?"

"I must tell you that I have served this country for years, given jobs to thousands of people. Jobs with bene-fits the state couldn't match in a hundred years. None of my retired workers have to queue for free healthcare or pump gas because their pensions don't meet the bills."

"I'm sure you're right," the general said, stuffing his plastic bag of bread into his overcoat. "You know, Mr Swiss, we live in very dangerous times. We never know what'll happen next. We'll speak again."

And with that the general turned and began to walk in the direction of the Pentagon, leaving Swiss stand-ing there, shaking his head at the ducks.

"I like it, but what the hell was that all about?" Les-ter said.

"Get a man confused and twitchy and he makes mistakes," Tom said.

302 STATE OF HONOUR

This was Tom's plan. His father wasn't exactly a model parent, but he was good at making someone feel nervous without pointing a gun at their head. Tom figured Swiss would be jumpy already after he'd told him about Hasni at the warehouse. Swiss had killed Hawks on the strength of it, after all. He just hoped that this little scene wouldn't push the man completely over the edge.

SEVENTY-TWO

THE CAR RIDE had gone on for another forty minutes or so. Khan guessed he was in some ISI-owned house, deep in the valleys. But the dimly lit room might as well have been anywhere in Pakistan. The ISI had numerous torture centres, most of which were not in their official buildings, and didn't show up on any government paperwork. To all but a very few people, their whereabouts were unknown. Officially, they didn't exist, just as the black sites around the world Khan had sent over thirty Pakistani men to as a result of the information he'd given to the CIA didn't exist. It was the way of things, the path he'd chosen; and now it was payback time.

He was naked and tied to a wooden chair, blood oozing from a large gash above his right eye where the torturer had punched him with a brass knuckleduster. He spat more blood from his mouth, and felt the jagged edges of broken front incisors with his tongue. The man was old-school, preferring scalpels and dental pliers to serums or electric shocks. He had them laid out on a wooden table in front of him; all part of the vicious game. He was jowly and heavily lined, with an obvious pot belly. He had a bad comb-over and a wispy moustache, like that of a teenage boy. He wore only khaki pants and a sweat-stained white undershirt.

Khan trembled involuntarily. But he hadn't been asked any questions as yet.

Apart from the torturer, two ISI operatives and a man operating a recording device, Brigadier Hasni now entered the room and stood roughly four metres away. Out of range of flying blood, but close enough to study the contorted face and hear Khan moan.

Khan worried why Hasni had arrived. The man had been a torturer in his time and was good at it by all accounts. But why do it yourself when there were others to do it for you? There were myriad other things in life more pleasurable, except for a sadist. But he knew that Hasni wasn't one; it had been his duty, he supposed. Besides, he knew that sadists made bad torturers. They lacked the empathy that was necessary to obtain a confession or information. If a victim merely thought the torturer was getting off on the experience, he or she would simply blurt out anything early on, or even before they experienced any pain. And there would be no way they'd shift from that initial position.

The man pulled off the bloodstained knuckleduster, keeping his black leather glove intact. He stretched his back, clearly tired by his physical exertions. He picked up a length of lead pipe from the table and waved it before Khan's eyes. He could see it clearly, because the man did not like to strike the eyes and had been fastidious to avoid them. The eyes don't lie, he thought. They betray, but they do not lie. He watched the man twiddle the pipe in his hand before looking at it with what appeared to be a degree of disdain. What could he do with it? Khan thought. Knock me out. Break my toes or kneecaps. It was crude, even for him. As if sensing this, the man placed it back down and lifted up the pliers. This was a different matter, and Khan winced at the thought of it. *The teeth*, the ISI operatives in the car had said, *he likes the teeth*.

"Wait," Hasni said, holding up his hand.

Khan saw Hasni walk over to him, stopping by his side. He bent over and whispered, "I know it was you, Khan. You told the Americans where she was, didn't you?"

Dear God, Khan thought. He knows. But how does he know? He'd only relayed the whereabouts of the US Secretary of State to one person. His CIA handler.

Hasni straightened up and move backwards a few steps. "You have no children."

Khan shook his head. "No."

"A man without children is like a car without an engine. What's the point?"

Mahmood, Hasni's son, Khan thought. He knows everything.

"Ah," said Hasni. "Right there, just a flicker. You've got it, haven't you?"

"I don't know what you mean," Khan said, weakly.

"Oh, yes. Yes, you do. You told the American about my son."

He felt utterly hopeless. But what he did now know was that he was being tortured for Hasni's revenge. This wasn't about how long he would take to break, or what needed to be reduced to raw meat, twisted, mangled, shredded or smashed beyond repair. There was no breaking point applicable, no sense of rationality to the concept of breaking in time. And he began to weep, knowing that no truth, no piece of intel or name would be an antidote for the pain that would be visited upon him.

Hasni walked over to the far corner of the room, which was a dark recess. He stopped and began to talk with someone who was hidden there. When he saw the man come out of the shadows, Khan gasped, the intake of air causing intense pain in his broken teeth as it raced over the exposed nerves. He shook his head, both in disbelief and to relieve the pain, but mostly because he could not believe it. He was dead. Of that there was no doubt now.

The man standing a little way out of the shadows, a metre from Brigadier Hasni, was his CIA handler. Dan Crane.

SEVENTY-THREE

In the back of the VW, Karen monitored the signals from the GPS tracking device she'd placed under Swiss's Range Rover at the warehouse, and ensured that the small acoustic super-sensor pickup placed there, too, was at its full capacity. An amplification up to 200x via the portable ten-watt RMS amplifier. Tom sat beside Lester, who was driving in heavy traffic now. They each had a small wireless earpiece, allowing them to hear any conversations in the Range Rover four cars ahead, travelling at no more than twenty miles per hour. Light rain began to fall, the tiny drops speckling the windshield. After the static had cleared, Swiss could be heard cursing their slow progress and shouting at the driver to pull off the highway and take a back-road route.

"You think this'll work?" Lester asked, glancing at Tom.

"If it don't, we're screwed," Tom replied.

"Won't Swiss try to do a deal now?" Lester asked.

"I just hope he ain't that shaken up."

"Swiss is calling someone on his cell," Karen said.

"Can you turn the volume up on that thing?" Tom asked, turning around.

"It's on full already."

"Are you double-crossing me?... Yes, I know you told me how that special agent got my man's name. But

I've just had a conversation with someone and I have a very bad feeling..."

Tom knew that Swiss was referring to him and Hawks, and the encounter Swiss had just had with his father. By the sound of it, he was talking to Hasni, and Hasni hadn't attempted to cover anything up. But at least Hasni hadn't lied about Hawks's involvement.

"No, I won't calm down. I took you at your word about that man's son. But I warn you, if this goes bad, you're coming down with me."

Not Hasni, then, Tom thought. *That man's son* was a reference to Hasni and Mahmood. So who is he talking to? he thought. Maybe Swiss wasn't in direct contact with Hasni. Maybe Hasni had never met or talked with Swiss. Maybe the ISI had dealt only with Hawks, just as Hasni had told him when he'd held Mahmood at the lock-up. The only thing he did know for certain was that the person Swiss had just talked to had to be integral to the kidnapping. But there was no way he could find out who it was, at least not in the short term.

"Your father sure did spook him, Tom," Lester said.

"He's making another call," said Karen. "He's speaking in French."

"What's he saying, Tom?" Lester asked.

"He's asking if everything is okay... He said they should ensure there's twenty-four-hour security on the gate... That's it."

"Is everything all right, sir?"

It was a woman's voice, with an Eastern European accent.

The bodyguard, Tom thought.

"Yes," Swiss said.

"The chateau is a good place," she said.

"Shut up!" Swiss barked back.

"I've lost the signal," Karen said.

Tom saw the Range Rover pull off the highway.

"You want me to follow them?" Lester asked.

"No. They'll clock us."

"What now, Tom?" Karen asked.

"Chateau in French means a manor house," Tom said, taking out his earpiece.

"So she's in France?" Karen asked.

"Could be, and it would make sense. Swiss was born there, after all," Tom said, his mind racing around to find other connections.

"France is a big place," said Lester. "The hell are we gonna find her there?"

"I'm on it," said Karen.

"On what?" Lester asked.

"Chateaux owned by ADC or Swiss in France."

"We did that already with the warehouse," Lester said. "Something tells me that Swiss wouldn't be dumb enough to keep the US Secretary of State at a chateau directly traceable to him or his business."

"You're right," Tom said. "This guy is alotta things, but dumb he ain't."

He knew that there was a chance that Swiss would escape out of the country before they were able to get to the secretary. But he figured the man's options would be limited and that he'd get what was coming to him sooner or later. He sure as hell couldn't risk lifting him.

"I know what you said, Tom, but there has to be some kind of trail," Karen said. "You can't organize something like this without a trail."

"Lester, you said you were seconded to the Legion," Tom said.

"Yeah, for six months."

"Do you have any contacts there?"

"Too long ago," Lester replied, taking his left hand off the wheel and scratching his head.

"What are you thinking, Tom?" Karen asked.

"I dunno. It's what you said about a trail. I'm missing something. Wait, the secretary could only be taken to France that quickly by air."

"I know a guy who did a spell with the French Air Force in Lyon a couple months back, teaching airfield security systems. He's a freelance consultant. We worked together in Afghanistan for a while," Lester said.

"That's good, Lester. Can you call him?"

"Sure. My bluetooth is in the glovebox there."

Tom opened the glovebox and took out the handsfree headset, handing it to Lester.

"What you want me to say?"

"Ask him if the French Air Force has links with its Pakistani counterparts," Tom said.

Lester checked his cellphone, steering with one hand again.

"How you doin', man? It's Lester… Listen up, that time you spent with the Frenchies, they have links with the Pakistanis?… Yeah, I know it's a weird question, but did they?… Hold on a minute there, brother."

Lester took off his headset. "He said the French are tight with the Pakistanis. The Pakistan Air Force used to be equipped with French-made Mirage III and Mirage 5 jet fighters."

"Ask him if the French have any airbases in or near Pakistan," Tom said.

"That it? I don't wanna be cutting him off every few seconds. He'll think I'm playing with him."

"That's it," Tom said.

"Hey, man, this is weird, too. Those Frenchies have any bases in or near Pakistan?... Yeah, I'm serious... No, it ain't a job... Thanks, man. Listen, I got a bottle of Jack with your name on it the next time you're in DC. Good. Stay safe, you hear." Lester removed the headset once more. "Put that back, willya, Tom?" he said, handing it to him.

"Well, what did he say?" Tom asked, taking it from him.

"Not in Pakistan. The closest is in Abu Dhabi."

"That's just across the Gulf of Oman from Southern Pakistan," Karen said. "About five hundred miles. As you said, Tom, the secretary had to be taken to France by air. A military airbase could be a good option. Swiss could have insiders there."

"Pull over," Tom said, seeing a sign for a diner up ahead.

SEVENTY-FOUR

OVER SEVEN THOUSAND miles away, Brigadier Hasni was at the Royal Embassy of Saudi Arabia at House No.14, Hill Road, F-6/3, Islamabad, meeting with the ambassador, Rahul Al-Dhakheel. It was the early hours of the morning and both men hadn't slept properly for two days.

The ambassador wore a blue suit and a pair of brown, tasselled loafers, preferring Western clothes to a dishdasha when he wasn't on official visits. He sat on a padded armchair in a room with a marble floor and mahogany chests, the sealed windows covered by slatted blinds. As Hasni sat down opposite him on a leather sofa he noticed the Arab's attentive eyes on him, so black that they appeared to be all irises, reflecting the bright artificial light eerily. Like an alien's.

"I had a conversation with Swiss. Well, to be truthful, Brigadier, it was more a one-sided shouting match. I'm worried that he's getting overly nervous," the ambassador said.

"I have apologized for what happened. The American special agent was going to kill my son, Mahmood," Hasni replied, referring to Tom Dupree.

"I know. I am grateful for your honesty. Swiss isn't."

"They have never understood us."

The ambassador nodded. "I know you think we have been excessive by asking you to assist, but I'm sure it will turn out to be the right thing to have done," he said. "The Americans will go to war with Iran and do the killing for us. Just as they did in Saddam's Iraq. They can't help themselves, you know."

"Let us hope so."

Agreeing to have the secretary kidnapped in Islamabad had been a huge gamble. Hasni knew the plan was in danger of breaking apart now. Swiss might speak out, if only to save his own skin. Even though he had never met the man or had a conversation with him, it was a fair assumption to make. But he also knew that Swiss and the ambassador's business relationship was strong, Swiss's company selling millions of dollars' worth of arms to the ever-nervous Saudis.

"So, Brigadier. I can safely leave this in your capable hands, yes?"

Hasni was used to diplomats speaking indirectly, but he really didn't know what the Arab was referring to. He was sure his face hadn't shown any emotion, something his military father had trained him not to do in childhood. But he needed clarity. "Mr Ambassador, I'm not sure what you mean."

The Arab grinned. "Forgive me. You must take care of the unbelievers."

"All of them?"

"Indeed."

"The same terms?" Hasni asked.

"Of course."

Hasni nodded once. He understood now. As far as the minor players were concerned, he was already on it. But whether it was just a glitch or something worse, Swiss and those who knew too much would die as well now. No one would be left to talk. The alternative was to risk being found out. And he had a lot to answer for. Due to his political influence, together with the customary bribe, he'd persuaded the new Prime Minister to invite the Secretary of State to Islamabad at precisely the time the Arab had asked him to. But they had absolutely no intention of handing their nuclear weapons over to the US. It had been a ruse.

That act alone had bagged Hasni one million US dollars from the Saudi. After he'd ensured her abduction outside the children's hospital and subsequent removal from the country, he'd gotten another million. Once he'd disposed of the Westerners, he now had the promise of the same amount again. Good money. Too good to pass up. Besides, it suited him for the US to go to war with Iran. The thought of those Shia lunatics invading south-west Pakistan and taking their natural resources was intolerable.

The Arab's right, he thought.

It was, after all, the definitive insurance policy against someone becoming a squealer. Yes, he thought, a clean shot between the eyes, just as he'd done to Sandri Khan. But not before he'd had all of his teeth removed with pliers. If the American special agent Tom Dupree had badly injured Mahmood, he would have ensured that Khan's death had taken days.

SEVENTY-FIVE

LESTER EASED INTO the slip lane and drove slowly into the diner's parking lot, which was surrounded on three sides by monkey-puzzle trees and large concrete pots brimming with goldenrods and Russian sage. The lot was crammed with trucks and cars whose owners, Tom guessed, preferred to drink coffee and eat burgers rather than watch their gas monitors drop as they crawled along the highway.

He quickened his pace across the tarmac with Lester and Karen to escape a downpour. In terms of motive, he could see that Swiss had one now. What his father had said about Swiss's business making money out of a war had gotten him thinking. If the cuts bit as deep as his father said they would, Swiss's business would lose billions. Men and women killed and died for a tiny fraction of that, he thought. If the secretary died, thousands, maybe hundreds of thousands, would die as well. America would go to war again.

After entering the diner, they sat at a window booth, the oblong table finished in blue Formica, a bunch of laminated menus in a red plastic holder. It was noisy and cramped, the place packed with families, truckers and suits. Karen opened up her laptop and began typing.

"So this is what we have," Tom said, rubbing his eyes.

Karen stopped typing and looked up.

"She's being held at a chateau," Tom went on. "She

was likely flown from Pakistan to a French military airbase in Abu Dhabi, and from there to a base in France. So for openers we're looking for French military airbases located in France. I guess there's maybe twenty-five sites."

"Thirty-eight," Karen said, her hands flying over her laptop again. "And we need to find out what military transport planes left the base in Abu Dhabi in the last forty-eight hours and landed at one of those sites. The base in Abu Dhabi is called Air Base 104 Al Dhafra."

"And how do we do that?" Lester asked. "You can't find that on your computer, right?" He scratched the top of head, his eyes squinting.

"Not in our current timeframe, no. But listen to this. CDAOA. That's France's Air Defence and Air Operations Command. It's responsible for all air operations, both public and military. Based in Paris," she said, reading from the screen. She looked up at Tom. "You make out you're a high-ranking Air Force officer. You act arrogant. Some clerk will put you through to air-traffic control. The flight has to be cargo. It's already happened. There is no security risk. The chances are they'll tell you where the plane landed. Then we go from there."

"You're smart, Karen," Tom said. "Real smart."

Karen wrote a number down on a napkin and gave it to him.

A middle-aged waitress came over, her hands holding a pencil and pad. She wore thick glasses and had a bad perm, a mass of blonde frizz above her red forehead. "What can I get ya?" she asked, taking the menus from the holder and putting them down on the table before using her fingers to place them under their faces.

"As we're here, we might as well get some hot chow," Tom said. "I don't know when we'll eat again."

They placed an order.

"I'll make the call outside," Tom said.

He got up, walked past the tables and booths to the automatic glass doors, the smell of fried food filling his nostrils. Sheltering from the rain underneath a concrete overhang, he made the call to the number that Karen had given him, speaking French. The woman operator put him through to a non-commissioned officer. It took Tom a few minutes of coaxing, badgering and veiled threats before the man confirmed that only one French military cargo plane had flown out of Air Base 104 Al Dhafra in the past forty-eight hours. It had landed at Évreux-Fauville Air Base, located about two miles east of the town of Évreux in Normandy, northern France. The base was home to two French tactical transport squadrons flying mostly cargo planes. Tom worked out the time-zone changes on the cell's calculator. If the secretary had been held for a while in Southern Pakistan, it fitted well.

He jogged back to the booth, excusing himself to a big guy heading for the restroom and a waitress carrying several plates up her forearms. He sat down next to Lester. The food and coffee had arrived, and Lester was shovelling eggs into his mouth as if he were trying to break a record.

"And?" Karen said, holding up her palms.

"It worked. See what chateaux you can find near Évreux-Fauville Air Base, Normandy."

"I gotta make a call, too," Lester said, wiping his mouth with a napkin.

"Who to?" Tom asked, his voice more abrupt and suspicious-sounding than he'd intended.

He glanced at Lester. He was staring hard at him.

"We all gonna sprout wings and fly across the Atlantic Ocean? Or maybe you think airport security will just turn a blind eye to the weapons I got in back of my van?"

"I'm sorry, man," Tom said, bowing his head.

"After I sort that out, I'm gonna take a leak. You wanna watch, just in case I got a wire down there?"

SEVENTY-SIX

IN NORMANDY, PROCTOR unlocked the large padlock and swung over the hinged metal arm that added strength to the door, which he felt was appropriate, given the secretary's previous escape attempt in Karachi. He bent down and picked up a plate of food—an overcooked hamburger and salad with curled leaves—before raising himself up and jerking open the door. Stepping into the makeshift cell, he saw her sitting on a wooden chair, reading the Bible that'd been left for her on the table. She looked up at him, but quickly lowered her eyes to the page.

"Good read?" he said, his tone thick with sarcasm.

"'Do not give what is holy to dogs, and do not throw your pearls before swine,'" she replied, grinning.

He found both her words and demeanour strangely unnerving, and placed the plastic plate on the floor, glad that it had been agreed not to give her cutlery.

"Eat it. When you do, I'll bring you some water."

She didn't respond.

"Did you hear me?"

She ignored him.

Proctor suddenly felt the urge to shock her into a response. The bitch's silence was condescending, and as a teenager from a public housing estate in the north of England, who'd joined the army as a private, he'd had his fair share of that in his life. Despite his military expertise and the fact that he'd learned to speak fluent Arabic and fly a helicopter, his past still made him feel insecure at times. Swiss, the man who'd hired him for the task, had phoned him when he'd gotten back to his office in Arlington County after the incident at the warehouse, and had told him about the secretary's head of security. He decided to use the info to get to her.

"Tom Dupree will be dead by now."

She didn't flinch.

"Tortured in ways you can't imagine and shot in the head."

With her head still down, she said, "He was the bravest man I knew."

"He was a little man; a flunkey."

"I know that by showing your face, I'm likely to be killed."

"Killed, yeah. In style. Just as it said on the video."

This time she looked up, her eyes defiant. "I'm ready."

"Sure you are. You want to know why?"

"What difference does it make?"

Her composure riled him. "You, missus, are a catalyst, the dictionary definition of which is a person or thing that precipitates an event."

"I know what it means."

He crouched down, so that he was level with her. "I suppose someone who has had a hand in sending thousands to their deaths finds it difficult to understand that they themselves can become a victim. I get that. But here's how it's going to appear. The Leopards won't get what they've demanded. The Iranians won't step in to save you. And after that, the people I work for won't lose billions in military contracts. You are the catalyst

"As we're here, we might as well get some hot chow," Tom said. "I don't know when we'll eat again."

They placed an order.

"I'll make the call outside," Tom said.

He got up, walked past the tables and booths to the automatic glass doors, the smell of fried food filling his nostrils. Sheltering from the rain underneath a concrete overhang, he made the call to the number that Karen had given him, speaking French. The woman operator put him through to a non-commissioned officer. It took Tom a few minutes of coaxing, badgering and veiled threats before the man confirmed that only one French military cargo plane had flown out of Air Base 104 Al Dhafra in the past forty-eight hours. It had landed at Évreux-Fauville Air Base, located about two miles east of the town of Évreux in Normandy, northern France. The base was home to two French tactical transport squadrons flying mostly cargo planes. Tom worked out the time-zone changes on the cell's calculator. If the secretary had been held for a while in Southern Pakistan, it fitted well.

He jogged back to the booth, excusing himself to a big guy heading for the restroom and a waitress carrying several plates up her forearms. He sat down next to Lester. The food and coffee had arrived, and Lester was shovelling eggs into his mouth as if he were trying to break a record.

"And?" Karen said, holding up her palms.

"It worked. See what chateaux you can find near Évreux-Fauville Air Base, Normandy."

"I gotta make a call, too," Lester said, wiping his mouth with a napkin.

"Who to?" Tom asked, his voice more abrupt and suspicious-sounding than he'd intended.

He glanced at Lester. He was staring hard at him.

"We all gonna sprout wings and fly across the Atlantic Ocean? Or maybe you think airport security will just turn a blind eye to the weapons I got in back of my van?"

"I'm sorry, man," Tom said, bowing his head.

"After I sort that out, I'm gonna take a leak. You wanna watch, just in case I got a wire down there?"

SEVENTY-SIX

IN NORMANDY, PROCTOR unlocked the large padlock and swung over the hinged metal arm that added strength to the door, which he felt was appropriate, given the secretary's previous escape attempt in Karachi. He bent down and picked up a plate of food—an overcooked hamburger and salad with curled leaves—before raising himself up and jerking open the door. Stepping into the makeshift cell, he saw her sitting on a wooden chair, reading the Bible that'd been left for her on the table. She looked up at him, but quickly lowered her eyes to the page.

"Good read?" he said, his tone thick with sarcasm. "'Do not give what is holy to dogs, and do not throw that will ensure that that happens. If the US Secretary of State can be murdered, the US public will feel as safe as a seal pup surrounded by great whites."

"You'll all rot in hell," she said.

"I got some living to do first," he said, easing himself upright.

He turned and left.

Walking down the basement corridor, he decided to shave his head again, as he always did before going into combat. A habit. A superstition. He had killed fifty-two men in war. In preparation, he felt no emotion, his mind fixed on wind speed, drag force and air pressure, calculating the bullet's trajectory over the given distance. By the time he squeezed the trigger, he might as well have been firing at mannequins. Poleaxed by a silent bullet from an unseen source, most of his targets were dead when they hit the ground. The aftermath involved filling out a report rather than digging a grave. It had been clinical.

But it will be different this time, he thought.

SEVENTY-SEVEN

BACK AT THE DINER, Lester was still absent, making his call, and Tom saw Karen looking at him disapprovingly.

"Lester's a sweet man and he loves you like a brother," she said.

Yeah, but he's got another side to him, Tom thought. They'd been in a bar fight down in Louisiana a couple of years after he'd dragged Lester out of the rubble in Nairobi. Some redneck with racoon shit for brains had started it after he'd accused Lester of making eyes at his girl. After Lester had taken out the redneck and three of his buddies, he'd looked disappointed that it was over. Lester lived for the action and that was a dangerous trait. Money, too. Maybe I'm getting too paranoid, Tom thought, even for someone trained to be so.

"Tom. You okay?" Karen said.

"What?" Tom said, shaking his head.

"You okay?"

"Sure."

As Lester came back and sat down he said, "We got transport."

"That's good, man," Tom said.

Karen, looking now at her laptop screen, said, "There's only one chateau close to the airbase you mentioned, Tom. It's called Chateau Asean. Looks like it's used by parties of tourists and business types for small conventions."

Then Karen pulled up a basic layout of the chateau from a plan on the site, followed by overhead satellite maps. They spent the next five minutes or so studying them together.

"Likely to be CCTV cameras on the walls," she said. "Either already there or fitted by Swiss's men after they took over the place."

If they did, Tom thought.

"I got that covered," Lester said.

"You have?" asked Tom.

"Trust me."

"What's the contact number?" Tom asked Karen.

Karen scribbled down the number and handed it to him.

Outside the VW, the light was starting to fade, but at least the cloudburst had stopped. Lester said their destination was an isolated airstrip twelve miles inside the Virginia state border, and that he'd organized a small plane to fly them to Normandy. That was the call he'd made at the diner, he added. They would land at a private airfield there, which catered for amateur pilots and shifty types, who might not want to pass through regular customs.

Tom took out his cellphone and thumbed in the number, reading from the napkin that Karen had handed him in the diner. After five ringtones, the call was answered by an elderly woman's voice. Her tone was business-like. She told Tom that the chateau had been booked by a private party for a week. Tom asked if it was his American friends, his cover being that he had lost the address and didn't have their cellphone numbers. He was glad that the woman was elderly. A younger person might have asked why he didn't have his friends' numbers in his cell. She replied in the negative. It was a party of mostly Frenchmen, or at least French speakers. Tom thanked her and disconnected.

"It sounds like we might have the right place," he said, and relayed the conversation to them.

Twenty minutes later, Lester pulled off the highway. After passing through several residential neighbourhoods with white picket fences, well-kept yards and wide drives, he took a right onto a minor road that led them into open country, Davina's voice guiding him all the way.

"We're here," Lester said, taking a left into a field.

The field was maybe five acres, surrounded by cedar trees and a grey-brown, stone-built wall. The runway cut a tarmac swathe through the middle, marked with white distance indicators and staggered stop-lines. Lester pulled into a small lot, linked to a timber-frame bungalow by an asphalt walkway. Beyond the bungalow was a green hangar and an outbuilding. A red wind cone flapped languidly against a steel pole between the bungalow and the hangar. Tom thought it looked more like a weekend flying club than an airport.

"Just gimme a minute," Lester said, getting out and walking over to the bungalow.

Karen turned to Tom. "If something does go wrong over there and I don't make it—"

"Don't say that, Karen."

"No, I know. But if I don't make it, will you promise me something?"

Tom almost said he wouldn't let anything happen to her, but stopped himself, feeling suddenly inept.

"Go ahead," he said.

"My parents never wanted me to join the military. It scared them, I suppose. They felt it wasn't what a girl should do. They're old-fashioned that way. I love them, but they have always worried about how I earn a living. When I left the army, they thought I'd seen sense. Anyway, I couldn't bear for them to see me dead on some news network, my face all bloody or whatever. I just couldn't bear that. So, if something does happen, please, Tom, just cover my face, would you?"

She moved her hand down to his and held it gently.

"You'll be fine."

"Promise me."

He nodded, slowly.

"Thank you, Tom."

SEVENTY-EIGHT

SWISS CLOSED THE panelled door behind him, leaving the chair of the Senate Committee on Armed Services sitting in his congressional office on the second floor of a fifties office block in the Capitol Complex, The Dirksen Senate Office Building. A seven-storey structure faced in white marble. The senator was fifty-eight years old with balding grey hair, reddened skin and a solid paunch. He'd cultivated a past that hinted of old money, although Swiss knew he'd worked the nightshift four times a week at a fish-processing factory in order to put himself through Stanford, and had spent the summers on construction sites in San Jose, the city of his birth. But he had power. The kind of power that could ensure the reversal of the military cuts and that revenge was meted out to the secretary's fabricated killers. The cutbacks would mean near-financial disaster for ADC, since it would hit mostly weapons-and-equipment procurement.

Swiss took the elevator down to the lobby. Outside, he stood on the sidewalk, away from the barrier and the black-metal security bollards, opposite the guarded parking lot. He watched his Range Rover pull up at the sidewalk on the other side of the road. He felt a chill go through him, put it down to the wind cutting across the intersection of Constitutional Avenue and 1st Street, and buttoned up his dove-grey overcoat. Grimacing, he took out a disposable cellphone and spoke in French to a guard at the chateau in Normandy, asking for Proctor.

After a few minutes, the Englishman said, "What's wrong?"

"I'm not sure yet. But something is."

"You want me to move her?"

"No. Besides, we don't have time."

"You want me to do it now?" Proctor asked.

"No. We have to proceed as planned. But when it's over I have a new job for you back here, if you're still for hire."

"Could be."

Swiss hit the disconnect button, thinking that he would get Proctor to work on the two-star general called Dupont. He'd find out what he knew and then order him killed.

Travelling in the Range Rover to his home a mile or so from Pentagon City, he still felt rattled. He'd had to kill a good man, Hawks, and all because Brigadier Hasni, the ISI boss, had ratted him out to the DS special agent called Tom Dupree.

If the whole plan was compromised as a result, he was finished. But dead men didn't speak, and he hadn't been called after leaving the warehouse. He guessed Tom Dupree really hadn't known anything. He could have stayed around, just to be sure, but he had no stomach for torture. Never had. When a gnarled-faced Legion sergent-chef, a veteran of the Battle of Kolwezi in Zaire in 1978, had suggested cutting the ears off a terrified Iraqi prisoner during the Gulf War in 1990, Swiss, who was then a young officer, had threatened to court-martial him for even suggesting it. His world had changed since then. Now he allowed such things, but only on the proviso that he didn't have to witness them firsthand. Just like every politician he had ever known.

Sitting in the back seat beside him, his Russian bodyguard took a call on her cell. He turned his head, saw her nodding silently, her face as white and hard as alabaster; her blue-green eyes unblinking.

"Our source at Pentagon says all leave cancelled for the Marine Corp and 101st Airborne Division. They put on twenty-four-hour standby," she said, disconnecting.

More good news, he thought. But he couldn't stop himself from saying, "The man's a useless leech. That kind of information could've been picked up from a private's wife at a grocery store."

The woman shrugged.

He thought about the Saudi ambassador. He'd been contacted by him six months ago. His proposition had been stark and ambitious: the kidnapping and murder of the US Secretary of State. If he could organize the men, the ambassador would ensure that the Pakistanis wouldn't interfere. They would, in fact, facilitate it. Apart from bringing about a war with Iran, which could only benefit ADC, the ambassador had promised him exclusive contracts with the Saudi military.

Although the survival and growth of his business was his overriding driving force, Swiss found it peculiar that the US had such close links with the Saudis. Politically, the country was essentially a feudal system, with no voting rights. Eleven of the fifteen hijackers in the 9/11 attacks were Saudis, after all. Women were forbidden from driving and people were still executed for sorcery. Saudi Arabia wasn't exactly a model state.

It was, he knew, the natural reaction to what the Saudi religious leaders had been preaching for years:

Wahhabism, an extremist form of Sunni Islam. The CIA considered it the soil in which al-Qaeda grew. And yet in the Arab world, the Saudis were seen as the most pro-Western state, despite being the biggest backer of anti-Western Sunni terrorist groups. A paradox, perhaps.

But Swiss knew that for years the Saudis had increased oil production in order to boost the US economy at times that coincided with presidential elections. The deal had been the same since Roosevelt had met with the founder of the Saudi kingdom: security for oil. Politicians had gained personal and family wealth from that arrangement. But it also meant that whereas Iraq and Afghanistan had felt the full force of US military might, the Saudis had escaped it. Whether the Washington elite had allowed personal gain to dictate US foreign policy was an argument he had no intention of getting into. For him personally, though, it was obvious.

As the Range Rover reached the gated entrance to his country spread—a seven-bedroom, single-storey ranch house with four paddocks, three lines of stables and miles of fenced grassland—he'd calmed down a little. The world was full of contradictions, he thought. But if selling arms for a living was deemed morally reprehensible, politics and the oil business were Faustian pacts.

SEVENTY-NINE

Tom watched Lester walking back to the van. Karen had opened the door and had slid out, saying that she had to check her bag. He decided to call Crane.

"Tom, it's good to hear from you, although if anyone is checking my calls they'll think we've got something going on between us."

"Are you done?"

"You can't last in this job without a little humour, Tom."

"The man responsible for the abduction of Lyric is called Peter Swiss."

"Wow, hold on there. That's a helluva statement to make."

"I got the proof. He's the CEO of ADC, the corporation that Hawks worked for."

"You said *worked* for."

"Swiss killed him."

"What?"

"I've got it on video. But don't bring him in. Watch the borders and airports if you must, but don't bring him in yet."

"Why's that?" Crane asked.

"Because those that have Lyric will likely kill her and disappear."

"And they are?"

"I don't know exactly. But I'm pretty certain she's being held in Normandy, France."

"I know where Normandy is," Crane said, his tone serious. "But what does *'pretty certain'* mean?"

"You of all people should know that nothing's certain in this game, right?"

As he was telling Crane the exact location, Karen opened the door and he held up his hand so that she wouldn't interrupt him.

"I gotta contact the DCRI," Crane said, referring to France's Central Directorate of Interior Intelligence. "But it'll take them hours to get organized, put a team together and arrive there from Paris."

"What about their Special Forces?" Tom asked

"They've got the 1st Marine Infantry Parachute Regiment. That's their equivalent of the British SAS. But they're based in Bayonne in the far southwest. I don't even know if they're at their base. Anyone else, it'll be hours, too."

"I thought they were fast-response."

"That generally means twenty-four hours. What are *you* gonna do, Tom?"

"I'm going to France. The French intelligence service ain't trained for sophisticated hostage situations."

"Neither are you. Unless you're not telling me everything. And I don't wanna bring you down too hard, but you got as much chance of hooking up with them as they got of bringing back the monarchy. Gimme one good reason why they gonna do that?" Crane asked.

"I'm still head of Lyric's protective detail. That's gotta mean something. Besides, I know something nobody else does."

"And that is?"

"I'll call you when I land," Tom said. "Just tell them

that. And I know I don't have to say it, but if the place is crawling with cops she won't get out alive."

"I can't guarantee the DCRI will go for it, but I'll do my best. Someone's gonna have to make a quick decision about how we're gonna get Lyric outta there. And, Tom?"

"Yeah."

"Steve Coombs had a bank account in the Caymans with three million in it."

Swiss's blood money, Tom thought.

"But that's not all, Tom. I got a hold of his medical records, too. He'd been diagnosed with brain cancer a year ago, told that he wouldn't reach his fiftieth birthday."

So it was the money, but not for him. His family, Tom thought. He disconnected the call, remembering Coombs complaining about headaches as they stood outside the secretary's temporary office in Islamabad the morning she was taken.

"How long before we get the plane?" Tom asked Lester as he came up to the van.

"Thirty minutes tops."

Tom jumped out and Karen came over to join them. Lester pulled out the two reinforced-plastic cases from the back of the van and lowered them onto the damp grass. He flicked open the clasps and lifted the first lid.

"These here are state-of-the-art lasers." Lester took out four separate shafts, which he proceeded to fit together into a long black tube, a full metre long. "This was adapted from a tank-based prototype used in the Gulf War," he said, smiling broadly and holding up the tube. "I call it the Stingray."

He explained that CCTV cameras could be taken out because they were imperfect mechanisms, susceptible to both what he termed blooming—where the camera sensor was overloaded—and lens flare, caused by light filtering into the internal glass. The CCTV cameras on the chateau's wall could be located by an anti-sensor laser, which picked up the glints of reflected light. They were disabled as the Stingray switched to a high-energy laser capable of overloading the sensor behind the CCTV cameras' lenses.

"And this," he went on, putting down the tube and picking up a shorter one about half as long and the circumference of a nightstick, "is an adaption of the US Air Force Saber 203. An antipersonnel laser used to dazzle."

"Dazzle?" Karen asked.

"That's a technical term for spot-blindness. It causes disorientation and enough delay for someone to stand, aim and pop a cap in enemy ass. And it ain't no coincidence that I got an M16 for you, Karen. This baby fits into the grenade-launch mechanism. The beam shoots out in line with the scope. Effective up to three hundred metres."

"Does it cause permanent blindness?" Tom asked.

"Nope. Unfortunately."

"What's in the other case?" Karen asked.

Lester opened the second lid, which looked like an outsized hatbox, and took out something that resembled a TV satellite dish. "This is anti-personnel sonic sound system."

"We gonna drive them mad with Gangsta Rap, Lester?"

"That ain't funny, Tom. And it's ancient history," he said, shaking his head. "The prototype was used against protestors in Tbilisi, Georgia, and against them Somali pirates. But, this, hell, it'll send a freakin' elephant to its knees." He grinned. "Effective up to a hundred-metre radius."

He tossed Karen and Tom a pair of ear defenders each.

"You got sensitive ears, Tom. You don't wear those, you won't have to worry about that no more, cuz you won't be hearing jack shit. Okay?"

Lester said the plugs were reinforced military ones, adapted precisely for use with the sound system.

"These are somethin', Lester," Tom said, referring to the weapons. "I'll give ya that. But we're hooking up with the French intelligence service if all goes well. We won't need them. We won't even be allowed to use our SIGs."

"Whatever," Lester said. "I'll show y'all how they work anyways. We got the time."

Lester spent the next twenty minutes teaching them how to use the equipment, which was surprisingly easy.

EIGHTY

A BOMBARDIER CHALLENGER business jet, black and shiny like a beetle's back, appeared out of a bank of cloud as dusk was fading. The plane could fly for four thousand miles and was capable of taking off and landing on an airstrip of a hundred and fifty metres or less. Three of them were on standby in DC for corporations and wealthy individuals twenty-four-seven. Tom wondered how Lester could have afforded it, but guessed that his business was doing better than he'd let on.

He checked his watch. 21:04. Fifteen hours to go.

The jet seated nineteen people in cream-coloured leather seats, with touch-screen entertainment, Internet access and fold-away teak tables. There was a well-stocked galley up front, and a baggage bay accessible in-flight in back.

After they'd loaded up and fixed their seat belts, Tom took out his small Buddha and began rubbing the mahogany surface with his thumb.

"That for luck, Tom?" Karen asked, sitting opposite.

"Not exactly."

She cocked her head to one side. "And?"

"It's freaky, you ask me," Lester said, sitting across the deep-piled carpet, fiddling with his iPod.

"That Miles Davis?" Tom asked.

"Who else?" he said, closing his eyes.

"So, Tom," Karen said, "you were going to tell me about your little friend."

"It's nothing, really," he sighed. "Okay. It's not a religion; more a psychological aid. It's about controlling emotions by controlling thoughts and behaviour. In this way, you can experience a calmer mind, although, I have to admit, it ain't working lately. But, for me, a calm mind is an optimal state of mind."

She nodded, and he saw something in her face that spoke of recognition; regret, too.

"I guess a calm mind is important in your line of work," she said.

Not exactly, he thought. But he refrained from saying that DS agents were taught to have a paranoid mind-set, at least on duty. It would only complicate matters.

They chatted for a further five minutes or more. She had a knack of getting him to open up. But in truth, he felt a need to. He told her something he hadn't told anyone for years. His mother had gone to the local store one day when he was a teenage kid. But she never returned. She died that day on her way home. As a result, he was brought up by his maternal grandparents in a small town in Louisiana, ten miles from where he'd lived with his mother. Good people, he said, generous with their time. His granddaddy had taught him to fly-fish; a helluva lot else besides.

"I joined the DS after college and got posted to Bang-kok. I met a woman there."

"A woman?"

"Not like that. She helped me to begin to come to terms with what had happened, I guess."

"Was your mother killed in a car accident?" she asked.

"No." He looked at her straight in the eyes. "I killed her."

Karen's forehead creased up. "I don't understand, Tom."

"I shoulda been there for my momma. I promised her I'd pick her up. I went fishing with a buddy instead. She decided to walk home. They found her body in a shallow grave less than a mile from our house. She'd been raped and murdered by an ex-con," he said, his eyes glistening over.

He realized he hadn't told anyone that.

Ever.

But the emotion it'd evoked hadn't been the one he'd imagined it would. It was cathartic rather than shameful.

EIGHTY-ONE

HOURS LATER, THE jet banked through grey, ribboned clouds before descending in steep steps, each one making Tom's stomach flip as he tried to pop his ears. For a man who travelled frequently by plane, his body had never quite attuned itself to altitude. He felt queasy.

Beneath the cloud line, the outskirts of Rouen were just visible in the distance, the capital of Upper Normandy, the Seine snaking through it like a dull brown cable.

"Down there," Lester said to Tom, pointing at five o'clock.

There was a large square of grass, edged by high hedges, with acres of fields beyond. The outline of two buildings was in the far left-hand corner. It looked like a farm. After giving Lester the thumbs up, Tom reached over and shook Karen's knee gently. She had fallen asleep less than an hour after take-off. As she blinked herself awake he checked the time difference. Paris was six hours ahead of DC, which, after the eight-hour flight, meant it was midday here. Seven hours and counting.

Karen stretched her arms and yawned. She made eye contact. "Are we here?"

Tom nodded.

They landed a few miles outside Rouen, some thirty miles from Évreux. Karen estimated that it would take them about an hour to get to the chateau. Lester told them to stay put for a couple of minutes, took their passports and left the plane, heading for a breeze-block building. The hangar next to it had looked like a barn from above. It struck Tom that it was purposefully deceptive.

"How is Lester going to get us through customs with all this firepower?" Karen asked.

"They don't have customs at airfields like this. They rely on people's honesty. It's a system of prior notification and permission, or not as the case may be. Just like back in Virginia."

"Places like these cater for small aircraft and they rely on honesty?"

"You can get searched, but it's rare. It's mostly just a paper exercise." He saw her scoff. "Yeah, I know, makes as much sense as asking a junkie to mind a drugs store."

"Are you okay, Tom?" she asked, reaching over and placing her hand on his.

He looked at her, found himself asking her to stay put in his mind again. But he said, "Don't worry about me." He took out his cell. "I gotta make a call."

"You want some privacy?"

He thought about it. "No. We're in this together," he said, searching the speed-dial numbers.

He called Crane, who said that he'd swung it before telling Tom the directions to the rendezvous point where he'd meet up with three operatives from the DCRI.

"Only three?" Tom asked.

"Trustworthy men I've worked with before. French Special Forces are getting it together as we speak. But it could be another couple hours before they arrive.

What's the one thing you know that nobody else does, Tom?"

"Something we can get them to ask Lyric to check she's alive if we have to."

"And?"

"She gave me a present in Islamabad the morning she got taken. A diamond-studded silver Omega. No one else knows that as far as I'm aware."

Tom still had it on him. He would keep the engraved message to himself for now: *To Tom with heartfelt gratitude. Linda G. Carlyle. US Secretary of State.*

"Don't do anything dumb."

"I'll call you in an hour," Tom said, disconnecting.

"Everything okay?" Karen asked.

"Everything's fine."

"I need some air," she said.

She got up and disappeared through the clamshell door. He saw her a few seconds later, stretching on the grass, her arms clasped above her head, her sweater and T-shirt riding up as she flung her head back and drank in the cool air. Behind her, Tom saw Lester emerge from the building and get into a dark-green Land Rover that was parked between a Citroën and a Fiat on the small lot adjacent to the building, thinking that his friend was…what? Too resourceful? He shook his head and dismissed the notion. The sooner this was over, the better. He felt as if his mind was deliberately playing tricks with him and he didn't care for it. He got up and walked down the short flight of steps to the narrow runway.

Lester parked the car next to the plane, so that they could unload the equipment into the large trunk space. He said that he'd agreed with the pilot and co-pilot that they'd hang around for six hours. They would refuel via the truck parked on the other side of the hangar. If they didn't get a call to stay longer, they'd fly back to the States. Tom put his arm on Lester's shoulder, leading him away from where Karen was still stretching her body.

"I went back to Islamabad the same day the secretary was taken. I met up with a Pakistani, a CIA asset. I nearly got captured by the ISI. A few hours later, a bunch of guys at a remote roadblock had my photo on their cells."

"They know you were coming?" Lester asked.

"A CIA guy in Kabul said his room had been bugged, so when we'd discussed the fact that I was going over the border, I guessed that someone was listening," Tom said, referring to Crane. "He figured my cell had been bugged, too."

"That's why you asked the DS agent I capped at Fresh Pond."

"Coombs, yeah. He coulda bugged the room. He sure as hell sent the photo of me to them." Tom kept quiet about the CIA woman, figuring it would complicate matters for Lester.

"So that's it, right?"

"I guess. But Coombs didn't admit to bugging the room."

"No, he didn't," Lester said. "He just made a noise as he was dying."

"And, Lester, let's just keep this between us. I don't want Karen getting spooked for nothing."

EIGHTY-TWO

RAHUL AL-DHAKHEEL WAS sitting at an ornate desk in a high-backed chair, the rosewood-panelled walls half covered with photographs of him shaking hands with the famous people he'd met in his career.

The room was the ambassador's study, with numerous leather-bound religious books in gilded cases. It was also a showcase for his collection of Islamic antiques: engraved brass coffee pots, calligraphic panels, silver vases and valuable murals; all protected from the world behind locked glass cabinets. He'd spent hours reading here; hours admiring the skills of the artisans who had created such exquisite works, too. But now his mind was on pragmatic matters.

The two-thousand-strong House of Saud had ruled his country since the kingdom had been established in 1932. Back then, he knew his nomadic grandfathers would've gladly traded land for camels; water, even. Now the absolute monarchy had the world's second largest oil reserves, and was ranked sixth in terms of natural gas. Allah had willed that they live in a desert, but He had buried enormous wealth beneath it.

They had used that wealth to expand their influence and defeat their enemies, usually by proxy, spending twenty-five billion dollars to support Saddam Hussein in his war with Shia Iran. That backfired after the tyrant attacked Kuwait. They feared they were on his target list. As a result, the then Saudi king invited 400,000 US troops onto their sacred land, an act that prompted bin Laden to become radicalized and led ultimately to 9/11. The ambassador knew the unofficial reason was that the White House believed that the invasion of Iraq would produce a Shia regime to be a pro-Western counterbalance to a Shia Iran. But the opposite happened. The Iraqi president was a friend of Iran, who'd backed the Russian opposition to the West's intervention in Syria. Added to which, the US removal of Saddam both led to the Sunni-Shia civil war that was raging in Iraq, and sparked the current region-wide Shia revival to get back at the Sunnis. But the world was changing and with it those who wielded power. The new king's links with the US were in danger of blinding him to that. Besides, as the ambassador knew well, within a few years the US would be almost self-sufficient in oil, due to its fracking operations.

As a result, he had decided to work closely with the so-called Brothers of Faith, a group of five of the king's nephews who were opposed to the monarch's lack of vision and decisive action. Just as Saddam's Iraq had been a threat, Iran had replaced it. But apart from encouraging the US to go to war, the king had refused to bend to the Brothers' promptings to go down a unilateral route. He wasn't alone. Without the US, many in the House of Saud believed that their influence in the Middle East would dwindle.

But the future lay, Rahul believed, with China. The Iranians knew that, too. China now imported fifteen per cent of its oil from Iran. Although the US was encouraging the Chinese to wean itself off this supply, the opposite was happening. China had become the world's largest importer of oil, and was hungry for natural gas. Due to geographical necessities, only Iran could pipe in the seemingly insatiable demand. The Chinese saw Iran as the new power in the region, and would, in time, protect them with its enormous and expanding military, he believed. Just as the US had protected his own country for decades, and for just the same reason. Military security for energy security.

Knowing he was already a trusted confidante, the Brothers of Faith had asked him what should be done about all this. To some, this would have been treasonous. But he'd convinced himself that it wasn't the case. The line of succession in Saudi Arabia was based on agnatic seniority, whereby the crown passed to the king's younger brother, rather than his eldest son. And since the Brothers were the king's nephews, one of their fathers would eventually succeed. In this way, Rahul was just protecting his future, too. And he'd been promised a ministerial post if everything panned out, something that had seemed unreachable in the past.

He had thought about the Iranian conundrum for a full four months. The Saudis had already stoked the sectarian divide in Pakistan, using the Madrassas, agitators, and pamphlet propaganda, together with carrying out bomb attacks on sensitive Sunni sites and blaming it on the indigenous Shia. That had been a successful strategy, leading to the military assuming temporary power and, in turn, sabotaging the Iran-Pak pipeline. But more had had to be done to paralyze Iran's exports and secure Saudi wealth and, more importantly, political influence in the Middle East.

The answer had come to him one night as he'd lain awake, listening to the chirping of cicadas. It was a simple matter of duplication. Turn Iran into something akin to the bloody chaos that was Iraq, the country's infrastructure so decimated by the US and the ensuing civil war that Iraqis had to heat their food in darkness over makeshift braziers.

The only way to do that, he'd told the Brothers of Faith, was to get the US to do it for them, and the only way to do that was to make the US fear and hate them. The Brothers accused him of being as weak as the king. But he outlined the full extent of his geopolitical plan. The Iran nuclear programme, which the Saudis were eager to exaggerate, although the threat was potentially extreme, went a long way to securing the former. The abduction and execution of the US Secretary of State would go a long way to securing the latter, he ventured. The Brothers had, of course, agreed.

He stood now and walked to the huge oblong window that overlooked the embassy gardens. He pulled a weighted string and the slatted blinds flicked open. The early-morning sun poured in. He smiled. His youngest son was riding on the back of an Irish wolfhound. His favourite hunting dog. His favourite son. The boy exuded a near-primal vitality. He was laughing, flinging his head back as he rode. The dog sensed it, too, obeying his son's every prompting. Both, he concluded, wondrously unsullied by the world around them.

Brigadier Hasni had told him once that he'd sent his son, Mahmood, to Harvard to enable him to think like the Americans. Rahul had decided to bypass that. His son would one day simply act like them: imperious and feared.

EIGHTY-THREE

THE THREE FRENCH DCRI operatives had done some initial covert surveillance of the chateau, with high-powered scopes and long-range listening probes, after getting the call from Crane hours ago. The operative in charge was called Philippe, a fifty-two-year-old with a weather-beaten face and the flattened nose of a boxer. He'd worked with Crane on a number of occasions, and both liked and trusted him. But something wasn't right. The men who'd rented the chateau had looked to him like flabby desk jockeys, rather than hardened mercenaries. There were no visible signs of an attempt at securing the place, either. Satellite observation had likewise come up blank as far as incriminatory evidence was concerned.

After checking in with HQ at Levallois-Perret, Paris, and saying that he felt they had the wrong location, he'd been ordered to make sure. He'd risked calling the local gendarmes, and had asked them to feign a casual passport-checking exercise, the law demanding that all nationals and visitors had to prove their identity if asked.

When HQ had scrutinized the names that had been emailed through, he'd gotten a call to say the men were all bona-fide computer-inkjet salesmen from Marseilles, who were on a team-building retreat. They were going to have some downtime in Paris before flying home.

But half an hour later, he'd taken another call on his

smartphone, and this time the news had been positive. The Normandy connection that Crane had filled him in on was crucial. On the strength of that, he'd rung Crane a few seconds after coming off the phone with HQ.

Philippe had told him that the DCRI had gotten a tip-off that something had gone down in Abu Dhabi. The source was a suspicious caporal-chef, who'd decided that national security overrode personal ambition, although the DCRI had asked that his unofficial smoking break be overlooked. The info had led to a search of the flight records. When the destination of the French Air Force transport plane had become known, the base's CCTV cameras had been checked. They had shown a civilian van.

After Crane's reference to Évreux had been factored in, the plate had been picked up by a traffic-monitoring camera as the van had left the capital en route to Normandy. Following an external search of chateaux within a thirty-mile radius by unmarked police cars, they had found one that might fit the bill. Men on the gate. Razor-wire. CCTV cameras. It was only twelve miles south from the chateau they had under surveillance. Finally, Philippe had given Crane the directions for a new rendezvous point where Tom should meet him.

Philippe had already agreed to meet up with Tom after the initial call from Crane, who'd asked him a special favour and had promised that the head of the secretary's protective detail wouldn't interfere. He was a loyal man, and deserved to be there when she got out. If it weren't for him, Crane said, they would never have known where she was. Besides, the DS special agent knew something that could ensure her identity. Following the most recent call from Philippe, Crane had phoned Tom.

BY THIS TIME, Tom, Lester and Karen had reached the outskirts of Évreux. Crane told Tom that the chateau had been checked out by the DCRI already. That was the bad news. The good news was that the French had found a chateau where she might be. But due to logistical considerations and the fact that it could be another dead end, no roadblocks had been set up as yet. The gendarmes were searching for other potential sites as he spoke. Then he told Tom the new location, saying that only the three DCRI operatives had arrived there so far.

"You can meet up with the DCRI at an intersection about a half-mile from the chateau," Crane said. "The road that passes due west by the chateau forks a hundred metres from the end of the perimeter wall. The left-hand road leads to a copse of trees with a rest stop about twenty metres beyond that."

"Thanks," Tom said.

"But listen to me, Tom. When you get there, you wait with the DCRI operatives, you hear? If no other sites are found and it turns out to be the right place, French Special Forces will go in."

"What's their ETA?" Tom asked.

"An hour, give or take."

Tom turned to Karen and gave her the details. After checking out satellite maps on her laptop, she said that the rest stop wasn't too far away. She gave Lester the location of both the chateau and the rest stop and he punched them into the Land Rover's sat-nav.

Twenty minutes later, Lester drove Tom through the narrow lanes near Évreux, the ancient oak trees overlapping above them and making it dark enough to warrant the headlights being on. Karen had been left a few miles back with the equipment, sitting in a field

beyond a rusted gate that hung off its hinges by a piece
of frayed rope. Tom had told her that if anything went
wrong, she should call Vice Admiral Theodore Birch,
the head of the Bureau of Diplomatic Security in DC,
and had given her the number to ring. He'd said to tell
him everything, then hand-deliver a note he had sealed
in a manila envelope, which stated everything else that
she didn't know.

Lester stopped the van at the entrance to a farm track
that ran the length of a field where cows grazed. He
slipped out and Tom got into the driver's seat, his mind
fixed on finding the secretary and taking her home. He
could sense that the next ten minutes or so would be
vital in achieving that aim. After remaining at the track
while he'd watched the second hand on his watch tick
away for three minutes, he drove off. He figured he'd
reach the rendezvous point in less than sixty seconds.

There were three men, just as Crane had said there
would be, their hands clasping stubby Heckler & Koch
MP7A1 sub-machine guns fixed with suppressors, extended magazines and EOTech holographic day-sights.
They were dressed in black fatigues, standing in front
of a dark-blue Citroën van with tinted windows.

Tom steered the Land Rover into the leaf-strewn rest
stop. As he got out the man he took for the trio's leader
stepped forward, a man well over six feet tall with a
thin mouth like a snake's.

"Mr Dupree?"

"Oui, je suis Monsieur Dupree."

"Parlez-vous français?"

"Oui, je fais."

They proceeded to speak in French.

"You're a foreign national. I'm afraid I will have to escort you to a hotel until this is over."

A set-up, then, Tom thought. He caught a glimpse of a French Foreign Legion tattoo on the well-muscled forearm of one of the men on the right, a green-and-red triangle containing the grenade emblem. He was a stocky guy all over, with sandy hair and ruddy cheeks.

"Did Crane send you?" he asked Snake Lips. He figured the only person who knew he was going to be there was Crane, and that he'd betrayed him. These guys weren't DCRI operatives. They were mercenaries.

"I don't know anyone called Crane."

"No, 'course you don't."

Snake Lips grinned.

"How about Peter Swiss?" Tom turned to the guy with the tattoo. "He's one of you, 2nd Rep."

The man shook his head.

"Is my French not good enough?" Tom asked.

"Your French is good," Snake Lips said. "But that doesn't change anything."

"You came from the chateau, right." Tom guessed that Crane had gotten these guys to take out the DCRI operatives.

Snake Lips smiled, revealing a gold molar. "On your knees. Hands behind your head, if you please, Mr Dupree."

Tom assumed the position on the ground.

EIGHTY-FOUR

THE TATTOOED MAN walked forward, flex-cuffs in his hand. As he bent down to restrain Tom his head jerked back, a spout of blood ejecting from his left temple. Tom sprang up and flung himself at Snake Lips, just as the second man, who'd turned in the direction of the suppressed discharge, was hit in the neck. He collapsed to his knees, his hand grasping his shattered carotid artery, as blood gushed over his fingers.

Tom had hit Snake Lips in the solar plexus with his forehead, winding him and pushing him backwards. As the Frenchman fumbled for his MP7, Tom launched himself into the air. He brought his knee up and simultaneously clasped the man's head in his hands, pulling his face down onto his rising lower thigh. His thigh impacted Snake Lips' nose with a loud crunch, and Tom knew the bone had shattered. As he collapsed sideways Tom finished the Frenchman off with a hook to the jaw. Snake Lips hit the ground in a twisting motion, groaning. Tom stooped down and pulled the gun strap over the man's head before slinging the weapon over his shoulder. He closed his eyes and breathed deeply.

He crouched back down again. *"Parlez-vous anglais?"* he asked, quietly.

"Yes," Snake Lips grunted, face up in the dirt and leaves.

"You wanna live?"

"Yes."

"Good answer."

Lester stepped out from behind an ivy-clothed tree trunk. A suppressed Marine sniper rifle, the bolt-action M40A5, with a scout sniper day-scope, held before his chest, the strap still wrapped around his left forearm.

Looking over, Tom said, "Nice shooting."

"Old habits," Lester replied, his face showing no emotion.

"Our French friend here would like to stay alive."

"He better be a talkative Frenchy, then."

"I don't think there are any other kind," Tom said.

They half carried the injured man into the surrounding undergrowth, and onto the edge of an evergreen forest about thirty metres from the rest stop. Lester secured him to a tree with a length of rope, the man's head lolling to one side, the blood still falling in clots from his broken nose.

"You do that so you ain't the only ugly one?" Lester said to Tom, gesturing to the man's broken nose.

Tom smiled.

After walking back to the rest stop, he and Lester carried the two corpses into the forest. Stripping them down to their underwear, they hid the bodies among nettles and long grasses. They picked up their fatigues and weapons, and walked over to where Snake Lips was tethered, squatting down either side of him.

Tom grabbed the man's cheeks with his hand, pushed his head back against the gnarled trunk roughly. "My friend here is going to work on you if you go dumb on us. Understand?"

"Yes," the man said, his eyes rolling as if concussed.

"Let's keep it short and painless and you'll survive this. You have my word. And my word is good. Deal?"

"Deal."

Tom leaned in close. "Is the Secretary of State still alive?"

"Yes."

"Do they intend to kill her today?"

Snake Lips nodded, dimly.

Tom slapped his face. "Stay with me. When?"

"Half an hour or less."

Jesus, Tom thought. They'd brought the timeframe forward by more than four hours. "How many men are guarding her?"

"Nine."

"Be specific."

"Two on the gate. The other seven are dispersed inside. One is a tech."

"At the chateau close by?"

He nodded.

"Weapons?" Tom asked, grabbing the man's jaw and jerking it up ninety degrees.

"Same as me. MP7s."

"Where is she in the chateau?"

"Basement cell."

"Locked?" Tom asked, staring into the man's eyes.

"Yes."

"Who has the key?"

The man closed his eyes, clearly feigning unconsciousness. Tom jabbed his finger into the pressure point under the Adam's apple, where the trachea passed just below the surface of the skin. Snake Lips began spluttering and shook his head.

"Proctor," he croaked.

Tom let go of him. "Proctor. An American?"

"English."

"Where are the DCRI operatives?"

"Dead."

"Whose orders?" Tom asked, readying himself to inflict more pain. But it wasn't necessary.

"Proctor's," Snake Lips replied.

"How did he know they'd be here?"

"I don't know. I swear."

Tom believed him. "You did good," he said, patting Snake Lips on the shoulder. "You'll live."

"You mean it?"

"I mean it."

He sighed long and hard. *"Merci."*

"But if you're lying, my friend will come back and give you a double tap. Understand?"

"I understand."

"Don't forget that now, Frenchy," Lester said.

Tom and Lester stood up and began to undress. They changed into the fatigues and walked back to the Land Rover, the dead men's MP7s over their shoulders.

"You drive the van," Tom said to Lester.

"You okay, Tom?"

"The CIA man I mentioned told me where to hook up with the French," Tom said, referring to Crane.

"He did?"

"The only person who could've turned this rotten is him. He thinks I'm working alone, so they were only expecting me."

"You figure he's some kinda double agent?" Lester asked.

"I'm not sure what he is. But I now know he's not to be trusted. And, Lester—"

"Don't say it. Just between us."

"Thanks, man."

Driving back to where Karen was waiting with the equipment, Tom rang Birch on his hands-free. He told him what had just transpired and how Crane had to have set him up. "He's a traitor, sir. I don't know who else in the CIA might be involved, so I suggest we keep it in the DS."

"I don't get it. Crane called in French Special Forces. No question," Birch said.

"I guess he was covering his ass. He knows they won't get here in time."

"They will, Tom. I'm sure of that."

"I…"

"What is it, Tom?"

"She'll be dead by then."

"I'm telling you not to do anything by yourself. You could endanger Lyric's life. And if you do, I won't be able to save you. That's a direct order, Agent. Stand down."

"Yes, sir."

But given the reduced timeframe, Tom knew he had to act.

He spent the next five minutes putting together a simple rescue plan. He was glad that Lester had pushed to show them how to use the weapons, because, apart from sounding seriously effective, they were of the disabling variety rather than lethal, and there was no way of knowing whether or not the secretary's location inside the chateau had changed.

EIGHTY-FIVE

PROCTOR FLUNG OPEN the door to the makeshift cell and saw the secretary lying asleep on the bed. He cracked his knuckles loudly. Startled, he saw her eyes flick open, her mouth drawing a sharp breath. But he couldn't tell now whether she was afraid or curious.

"Time for the game to begin, missus," he said, grinning.

"What game?"

"Come on, now, you're an American. There's only one game you know. Winner takes all."

As he moved towards her, he saw her flinch. She had a right to, he thought. By the time he'd finished with her, she'd be wishing she were still drugged in a coffin. She raised a hand as he reached her. A half-hearted if defiant act. He grabbed her fingers, snapping them back. He registered the tears forming in her eyes with satisfaction.

"Why are you doing this to me?" she breathed.

"Because I can," he replied. He clenched a massive fist. "If you relax, it won't hurt as bad. If you fight it, I'll get mad and hit harder."

He saw a blur and felt the fingernails of her free hand rake across his neck, drawing blood.

Grabbing her wrist and pulling it down, he said, "You just made a big mistake."

Knowing what was to come, he wanted to eradicate any spark of resistance and make her as docile as a lamb. Her last reaction had just confirmed that that was necessary.

EIGHTY-SIX

THE SECURITY GATE was wrought-iron and about four metres high, with a length of concertina razor-wire fastened along the top. The wire looked brand-new and Tom guessed that it'd been put in place by Proctor and his men, rather than being a permanent feature. Either side of the gate was a high wall, stone-built and encrusted with dull-green lichen. A few beech trees grew above it, their trunks rising from a grassy verge, which eased down to a flint-ridden pathway, but the branches had been cut back so that they didn't overhang. Beyond the gate, an acre of well-maintained lawns was bisected by a pink-gravel roadway, which led up to the façade of the chateau. The chateau was three storeys high, built in the neo-classical style, with four pillars flanking the arched entranceway.

Two men stood in front of the gate dressed in woollen overcoats. Their hair was cropped, and they had granite faces like bouncers. They carried two-way radios. They chatted to one another and paced about to relieve the boredom.

"They'll be concealing more than handguns under those coats," Lester whispered.

Tom nodded.

They lay enveloped in bracken on the other side of the lane that ran past the gate parallel to the wall. Their faces were streaked with camouflage paint. Tom held a field-scope, Lester his suppressed Marine sniper rifle resting on a bi-pod.

"I can make out one CCTV camera," Tom said, lowering the glass. "Likely to be more."

The cloud was high, the sky still completely overcast, which was perfect weather as far as Tom was concerned. There was no danger of the lasers that Karen would use glinting in sunlight, which could alert the guards on the gate. He checked the time. They had twenty minutes to get in and rescue the secretary before the deadline, if what the Frenchman had said was true, although Tom didn't have any good reason to doubt him.

He tapped Lester on the shoulder. "Time for your kickass weapons, buddy."

They snaked backwards, using their elbows and knees, slow enough not to cause more than the slightest ripple in the undergrowth, although the cool breeze was adding a welcomed dimension to masking their movement. Once they were a few metres from the vantage point, they flipped over and low-crawled another twenty before straightening up in a small clearing beside a brown-coloured stream. Karen was kneeling there, an MI6 carbine fixed with the dazzler in her hands. The two cases with the rest of the equipment that Lester had shown her how to work at the airfield were placed either side of her, her backpack on her back. She wore a camouflage windbreaker and military boots.

Tom tucked the scope into his webbed belt and Lester bagged his rifle before lowering it onto the grass. Tom lifted out the tubes of the large sensor from its case and eased them into his green backpack. Lester took the sound system. As Karen raised herself up Tom and Lester picked up the Frenchmen's MP7s with flash suppressors and, after checking the magazines, slung them over their shoulders. Lester handed Karen a Browning M1911 semi-auto, the stand-issue handgun of the US Marine Corps Special Operations Command.

"You only got seven rounds, but they're .45 car- tridges," he said. "So if you meet a smart grizzly in the woods, he ain't gonna wanna mix it with ya."

Karen nodded.

"We take out the ugly twins on the gate, Tom, that'll be six shooters left and the tech."

Tom glanced over at him. His friend's eyes were on fire.

EIGHTY-SEVEN

USING BRACKEN AND ferns as cover, Tom watched Karen scanning the wall along its visible length with the long anti-sensor laser. She signalled that she'd picked up two glints from the lenses of CCTV cameras hidden in the vicinity, in addition to the one that Tom had already located. She switched the military laser off before the cameras were disabled prematurely.

"They're pointing away from the guards," she whispered, "covering the wall."

"Guards first, then," Tom said. "I'll go left."

Tom took out a coiled, knotted rope with a hook at one end and hung it from his belt. He nodded to Karen, who pointed the M16 towards the guards on the gate. She hit both of their faces in quick succession with the disabling light.

Tom and Lester sprang up and ran forward. The two men, who'd been blinded temporarily, raised their hands to their eyes before reeling around like drunks. As Tom and Lester reached them, they knocked both of them out with quick sharp blows from the butt stocks of the MP7s, hitting them on the sides of their jaws. After they'd dropped, they secured them with flex-cuffs and gagged them before dragging them over to the nearest tree.

The gate was locked by a central control system and couldn't be scaled due to the razor-wire. Tom checked for signs of life, but there weren't any. He jogged over to the wall, signalled to Karen, who activated the probe, which automatically switched to a high-energy laser and overloaded the cameras, disabling them.

He didn't know what level of security the chateau had or had been added to by the tech. There could be infrared detectors or geophones, which monitored vibrations on the ground. There could be hidden microphones or cameras designed to look like flowerpots or rocks. But he just hoped that if they set something off before they reached the chateau proper, the tech would take them for guards. That was the plan. It didn't matter what the windows, doors or interior were protected by—pressure mats, broken-glass detectors and the like—since they'd planned to assault the building head-on.

Tom swung the knotted rope hook first over the wall. Once secured, he began scaling it, pushing his body out and taking the strain with his legs. His hands worked mechanically, the odd jutting-out stone assisting his progress. At the top, he lay flat and pulled the rope up before fixing the hook to the front of the wall and letting the rope fall to the far side. He rappelled swiftly down, crouching on the damp soil a metre or so from clumps of light-yellow peony bushes. He took the field-scope from his belt and checked the front of the chateau. It was clear. He wrapped the rope in an oval around his hand and elbow and, tucking the sharp hook into the middle of the coil, swung it over the wall in a wide arc for Lester. He heard a dull thud as it landed on the grass verge on the other side. Waited.

He saw Lester emerge on top a minute or so later, the sound system filling his backpack, such that his friend looked as if he'd grown a shell. After repeating the manoeuvre with the rope, he crouched beside Tom and slid the MP7's extended butt into his shoulder, aligning his eye with the holographic sight.

"It's quiet," he said.

Yeah, like a graveyard, Tom thought.

Karen appeared and rappelled down, leaving the rope dangling from the wall. Tom just hoped they wouldn't have to use it to escape the place if everything went wrong.

Karen crouched down beside Lester, who took out the sound system and placed it next to her. She would wait for Tom and Lester to reach the chateau, then run up to join them.

"We're gonna stroll up there like we own the place," Tom said, handing Lester a wet-wipe before taking out one for himself.

They scrubbed their faces clean of camouflage paint. Lester took out a black ball cap and pulled it down low so that it was no more than three centimetres from his nose. He squeezed out a line of pale foundation cream from a tube, using it to buff his face into something that could be taken for Caucasian, at least from a distance.

Karen took the initiative, using the laser to knock out two security cameras, which, she said, were perched above the eaves of the roof.

With that, Tom and Lester walked casually towards the chateau along the gravel path, still dressed in the black fatigues of the men Lester had shot at the rest stop.

They got about halfway up before a man wearing eyeglasses, jeans and a sweater emerged from a side entrance. Tom took him for the tech, since he wasn't carrying a weapon. He figured he was checking to see what the problem was after the cameras had malfunctioned.

He called out, and Tom and Lester waved. Before he had a chance to register that something wasn't right, Lester raised his suppressed MP7 and sprayed him with a burst, bringing the gun up in an arc, the rounds cutting into him from waist to shoulder. The man flipped backward and lay splayed on the grey pavestones to the left of the chateau's decorative façade.

They sprinted the remaining twenty metres or so to the right of the chateau's main entrance, crouching down in the narrow portico. Tom waved Karen forward.

EIGHTY-EIGHT

PROCTOR SAT AT an oak desk in front of a flat computer screen, slicing an apple with his Ka-Bar knife. Sixteen centimetres of stainless steel with a serrated edge. The windowless room on the ground floor was a library stacked with musty-smelling books, the high ceiling edged with moulded-plaster cornices.

He glanced at his knuckles. They were a dull red and ached a little. Although he'd worked over the US Secretary of State, something that he'd found strangely empowering, he was thinking that he'd never killed a woman before, let alone at close quarters. He was a sniper, and snipers picked their targets with precision. From a distance. Beheading a woman was something else. He consoled himself by deciding that no one would see the expression on his masked face as the blade sliced through her neck, despite the otherwise macabre theatricality of the spectacle.

A French guard burst in. A pinched-lipped guy with a thin face and a long nose whom Proctor had secretly nicknamed, "The Shrew".

"What's wrong with your radio?" he asked.

Proctor put down the Ka-Bar and picked up the PTT radio on the desk, pushed the activation button. "It's flat."

"We have a problem," The Shrew said.

"What is it?"

"Intruders. Armed."

"Police?"

"Unlikely. Just two men and a woman. But they've killed Jacques already and taken out the CCTV cameras."

"Alert the others. I'll be out in a second," Proctor said.

The Shrew darted out, a worried look on his ashen face.

Proctor took out his cell and phoned Swiss. After a couple of ringtones, he picked up.

"There's an issue," Proctor said.

"Tell me."

"Two men and a woman with attitude problems."

"So deal with them," Swiss said. "Ring me as soon as it's done. Don't fuck it up."

Proctor thumbed the red button, holstered his Slovakian K100 handgun fixed with a red-dot laser sight, stood up and walked from the room.

EIGHTY-NINE

LESTER PLACED THE thirty-centimetre-by-six-centimetre adhesive strip of breaching charge over the lock of the chateau's large oak-panelled door before inserting the delayed primary explosive devices. Karen moved up and crouched beside Tom. He could smell her hair, a slight waft of deodorant, too. It smelled good. When the door was blown off its severed hinges, she would hit the sonic sound system. She'd wait outside, covering the rear.

They all put in their earplugs, which Lester had supplied, and walked backwards, keeping their distance from the wall. Six shooters, Tom thought. It only took one to kill her. He figured their chances were less than fifty-fifty. But he'd known since he'd spoken to the Frenchman masquerading as a DCRI operative, and then Birch, that they were her only hope. French Special Forces wouldn't get here in time. I'm doing the right thing, no matter what Birch and the suits on the Hill have waiting for me, he thought.

If I make it back.

The door was flung outwards, sending shards of wood into the air with the smoke as the shock wave careered down the wall. A split second later, they ran forward. Karen knelt and activated the system, the sound like a mixture of a high-pitched wail and a ship's horn, causing the windows to rattle and ground to reverberate beneath them. Lester edged forward, using the stone archway as cover, and lobbed in a flash grenade. A couple of seconds after it had detonated, he and Tom rushed under the arch where the door had been. Inside, they hunkered down, covering either side of the flagstone vestibule as they moved forward, pointing their MP7s. Stopping just before the large entrance hall, Tom noted the knotted floorboards half-covered by a huge oriental rug, the high ceiling, and the wide wooden staircase leading to a carpeted gallery to the rear.

Once fully inside, he saw a man on his knees to his right, his hands on his ears, blood flowing from them. Lester ran over to him, his boot knocking him unconscious as it connected with his temple. Tom quickly secured his hands and feet with plasticuffs before picking up the man's weapon and slinging it over his shoulder. Despite the plugs, his eardrums were pounding, the constant pulse of the sound system creating a disorientating rhythm, and he struggled to stay upright and move in a straight line. After seeing an archway leading to a corridor to the left, a flight of uneven stone steps to the right, Lester pointed up to the gallery, the back wall draped in a massive mural of a hunting scene. Two men had appeared from either side with MP7s, but they were moving them around awkwardly, their faces contorted in silent screams.

Tom and Lester bolted for cover towards the left-hand corridor, just as a swath of bullets hacked at the floorboards, sending splinters through the air like a volley of blow darts. They crouched down beside an oak grandfather clock, the gilded woodwork gleaming. Lester unclipped a stun grenade and reached out to throw it. As he let go of the grenade he spun around.

His right arm hung limp. A random round had penetrated his bicep.

Tom dived out, falling into a forward roll. The two men were on their knees now, barely able to hold onto their weapons, although one got off a couple of rounds, which hit the lattice ironwork beneath the wooden banister rail, creating a flash of sparks.

Knowing he had just a few minutes to save the secretary, Tom took aim and fired two short bursts, saw them keel backwards.

Struggling up, he swayed back to Lester, who was propped up against the clock, his hand grasping his arm, the blood leaching out in ominous-looking streaks. Abruptly, the sound system stopped. Tom guessed it had malfunctioned. He fixed up Lester's arm as best he could with a makeshift tourniquet, using a handkerchief he'd pulled from a pocket of the fatigues. They both took out their earplugs.

"That mother coulda used that," Lester said, gritting his teeth.

"You wanna bleed out or get snot on your arm?"

"Well, you put it like that." Lester pulled out his SIG. "But I ain't done yet."

Tom pushed Lester to the floor, covering him with his body, as two men came running up the corridor behind him.

"Tom?"

It was Karen's voice. He heard her as she ran through the vestibule, the thud of her boots echoing as they hit the flagstones.

"Get down, Karen!" he shouted.

Covering Lester's head with his forearms, he let off a burst from the sub-machine gun, hitting one of the men in the legs as the other ducked into an alcove. The man he'd hit cried out and buckled to the floor, his weapon falling out of reach.

"Jesus, Tom. Let me up," Lester said.

Tom glanced around, saw the telltale red dot on Karen's chest, emanating from an optical laser-beam sight. She was scanning the hallway with the Browning, but the man with the gun was obviously hidden.

"Karen!"

Lester heaved him off and aimed his SIG at the alcove. "Help her," he said.

NINETY

Tom STRUGGLED UP, hearing the discharge before he could break into a sprint. He saw the Browning fall from Karen's hand. Then another shot rang out. Her body collapsed to the ground, an agonized expression creasing her face.

"Jesus, no," he said. "Karen!"

As he was about to run to her, Tom heard Lester hammering down the corridor behind him, emptying half a clip as he did so. He glanced over his shoulder, almost involuntarily, just as Lester put a round in the head of the man in the alcove. His near-suicidal charge had been successful only because the man had risked ducking out rather than blind firing, conscious, perhaps, that if he missed he would be vulnerable. They had both acted recklessly, and Lester was lucky to be alive.

Tom turned and glimpsed a shaven-headed man disappearing down the stone steps to the basement. The last man. He saw Karen lying on the rug, her body twitching in spasms. He ran towards her, jumping over the body of the man he'd secured earlier. As he got to her, he bent down. Her eyelids were fluttering, her camo windbreaker soaked with blood around the two scorched entry holes.

"Go on," she said, blood oozing from her already blue-tinged lips. "Find her." Her breath was laboured, her voice a murmur.

"Karen, hold on. Just hold on," he said, cradling her head. Her eyes closed, a ghostly moan emerging from her mouth. Then she went limp. He put his hand to her nose, felt nothing. Tears welled in his eyes.

"She's dead," he said, hearing Lester come up behind him.

"We gotta move, Tom," Lester said, putting his hand on Tom's shoulder. "We gotta move now."

"He went down the steps. That's where she is, in the basement."

"C'mon, Tom. We gotta finish this."

Recalling Karen's words to him at the airfield, Tom took off his jacket and placed it over her neck and face. He slumped down afterwards, the impact of the shock of her death making him lose focus. He held her flaccid hand, willing her to somehow open her eyes.

"The secretary," Lester said, dragging Tom up. "He's gone to kill the secretary."

Tom shook his head, took a deep breath and stared blankly at his friend.

"C'mon, Tom. We gotta move," Lester said, grabbing Tom's forearms and shaking them like a pair of maracas.

RUNNING DOWN THE stone staircase with Lester, Tom felt as if his head were about to explode, as if he had come to the limits of his physical and mental self. It was all he could do to stop himself from passing out. But he had to go on. To find her. To fulfil his promise to her. He hadn't had the opportunity to save his mother, although he would've gladly died in the process. If he knew anything at all now, it was that he had to go on. To take revenge on the man who'd killed Karen, too.

As they got to the foot of the steps the corridor went left and right. Tom and Lester hugged the opposite supports beneath a large stone lintel.

"We'll split up," Tom said, his head still buzzing.

"I'll go right."

Tom watched Lester run down the corridor, drops of blood leaving a scattered trail from the entry wound. Looking left, he saw the dim corridor, a few lights affixed to the low ceiling in wire cradles. The gas pipes were exposed against the off-white walls, the floor grey-slate slabs, uneven and cracked with age. As he got halfway down he saw three rooms to the right, another corridor leading off to the left. Uncertain of how to proceed, he crouched down. The chain of events that had led him here were a wake-up call. Many people from Pakistan to the States had been involved in the secretary's abduction. Some were dead or captured. The rest would follow, he told himself.

Hearing footsteps behind him, he glanced around, seeing Lester jogging back along the corridor, shaking his head. Five seconds later, his friend knelt down beside him, breathing heavily and grimacing as he tightened the makeshift tourniquet with his good hand.

"A dead end," he said. "A windowless, granite wall."

"You check the corridor off left. I'll check the rooms," Tom said.

With that, the middle door swung open slowly.

"That's spooky shit," Lester said.

"No, that's flesh and blood that wants us to walk into somethin'."

Tom sighed. He figured she had to be in the room. There was no other reason for the man who had shot

Karen to come down here. Nowhere else for the secretary to go, either.

"What now?" Lester asked.

Before Tom had a chance to answer, a voice called out.

"You got ten seconds. Then I'll blow her face off."

"An English accent. The guy the Frenchy called Proctor. He'll know we won't go in shooting," Lester said.

"I gotta go," Tom said, standing up.

"We come this far. I say we go together."

"You've done a suicide run already, old friend."

"He killed Karen. Your blood is up. That means you ain't thinking straight," Lester said.

Tom figured he was right. They got up together and walked side by side down the corridor towards the open door.

NINETY-ONE

THE ROOM WAS the makeshift cell she'd been kept in, a rank smell of body odour and damp filling it. The secretary sat gagged on a wooden chair. Her body was covered in blankets. Apart from her cut hair, her nose had been broken, her cheeks scarred and bruised. Her face was smeared with blood. Her appearance shocked Tom, but he did his best not to show it.

Proctor was standing beside her, holding a handgun to her head. Tom noticed the laser sight and flinched. It could only have been Proctor who had killed Karen, the shaven-headed man he'd glimpsed running down to the basement, but the physical confirmation had sent a jolt of aggression through him. He wore green fatigues and high, laced combat boots. He had a childlike smirk on his ugly face, his thick neck protruding from his clean-shaven jaw-line. Tom switched his eyes to the secretary.

"Don't worry, ma'am," he said. "I'll keep my promise."

Her head flopped forward as she appeared to pass out.

Tom sucked his teeth, stared hard at Proctor. "You'll pay for this."

Proctor nodded. "You want revenge; I'll fight you for her. I win, she goes with me. You win, you take her home."

"That's not gonna happen," Tom replied.

Proctor's eyes darted from Tom to Lester, his handgun pressed against the back of the secretary's head.

"How about this, Yank? Let's say it's still me and you, man to man. I win, you give me twenty minutes before you raise the alarm. You win, you can leave me for the French."

Tom thought about that for a moment. "And the secretary goes with us either way?"

"As I said."

"Don't do it, Tom," Lester whispered.

But Tom figured it was his best option in the circumstances. The secretary would live whatever happened. If Proctor took his chances with the French, it was likely he'd be picked up and either extradited, or do serious time here. But at least he could finish it without risking her life, which was something he would have jumped at just an hour before. Still, if Proctor was prepared to release the secretary so they could go at it, he wanted to know why this man thought he and Lester would keep up their end of the bargain. Although Lester had a bullet lodged in his arm, he still looked as if he were about to turn the Englishman's face into hamburger meat.

"Why the trust?" he asked.

"A man gets a reputation. Yours is being a man of your word."

Crane, Tom thought.

"And you gave her a promise, after all," Proctor said, gesturing to the secretary. "Looks like you've kept that, too."

"You hear that, Lester?" Tom said.

"I did. But I don't like it," Lester replied, his SIG pressed against his thigh. "And y'all ain't agreed the rules."

"The rules?" Tom asked Proctor.

"A submission," Proctor said.

"Now take that damn gag off her," Tom said.

"All right, but she stays in the cell until this is over. And the cell stays locked."

NINETY-TWO

As PROCTOR UNTIED the secretary's gag she groaned loudly. Tom rushed forward, ignoring the Englishman, and picked her up in his arms. He lowered her gently onto the bed pressed against the bare-brick wall, manoeuvring her so that she was in the recovery position. Close up, the extent of her beating looked even worse, and Tom noticed that her irises were a milky-white, the green pupils rolling as if she was drugged. He clenched his teeth. But Proctor was a big guy and trained, no doubt. He told himself to bury the anger. It would slow him down and cause him to make mistakes, just as Lester had said.

Tom walked backwards, joining Lester at the open doorway. As Proctor stepped forward Tom and Lester eased back out of the room. Proctor shut the door, swinging over the metal arm and locking the padlock, leaving the key in place. He led Tom and Lester into the adjacent room, which like the cell had a wooden table, although it was three times the size and had a dozen unwashed dishes on it, together with empty bottles of wine and water. The only other item was a compact DVD player. Proctor walked over to the table and lifted it, using his muscular thighs to take the weight, as he lent back and carried it over against the far wall. Clenching his jaw, Tom watched Proctor kneel down and slide in a DVD. As he pressed a button he said he thought it was a good idea to mask the sound of the fight; the secretary looked a little fragile as it was. With that, the sound of heavy metal blasted out.

"Didn't think it would be Miles Davis," Lester said, above the din.

"Anything goes wrong, get the secretary outta here."

Lester nodded and leaned against the whitewashed wall, cupping his injured arm. Tom removed his backpack, the MP7s, his field-scope and SIG. He walked into the centre of the room where Proctor was waiting for him.

They faced one another, a heavy drum beat and a screeching guitar cutting through the air. Proctor cracked his knuckles, threw a right hook. Tom ducked, hit him just below the heart with a stinging jab, and heard the man groan. As he straightened up he punched Proctor in the left eye, temporarily disorientating him.

He waited a second, watched the Englishman raise his guard before kicking him with the instep of his boot, connecting with Proctor's exposed ribs. Proctor winced, but lunged forward, and, throwing a blur of combinations, brought his right boot up deceptively, catching Tom in the lower stomach. He doubled over.

Proctor unleashed a powerful uppercut, sending Tom reeling back as his teeth crunched together. He rushed at Tom, his face contorted in an ugly glare, and grabbed him around the thighs, lifting him, his momentum sending them backward. They crashed into the table, the DVD missing a few beats before starting up again. As the table rim cut into his back Tom grimaced. Proctor let go of him and weaved upward. He punched Tom on the temple with a vicious hook, which spun him around. Before he could recover, Tom felt his head being grabbed about the ears. A split second later, his forehead was smashed into the table.

Tom felt dazed and nauseous; a rivulet of blood oozed from his lacerated head. As Proctor let go of him he collapsed. Blinking as the blood seeped into his eyes, Tom glimpsed Lester raise his SIG. He just managed to shake his head a fraction, willing his friend to back off.

"Don't get up," Proctor said.

"I'm not done," Tom replied, his voice barely more than a murmur.

But he couldn't see where the next attack would come from. A swinging boot soon put paid to that disability. It crashed into his mouth, jarring his head. He spat more blood, flayed about with his right arm hopelessly like a blind man. The second kick landed between his open legs. He sucked in air and curled up into a ball, the pain so acute that he wished he'd capped Proctor when he'd had the chance.

"You had enough?" Proctor asked, backing off.

Tom moaned on the floor.

Then he calmed himself as best he could, zoning out. The pain eased a fraction. He struggled up, although his head was still a blur, his breathing reduced to short gasps. He put his arms out to steady himself. But Proctor rushed in once more, hitting Tom with a shoulder barge and grabbing him around the waist. The two men stumbled sideways, Tom vaguely attempting to elbow Proctor in the nape of his neck but failing. As he released the bear hug Proctor flipped his head up and caught Tom with the back of his skull under the chin. Tom fell again, hitting his head on the tiles, the searing pain making him almost retch as his heart rate spiked.

Proctor loomed above him and kicked him in the

exposed right kidney. Tom let out an agonized cry. As he felt his head swim Proctor pulled his right leg back to kick him again. Knowing it could be his last chance, Tom galvanized his depleted strength into one action, lashing out with his leg, hitting Proctor squarely on the side of the kneecap with his toecap. Buckling, Proctor screamed out in pain. Tom willed himself up, blood covering his body, as he soaked up a hit of dopamine. Twisting sideways to lessen Proctor's strike options, he feigned a right. Proctor's head tilted to avoid it, and Tom hit him in the exposed jugular vein with a hook, swivelling his right side from the foot up, increasing the momentum and power. Proctor crumpled, moaning morbidly.

He hit the tiles hard, his head bouncing. Kneeling down behind him, Tom went for a sleeper hold. He wrapped his arm around the Englishman's throat, his bicep squeezing against the right side of Proctor's neck as his forearm pressed against the left.

Simultaneously, he used his free forearm to press the man's head down.

He began to crush the windpipe. Proctor gasped for air like a beached fish. Bending sideways, Tom saw panic flicking across his pale-blue eyes. He knew he couldn't find an angle of attack, and that the Englishman's strength was ebbing fast. Proctor made a mewing sound, and began to tap the floor as best he could with his right hand: I submit. But Tom kept up the pressure. He bent forward again, and, as he saw Proctor's eyes rolling back, he knew he was seconds away from unconsciousness. A minute or so after that and Proctor would be dead.

But he released the sleeper and rolled off him. He

heard Proctor moan and then gasp as the air was drawn into his starved lungs. He watched Lester kill the music before lying flat, feeling as if his body had been crushed in a vice: every bone seemingly on the cusp of fracturing.

NINETY-THREE

"You really gonna let him live?" Lester asked, pulling Tom up.

"Yeah," Tom said, wiping blood from his forehead.

"That'll need stitches."

Tom bent over at the waist, breathing hard to clear the haze and reduce his pulse rate.

"I thought you were gonna kill him."

"I guess I prefer protecting people more than killing them."

"Sometimes that's one and the same thing," Lester said.

Yeah, I know, Tom thought. But not this time. He eased his torso up, his hands pressed against his lower back as he cricked his neck. "Let's get you fixed up. Take the secretary home."

"Me? You need a mirror, man. And what about Karen?"

Tom closed his eyes and massaged his temples. He consoled himself by thinking that her body would be cared for by the French. Besides, there was no alternative. If they took her body on the jet with them, rigor mortis would set in after three hours and bloating after that. The thought made him almost gag. After what she'd said about her parents, he didn't want them to see her in that kind of state. Leaving her behind would've been what she'd have wanted. She would be preserved as well as possible in the local morgue, the made-up cadaver a less gruesome sight for her parents to identify.

Wiping spittle from his lips, he said, "The French will take care of her. We ain't got the facilities on the plane. You know her parents?"

"No. But I'll track 'um down real quick."

"Thanks, man."

Tom looked at Proctor. He was in bad shape, still semi-unconscious. He'd leave him for the French. His word was good.

Lester stared hard at him. "You shoulda killed him. For Karen."

Tom sighed, patted his friend's good arm. Shaking his head, Lester said he'd go ahead to fetch the Land Rover, adding that he could manage it for the short distance to the chateau, and that it wasn't the first time he'd had to drive wounded and one-handed.

With blood falling in small clots from his forehead, Tom walked out of the room. As he got to the make-shift cell he turned the key, swung back the hinge and opened the door. He saw the secretary lying on the bed. She was still suffering from some form of drug. He guessed that she'd been sedated to enable her murder to be carried out more easily. That and the beating Proctor had given her.

Her eyes flickered open and she gasped as she registered him. He could see even more clearly now that her captivity had taken its toll, her face almost unrecognizable. He picked her up in his arms and carried her from the cell like an exhausted child.

"We should be in DC in the next nine hours, ma'am," he whispered.

As he walked towards the vestibule he passed Karen's shrouded body in the entrance hall. He closed his eyes and tried to imagine her in the afterlife. He'd grieve for her, although now wasn't the time. He'd go home to Louisiana, hang out for a couple of weeks. Mourn her there.

When he got outside, a light drizzle was falling.

He stood still, holding the secretary in his arms, the moisture playing upon his face. He thought about his mother. He'd saved a woman's life, but one he had grown to care for had died in the process. But he was just a man. And men had no right pretending to be anything else.

Attempting to clear his mind of extraneous thoughts, he saw the car heading up the gravel roadway. As Lester got out and opened the rear passenger door Tom laid the secretary onto the back seat, feeling her body trembling beneath the blankets. He asked Lester to gather up the guards' cellphones, if he could manage it.

Watching his friend walk back into the chateau, he phoned Birch. Birch went into a rant at first, but calmed down after Tom confirmed that the secretary was safe and that he was bringing her home. He relayed everything that had happened, including the whereabouts of those kidnappers who'd died and those who were still alive, emphasizing where he'd left Proctor. Birch ordered him to wait there for the French to arrive, but Tom said that he didn't trust anyone at this juncture and that he wasn't going to let Lyric out of his sight until they'd landed in DC, even if it meant his pension. He cut Birch off then.

With a reddened piece of torn cloth around his head like a bandana, Tom drove the Land Rover back to the private airfield near Rouen, due to Lester's bullet wound. The trunk was loaded with the seized weapons, the lasers and sound system. The secretary was lying across the back seats, her head propped up on one of the backpacks against the door. Sitting beside Tom, Lester was tending to his injury as best he could with the contents of a med kit he'd brought with him from onboard the jet. But Tom knew he'd been hit in an artery, and that he might have to risk a detour to the nearest hospital.

No one had spoken since they'd left the chateau. The drizzle had turned to rain and the car's wipers were on full power. Tom turned off the highway to Rouen onto the back roads that led to the airfield. After thirty seconds or so, the sound of a helicopter could be heard as it passed above them, although the overhanging branches meant that it couldn't be identified.

"That French Special Forces?" Lester asked.

Tom pressed the electric-window switch and craned his neck on a straight section of road, the raindrops splashing on his face. He still couldn't see the helicopter, but it was clear from the noise that it was heading in the same direction as them, rather than towards the chateau.

"If it is, they need a new navigation system."

"Good job we acted when we did, then," Lester said. "Just wish Karen had been going home with us, too."

So do I, Tom thought. So do I.

He put his hand in his pocket and pulled out the watch that the secretary had given him back in Islamabad. He thought he'd use it as a tool to break her silence. He flipped the watch over, glanced at the back: *To Tom with heartfelt gratitude. Linda G. Carlyle. US Secretary of State.*

"I still got it, ma'am," he said, holding it up behind his head as he drove. "Your middle name, ma'am. Maybe I've earned the right?"

He put the watch back and adjusted the rear-view mirror. The secretary looked blank and closed her eyes, coughing.

It was the look, a split second, no more. But it was enough for Tom.

"Ma'am," he said. "What does the T stand for?"

The secretary coughed again.

"The T, ma'am?"

"Hey, Tom, ease up, man," Lester said.

"The T?" Tom said, ignoring him.

"Theresa," she mumbled.

"Jesus!" Tom said, smacking the steering wheel with his palm.

"What's up, man?" Lester said, pulling out his SIG and checking for a tail.

Tom slammed down the brake pedal. The car juddered to a stop by a grass verge. The woman fell into the footwell.

"Why you stopping the goddamned car?" Lester asked, rebounding back in his seat.

"The secretary's middle name begins with a G," Tom said.

"It's the drugs, man. Drugs do that. Least as far as I recall they do."

Tom drew his SIG, turned and stared hard at the woman as she struggled up onto the seat. "If you got a weapon, take it out with your thumb and forefinger."

"A weapon? Tom, you lost it or what?"

Tom didn't blink. The woman put her hand behind her back and eased out a Ruger LCP. The Ruger was a six-round pocket pistol that weighed a little over a quarter of a kilo. But Tom knew it was as deadly as a Glock at close quarters.

"Toss it in the footwell," he said.

She did so.

"Now take it off," he barked. "All of it. Or I'll do it for ya."

The woman removed the green-coloured contact lenses before licking her fingers and digging them into her face, ripping off blemish-ridden skin-like layers, false scabs, a plastic lesion and a made-up bruise. Lastly, she rubbed her face clean.

Tom froze, his heart racing. Then he blinked, shook his head. He couldn't believe it. He felt bile rise in his throat, choking him.

"You gotta be freakin' kiddin'," Lester said.

It was Karen.

NINETY-FOUR

As Swiss's Range Rover took a sharp right-hand bend into a field a mile or so from his apartment in Pentagon City, he saw his private helicopter parked on the asphalt helipad about thirty metres away. I'm safe, for now, he thought. The allotted time for the secretary's death had passed, but no one had rung him to confirm the kill. Nothing had appeared on the Internet, either. Briefly, he wondered if the Saudi ambassador had decided to have her killed in accordance with the time-frame imposed by the video, but dismissed the idea. He was the conduit to Proctor and his men. He wouldn't be bypassed on such an important decision. Besides, Proctor had no notion of the ambassador.

When he'd tried to contact the chateau, no one had picked up. Likewise the various disposable cells of his men, which had been switched off. He knew that something had gone wrong. The operation had been compromised, not because it was a flawed plan, he'd thought, but because someone knew something.

He'd been unsettled by the conversation with General Dupont; and the special agent, Tom Dupree, might have talked to someone before he'd been taken to the warehouse. Although if he had, he'd taken it to the grave with him. But Proctor had told him that there were three intruders at the chateau. He couldn't conceive of how two men and a woman could've overpowered his men there. They were the best he had, handpicked especially for the task. But there had been only one option for him in the short term. Get to somewhere safe, find out what exactly had happened, and take it from there.

The car hit the tarmac roadway that led over the field to the helipad and Swiss unbuckled his seat belt. He heard the sound of the sirens before the buckle strap snapped back into place. He turned and saw three black SUVs speeding up behind. FBI, he thought. Even if his two bodyguards managed to kill them all, the helicopter would be tracked, forced to land, or shot down by an F-35 stealth fighter within the hour. But then he figured the chance of his bodyguards taking out a dozen or more agents was about as likely as him getting invited to the next presidential dinner at the White House.

"Don't resist," he said.

"But, sir," the Russian woman said.

"It'll be the FBI. I'll take my chances. Stay in the car."

"Are you sure?" the male bodyguard asked.

Swiss nodded, rubbing his clammy palms together.

The Range Rover slowed to a stop and Swiss saw the cars encircle them. Suited agents wearing shades, ball caps and FBI emblazoned windbreakers disembarked. They crouched down, raising handguns, pump-action shotguns and MP5s. He opened the door and stepped out. An agent eased himself up and walked over, aiming his handgun and shouting at Swiss to get down and put his hands behind his head. Obeying, he knelt down, although he raised his face to the morning sun before assuming the position on the tarmac. He didn't know how long it would be before he'd feel its warmth again.

The agent ran over and he was cuffed brusquely.

After his two bodyguards and driver received the

same treatment and had had their weapons removed, Swiss was dragged up and manhandled towards one of the SUVs. His head was pushed down and he was told to get into the rear passenger seat.

As the car drove off he said, "I want to make a call to my lawyers. Now."

There were four agents in the car. Apart from the driver and the one who'd used the cuffs, the two other agents sat either side of him. The seats were covered with plastic sheets, the footwell, too. It struck him as odd, that and the fact that no one had apprised him of his Miranda Rights.

"Are you arresting me?" he asked.

The agents didn't speak. But the one sitting to his left took out a cellphone and played a video of the scene at the warehouse where he'd shot Hawks and ordered Tom Dupree beaten and murdered. How the hell did they get that? he thought.

"You do not need lawyers," the agent in the front passenger seat said. "Not unless they can bring back the dead."

"That's funny," Swiss said. "Where's that accent from?"

The man in front turned around and Swiss saw the handgun fixed with a suppressor. The two men sitting either side of him acted in unison, pushing his shoulders back and keeping his head level.

"Pakistan," the man said.

Swiss attempted a smile, but closed his eyes at the last moment. The bullet entered his forehead between his eyes and killed him instantly.

A second later, the shooter took out a secure satphone and rang Brigadier Hasni's office, informing an ISI operative in code that Swiss was dead.

In Islamabad, it was late afternoon and Mullah Kakar was feeling isolated and nervous because one of Brigadier Hasni's men had called him and had said that he would be picked up outside a hookah lounge on the outskirts of the Blue Area in an hour. That meant alone. The man hadn't said why. They never did, and Kakar knew that it would have been pointless to have asked.

He sat in his dim house and thought about what had happened and who might have talked already. In truth, it didn't really make any difference, since, if the West found out he was in fact alive, he was already one of the most wanted men in the world. Besides, the war would go on irrespective of the fact that ISAF had left Afghanistan. As far as he was concerned, the war with the West would go on for decades. There were other hotspots he could utilize to mete out his lust for revenge: West Africa, Egypt, Syria…the list was growing rather than diminishing. And there were an increasing amount of unlikely allies, too. Leftists, disillusioned Westerners, anarchists. He didn't like it and the allegiances wouldn't last, but he would use whatever was available to him for now. He'd already done so.

After meeting Proctor in the foothills of the Hindu Kush, he'd taken him to the training camp at an ISI-owned cluster of buildings twenty miles north of Islamabad. At the camp, the Englishman had joined up with other foreign mercenaries and ISI paramilitaries. Kakar had tutored them in the techniques of terrorism, including IEDs and kidnapping. When he'd been satisfied of their readiness, he'd reported to Hasni, a few days shy of a month before they'd kidnapped the secretary in Islamabad. It had been his passion.

But now he was preoccupied with what was going to happen in the next hour or so.

As the black Mercedes pulled up outside the hookah lounge he slid onto the rear passenger seat. The driver was the same one who'd picked him up the first time he'd been driven to Brigadier Hasni's house. He was still chewing gum and wearing shades. Kakar didn't bother attempting to strike up a conversation with him, knowing the man wasn't so much taciturn as ignorant.

Less than five minutes later, as the car slowed down at a red stop, Kakar saw someone standing on the wide sidewalk. They looked a little strange, dressed in a ball cap and Coke-lens eyeglasses, their left hand carrying a cellphone. In truth, he couldn't tell if it was a man or a woman. Seeing the car, the person sprinted towards a narrow alley bordered by high walls.

"There—" Kakar said, pointing.

It was the last word he said. The car exploded in a ball of flames and rose three metres into the air, the blast shattering the chassis and turning the metal into lethal shards that travelled upwards. Kakar's already dislocated and fatally wounded body was shredded into a hundred pieces.

NINETY-FIVE

"WHY?" TOM SAID, his voice tremulous.

"Why? You haven't worked it out yet, Tom?" the woman replied.

"No," he said, shaking his head, wondering whether his eyes were playing tricks. He still felt nauseous, and cold sweat beads had broken out on his skin.

"I'm a patriot, just like you."

"ISI. You ISI?" he asked, knowing that, despite the shock to his system of her deception, he had to focus now. Hard.

She grinned.

"You're one piece of work," Lester said.

"That from a thug with a dishonourable discharge," she said, her face full of contempt.

Lester looked at Tom. Tom knew what that look meant. He nodded. They had very little time to find the secretary now and he wasn't in the mood to go through the motions. If, in fact, she was still alive.

Lester shot the woman in the foot.

She screamed. "You bastard. You shot my foot."

"I'll work my way up," he said.

"You haven't asked me anything, you jerk," she said through gritted teeth.

"Shoot her in the shin, Lester," Tom said, figuring she'd crack before he'd have to.

"Wait!" she said, putting up her hand.

"The secretary?" Tom asked.

"Just give me a second."

Something clicked. "That helo is heading to the airfield with the secretary on board. I'm right, ain't I?"

Tom knew most helicopters had limited capabilities in terms of height and distance. If they wanted to take her to somewhere remote abroad, they'd need a plane. Lester's plane. He discounted the possibility of a midair refuelling linkup, although he'd seen it done once or twice.

"I'm right, yes," he said.

She nodded.

"She plan on killing us at the airfield?" Lester asked.

"Yeah, I reckon. Is Proctor on there with her?" Tom asked.

"Yes," she said, breathing heavily, grasping her shattered foot.

"Why?" he asked.

She shrugged.

"Shoot her in the head, Lester."

"Okay, okay," she said, holding up her hand again. "A clean-up."

Tom winced. The woman was an ISI operative. He realized that she'd wanted him to find the secretary, since the ISI wanted to cover their tracks and kill everyone who might point the finger at them. And that meant him and Lester, too.

"Where's he planning on taking her now?"

She fell silent again.

Lester raised his SIG.

"Yemen. She will be flown to Yemen," she said, miserably.

"And murdered?" Tom asked. "Filmed?"

She nodded.

"Your real name?"

"Major Durrani."

"How the hell did you know I was linking up with Lester?"

"Steve Coombs. He bugged your phones and computers. When you rang Brigadier Hasni, I got involved."

Tom got out and ripped off the arm of his shirt. He opened the passenger door and, after shrinking back at first, she allowed him to lift her off the seat. He turned and lowered her onto the grass verge, saying nothing. Bending over her, he used the cloth to stem the flow of blood before taking out a phial of morphine and a hypodermic syringe from her bag in the trunk and handing it to her. Being a trained medic was probably the only truth she had spoken to him when he'd let her join up.

Lester got out and came around to the verge just as she injected herself. "Why don't we trade her skinny ass for the secretary?"

She laughed, mockingly. "They'll let me die. They'd let a hundred like me die to keep her."

"We gonna just leave her here?" Lester asked.

"She sure as hell ain't going anywhere," Tom said. "The French will deal with her."

"Whatever you say, Tom."

He looked down at her. "Why did you give me the name of the wrong chateau at the diner?"

"So the French were sent to the wrong place. I didn't know they'd find out the right place as quickly as they did."

"But we would've ended up at the wrong place, too."

"You thought I was smart, Tom. I am. I would have gotten us to the right place before the French."

"And when we didn't?"

She inhaled deeply. "I texted Proctor. Told him where you were meeting the DCRI operatives. His men killed them and waited for you. I had to hope that you and Lester would kill them in turn before they killed you. I have to think on my feet, you see. Least I did before your attack dog shot me. As I said, I'm a patriot. The Iranians would gladly slaughter my people. I can't allow that to happen. The secretary was the only way."

Tom ordered her to hand over her cell, which she did. He checked the sent box, saw the text she'd sent Proctor, before removing the SIM card and battery and throwing them over the hedge that abutted the verge.

"Let's get outta here, Lester. The air stinks," he said.

Walking to the car, Tom guessed she was probably telling the truth. But she would've killed him and Lester with the Ruger, of that he had no doubt.

As Tom drove off Lester said, "Upside, Karen ain't dead. Downside, Karen ain't Karen. But you never did have much luck with the ladies, did ya, Tom? Maybe you should ditch the Buddhism and become a Mormon or somethin'."

Tom felt like exploding, but stopped himself. He knew it was the way military types like Lester dealt with situations like this. The black humour was a way of keeping their heads straight.

"Did you know her well?" Tom asked.

"I knew of her. She contacted me for a job. I said that I had something and she talked me into it."

"Jesus, Lester."

Lester held up his good hand. "You fell for it, too, am I right?"

"I guess."

"Still, that was some make-up job. Had me fooled."

Tom recalled someone saying that the CIA and other foreign intelligence agencies had teams of graphic artists who designed disguises for operatives in the field. They had to be good enough to pass close scrutiny and, if necessary, save their lives. At firsthand, he had to admit that the deception had been complete. After he'd told Lester what he'd remembered, he realized that if he hadn't asked her about the watch, he wouldn't have known.

"You're driving too fast," Lester said.

"I'm only doing seventy."

"Like I said. She do the switch when you was fighting, Tom?"

"Yeah. That's why Proctor wanted to dance to music. That's why he wanted to leave the secretary in the cell and why the major wanted me to cover her face. I reckon she drugged her or just knocked her out before putting her in the hall," Tom said, speeding up.

"After what she said, does that mean the CIA guy is off the hook?"

Tom thought about it. She had set the DCRI operatives up. Not Crane. But he just didn't know the answer to that question.

NINETY-SIX

THE ASR, AN imam's late-afternoon recorded call to prayer, played out from atop an ancient sandstone minaret. It could be heard for miles across Ta'if in eastern Saudi Arabia. As the sun baked the aerial-ridden flat roofs Dan Crane left a cab and walked across a marble-tiled quadrangle decorated with date palms and water features. He wore a pair of taupe-coloured pants and a matching sports jacket, and was carrying an empty black-leather sports bag.

When he reached the revolving doors of the local branch of the Arab National Bank, the doorman nodded to him, a wry smile crossing his lips. Crane was sweating like a steelworker.

At a private booth, he handed over his passport to a female teller and accepted a glass of water. Ten minutes later, he placed the crisp stacks of hundred-dollar bills into the bag, his arm dropping down under the weight as he lifted it off the table, even though he was only carrying a tenth of what had been deposited for him. The money had been transferred there by the ISI, and everything had been in order.

Leaving the bank, he felt the damp patches under his arms begin to seep sweat. The air was still and dusty, the temperature in the early hundreds. Walking slowly to the kerb, he saw a black Lexus with tinted windows cut out from behind a parked truck and race towards him. The front passenger window was down, a handgun just visible as it got level with him. He struggled to lift the bag in front of his face and took two rounds in the chest before toppling over. As the car screeched away a small crowd gathered around his still body.

Across the street, a Pakistani core collector dressed as a local in a dishdasha and keffiyeh headdress lowered his cellphone, having just videoed what had transpired. Ten seconds later, he emailed it to the ISI HQ in Islamabad.

AT THE SAUDI Embassy in Islamabad, Hasni sat opposite the ambassador, who'd told him that the ISI had done well. Well! Hasni thought. His people had killed a wealthy arms manufacturer, Swiss, and worst of all, as far as he was concerned, a top CIA man, Crane. He could think of a lot of words to describe what had happened, but that adverb wasn't one of them.

The two men drank coffee and discussed their families then, but Hasni's mind was on other things.

The Saudis had risked a lot. He'd wondered at first why they'd decided to go down this route. Then it had struck him. The Shia-Sunni civil war in Iraq was going one way. The Shias would win within a few months. That meant that allied to having Iran facing them just across the Persian Gulf, the Saudis would have the Shias stretched across their northeast border. Despite his innate intelligence and grasp of international affairs, he had no idea of the Chinese dimension, and probably would have dismissed it even if a Saudi asset had whispered it to him. He trusted the Saudis on their rationale for the secretary's abduction, if nothing else.

The threat of the Iraqis pouring jihadists and ordnance over the border had sent the Saudis into over-drive, he thought, fearing their own country would erupt into civil war as half the Middle East had already. Cutting off the head of the Shia snake was the only way to ensure the body died.

Ten minutes later, as Brigadier Hasni left the embassy en route to his meeting with Mullah Kakar at his home in the Blue Area, he saw an elegant young woman walking along the sidewalk, whom he took for a well-educated Pakistani citizen. She reminded him of his daughter, Adeela. She wore a turquoise pantsuit and a silk hijab, her gold jewellery shimmering in the sunlight. As the door to his armour-plated limo opened she appeared to trip on a groove between the paving stones, her ankle twisting.

Leaving his bodyguards standing still, he rushed over to her and helped her to her feet. She smiled and thanked him. It was only a second or two later that he realized he'd pricked himself, probably on a brooch or hem pin, he imagined. Maybe even a sharp edge on a piece of her expensive jewellery.

As the limo drove off, sandwiched between four SUVs, a dozen police motorcyclists front and back, he rubbed the mark, which had started to turn red, a circle about the size of a dime. It itched like crazy. Twenty seconds later, he felt nauseous. A minute after that, he was throwing up and sweating. A bodyguard told the driver to head for the nearest hospital. Hasni held his chest, thought he was having a heart attack. Two minutes later, he died of cardiac arrest.

The woman was an operational officer in Al Mukhabarat Al A'amah, the Saudi secret service. In a secluded alley, shaded from the sun, she took out an adapted cellphone and rang the Saudi ambassador.

"Plato will die of a heart attack, if he hasn't already," she said, using the pro-word for Brigadier Hasni.

"And the mullah?" the ambassador asked.

"His body already covers half the street."

NINETY-SEVEN

PROCTOR HAD LANDED the helicopter in a grass field opposite the small airfield, and had carried the secretary over to the metallic-black Ford Fusion parked in an adjacent lane. The helicopter had been situated behind a barn at the end of the chateau's three-acre, ornate garden. Ostensibly, it was to be used to evacuate his men as soon as the secretary's murder had been carried out.

After driving the short distance to the airfield, he saw the pilot and the co-pilot, whom Lester had hired, standing outside the business jet. They were drinking coffee poured from a stainless-steel Thermos. He heard the secretary reviving on the back seat, mumbling something that sounded like a prayer or some words from the Bible. He'd revived himself with what had been left of the smelling salts that he'd used on her. He wasn't as badly injured as he'd made out after the Yank had eased off, but for a moment he'd actually thought he was going to die. And yet it had all fallen into place. The man just couldn't do it, and apart from the money that he'd received from Swiss already, Brigadier Hasni had promised him twice as much again. That and his life.

The substitute pilots would be waiting in the hangar. A couple of Pakistanis. Not ISI operatives, but ex-Air Force down on their luck, who had driven the fifty miles from Paris once Major Durrani had texted him from the States, confirming that they had air transport.

He drove up to the parked jet and got out. The two flight crew looked at one another.

"There's been a change of plans," he said.

"The hell are you?" the co-pilot said, a thickset man with pallid skin and a bald head.

Proctor pulled out his handgun still fixed with a laser sight, together with an added suppressor, and poleaxed him with a head shot. The pilot, a younger man wearing shades, dropped his cup of coffee.

"Oh, Jesus," he said.

The round hit him in the throat and he fell on top of the co-pilot. Proctor popped the trunk and heaved both men in before driving back to the hangar, as casually as a man about to go on vacation.

As he reached the hangar, its curved roof painted a dull green, two Pakistani men dressed as civilian pilots stepped out, looking a little too nervous for his liking. But there was nothing to stop the secretary being flown to Yemen where she'd be beheaded. Later than planned, given Tom Dupree's interference. But late or not, if that didn't go viral on the Internet, he didn't know what would. Besides, the major would have dispatched Dupree and his black sidekick by now. She'd drive back to Paris in the Ford, where she'd take a scheduled flight to Islamabad, dumping all four bodies en route.

His cellphone rang, a number he didn't recognize. He hesitated before taking the call.

"Brigadier Hasni has been assassinated in Islamabad," a woman's voice said.

"What the fuck...? Who is this?"

"A water lily," the woman said, the agreed code for a friend.

"Okay."

"You will proceed as planned," she said, matter-of-factly.

"Who killed him?"

"A Shia bitch."

BY THE TIME Tom and Lester reached a small yew tree sunk into the hedge abutting the airfield, the jet was rising towards a mud-grey cloud miles in the distance. Tom cursed under his breath, slamming the butt of the MP7 into the tangle of bushes. With that, Lester slumped to the ground. Tom dropped the MP7 and crouched down beside him, cradling his head.

"I'm sorry, Tom." Lester's voice was wheezy and a sheen of sweat had broken out on his forehead. He was struggling to find breath, his face contorting.

Tom put his hand over his friend's wound, but the blood seeped between his fingers, black-red and pus-like. "Stay with me, Lester."

Lester's eyelids were fluttering and he was clearly close to unconsciousness. Tom knew that if he didn't get his friend to a hospital soon, he'd bleed out. He pulled out his cell and called 112, the French equivalent of 911. He gave the operator their location and was told that a hospital-based ambulance would be on its way in less than five minutes. The ETA was thirty-five minutes.

After making Lester as comfortable as he could, covering his body with a blanket and giving him some water from a plastic bottle that was in the trunk of the Land Rover, Tom called Vice Admiral Birch and filled him in on the details. The head of the Bureau of Diplomatic Security simply listened until Tom finished. Tom had expected him to bark a string of expletives down the cell before telling him to turn himself in to the US Embassy in Paris. To his surprise, he didn't.

"I'll divert the SEAL platoon," Birch said, calmly, referring to the US Navy's Sea, Air, Land Teams, and principal Special Operations Force since their inception in the Vietnam War. "You *will* wait there until they arrive."

Tom had no idea what a SEAL team were doing on French soil. "What about the French?" he asked, more than a little fazed.

"POTUS pulled in a favour from his French counterpart. The SEALs were on a joint training exercise with the British SBS," Birch said.

Tom knew the Special Boat Service was the Royal Navy's Special Forces unit, made up almost entirely of Royal Marines.

"The SEALs were going to liaise with French Special Forces and help out," Birch went on. "But they ain't carrying weapons. The French President was worried about political fallout if they killed French citizens. I guess, after what you've just said, I better tell her that three of her DCRI operatives are dead."

"Can we get them to intercept the jet?"

"It'll be outside their airspace by now. And why would it land? Those onboard know we won't order it shot down."

"What about Crane?" Tom asked.

"He's dead, too. Killed in Saudi Arabia while collecting his blood money from a bank."

Tom was stunned by Birch's statement, taking a few seconds to focus. "Blood money?"

"He turned a CIA asset over to the ISI."

Tom couldn't help feeling sad that Crane had turned

out to be a traitor, despite his previous suspicions. He swallowed hard as he joined the dots. "What was his name, sir?"

"What difference does it make?"

"I'd like to know, that's all."

"Sandri Khan. Crane got half a million dollars for betraying him. Khan was the one who told us where Lyric was being held in Karachi. I guess that signed his death warrant."

"Who killed Crane?"

"ISI," Birch said. "So stick with the SEALs. They're just about the only people you can trust right now."

Tom clenched his teeth, feeling rotten. Khan had saved his life and Crane had turned him over to be murdered at the hands of butchers. At least I have an answer, he thought. But it all seemed irrelevant now, given that he'd failed to save the secretary's life. He guessed she was on the way to Yemen, just as the ISI major had said. He sank to his knees, watching Lester cough up blood.

NINETY-EIGHT

THE SEAL OPERATORS arrived in unmarked helicopters just over fifteen minutes later. They were dressed in civilian clothes: jeans and windbreakers. Sixteen men whose ages ranged from about thirty to forty, with regular haircuts and facial hair in order to disguise the fact that they were military personnel.

As a medic attended to Lester the others checked the area methodically. One forced open the Ford's trunk and hauled out the bodies of the two American pilots whom Proctor had murdered. Tom grabbed Lester's hand just as the medic gave him a shot of morphine. He watched his friend blink erratically.

"You give people hope, Tom. You remember me saying that?" he said, his voice tremulous.

"I do, old friend," Tom replied.

"And that's a gift. Don't ever change."

As Lester was lifted onto a stretcher and carried to one of the helicopters' cabins, Tom's mind was reeling. But then he swore under his breath, "The major!"

Leaving her at the roadside had been a mistake, that and not interrogating her fully. He told himself that he'd been anxious to get back to the airfield, to be the one to save the secretary. At the very least, he should've brought her along, sucked up his contempt and thought straight. But if she was still there, he might be able to convince her to redeem herself.

And me in the process, he thought.

He watched the guy he took for the SEALs' leader, a tall, sinewy man with three-day-old stubble, as he walked towards him.

"Dude, did you get hit by a truck or what?" he asked.

Tom said that it'd been a rough few days. The SEAL said he was a platoon chief and that his name was Nathan. He told Tom that his men were part of SEAL Team 7, with worldwide deployment duties, but it looked as if their flight across the English Channel had been a waste of time.

"Maybe. Maybe not."

Nathan shook his head and spat on the ground.

"Listen to me," Tom said. "There's a chance we can find out where Lyric is being taken. The exact location."

Nathan thought for a moment. "My orders were to take Lyric to England."

"So think outta the box."

Nathan stared hard at Tom. "Over my pay grade, dude."

Frustrated, Tom called Birch once more. He asked him if he could follow the lead. Birch was reluctant, but said he'd make some calls.

After pacing around and doing his best to persuade Nathan that the delay was necessary, a matter of life and death in fact, Tom got a call from Birch. He told Tom that he should do what he could, but that a Navy commander was going to call the SEAL platoon chief and that it was their shout.

"And, Tom," he said. "This isn't official, but I think you should know. The head of the ISI, Brigadier Hasni, has been assassinated in Islamabad."

"Hasni! Who killed him?"

"That's classified."

"It could be important, sir. I might be able to spook the major with that kind of info."

Birch hesitated. "It's still one step up from a rumour, but the word is it was the Saudis."

That makes no sense, Tom thought, disconnecting.

Five minutes later, after Nathan had gotten the go-ahead from his commander, he and Tom, together with four operatives, flew in a red helicopter to the narrow road where Major Durrani had been left with a round in her foot. After the helicopter had landed in an adjacent field, Tom and Nathan exited first and ran across the grass to a two-metre-high bank, speckled with wild flowers, which abutted the verge on the other side. Tom had spotted Major Durrani still lying on her back about ten seconds before landing.

MAJOR DURRANI'S FACE was covered in a sheen of sweat. Despite the morphine that Tom Dupree had given to her just over an hour before, she was struggling to remain conscious. She'd felt ants start to crawl over her legs already and crows had perched on a nearby branch of an overhanging oak tree, squawking portentously. She guessed the helicopter contained French Special Forces and thought seriously about taking the razor blade she had concealed under her hair and ending it before they reached her.

But she had an extended family—impoverished farmers who lived in Punjab Province—who relied on her. She'd excelled at the charity-run school she'd attended from the age of eight, and had won a scholarship to Gurjat University. Ever since she'd joined the civil service, five years before being recruited by the ISI, she'd sent money home. Her father was ill. A rare form of colon cancer. He needed specialist treatment, which accounted for more than half her monthly salary. Picturing her mother cooling his emaciated face with a damp cloth, she decided to think of a story to tell the French.

She heard a rustling sound behind her, knowing it came from the movement of humans rather than rodents. Bracing herself, she turned her head and saw two men atop the bank. She recognized one of them instantly. It was Tom Dupree. Part of her felt relieved; the other part desperate.

TOM KNELT BESIDE the major's head. He noticed that her eyes were turning a muted yellow, her skin pallid. Nathan stood above them, scanning the country road for any sign of a vehicle or pedestrian. The other four SEALs had stayed behind the hedge, so as not to draw too much attention.

"Where in Yemen?" he asked.

She made a dismissive *hiss* between her teeth. "Only Proctor knows that."

"Brigadier Hasni is dead. Murdered by the Saudis. Betrayed."

She looked strangely uninterested. She winced and wiped the sweat from her cheeks.

"So, the old tyrant is dead. I never did like him. As for the Saudis, you've been courting them for years, even though you know they produce more jihadists than anywhere else."

Nathan tapped Tom on the shoulder and pointed a calloused finger down the road. An ancient Renault was heading towards them. A few seconds later, it slowed to a stop as it reached parallel, exhaust fumes spewing over the rusted paintwork. A man in blue overalls poked his large head out of the wound-down window, his jowly face a mass of spider veins.

"Ce qui se passe ici?" What's happening here?

Staying put, Tom said, *"Si vous voulez frapper le bar ce soir, continuer à avancer."* If you want to hit the bar tonight, keep moving.

"Mademoiselle?" he said, staring at the major.

She made a pushing movement with her hand. "I'm okay. I'm okay."

Reluctantly and swearing under his breath, he drove off.

"Whatever you gotta say, say it quick," Nathan said.

"Tell me where they're taking her in Yemen and I will vouch for you. Otherwise it'll be life in a cage, or worse," Tom said.

He saw her mind working, her eyelids blinking. Then she grinned.

"No, Tom. You'll get me a presidential pardon and you'll do it now. That and safe passage for my family to the US."

NINETY-NINE

THE HELICOPTERS HAD landed back in England on a dis-
used runway illuminated by an infrared strobe at RAF
Alconbury in Cambridgeshire, a non-flying facility
under the control of the 423rd Air Base Group of the
US Air Force in Europe. Lester was stretchered off and
taken to a nearby hospital for emergency surgery. Tom
had received stitches to his forehead and been told that
the wound would heal with time, although, if he didn't
want a Frankenstein-like scar in the interim, he might
want to opt for plastic surgery.

He sat in a small office now, surrounded by dull-grey
file cabinets and framed photos of a young US Air Force
officer's family. He figured it was the end of the line.
Birch was going to call him on a secure satphone that
lay on the chipped wooden desk in front of him. He was
convinced the head of the DS would order him to report
back to DC, despite the fact that Major Durrani had pinpointed a location. Whether it was where the secretary
had been taken, or a lie to buy her time, was something
that would become clear soon enough. But she'd gotten her presidential pardon, although it was conditional
upon her being accurate. She'd also agreed to undergo
a polygraph, and be subjected to weeks of non-violent
questioning about everything she knew. As a result, there
was a general consensus that she was telling the truth.
But whichever way he looked at it, Tom believed he'd

failed personally in his mission. He figured the chances of the secretary being rescued were now close to zero.

When the phone rang, he left it a full ten seconds before answering it.

"You got friends in high places, Tom?" Birch asked.

"Not that I know, sir," Tom said, wondering vaguely if his father had something to do with what Birch was going to say.

"You'll accompany the SEALs to Yemen. But strictly as an observer. The platoon chief is in command. You so much as question his judgment, and he's got orders to cut you loose. Understand?"

"Yes, sir."

"And don't think that your illegal attempts to go it alone have endeared you to anyone. They haven't. But given what you told me about her physical appearance, you're deemed the only person capable of a positive ID. I suppose I should say good luck. But I'll be honest with you, I was dead against it."

Tom found it difficult to believe that the US authorities were letting him go along. But what Birch had said was true. If she was still alive, the White House sure as hell couldn't afford the embarrassment of rescuing the wrong woman, and only he and Lester had seen the result of Proctor's brutal handiwork. He guessed that that paranoia had been exacerbated by what he had told Birch about Major Durrani's disguise. Anything was possible now, including another monumental screw-up of the facial-recognition variety.

Ten minutes later, Tom and the operators were sitting on plastic chairs in a blacked-out chow hall, with white-washed cinderblock walls and blue tiles. A flat-screen monitor had been rigged up behind Nathan, showing the first slide of a hastily prepared PowerPoint presentation, a laptop perched on a stool by his side. The subject-matter of the meeting wasn't so much classified as completely off the radar to all but a few people in the US intelligence community. As a result, a section of trucked-in Redcaps had been ordered to surround the building armed with SA80 A2 assault rifles. It wasn't exactly a secured conference room, so US Secretary of State Linda Carlyle had been given the upbeat pro-word, Phoenix, and all the operators had been asked not to use anything else. Tom had already come to the conclusion that they were the type of guys who didn't need to be ordered around or told twice.

"I'll do a Q&A at the end of the briefing," Nathan said. "The most recent photographs we have of the rescue site are these." He tapped a key on the laptop and the first satellite-generated image came up on the screen behind him. "You can gather round for the drone feeds later. Now the detail…"

The distance to western Yemen was almost three and a half thousand miles. A five-man reconnaissance and sniper SEAL team had been deployed there already. The country was ravaged by internal conflict, chiefly between the north-western Shia tribesmen and the al-Qaeda backed Sunnis in the south. At the behest of the State Department's counterterrorism unit, the SEALs had been sent there to monitor the situation. If what Major Durrani had said was correct, the secretary was being held at a small hamlet in southwest Yemen on the Red Sea coast.

Opposite Yemen, a mere eighteen miles away across the Bab-el-Mandeb, the strait between the Red Sea and the Gulf of Aden, was the small African state of the

Republic of Djibouti. An Islamic, US friendly country sandwiched between Eritrea and Somalia on the Horn of Africa, it had been used as a so-called black site in the Global War on Terror, housing secret prisons used by the CIA for the interrogation of jihadists. It regularly allowed US forces to strike at al-Qaeda sympathisers in Somalia and Yemen. Since the insurgencies in Mali and Algeria, the base had been deemed even more important and strategically placed.

An RAF Hercules would transport Tom and the operators to Camp Lemonnier, a former French Foreign Legion outpost, which occupied an area bordering the Djibouti-Ambouli International. Lemonnier was utilized as a base for the Combined Joint Task Force—Horn of Africa, the only US base on the continent. From there they'd cross to Yemen by sea. They'd meet up with the team inside Yemen, who were heading towards the rendezvous point, and the combined force of twenty-one SEALs would assault the hamlet, hoping to free the secretary in the process. The assault would be carried out on foot, with, if necessary, aerial back-up from armed Reaper drones. The Yemeni president was a friend of the US, but given the secrecy needed to secure any chance of a successful outcome, together with the possibility that innocent Yemenis might be killed in a firefight, it had been decided by the NSC that he wouldn't be informed of the mission until after it had concluded.

Nathan wound up by saying that there'd be a quartermoon, which mean that there'd be enough ambient light to use their night vision effectively, but also meant that they could stay relatively hidden. Tom knew he was referring to their goggles, because they all had thermal or infrared scopes, which worked perfectly in total darkness. While he worked primarily in the open during the day, the SEALs adopted feline tactics. They attacked at night, utilizing surprise and stealth. The Delta assaulters back in Pakistan had had no option but to go in the way they had, due to the occupation of the land around the fort by the Shia refugees. But the majority of Special Forces' ops were the opposite.

As he stepped out into the overcast daylight once the briefing had ended, he saw an Air Force officer walking towards him. She was in her late thirties and wore tortoiseshell-framed eyeglasses. Her blonde hair was up in a neat bun at the nape, although her uniform was struggling to contain her Munroesque curves. After confirming his identity, she informed him that a local hospital administrator had rung to say that Lester's condition was described as comfortable and that he had a good chance of pulling through.

Despite the secretary's circumstances, Tom could barely conceal his relief.

ONE HUNDRED

To Tom, the payload compartment of the C-130 Hercules, or the Herky Bird, as the military had nicknamed it, looked even more basic than the Chinook he'd flown in to the Upper Kurram Valley. With its exposed-aluminium conduits, metal plate boxes and lengths of clad wiring, the cabin resembled a basement generator room. But it'd been relatively stable, even at eight thousand metres, and had decent AC. While he'd been unable to close his eyes for the duration, the operators had taken sleeping pills and had spread out on the deck close to where their gear was strapped down, and had fallen unconscious from barely after the plane's chassis had retracted.

He wondered if he'd been wrong to try to do things by himself. Perhaps the US intelligence community would have had her safe by now if he hadn't intervened. But if they'd had a better source of intel, he figured he'd be facing a federal indictment, or even occupying a cell at a black site, instead of flying towards the African continent with a bunch of the Navy's finest.

Resting against the back of the red canvas seat now, he watched a brawny crew chief in a massive aviation helmet hold up two fingers to the SEAL sitting closest to him. Due to the loud whine from the engines, the arrival time was passed down the line of operators in the same fashion. Then they grasped the alloy bar either side of their thighs, so that they wouldn't injure themselves before the mission if the plane hit the runway like a lineman taking out a wide receiver. Tom did likewise, bracing himself for the landing.

The Hercules landed heavily, as it always did, the screech and roar of the four turboprop engines in reverse thrust making it sound as if the fuselage were imploding. After the plane had taxied on the runway, they all moved to the aft cabin.

The operator next to Tom was a short guy, perhaps five-six, with wavy hair that fell over his ears, and a pale-pink scar on his jaw-line. He held a weapon that Tom didn't recognize. It was less than a metre in length and looked like a mini-cannon, with a laser rangefinder on top. Unlike the other small-arms weapons the men had, which were camouflaged in a tan-desert pattern, the stocky weapon was jet-black.

"That heavy?" Tom asked.

"Nope."

Tom sighed. "So what does it weigh?"

The operator looked over at Nathan, who nodded to him.

"6.35 kilos. It's called the XM25 CDTE System. That's Counter Defilade Target Engagement. An air burst grenade launcher. Fires 25mm shells with microchips programmed to detonate mid-air at a specific range. Over five-hundred metres if fired straight from the shoulder. Designed to take out targets hiding behind impenetrable obstacles like reinforced walls. Heckler and Koch smart tech."

"Effective?" Tom asked.

"We call it the Punisher. Real motherfucker."

As the cargo door swung up and the heavy rear ramp

lowered to the tarmac, Tom shivered. The daytime temperature had plummeted to something like November in New York.

Camp Lemonnier was situated on the southernmost end of Djibouti airport, an outcrop of volcanic rock at the base of the Red Sea. The five-hundred-acre site was home to three thousand US military personnel and Department of Defense contractors, who occupied lines of adapted shipping containers known as Containerized Living Units, or "cans". As they disembarked Tom saw them illuminated beneath the floodlights a hundred metres or so ahead. To the left, a military truck was parked on a nearby gravel road in front of "Thunder Dome"— the massive hangar-shaped structure used as a basketball pit—a group of five US Marines dressed in desert camouflage stood around it. The hum of generators filled the cold air, and Tom felt suddenly incongruous.

Nathan came up to his shoulder. "The rest of our gear," he said, nodding towards the vehicle.

"What's the up-to-date intel?"

"Nothing's changed."

"How long?" Tom asked.

"A helo will be flying us out in thirty minutes. We'll be at the Y at zero two ten," Nathan answered, referring to the point from where they'd proceed on foot to the hamlet. "There'll be an interpreter in Yemen. Stick with him."

"You think I'm a liability?" Tom asked, a little rattled.

"I respect what you do. But this is a military op," Nathan said. "Nothing personal, dude."

He walked off towards the truck, took his hands out of his cargo pockets and gestured to the Marines to unload the gear.

He's right, Tom thought. It'd struck him that although he was the head of her protective detail, he'd been as much use as an interpreter in preventing her kidnapping in the first place. Now he'd be a bystander again, same as at the Shia fort in the Pakistan Tribal Areas. But, in truth, he was fortunate to be even that.

ONE HUNDRED AND ONE

THE SAUDI AMBASSADOR sat deep in thought as the Land Cruiser moved in a small convoy across a flat, arid plain in western Yemen, bordered by high sand dunes. The xenon headlights lit up the clear night air seemingly for miles. This was the Tihamah, the hot lands on Yemen's Red Sea coastline. He'd stopped at a small village en route, constructed entirely of stamped clay and sun-dried mud bricks. Sitting on palm-leaf matting, he ate a light meal of goat meat and lentils, and drank the strong sweet tea. He thought the village smelt like a dung heap and was glad to return to the hermetically sealed car, and feel the AC on his face. But at least he hadn't been at risk from the northern Shia. If they'd gotten hold of him, he would've likely lost his manhood.

With his keffiyeh-wrapped head tilted backwards against a rear headrest, he ruminated upon the recent events that had led to him being in this unlikely and primitive place. Despite all of the meticulous planning and loss of life, the secretary had almost been rescued. He found it difficult to believe, especially given that the head of her protective detail was supposed to have been killed by Swiss's men in the US. As a result, he had blood on his hands, including that of Brigadier Hasni and the jihadist, Mullah Kakar. Part of him felt disloyal. But he couldn't risk anything coming back on him, let alone the Brothers of Faith. That would not only lead to his probable death, but also, and more importantly, the complete negation of all he wished for his son.

After landing back in Riyadh, he'd had a meeting with the Brothers. They had ordered him to oversee the secretary's killing personally. A poorly veiled repost, he'd thought at the time. Besides that, he hated Yemen. He called it the sick dog of the Gulf. Dirt poor, unstable, dangerous and corrupt. All the things his country would have been without oil and gas. He'd thought he'd be going back to Riyadh to watch the beheading on the Internet like half of the computer-savvy world. Instead, he'd been flown to Sana'a, the Yemeni capital, ostensibly on a personal visit to the Saudi embassy there.

It had taken fourteen hours for the secretary to be flown from France to Yemen and then driven overland to the remote hamlet. His journey would add another six hours to that. The difference between the time that she should've been beheaded online, and the actual time it would take to get it done and transport the video to an area with Internet connection, would be close to a day and a half. The only possible advantage would be that the US would consider the threat to be a bluff, one that would be all the more dramatic when it was in fact carried out. Still, he took off his Ray Ban sunglasses, which he wore to help him relax, despite the darkness, and barked at the driver, ordering him to put his foot down. He wanted the grisly errand over as soon as possible.

LINDA COULD BARELY breathe, the dry air being heavy with dust. It was dark with no artificial light. She'd heard insects scuttling around her since she'd been dragged here. It had been stifling at first, and she'd felt as if she were being slow cooked. But now she was freezing, her teeth chattering as she lay on the hard concrete floor. Wearing the burqa, although her head was bare, she was chained to a brick-built pillar in a square room. She hadn't had any food or water since the group of masked men had brought her here. Despite not seeing the sky since leaving France, she knew she was in the desert, close to the coast. She could smell the sea and sand had leaked into the room.

The Muslim men who'd carried her from the jet at another unknown location had been different from those who had held her previously. Although they too had refrained from speaking in her presence, they'd manhandled her roughly for most of the time and had even kicked her on a couple of occasions. She'd been blindfolded and gagged before being thrown onto the bed of what she'd guessed was a pickup truck and covered with a mouldy tarp. She'd wept then, partly due to the pain in her shoulder and knee as she'd landed heavily, and partly due to a rising sense of fear. But weakness wasn't going to save her life now, so she closed her eyes and tried to clear her mind.

She felt around with her feet, an act designed simply to distract her. But after a minute or so, she felt something sharp and cold like metal. She examined it as best she could, guessing it was a nail. She eased it up with her toes, so that as she extended the chain to its limit she was able to manoeuvre it into her hand.

It was a nail. She hid it beneath the folds in the burqa. Fleetingly, she thought she might get a chance to pick the lock with it. Then she thought that was a ridiculous notion. She didn't have a clue how to do that. Still, she would keep it.

Less than a minute later, she realized that keeping up

her spirits was an impossible task. It was little more than a pretence. Her mind was on the cusp of closing down and making up a new reality to save it from further trauma. After Tom Dupree had appeared in the room where the Englishman had abused her, she'd actually thought her nightmare would end. But she guessed he was dead now, and all hope had disappeared as a result.

She heard the wooden door being unlocked and opened. She trembled involuntarily. Someone shone a strong beam of light from a flashlight onto her face but said nothing.

"Water," she said, although it sounded as if someone outside her body had spoken.

The figure stepped forward and blindfolded her with a length of rag that smelt faintly of male sweat before gagging her with another piece. The door was closed and locked. She guessed her death was near. She couldn't help herself.

She began to weep. In truth, she didn't know if she was weeping for herself, or for the pain her daughters would feel at knowing they would grow up motherless; for John, her husband, perhaps, or the thousands that would die once her death became known.

Where is God in all this? she thought. Where is He?

ONE HUNDRED AND TWO

THE NIGHT SKY was brocaded with tight clusters of luminous stars. On this part of the north-east coastline of Djibouti, the white-sand beach was speckled with stunted trees and scrub, and was edged by squat, stone cliffs. Abandoned fishing boats were upturned beneath them, their barnacle-ridden hulls resembling a pod of beached whales.

Tom and the operators were dressed in civilian Yemeni clothes: hand-woven turbans, short, sheepskin coats and cotton breeches. Underneath their baggy shirts, they all wore modified ballistic vests. The equipment—radio sets, portable SATCOMS, an array of small-arms weapons and IR and thermal lasers—was lying on light-brown poncho liners, ready to be passed out among the men.

Tom watched as a Mark V.1 Special Operations Craft, a twenty-five metre transport boat armed with M60 7.62mm machineguns, was lowered from the triple-hook system of a special ops Chinook, just beyond the surf thirty metres away. A Chinook was the heavy lifter of helicopters, versatile and dependable. The rotor blades whipped up the water into a surface whirlpool and flecks of sand stung Tom's face. He turned his head, seeing the operators apply stripes of black face camo before checking the chambers of their assault rifles and sub-machine guns.

Nathan had informed them at the briefing in England

that the Yemeni navy was insignificant, consisting of just thirty-five vessels, most of which were patrol boats. Given their extensive coastline, the chance of being spotted by one of them was remote. Added to which, the Mark V's angular design and anti-radar cladding should ensure that they'd avoid the Yemenis' Selex Coastal Defence System, he'd said, with a wry smile.

But as Tom waded through the warm shallows towards the craft, he knew he was heading for a kill zone.

After he strapped himself into one of the eight seats on the port side, the Mark V was soon travelling at over sixty-five knots, the sea spray all but soaking the occupants. The craft was used extensively as a SEAL launch facility and the seats were designed for maximum impact resistance, but the shock waves from the aluminium hull slamming through the waves sent jolts through Tom's spine.

Nathan, who was sitting in front of him, turned around. "Clench your teeth," he said as he grabbed the gunwale, "or you'll bite your tongue off."

The platoon chief put on a pair of headphones, the wire affixed to a VHF radio backpack propped up against the spare seat next to him, enabling him to use a secure frequency.

About ten miles out from Djibouti, Nathan confirmed that their fellow SEAL Team 7 operators had arrived at the rendezvous point. The landward edge of a secluded lagoon eighty-nine miles south of Al-Hudaydah, a seaport and Yemen's fourth largest city. The Mark V's engine was killed and the two CRRCs, combat rubber raiding craft, were manoeuvred onto the ramp on the stern. The craft, powered by outboard motors, would take them the remainder of the distance, where they'd be slashed open and buried. The motors would be cut a mile out and paddles would be used to reach the shoreline. If all went to plan, they would be flown from the hamlet in Black Hawks and be back on the African coast way before dawn.

About an hour later, the oil-black waters of the near-stagnant lagoon could be seen separated from the expanse of sea by a coral reef little more than fifteen centimetres below the CRRCs. Beyond, the muted moonlight had turned the dunes into huge piles of dark-red spice. During the day, the lagoons were teeming with mosquitoes, but the species that lived in sandy environments didn't feed at night, and Tom and the SEALs hadn't needed to apply repellent.

As a couple of operators paddled towards the beach, Tom, who was surrounded by bagged covert ops gear and ordnance, saw a small group of men emerge from the dunes and crouch down into a diamond shape on the dry sand. The deployed SEAL team, he thought. Nathan, who was sitting in the stern, resumed radio contact with them, speaking in short sentences peppered with code words and military acronyms. Apart from him, no one else spoke.

After landing on the sandy beach, the operators dug two large holes with short-handled shovels to hide the deflated boats. A couple of them had heaved out a large black box beforehand, which had been handed over by the CIA at Camp Lemonnier. When Tom had asked what it was, he'd been told by a bearded SEAL with densely tattooed forearms that it created enough interference to block cell and satphone signals. But it wouldn't mess with their voice-activated radios, so, even if the rescue site could be used to communicate from, the Arabs were screwed.

One of the men on the beach was the Yemeni interpreter that Nathan had mentioned, a man of about twenty with eyes like polished chestnuts, a prematurely lined forehead and wispy facial hair. His name was Khaleed Thabit. The operators called him Kali. He'd told Tom that he loved the US president and that he was going to marry an American girl and bring up a family in Santa Monica. Tom figured the guy was hoping for a Green Card. If the Yemeni survived the next few hours, he guessed he'd get his wish.

Nathan liaised with the team leader on the ground, a broad-shouldered man in his early thirties with a thick beard. He was wrapped in a traditional Yemeni shawl and carried a big-barrelled M79 grenade launcher with a customized pistol grip. An HK 45c handgun was holstered on his thigh. He looked as if he'd just stepped off the set of a spaghetti western. Nathan told Tom afterwards that the guy was a seasoned master chief, who was famous among assaulters for never carrying anything into battle apart from his handgun and beloved launcher.

The SEALs who had travelled with Tom handed out extra gear and ordnance to their brothers in the troop, including fragmentation grenades, suppressors and ballistic vests. The hard ceramic armour was uncomfortable and would slow them down some, but it would help to save their lives. Their backpacks had ballistic shields woven into them, which would be used to protect their heads as they fired around them. But like Kali, Tom remained unarmed. Nathan had said from the off in Djibouti that his orders were that Tom couldn't use a firearm in combat in Yemen, and, although he didn't care for military rules, this one was non-negotiable. Kali refused to wear a ballistic vest, too, saying that he was a Muslim and would put his faith in Allah. No one tried to persuade him to do otherwise. But everyone, including Tom, was given a med kit.

The hamlet was an hour's drive away by Desert Patrol Vehicles: high-speed buggies that looked like souped-up sandrails fixed with M60 machine guns. They'd stop the DPVs a mile or so from the rescue site, just close enough for the black box to operate. They'd walk on foot to ensure the terrorists there wouldn't be spooked by the roaring sound of the DPVs' air-cooled 200 hp VW engines.

Tom motioned to Nathan, who walked over to him, "How's it lookin'?" he asked.

"Like we're in the middle of a *Mad Max* set," Nathan said, grinning, as he put his hand on a DPV's roll bar. His expression changed to stern resignation. "We don't have a positive ID. The mission is flawed, you ask me. If she's there, I'd say there's a ninety per cent chance they'll kill her before we get to her, or she'll die in crossfire. And there's three unidentified vehicles heading toward the hamlet, less than twenty klicks away."

"Can't a drone take them out?" Tom asked.

"No problem. But she could be in one of them. Would you make that call?"

No, Tom thought.

"That could be an extra fifteen fighters. But successful or not, we won't leave any of them alive. That much I'm sure of."

Tom nodded, although he felt mentally numb.

ONE HUNDRED AND THREE

NO MORE THAN a quarter of a mile from the Red Sea, crescent-shaped sand dunes surrounded the hamlet on three sides, the fourth being open to the hundreds of barren square miles of the so-called Empty Quarter. There were no perimeter fortifications, just a few make-shift goat pens made from thorny scrub and jagged stones. The hamlet had five African-style mud-and-thatch huts, together with a central timber one. Fishing nets and woven pots lay in clusters between them. Two metres from the wooden hut, smoke-tipped orange flames rose from an open fire. Three Yemenis were huddled around it, smoking cigarettes. Nearby, a pair of small dogs pulled at either end of a discarded bone, their lips curled back, snarling.

Atop the southern sand dune, Tom lay between Kali and Nathan, who was scanning the hamlet with his panoramic night-vision goggles. Global Hawk spy planes, equipped with advanced synthetic aperture radar, and high-altitude Reaper drones with thermal imaging systems, were feeding him with real-time information via pilot operators at Camp Lemonnier, but an on-site confirmation of the layout and the number of occupants was essential. Nathan had a HK416 carbine fixed with a thermal scope and a red-dot infrared laser, which was invisible to anyone without night-vision. Although he'd told Tom that his orders were that he'd have to remain unarmed, he had relented once the DPVs had stopped, and handed him a SIG P226 handgun, saying that if anyone asked, he didn't get it from him. It was for self-defence only. He reiterated that he couldn't become involved in the mission proper. Tom had thought that a decent gesture.

The sound of the fire crackling and the Yemeni guards sitting chatting around it seemed to be amplified threefold, Tom thought. He heard his heart pounding in his chest, his breath through his nose, and did his best to mentally calm himself as he sensed the adrenalin coursing through his veins.

Nathan had split his SEALs into three attack squads. Alpha squad covered the only way in for the vehicles, which were only a few minutes away, while Bravo and Charlie squads occupied the dunes on the southern and northern slopes of the hamlet proper. A fourth squad, made up of the master chief's snipers, was situated on the dune leading to the coast. They all wore headphones and cheek microphones.

Sensing movement around him as the assaulters finalized their positions, Tom picked up an infrared field-scope and held it to his right eye. The images cut to a muted green. Eleven occupants. Two moving. That's nine possibles, he thought, discounting the possibility that the secretary was travelling in one of the approaching vehicles. Then there were the three around the fire. That left six possibles. One emerged from the hut at four o'clock. He walked a few paces before hitching up his sheepskin jacket and urinating, which left five possibles in the huts.

The secretary could easily be disguised as a man, but it had been agreed that the chances of her being allowed to roam about the site freely were so low that the figures outside were deemed hostile. But he knew that without a positive ID, Nathan would have to risk the vehicles getting here before his men moved in. Although the black box would prevent the fighters in the hamlet from alerting them by cellphones, and the SEALs' weapons were suppressed, the occupants of the vehicles would see or hear the discharges from the Yemeni's weapons miles away.

Tom lowered the scope, about to check the SIG's chamber and magazine. But before he released the clip fully from the well, the headlights of three vehicles appeared out of the darkness. This is it, he thought, pushing the magazine back into place.

The Land Cruisers skidded to a halt and armed men in suits exited at speed. Nathan ordered the attack and suppressed flashes flickered in Tom's peripheral vision. The guards who were in motion around the hamlet's cluster of huts fell in quick succession, their bodies landing with soft thuds, taken out by the snipers.

The three Yeminis by the fire grabbed their AKs and lay flat, firing randomly into the night. Then they threw smoke grenades towards the perimeter as they rushed into the nearest mud hut in the melee. With that, a massive explosion boomed through the night air. The beachside dune had erupted, sending up a huge, sand-filled cloud. As it settled Tom could see that the top quarter of the dune had disintegrated, leaving an uneven, crater-ridden series of sand hillocks.

Nathan swore under his breath. Tom knew that none of the master chief's snipers could have survived such an impact. He reckoned that the Arabs had rigged the dune to prevent a seaborne assault. He turned towards the vehicles, forcing himself to concentrate on the unfolding events, rather than dwell on the carnage that had just occurred.

The men from the vehicles who hadn't been cut down as they'd exited had half flung themselves to the ground, or had begun scaling the surrounding dunes. The area erupted into a seemingly chaotic firefight. Tom watched as the shadow-like figures of the lead operators moved down in unison from the dunes; he knew this was the most crucial time.

There was a series of half-muted explosions. Tom guessed the sand around the perimeter had been peppered with IEDs or landmines. "Jesus," he muttered. The twisted bodies of three assaulters writhed on the ground, while others lay motionless, their legs severed. Nathan hadn't put any contingency plans in place for such an eventuality at his briefing, and the secretary's life was hanging by a cotton thread.

After telling Tom to stay put, Nathan flipped up his NVGs and removed the lens cap from the thermal sight, which would allow him better vision in the smoke. He pulled out two fragmentation hand grenades from his pocket and handed them to Tom, saying that he should use them if their rear was compromised. Tom nodded before looking over at Kali. The interpreter's hands were shaking, his eyes wide. He looked as if he were on the verge of screaming. Nathan launched himself down the slope, heading for the master chief, who'd been hit by shrapnel and was dragging himself back to the base of the dune, rounds hitting the sand around him.

ONE HUNDRED AND FOUR

TOM PICKED UP the scope again. The thick smoke haze, exacerbated by the small-arms discharge and explosions, obscured his view in front, so he checked around the vehicles. An operator knelt about two metres from the base of the dune. He aimed his HK at the rear vehicle. The suppressed cracks from the muzzle meant he was attempting to disable it and cut off a retreat. But after the burst had ripped into the side-on tyres, the vehicle reversed. Tom figured the car must have been fitted with run-flats.

Nathan had said that the wooden hut held one occupant, which was likely to be the secretary. The drones had picked up a heat signature there, which hadn't moved since it'd been monitored. But she could be in one of the other huts, or the two remaining vehicles. He just hoped she wasn't in the one that had been scared off, although had no way of knowing for sure.

He glanced sideways. Kali had his eyes closed now, and appeared to be content to leave matters to fate, although he was making a faint mewing sound, like a puppy, as he shielded his ears with his hands.

Feeling impotent, Tom watched a group of Arabs retreat and crouch down behind the second vehicle. Too close, he thought, knowing they were susceptible to ricochets and flying metal shards from rounds hitting the bodywork. He spotted the SEAL with the scar emerge from the nearest dune, aiming the grenade launcher, the XM25 CDTE. A couple of seconds later, a microchip shell exploded in a white flash a metre or so from the rear of the vehicle, the noise loud enough to wake a hibernating bear. The men were scattered like bowling pins as the blast and shrapnel hit them, their screams hysterical and unnerving.

Tom focused back on the hamlet, where the smoke had thinned a little, but almost immediately noticed movement in his peripheral vision on the crest of the dune to his right. He jerked the scope away.

An Arab from one of the vehicles was aiming a submachine gun at Nathan's back. The platoon chief was heading towards the nearest hut after dragging the master chief a quarter of the way up the dune and covering his head with his own ballistic vest. As the Arab aimed Tom jumped up from behind Kali's trembling body. He couldn't risk shooting over him, since, if he missed, the interpreter was clearly incapable of defending himself or even rolling down the slope.

As he ran along the crest he pointed and fired. Nathan turned just as Tom's third round hit the sand by the Arab's head. But then the handgun jammed. The sand, he thought, knowing that if it stuck to a cartridge it could prevent the breech mechanism from working. He cursed himself for not checking the clip. With that, the area was lit up by an airborne flare. It must have been ignited by a fighter, Tom thought, because all the operators had NVGs and thermal imaging scopes.

But he kept running, despite the sand collapsing beneath his feet. He saw that the Arab was turning the weapon in an arc towards him. Before he could fire, Tom launched himself into the air, landing onto the still-outstretched gunman. He grabbed the muzzle and thrust it up. The Arab shouted out and headbutted Tom's hand. He winced as it connected, the metal preventing a give. As the Arab sank his teeth into Tom's exposed thumb he used the butt of the SIG to bludgeon him. After the third hit, the man was rendered unconscious.

He tried to prise the Arab's fingers from the weapon, but, despite the man's state, they seemed to be lodged tight. A round hit the sand by Tom's shoulder. A split second later, another pinged over his head. Tom dived a metre or so down the leeward slope and began scrambling his way back to the interpreter.

By the time Tom got to Kali, he was still ducking his head down and the mewing had been replaced by feverish praying in Arabic.

Tom released the clip on the SIG, and blew on it furiously, removing the disabling grains before slipping it back into the well.

Then Kali freaked.

Screaming, he swivelled around and got up onto his knees, about to bolt down the leeward side of the dune. Tom twisted at the waist and grabbed him by his pants. A shot rang out and Kali toppled sideways, half covering Tom with his twitching body. Peering down, Tom saw three men scaling the steep slope beneath. He struggled to pull the pin on one of the hand grenades before lobbing it down towards them. The grenade exploded as he eased Kali off him. The Arabs' bodies were shredded by the shrapnel, the blast flinging them backwards. He drew the SIG and fired two rounds into each of the splayed bodies before turning his attention back to the interpreter.

Kali had an entry hole in his chest, but was still breathing. The air was being drawn into his chest cavity through the hole, making a distinctive gurgling sound. Tom knew a sucking chest wound would collapse the man's lungs if left untreated. He didn't have a radio to call over one of the medics, even if that had been a possibility.

He took out the med kit from his pocket. He removed the sterile latex gloves and a pre-packed Asherman Chest Seal, a disc-shaped dressing consisting of an adhesive seal with a one-way valve in the middle. Cleansing the wound of blood, he applied the seal, ensuring that the valve was working, allowing air and blood to escape without re-entering. Then he gave him two shots of morphine.

With Kali stabilized, he focused back on the hamlet. A SEAL stooped down in front of the wooden hut, a pump-action shotgun in his hands. He blew the door off with a couple of breaching shells called TESARs, after aiming at the hinges. The shells were designed to disperse into a harmless powder once they had impacted with the target. But before the operator behind him could move in, both men were felled by rapid fire, the rounds slamming into their unprotected legs.

About three metres away, Tom watched a man lower an assault rifle before crawling towards the wooden hut, the weapon resting in the V between his forearms and biceps as he utilized the odd pocket of heavy smoke that still lingered above the sand for cover.

The secretary, he thought, lowering the glass and grasping the SIG.

Three of Tom's rounds hit the sand around the man, the impact of each flinging up a handful of grains.

Just as the shooter raised himself up at the entrance to the hut, a flicker of sparks signalled that one of Tom's rounds had hit the muzzle. The rifle spun out of the fighter's reach, but he flung himself forward, bursting through the opening and disappearing from sight.

Tom decided to act, despite Nathan's words. As he pushed himself up, preparing to run down the dune, he twisted his head. Another Arab from one of the vehicles had reached the crest about twenty metres from him, his hands clasping an MP5K sub-machine gun.

Aiming the SIG, Tom heard a nearby burst. The man's chest erupted, his weapon landing to his left. Tom stuck the SIG into his pants and crawled over to where the MP5 had landed, hoping it was still functional. He checked the chamber and the clip before wrapping the sling around his hands instinctively and turning his attention to the hamlet below, readying himself to run down the dune and join the ongoing gunfight.

As operators stormed the outlining huts, gaining the upper hand, he knelt onto one knee, aiming at a fighter who was shooting from the hip as he raced between the huts. But before Tom could squeeze the trigger, an intense pain erupted above his ribcage. The ballistic vest covered his torso, but as he'd raised the weapon he'd exposed an area about the size of a fist under his arms. A split second later, the pain seemed to career throughout his whole upper body, as if it had travelled in his blood vessels.

And then Tom was rolling down the steep, leeward slip face, the sounds of the ensuing firefight muted and remote now, each turn making him grit his teeth and moan as the entry wound made contact with the sand.

Finally, he was lying on his back, the MP5's strap

still wrapped around his hands. He went into a spasm. The night sky turned red, as if blood had filled his eyes.

He blacked out.

ONE HUNDRED AND FIVE

WHEN THE WOODEN door had been blown off its hinges, Linda had flinched and gasped into the cloth gag. Sitting upright on the concrete floor, still blindfolded, she'd prayed that her captivity was at an end. The US military have finally come for me, she'd told herself.

Gunfire and the screams of the dying and injured assaulted her ears. But now, just above the fearful racket, she heard something like a trapdoor being pulled up a metre or so by her head, and a waft of air brushed her face as it crashed to the solid floor.

Her shackles were released and a large hand yanked her up.

"We're going down, missus. Just me and you. So relax or I'll open up those healing wounds of yours."

She recognized the voice instantly. It was the man who'd beaten her at the chateau. The Englishman. But the thought of going under something as unstable as sand filled her with a terror far greater than being in his presence again. She shook her head frantically, screaming into the gag, and flailed her arms about. But she was grabbed by his muscular arms in a bear hug. Smelling his tobacco breath a few centimetres from her, she was picked up. Sensing he was manoeuvring her into position, she braced herself as best she could for what she guessed would be a fall.

Tom BLINKED OPEN his eyes. The pain was still intense, but the red haze had faded. Snapping back to reality, he gripped the MP5, testing his strength. His hands were weak. He heard the crack of gunshots and realized that he'd fallen backwards, because the now intermittent small-arms fire was coming from the other side of the dune.

With the acrid smell of battle in his nostrils, a descending flare half illuminated the area around him. He squinted, then focused. The ground was rising less than twenty metres ahead of him. He figured he was hallucinating. But then the unmistakable shape of the back of a man emerged from the sand. Then another person. A woman dressed in a burqa. Just before the glare from the flare fell beyond the dune, the man turned sideways. Tom sucked in air and clenched his jaw muscles. It was Proctor. And that meant that the woman in the burqa was likely to be the secretary.

He kept perfectly still. Proctor appeared to be unarmed, but he could be concealing a handgun under his woollen jacket. Forcing himself not to groan, he saw Proctor walk in the direction of the beach, the woman he took for the secretary being hauled behind him.

He struggled up, seeing that the sand was wet with blood where he had landed. He began to drag himself after them along a scratch, the narrow trough between the dunes, the pain almost making him pass out. After about ten metres, he dropped to his knees, blood leaching from his wound, his breath laboured and ragged.

Proctor reached the crest of a sinuous sand ridge with the woman by his side, the man's hand grasping her upper arm. It was then that Tom made out the sound of a powerful outboard motor. Proctor was making his escape. If they passed over the ridge, she'd be gone for good. He guessed it was a contingency plan, which had been activated once it was obvious that the hamlet was under assault. He knew he had to act, too. The effective range of the MP5 was two hundred metres, he recalled vaguely. It fired nine hundred and fifty rounds a minute. He hoped that with a lot of luck, he'd only need one.

Still kneeling in the sand, he raised the weapon, extended the retractable butt, and pressed his eye against the reflex sight, aiming for the middle of Proctor's shoulder blades. His actions were pure muscle memory now, his brain unable to cope with the hormone burst. As he squeezed the trigger he winced and coughed up blood at the crucial moment. The MP5 jerked in his hands and, for a second, his vision was clouded as he squinted involuntarily.

By the time he looked back, they'd both disappeared from view. He cursed himself again. He couldn't tell if he'd hit him.

Tom's eyelids became heavy; his head lopped forward. But he forced himself to stand up and, wavering from side to side, lurched towards the ridge, taking advantage of a late dopamine dump. The soft sand would have been heavy going for an able man, but with the disability imposed by the wound Tom was reduced to crawling up the slope on his hands and knees, sweat dripping from his creased-up face. He stopped halfway and manoeuvred the MP5 onto his back after it had fallen forward. He spat something that tasted like bile, his lungs heaving. He glanced back, seeing the dotted trail his blood had made before moving on again.

As he got to the top of the sand ridge his vision was blurred. He pulled the strap around his torso, his arms barely able to hold onto the MP5 as he raised it. As he staggered up his legs felt as if the muscles had turned to gel, and the bleeding from the entry wound had increased significantly. About three metres down the gradual incline of the windward slope, the woman was lying face up, her eyes covered by cloth, her mouth gagged. For a moment, he wondered if he had killed her by mistake, his shot so skewed by his involuntary cough that the weapon had veered to the right. But then he saw Proctor, the back of his thigh seeping blood from a centimetre-wide entry hole in his cotton pants. The man started groaning.

"Put...your hands...behind your head," Tom said, his voice guttural and slurred.

Proctor just moaned. Tom knew the seriousness of a leg shot. Most people bled out quickly. Proctor wouldn't be any different. But his adversary was tough, probably ex-military, he thought.

He sidestepped down the slope, every movement making him wince with pain. When he was a metre from Proctor, the man rolled, growling like an angry dog as his thigh touched the firm sand. Tom caught a glimpse of the flash of steel as Proctor's arm snaked out. He recognized the knife instantly. A Ka-Bar, a favourite of British Special Forces. With his back to the sand, Proctor was holding it against the woman's throat. Tom inched forward. Proctor's eyes were blood-shot and filled with hate.

"Drop it," Tom said, aiming the MP5.

Proctor looked shocked when he registered Tom's face. Tom figured he'd thought that Major Durrani had killed him. But then Proctor grinned insanely.

"I'll bleed her like a pig," he said.

Tom heard the woman's breath quicken. It had to be her, he thought. It was then that he realized that the firing had stopped at the hamlet. At the same time he heard the spluttering sound from the outboard. Allowing himself to glance up, he saw the speedboat ticking over in the shallows, three dark-skinned men sitting in it.

"It's...over," he said, struggling to keep the extended butt of the weapon tucked into his shoulder.

Proctor screamed and jerked his arm away. Seeing that the woman had stabbed what looked like a nail into the man's forearm, close to the elbow joint, Tom sank to his knees involuntarily, one eyelid closing over, the MP5 falling into his lap. Vaguely, he watched her scramble up, still gagged and blindfolded, and, teetering back and forth, she moved away from her kidnapper.

Tom tried to call out, but his words didn't leave his mouth. *Run up the slope. Just run.*

But Proctor wasn't done, either. He pushed himself up with his free hand and twisted his body in the direction of the woman, who'd only managed to hobble a couple of metres away. He swivelled the knife, manoeuvring it deftly between his thumb and forefinger. Pulling his arm back, he readied himself to throw it at her exposed back, a macabre smile breaking on his face, revealing nicotine-stained teeth.

Finding a last modicum of strength, Tom used his left hand to raise the muzzle as his right forefinger squeezed the trigger.

There was a short burst.

Then he collapsed sideways.

WHEN HE MANAGED to open one of his eyes, he saw the knife lying on the sand, a few shafts of moonlight glinting off the blade. Proctor's prostrate body lay a few inches from it. The Englishman's big, shaved head was facing him, blood oozing from the lips.

Tom eased himself up, the pain making his head spin as the wound seemed to widen. The woman was nowhere in sight. He heard the boat's powerful outboard engine roar away. For a few seconds, he thought the worst. But then he heard her weeping and realized she was lying on the other side of Proctor's corpse. The trauma had gotten to her at last; that and physical exhaustion, the result of lack of food and sleep, he guessed.

He sensed movement behind him and, grimacing, turned his head around as best he could. Nathan and three operatives were barrelling down the slope towards him.

"Is it her?" Nathan called out.

Unwrapping the MP5's strap from his hands, Tom crawled around the dead body, dragging his legs behind him. She was curled up on the sand, her facial features still obscured. It had to be her, he thought. But he had to be sure.

"Your middle…name, ma'am?" he asked.

She struggled to pull the tight blindfold from her eyes. Then the gag was removed. He recognized her.

"It's Gertrude. My middle name is Gertrude," she said, faintly.

As Nathan reached him Tom nodded his head a fraction.

Nathan spoke into his cheek mic. "Affirmative ID," he said. "Phoenix is safe."

LYING ON A poncho liner, Tom heard a muffled explosion and glimpsed a flash of white about two miles out at sea. Standing over him, Nathan said that the escaping speedboat had just been hit by a Hellcat missile fired by a Reaper drone. A few seconds later, the suppressed sound of fast-approaching helicopters could be heard faintly offshore. Tom looked past Nathan, but, with their navigation lights switched off, the inward MH-60 Black Hawks resembled two massive hornets as they travelled low to the water from the west.

After Nathan had shielded him from the mini-sandstorm blown up by the rotor wash, Tom saw a crew chief from the Special Operations Aviation Regiment appear from the side door of one of the Black Hawks, wearing night-vision goggles. He stood beside a skinny guy with a blacked-out face, who was scanning the beach with his M-240B machine gun. The crew chief called Nathan over, informing him exactly how his men should proceed. Navy SEALs were respected throughout the military, but this was his gunship.

As TOM AND the secretary were carried towards the fuselage of the rear helicopter, he heard other explosions coming from the hamlet, knowing the operators had just blown up the fighters' weapons and vehicles.

Nathan came up beside him once more, patted his forearm gently.

"Your men take their snaps back there?" Tom asked, remembering that the Delta assaulters had done so for evidence at the fort in the Kurram Valley.

"For a civilian, you know too much. But the guys wanted me to say that you got a night of hard drinking to look forward to when you're up to it."

"Sounds good," Tom said, nodding. "Kali?"

"He'll live. Thanks to you, dude."

Within a couple of minutes, they were safely in the air.

He looked over at her. Although it was dark, the only light emanating from the illuminated dashboard in the exposed cockpit, he could see her body lying strapped to a stretcher pushed against the side of the cabin. She was wrapped in blankets, her eyes closed, her breathing shallow but not erratic. A medic was crouching down by her side and had set up a drip-feed.

As he lowered a respirator to her nose and mouth she resisted him, flinging her head from side to side.

"Tom," she said, desperately.

He stretched his hand over towards her.

"It's all right, ma'am. We're going home."

After getting berated by another medic for that, he felt the morphine take effect as he saw his own respirator being lowered to his face.

He breathed deeply, anxious for the ordeal to be over.

But as he closed his eyes the pitiable faces of the dead came to him. He shivered.

Their eyes were hollow, their expressions reproachful.

ONE HUNDRED AND SEVEN

BACK AT CAMP LEMONNIER, Tom lay in a steel bed in the Navy Expeditionary Medical Field Hospital, a cream-coloured, single-storey building, surrounded by raised concrete walkways. The room was painted white, with square-shaped fluorescent lights and an AC vent in the low-level ceiling. Apart from a piece of abstract art on the wall and a large pot containing a branched yucca plant, the space was stark and minimalist. A Navy surgeon had just left, after saying that the X-rays had shown that the bullet had missed the major organs. He'd be flown back to the States to recuperate.

The door opened and Tom heard footsteps stop half-way across the room.

"Don't tell me. They weren't my X-rays," he said, jokingly.

The person didn't answer.

"Who's there?" he said, struggling to raise his head.

A man in a straw fedora walked over to a table where a bowl of fruit lay, his hands stuck in the pockets of his white-linen pants. He picked up an apple and turned face-on, tossing the apple in his hand.

Tom frowned, his eyes narrowing. When he recognized the face, he stopped breathing and his body tensed, a sense of the surreal overtaking him temporarily. He saw a ghost standing before him. But a ghost with a beating heart and a name.

Dan Crane.

"The jarheads call this place CLUville, due to the Containerized Living Units and the link with France. Smart, huh?" he said, his tone rasping.

"What the hell's going on?" Tom asked.

"Guess I'm just hard to kill."

Then Crane explained that a source had informed the CIA that the ISI were going to kill him in Ta'if. A radical group within the House of Saud called the Brothers of Faith had been up to no good, and the pro-Western king had been persuaded that the operative who'd been sent to murder him there should be replaced. Crane's death was staged for the benefit of the ISI. He had worn a ballistic vest when he'd been shot at with blanks. But his sports bag had been lined with bulletproof shields just in case. A shot of adrenalin had stopped the risk of a heart attack.

"Though I was sweating like a dog walking past a Korean restaurant. And not just from the heat, either," he added.

"I don't get it," Tom said, resisting the urge to scratch the stitches on his forehead.

"Perception, Tom. As I told you back at the Ariana, everything is perception."

Tom stared hard at Crane. "You gave Khan to Hasni. Are you denying that? Denying you got paid for it?"

"Don't get your blood pressure up there, Tom. And, no, I ain't denying it. But he got paid for telling us where Lyric was in Karachi, and then by the ISI for telling them that we were on the way. Khan was playing both sides. That's why he gave you Hasni's son." Crane looked a little distant. "There's nothing double agents like more than the vulnerability of their employers. I guess he knew you wouldn't kill Mahmood, but he wanted to show Hasni just how vulnerable he was. Hasni played along in the game, made out like Khan wasn't one of theirs. Besides, Hasni wanted revenge for his son. There are certain unwritten rules, even for spooks. You and Khan broke one of them. So, yeah, I turned him over to Hasni, just as Birch said. I had to play along, too. Hence my visit to a bank in Ta'if."

Tom couldn't quite take it all in, said, "Birch didn't trust me?"

"Everybody trusts you. It wasn't a matter of trust. Until Hasni and a terrorist called Mullah Kakar were taken out, it wasn't safe to tell anyone the truth. We were just beaten to it. Ordered by the Saudi ambassador to Pakistan." Crane glanced at his watch. "But he died just over six hours ago back in Yemen. Hit by a drone strike as he was escaping from you and the SEALs. I guess he never knew his masters sent him to his death. I think you should know that Peter Swiss is dead, too, Tom. The corruptibility of money, huh."

"Was it just the money?" Tom asked, regaining some of his composure.

"We believe that that was the primary motive. For Swiss at least. But by the time the feds have finished crawling over ADC, it won't be worth a dime."

"Why are you telling me this?" Tom asked.

"I didn't want you getting the wrong idea about me if we bumped into each other in the future. Besides, a man like you got a right to know the truth sooner rather than later," he said. "You did good, Tom. I'll bet good money that the Iranians will agree to back off. They were barked at for an hour after we thought the Leopards had taken Lyric, that they were involved, too. It was made very clear to them what we'd do. After that, they realized we weren't done in the region, despite two wars. It won't take much to persuade them that the same will happen if they invade southern Pakistan, you ask me. But if you hadn't rescued Lyric, alotta people would have died, that's for certain. Leopards, Iranians... Our own."

Tom sighed. "What about the Pakistanis?"

"The president has agreed to a five-billion-dollar arms package to assist them with the ongoing threat to their national security, and the security of the region in general. Politics, Tom. Now I gotta leave ya. Say hi to the general when you see him."

To Tom it was a double shock. Not only the appearance of the man whom Birch had said had been killed just a day earlier, but also by the fact that he clearly knew his father.

"How come you two know each other?"

"Your father didn't always sit behind a desk," Crane said.

"I said how do you know him?"

"Before I joined the CIA I was in military intelligence. He was my boss," Crane said. "You see, Tom, your father kept a promise, too."

Tom thought about that for a moment. "Did he get you outta Beirut?" he asked.

Crane grinned, took a bite of the apple and walked towards the door. After five steps, he stopped, but didn't turn around.

"If it weren't for your father, I would never have let you go over the border, let alone everything else you've been up to. But as it is, well, that was a good move. You live in a state of honour, Tom," he said. "And that's a damn fine thing. You ever get fed up with the bureaucracy at the State Department, look me up."

EPILOGUE

THE SMALL LOUISIANA cemetery was shaded by oak trees, their fat trunks clothed in damp lichen. The air was humid, filled with the songs of waterthrush and blue jays. Tom came here when he could, but his grandma tended his mother's grave lovingly every Sunday afternoon after church, polishing the brass surround latticework and washing down the marble headstone. The general had never been here before. He bent forward now and placed a bunch of white roses at the base of the headstone; her favourites, Tom had said when they'd stopped at a florist's a hundred metres from the entrance.

The inscription read simply:

In Loving Memory of Melissa Dupree
Who Died in Tragic Circumstances
Rest in Peace in the Arms of The Lord
1950–1988

"I'm sorry for what I did," the general said. "I'd like you to forgive me."

Tom looked down at his mother's grave. "It's me who should be asking forgiveness."

"I don't know what that means, and, I tell ya, I don't wanna know. Whatever you did or didn't do, you were just a kid." He put his hand on Tom's forearm. "We'll make some regular time for each other, Tom. That much I know."

They turned and began to walk away from the simple gravestones, along a flint-ridden path edged with low iron railings. Here, the older graves of the rich lay a few metres back. Moss-stained, stone sarcophagi decorated with angels and laurels. Untended now, the dead no longer even a memory. Tom thought about all those who had sacrificed their lives, although Lester had survived, due to a surgeon's expertise. When they'd met up in a bar in DC, he'd thought his friend appeared to have lost ten pounds or more. But Lester had spent the time joking and saying how fine the nurses were. As for the secretary, her wounds were mainly superficial, at least the physical ones, and she was recovering with her family at Camp David for security reasons. Tom had been asked to visit, but as yet he hadn't. He would, soon enough, though; he knew that.

Twenty minutes later, the general drove them to a small town thirty miles or so from Baton Rouge. The main street was bordered by two-storey buildings, mostly unkempt retail stores with timber-frame accommodation above. Tom's grandparents lived in a detached bungalow set back about twenty-five metres from the road. They passed the old whitewashed church with a green-tiled, pitch roof where Tom had sung in the choir as a boy. Nearby, surrounded by short grass, a huge bell was still on a brick plinth. The bell was going to hang in a larger church, but the church hadn't moved on any more than the town had.

As the general parked the Buick Tom asked his father to give him a minute. He got out and walked up a stone path, feeling the sticky heat of a Louisiana afternoon start to encroach on his body. He saw his grandma sitting on the porch in a wooden chair. Her grey hair was up in a bun and she wore a plain beige dress. He hadn't told his grandparents specifically what he did for a living, other than saying he worked for the State Department. He hadn't wanted to worry them. She smiled and waved as she always did, getting up and stepping forward to give him a hug.

"Good to see you, Tommy. Dear Lord," she said, registering his beat-up face. "What happened to you?"

"I fell down some stairs."

"Drunk?"

"No, ma'am."

"You lost weight, too."

"Where's Granddaddy?"

"He's watching TV," she said. She hollered out behind her, telling Tom's granddaddy to come outside. "You want some lemonade?"

"No, thank you, ma'am."

She tried to run her fingers through his dark hair. "You cut your hair too short. You ain't in the military. No need to."

He scratched the back of his head.

"Your momma wouldn't like it."

"Momma's in heaven, Grandma. She don't fret about such things."

Tom's granddaddy appeared and, after glancing at his strapped shoulder, slapped him on the opposite one and shook his hand. His shake was firm and the dark-brown eyes Tom had inherited from him sparkled like sunlight on the Mississippi.

"You look well, son," he said.

"You're blind, Daddy," his grandma said. "You can't see his scars?"

"He ain't dead though. Don't fuss, Mother."

Tom grinned, hearing the Buick's door slam shut. He saw his grandparents looking behind him.

"Who'd ya bring along, Tom?" his granddaddy asked.

"Let's all go inside," Tom said, gesturing to his father to join them.

Despite what his father had said at the cemetery, he knew now that opening up about his part in how his momma had died would give him a peace that he'd longed for.

* * * * *

Get 4 FREE REWARDS!

We'll send you 2 FREE Books
<u>plus</u> 2 FREE Mystery Gifts.

Harlequin® Intrigue books feature heroes and heroines that confront and survive danger while finding themselves irresistibly drawn to one another.

FREE
Value Over
$20

Get 4 FREE REWARDS!

We'll send you 2 FREE Books plus 2 FREE Mystery Gifts.

Harlequin® Romantic Suspense books feature heart-racing sensuality and the promise of a sweeping romance set against the backdrop of suspense.

FREE Value Over **$20**